roommate's guide to love

Guide to Love

Book Three

chelle sloan

Cover Design: Chelsea Kemp Art

Editing: Kiezha Smith Ferrell, Librum Artis Editorial Services

Proofreading: Michele Ficht, Pin-Up Proofs

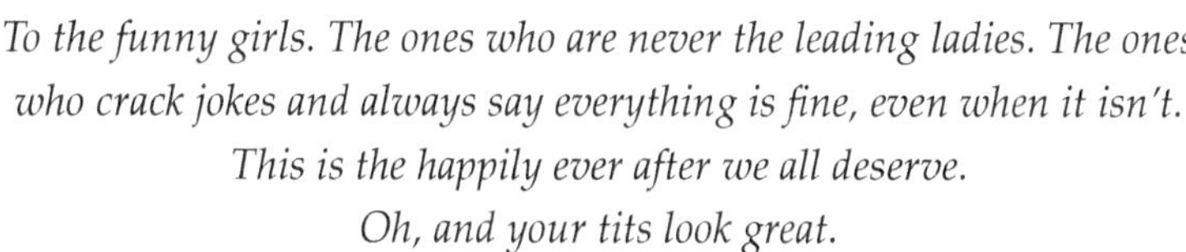

To the funny girls. The ones who are never the leading ladies. The ones who crack jokes and always say everything is fine, even when it isn't. This is the happily ever after we all deserve.
Oh, and your tits look great.

guide to love rule #24

One more time never means one more time. Especially when orgasms are involved.

prologue

Quinn

I am a weak, weak woman.

Both in the head, heart, and because of the positions I was just put in, legs.

I thought I was strong. I live on my own. I kill spiders. I build IKEA furniture without help—and sometimes there aren't even pieces left. But there's something about the moment that I step back into Rolling Hills, Tennessee, that makes me a weak, horny woman.

And that something is Porter McCoy.

"Jesus Christ," Porter says, both of us still panting after the round we just went through. "I think you nearly killed me."

"No murder charges here," I say, making no attempt at moving or rolling over from my spot on his mattress. "I've gone this long without an actual arrest record, and I'd like to keep it that way."

"Really?" he says as he kisses my shoulder before rolling to his side. "Hurricane Banks has never been arrested?"

I hate that nickname, but I'm too orgasm-drunk to fight him on it. I barely have the energy to turn to face him. Though I'm glad I do. The sight of a shirtless and sweaty Porter is never a bad one. "I haven't. Close, a few times, but I technically have a clean record."

This makes him laugh. "I think that might be a bigger surprise than you showing up at the bar tonight."

I smile as I brush my finger up and down his sternum. I rarely take the time to just lie back and admire Porter's body. His muscles are defined but not intimidating. There's a smattering of chest hair that I love feeling against my skin when he's on top of me. And even in the darkness of his bedroom, I can see a twinkle in his brown eyes.

The weak woman thing is starting to make sense…

"You can thank my new brother-in-law for that one. Surprise wedding dinner for him and Maeve required each family member to be there. And I figured since I was in town…"

"You'd come to your favorite bar for a nightcap and chicken wings?"

I smile at his use of our favorite code word. "Exactly."

"Well, thank your new brother-in-law for me. Tonight was very, and I mean very, unexpected. And very, and I mean very, pleasant."

Porter leans down to kiss me again, and because the theme of the night is me being unable to stop myself from doing things that probably aren't the right decision, I let him. And I deepen it. Because eight years ago, when we started this, Porter put a spell on me. But instead of a wand, he used his dick.

And fingers.

And mouth.

God, that mouth…

I don't know how I got so lucky as to have a fuck buddy who makes it his mission to make me his snack every time we're together, but I'm not one to look at gift horse in the mouth.

Especially if he's not tired of it after all this time.

Eight years is a long time for anything. Many marriages don't last that long. But yet, Porter and I and our perfect arrangement have stood the test of time. Probably because we have our formula down.

I come home from where I live and teach in Arizona at least twice a year. Once around the holidays, once in the summer, and the occasional drop in, like tonight.

While here visiting my family, at some point I end up at The Joint, the neighborhood bar where everyone knows your name. There, I see the owner, Porter McCoy, who not only knows my name, but knows how to make me come in point-five seconds.

Each time I'm in said bar, I give myself a pep talk that just because I'm home doesn't mean I *have* to fuck him. Then he gives me a look. Or a wink. Or he just exists as I sit back and remember that no man knows my body better than he does.

So, eventually, I saunter up to the bar, trying to look as nonchalant as possible, and tell him that I'd like to order chicken wings.

Which means sex.

I order sex.

From a bar.

Because that's who I've become. A thirty-four-year-old childless cat lady who doesn't date, but has had an eight-year secret situationship with the boy she had a crush on in high school.

Yes, I know it's fucked up. Eight years is a long-ass time. Yes, I should talk to someone about this. However, I'm not ready to tell a therapist that I'm avoiding commitment by sucking on the same dick twice a year with no attachments.

In my defense, it's a really nice dick.

"Porter?" I ask, his face between my tits.

"Yeah?"

I want to laugh at his mumbled reply, but the thought I'm having is serious—one I don't know if I've ever been ready to vocalize until right now.

"What are we doing?"

This makes him pause, and he slowly brings his eyes to me.

"Currently? You're lying back while I reacquaint myself with my two best friends."

I sit up, which naturally pushes him back. "I'm being serious. What is this? How have we let this go on for eight years?"

Porter nods and sits up, though he does a fantastic job of making sure that his dick is *just barely* covered by the sheet.

"I thought this is what we both wanted? Nothing serious. Just fun. Right?"

Everything he's saying is exactly what we've talked about before. Hell, I'm the one who put down most of the rules. "It's just… I don't know. Maybe it's because two of my sisters are now in healthy and happy relationships. Even Simon is settled down. I feel like what we're doing is something people do in their twenties. Not in their thirties."

Porter's fingertips brush down my arm as he places his fingers through mine. "I get that. Things change. Has something changed for you? Do you want something more?"

It might be the darkness of the room, but I swear for just a split second I saw something that looked like hope in Porter's eyes.

Hope for more? Or hope that I'm about to call this off? Not really sure.

"Nothing has changed."

"See. Who's to say this is wrong?" Porter scoops me up and somehow, despite my size, places me on his lap. "Just because what we have isn't conventional, doesn't mean it doesn't work for us. And I think it works pretty well, don't you think?"

"It does," I admit.

"Then don't worry about anything else. Don't let what others are doing get in the way of what we are," he says as he starts kissing across my chest and up my neck. "Just relax and have fun. Stay. Let's enjoy this impromptu visit a little longer."

I melt into the feeling of Porter's lips traveling up and down my naked body as he lays me back on the bed. I know I should leave. I don't stay the night. Ever. Porter knows that. And he didn't mean "stay" as in "stay the night." I know he meant stay for round two.

And I want to—God, I want to. Especially because the first round was so chaotic and hot that I didn't get to enjoy him like I really wanted.

So why is my head being a bitch and trying to be responsible? Is it really just because Maeve's now married? Or that Stella is living with the love of her life? I mean, I love my sisters and I'm happy for them. But I didn't think their happiness would make me question what I've decided to do with my sex life.

My mind is going back and forth when Porter's kisses suddenly stop.

"What?"

"I can hear your brain working."

Porter sits me up in bed, his hand gently grazing down the slope of my cheek. "I know what we have isn't traditional. But that doesn't make what we have wrong. We're two adults who enjoy each other. A lot. What we have works for us. Fuck everyone else."

I nod. "You're right."

"See? So how about this? You get out of that beautiful head of yours, stay a little longer, and let me remind you of all the reasons why we're so good at what we are."

Words fail me as Porter's mouth goes to work again. My hands immediately go into his hair, running my fingers through his chestnut brown locks as he sucks and laps my nipple.

This shouldn't feel as good as it does. *He* shouldn't feel as good as he does. Hookups aren't supposed to make you feel some sort of way. They're supposed to scratch an itch and then you go about your day.

And maybe that's why I keep coming back. Keep going back on my word. Because no one makes me feel like Porter. No one knows my body like him. No one has ever made me scream or talk in tongues.

But he does. Every time.

Maybe he's right? Why would I walk away from something that works? That's just silly.

And I'm a lot of things—chaotic, wild, spontaneous. But I'm not silly.

"What do ya say, wanna stay?"

I grin as I push him back down on the bed, allowing me to straddle him.

"Depends," I say. "What do you have in mind?"

He crooks his finger, bringing me closer.

"Sit on my face and let me show you."

guide to love rule #52

Most things in life can be solved with a good book and a slice of pizza.

1

quinn

"Students, raise your water bottles high in the air."

My sixth-grade class snickers as I clear my throat, doing my best to get their attention for the toast I'm about to make.

"I want to take this moment to congratulate you for completing your sixth-grade state testing." The room cheers, but I signal for them to keep it down since we're the only class in the hallway having a pizza party today. "Y'all worked and studied so hard! I know testing isn't easy for a lot of you, and no matter what the scores say, I just want to show you how proud I am of all of you for doing your best. So I want you to enjoy this pizza and treats, let's play some games, and say congratulations to each other for surviving state testing!"

The class cheers again, and this time I don't bother telling them to keep it down. Let's be real, the only person that's going to be mad that there's noise is the math teacher, because she's always claiming to be behind on where she should be in her syllabus. One day of outside noise isn't going to stop that.

Honestly, I don't care if anyone complains. My kids just worked their asses off for the past however many months to prepare for a state test that's going to generically tell them their aptitude and dictate their lives. Oh, and it will give the state something to hold over the school's head. The least I can do is spend a few bucks and get them pizza, veggies, fruit, and cupcakes as a reward for their hard work.

I quickly take a look around the classroom. The air is different today. They're eating, laughing, and mingling. They don't look stressed. They don't look worried. They look like kids. Which is exactly what I wanted for today.

That is, except for one student, who is standing and staring at the table of food like it's going to come alive and eat her instead.

"Makayla? Everything okay?"

She shrugs but doesn't make eye contact. "I miss pizza."

That takes me by surprise. "I get that. I miss pizza every day, and that's even when I bring it for lunch."

My joke doesn't work. In fact, it might make her more sad.

"Is everything okay? Can you have pizza? I didn't see any allergies or dietary restrictions on your forms."

She lets out the biggest sigh I've ever heard. "My mom says we can't have it because of gluten. Even though we had it two weeks ago. Now, apparently, we're going to die from it."

Now, I'm all for people who stay away from gluten because of allergies, celiac, or other medical issues. Or even parents who have devoted time and energy into seeing if that kind of food and lifestyle is right for their family. Who am I to judge? I like to live my life by the phrase "not my monkeys, not my circus."

However, I would bet my car and my cat Turtle that Makayla's family fits into neither of those categories.

Also known as, her mother has struck again. The woman, who is a known menace to teachers, is a family vlogger who likes to invent new things every week about their family in terms of diet, parenting, and lifestyle. I'm guessing this week's trend is gluten free.

Unfortunately, I can't assume that. I have to go by what she's saying. Luckily for Makayla, and her pain in the ass mother, I have backups.

"No worries," I say as I grab a hidden box of pizza I had

ordered for a previous class because I have a student who is *actually* gluten free. "This is gluten-free. Have as much as you want."

Makayla's eyes go wide, and her smile is bright as she takes two slices and puts them on her plate. "Thanks so much, Miss Banks. You're the best."

She gives me a one-armed hug, which I return because her mother might be a pain, but she's a sweet kid. Somehow. "You're welcome. Now go enjoy."

Makayla heads toward her friends as I sit back and let my brain wander a bit. With the middle of April comes the end of state testing. But more importantly? This is the official beginning of the countdown until the last day of school.

Twenty-one school days until the students say goodbye.

Twenty-two days until I can sleep in past six in the morning.

Twenty-three days until I'm on a plane for a well-deserved vacation. I can smell the freedom from here, and it's giving notes of piña colada and suntan lotion.

"Hey, Miss Banks?"

I look over to see where the voice came from, though I should've known it was Diego. The boy asks me the same question every day around this time.

"Yes, you can use the restroom. Please sign out."

He sets down his pizza, and I go back to making sure nothing crazy is going on with my other twenty-five students. Do I think he's actually going to the restroom? I don't know. I do know that he asks to go every day, and I'm pretty sure it's just because he needs to take a lap and decompress. So I'll never say no. I get it. Sometimes I need a minute too.

A few of my fellow teachers give me snide looks for giving the kids breaks like that, but I really don't care. I take that back; maybe in my first year I did. I think every rookie teacher wants to follow the rules, show that they're the one teacher who's going to keep every student engaged for every minute of the class block.

I think that lasted one day with me. And today, as I'm closing in on year twelve? It's out the door.

Kids are different these days. Attention spans are short. Home lives are sometimes rough. Some learn faster and some need more time. And they aren't the only ones different. So am I. Yes, I still want to make sure every kid leaves my room feeling a little better about themselves. I want them to learn. I want them to love books just as much as I did when I was their age. But I'm also hardened by years of middle school insults, state recommendations that were given by people who've never stepped foot in a classroom, and asshole parents who think they know everything because they possess two things: a stick up their ass and audacity.

But with all of that comes knowing how to handle everything. Outside of the classroom, I know which parents to placate by pretending I'm going to take their advice and the ones who truly want to help their children grow. I know which professional developments actually matter. And inside the classroom? I know when to just let the kid pretend to go to the bathroom.

"Miss Banks? What are we doing now?"

I look over to Daniella, one of my more inquisitive students. "Do you mean now or tomorrow since we're done with testing prep?"

"Tomorrow," she clarifies.

This gets me excited, and I sit up a little straighter. "We're starting to read my favorite book, *The Westing Game.*"

Every one of my kids looks around in a bit of confusion, probably because they've never heard of it. Little do they know I'm about to change their lives.

"What's it about?"

"It's a mystery book about a man who is murdered, and when people come together for the reading of his will, they find out it's a contest. And that's all I'm going to say because I don't want to spoil it."

A little chatter begins with them until Axel, the unspoken

leader of the class, speaks up. "You read that with my older sister's class too. She still talks about it, and she had you three years ago. This is going to be dope."

Axel's stamp of approval gets everyone excited, and I just sit back with a smile on my face. Because for the tenth year in a row, my favorite book is coming in to save the day.

I realized around my third year of teaching that April is exhausting. You're burnt out from testing and you still have a month to go. So, I thought, what better way to make sure that I was excited to come to school than by teaching my favorite book from when I was their age.

Because it's a mystery, both the boys and girls really get into it. I have a whole lesson on using context clues to try to solve the mystery. But my favorite day is when they find out the ending. Every year they're floored. That day is always filled with constant conversation, excited eyes, and kids begging to go back and read certain chapters to see the clues they missed.

And if I'm being honest? It's what's getting me through these last few weeks. This year has been overly exhausting, both in the classroom and out. Whether it's waking up to news of another book that's been banned, or parents questioning what me and the rest of my colleagues are teaching, I feel like every day has been a battle. I've never read the word "indoctrination" more than this year. And I'm not just talking about around the country. No, this was personally in our school district due to the group of moms—who might or might not have named themselves with an acronym of a specific male appendage—who have made it their mission to make our lives miserable.

Newsflash: I can't get these kids to remember to write their names on their papers. I'm not convincing them to make life-altering bodily decisions.

And then there's my personal life. Oh, who the hell am I kidding? I have no personal life. I don't try and date because I've learned that trying to date as a plus-size woman is laughable. The closest thing I have to a relationship is the few times a year I go home and hook up with Porter. I do have my book club, but it's slowly starting to dwindle down because everyone else has things they need to do with their families.

Needless to say, my soul needs this lesson. And this slice of pizza I'm about to scarf down. Because as a proud millennial, I grew up knowing that books and pizza go hand-in-hand.

The noise in the classroom is starting to get a little loud, but it's quickly quieted by the alert sound through the P.A. system.

"Miss Banks?"

A chorus of "oooohs" fills the classroom as they recognize our principal's voice. I wave my hands to shush them, but that only gets me snickers.

"Yes, Mrs. Hargrove?"

"After the final bell, can you please come to my office?"

Sounds serious. Wonder what I did this time. "Sure thing, Mrs. Hargrove."

The students are silent until they hear the click of the intercom disconnecting. And that's when all hell breaks loose.

"Bruh! You're in trouble!"

I shoot a look to Antonio, the student who most teachers warn you about. He can be mouthy, disruptive, and knows his way around the detention room.

I know his type. I *was* his type.

"First off, you owe the Bruh Jar," I direct.

"Worth it," he says as he saunters up to my desk and drops in the quarter. An appropriate fine for the kids to maybe stop using that fucking word. Little do they know that jar is funding their end of the year party.

"Second, what makes you think I'm in trouble? Maybe she wants to talk to me about you."

This is what Antonio and I do. He jabs me. I slightly jab him back. I let him think he's the winner. In return, he does his homework, and I'm one of the few classes he's passing.

"Nah, Miss Banks. I've been good this week. Haven't been to

the office yet. This is all you. Plus, you know that no one's safe when they're called down to Hargrove's office."

He's right about that. No student is safe when a summons from Principal Hargrove is given. But that's for students. I'm an adult. A teacher. A molder of minds. Voted one of the Teachers of the Year last year in the district. I'm not in trouble.

Probably.

Maybe.

I don't think.

"I'm sure everything is fine," I say. "Please make sure you clean up, and I'll see you tomorrow. It's *Westing Game* time!"

The bell rings and all of the students grab their things and quickly exit my room. I follow behind them, bag and keys in hand so I can make a quick exit whenever I'm done with whatever this is about to be.

As I make the long walk to the principal's office, I can't help but have flashbacks to my time at Rolling Hills Middle School.

I was a frequent flyer in detention. I had a gift for prank-pulling and general rowdiness. What can I say? I'm the middle child. And a Banks, for that matter. Teachers should've known what they were getting into after having my brother Simon.

To say that I saw my fair share of detention is an understatement. Though now as I look back at those years, I know I was just bored. Not in the gifted sense so I'd act out. I was the farthest thing from a straight-A student. But nothing kept my interest. So I'd act out.

Then one fateful day I had detention in the library, and everything changed.

I didn't have any homework, so I started browsing the shelves. The librarian—a wonderful woman named Mrs. Metcalf whom I think should be considered for sainthood—asked me if I'd like to read a book.

And she handed me *The Westing Game.*

It was over after that.

Now, my pranks didn't stop. Those continued on well through my high school and adult years. But books calmed me. They gave me something to look forward to. And for the first time in my young adult life, I felt like I wasn't just existing when it came to school.

That's why I decided to become a teacher. I wanted to help kids find their way. To show kids that finding an outlet, whether it be reading or art or music or whatever it is, could help fill voids you didn't know you had.

And if it's in the form of a book? Even better.

I wave to a few of my fellow teachers as I enter the principal's office. I don't bother her secretary, who's standing in front of the opened doors to the copier with a scowl on her face, as I open the door.

Though the second I walk in, I realize this meeting is not to congratulate me on being a two-time Teacher of the Year.

No, I'm standing in front of the firing squad.

Also known as the P.E.N.I.S. Posse.

"Please sit down, Quinn," Hargrove says. "We need to have a discussion."

guide to love rule #74

Stand up for what's right. Giving a middle finger for emphasis never hurts.

2
quinn

Being no stranger to a principal's office growing up, I got good at picking up on cues for how much trouble I was actually in. If the principal was still working on something, or taking a call, when I walked in, it was going to be easy. Just a warning or maybe even a curiosity of how I was able to wrap his car in cling wrap while not missing a single class.

Then there were times I knew I was in trouble. The mood was tense. Sometimes my parents were there. And always the first words I was told were, "Sit down, Miss Banks."

This is neither of those.

Principal Hargrove is sitting at the edge of her desk, arms crossed and looking her normal stoic self. What is throwing me is the cold gust of air I feel emanating from the three sets of eyes staring at me, lips snarled, injected, and pursed.

"I didn't know it was a P.E.N.I.S. Posse day! How we doing, ladies? What's the hot gos?"

All three women narrow their eyes at me even more. They don't like any teachers, but they hate me.

Probably because of the nickname I gave them.

P.E.N.I.S.—the horrible acronym for the mom group called Parents Ending the New Indoctrination of Students—should just be called PITA for Pain in the Ass. They're a group of around fifteen parents who've been in every teacher's business this year from kindergarten through twelfth grade, complaining about one thing or another. Christmas was a nightmare; they threw a fit when I gave a dyslexic student the option to listen to the book that we were reading; and tried to go to the local news, telling them that I was forcing every student to speak Spanish as their primary language.

I did no such thing. I just found some worksheets that were also in Spanish because half of my class has Mexican parents. Because we live in fucking Arizona.

And that's just me. I know they've driven the science teacher up the wall. They made a second-grade teacher cry. They tried to get the Halloween parade banned because of the obvious devil worship we do here. I think the only one they haven't fucked with is the math teacher, and that's because she's downright terrifying. Basically, they're horrible people with bad lip filler who were mean girls in school and don't know their life's purpose without causing some sort of drama.

"Monica, so good to see you," I say to Makayla's mother, who I'm certain is fresh from filming her daily vlog. "I didn't realize you were a P.E.N.I.S. member. Congrats! Is it true you get a bedazzled Stanley upon joining? Or is it a more discreet gift based on your acronym? I have one I think you'd love. It has—"

"Sit down, Quinn."

I give Monica a fake smile as I do what Principal Hargrove asks. But only so we can move this along. A new episode of my show dropped today, and it's not going to watch itself. "Are they going to sit or are they going to loom over me like the witches they are?"

"See! Witches!" That comes from Taylor, the leader of the group, whose youngest is in first grade and oldest is in fifth. She's the Halloween hater despite us teachers finding pictures of her, before kids, in a slutty nurse costume. "Why would she say that if she wasn't teaching it?"

"Now ladies, let's have a seat." The three of them squeeze on a couch meant for only two people. I want to laugh, but I'm going to read the room, put my smartass card away, and deal with whatever bullshit they're about spew.

"Can I ask why I'm here?"

Before Hargrove can answer, Regina, the mom of Irish triplets, speaks up. Yes. Three kids in three calendar years. And I had them all, with the last one leaving my classroom last year. "Because you're about to start that murder book, and we're here to ban it!"

I stare at Regina, waiting for her to say the punch line. When she doesn't say anything else, and the other P.E.N.I.S. members give me the same smug look with their arms crossed, I can't help but burst out into laughter.

"Quinn!" Hargrove hisses. "Pull yourself together."

"I can't," I say between laughing fits. "She thinks she can just come in here, snap her fingers, and ban me from teaching an acclaimed and award-winning book that I've been teaching for years? How can you not be laughing? They're ridiculous."

I laugh for another minute, I think I even slap my knee once or twice, but when I'm finally able to calm myself down, I realize that I'm the only one laughing.

"Quinn, you're teaching a book about murder? This wasn't in your lesson plan."

I look over to my principal, who apparently has never actually *read* a lesson plan that I've been forced to turn in every week for twelve years.

"It's not a book about murder," I defend. "And it's on there. Every year. You should know that."

"But a man is murdered!" Regina speaks up. "I read it last year!"

I don't make a point that two of her other kids already read it. Pretty much because Monica speaks up before I can.

"I refuse to have my precious Makayla read a book about such a gruesome act of violence."

I shoot a look to Monica. "Really? Ever watched *The Lion King*? Or *Bambi*? Last I checked that was all about the murder."

"Ladies!" Hargrove interjects. "Before this gets out of control, let's get back to the topic at hand."

"Yes, thank you, Principal," Taylor says, clearly needing to reinsert herself as the Head Bitch in Charge. "We in the Parents Ending the New Indoctrination of Students—"

"P.E.N.I.S." I say, which of course earns me three dirty looks. Worth it.

"As I was saying," Taylor continues. "We feel that a book like this is just too violent for our darling babies to be reading. And we are demanding that Miss Banks not teach it."

Okay, I've had it. "Do you know anything about this book? And I'm not talking about the generic plot that you asked Alexa about or the likely bad skim reading Regina says she did last year. Do you know anything at all about this book?"

"We know all we need to," Monica says.

"Of course, because y'all know everything," I say sarcastically. "It's an award-winning book. It's been taught by me and others for decades. And just in my experience, the students love it. It gets them reading. It gets their minds curious. There are life lessons in every book, including this one. Older brothers and sisters tell their younger siblings about this book, and it's the thing they can't wait for each year. What's so bad about that?"

"Murder is a life lesson?"

"Oh, for fuck's sake! He's not even fucking dead!" Spoiler alert for the book, but it's not like this group is ever going to read it.

"Quinn. Language."

I look over to my principal, who at this point I wish would say something in my defense. "I'm sorry, but this is ridiculous."

"Is it though?" she asks. "Maybe there's another book you can consider?"

My eyes go wide, and I'm pretty sure I stop breathing. "Really? I've been teaching this for years with literally no complaints. Every one of Regina's children has read it, and she *never* spoke up about it until now. Though at that time she didn't have any P.E.N.I.S. in her life. Maybe that's the difference."

Yes I know the double meaning of the dig. I don't know if Regina does though.

"That's not true," Regina stammers out. Okay, maybe she did. "All of my children complained every day! Justin especially."

"Really?" I highly doubt that. For example, Justin, her son I had last year, was a good kid. Decent student. But he didn't love reading or English, which is normal for sixth grade boys. But I remember him getting more and more excited every day we read a little more. And if my memory serves me correctly, her other two children were just as excited. "What did he complain about?"

"Well…he…I don't remember specifics. But I know he felt forced to read it."

I let out a groan. "Every kid is technically forced to read in school. It's called lessons."

"Quinn," Hargrove interrupts. "Since this is an *optional* lesson that you're teaching, and given that it might not have the best subject choice, maybe we can pivot. Come to a compromise that will work for everyone's liking?"

I stare at my principal, my jaw slacked as I hear what she's saying. This isn't the first time she's caved to the fucking P.E.N.I.S Posse. They've had lady boners all year about books in all grade levels, and this school has submitted to them more times than not.

But this is it. My final straw. If she's going to let these fucking dildo-nicknamed, bleach blonde bitches ban my favorite book, I'm out. I won't let this stand. This is the hill I'm going to fucking die on with two middle fingers in the air.

"No."

Everyone's eyes go wide as Hargrove follows up. "Excuse me? Did you say no?"

"That's right. I said no. I'm not changing the book. I'm not changing the lesson. And if you don't want me to teach it, you'll need to find another sixth grade ELA teacher for the rest of the school year."

I sit up a little straighter, because saying just those few words gives me the confidence that has me ready to go to war.

And not just for me. But for my kids. For books. For every person in their lives who have been pushed around by the mean girls.

Because fuck them and high horses they rode in on.

"You can't say no," Regina says. "We don't want it taught. Your principal doesn't want you to teach it. Therefore you have to listen to us."

I let out an exasperated laugh. "Actually. I don't. Because you have no power here. You're just a group of loud, obnoxious, bitchy mothers who want to set curriculum but didn't even realize you have the fucking word *penis* for the acronym of your group. You know, the word that makes every middle schooler snicker when it's said? Imagine your children having to hear every day that their mother loves P.E.N.I.S. Oh wait, they do."

They audibly gasp and actually clutch their pearls. I'm from the South, and I've never even seen that in real life.

"You can't talk to us like this," Taylor sputters.

"Oh, but I can," I say as I stand up, because no one delivers a good monologue sitting down. "You're just pissed that you've run for school board for the last five years and you lose every single time. So you had to gather some cronies up at Pilates class and make everyone's lives as miserable as yours."

"How dare you—"

I cut Monica off. "Don't *you* dare start with me. You've been a pain in my ass all year, but worse, you can't even see what harm you're doing to your kid. Makayla is a good student and classmate who I can tell is going through something. Now I'm not a psychiatrist or a Keebler Elf, but I'm pretty fucking sure it has to do with her mother trying to force new lifestyle changes on her all in the name of a four-subscriber YouTube channel."

Monica gasps, and I see Hargrove stand up behind her desk. I'm probably about to be fired, but I'm not done yet. If I'm going to get fired, I'm going out in a blaze of glory.

"Oh, and now you, Regina. The bane of my existence for the past three years." If I had to place a bet on who laid the egg for this takedown, it was her. She never liked me. Probably because I wouldn't cave to her fake demands and constant nagging of my teaching methods. "Each of your children loved my class, despite you trying to sabotage me at every turn. Your oldest still pops his head in to say hello when the high school comes to visit. Justin? The one you claim hated the book? He asked me last year if he could keep his copy, because he wanted to read it again over the summer. I know I want to keep books I hated. So really, what's your fucking problem? Mad they learned something outside of your pea-brain views? Mad that I'm their favorite teacher? Or are you just generally unhappy with life because it's the worst kept secret in this town that you're a beard for your husband and you forced him to have three kids so people would stop talking? Which is it? Whatever your answer is, I know for a fact that me teaching this book is not the source of your misery, but because you have nothing better to do between Botox appointments than make other people's lives miserable, here you are. Well, guess what? I'm not caving. I'm not budging. So I either teach the book or I quit. Your choice."

That apparently gets my three enemies excited.

"Oh that would be wonderful!" Monica chirps up. "We just wanted the book gone, but having this teacher who forces her ideals and beliefs onto our children…"

"And teaches murder!"

The three of them nod, because they all just think they walked away with the win.

They might win the battle of having me gone, but enemies of Quinn Banks don't win wars.

"Quinn," Hargrove says, her voice now pleading. "Don't teach the book. Or else you'll leave me no choice."

I'm flabbergasted by the words of my principal right now. So much for being on the side of your teachers. "Really? No choice?"

She thinks I'm going to stay. She thinks I'm going to cave. Sorry, Hargrove, you picked the wrong day and the wrong bitch.

And maybe some other cause, I might've caved. But not this one. And not today. Today I stand up for every teacher not only in this district, but in America, who are dealing with P.E.N.I.S.s all over the country.

"You know what? Fuck you. Fuck *all* of you. I quit."

"Quinn," Hargrove says, her voice now suddenly panicked. "Let's not be rash."

Now it's my turn to read her for filth. "Let's not act rash? Two seconds ago you were telling me 'or else.' What was 'or else?' Please. Enlighten me. Because I know it wasn't about to be you actually being on the side of your teachers for once. Or maybe doing two seconds of investigating to look into what I'm doing versus what the P.E.N.I.S. bitches are complaining about. You've let them take over this school because you're too chicken shit to stand up for yourself. And I refuse to work for a woman who doesn't have my, and my fellow teachers' backs. So yeah. I quit. I'm fucking done."

"Quinn…what about your students?" Hargrove's voice is now pure desperation. "You can't possibly leave them."

This makes me stop in my tracks, and I know this is her attempt of guilting me into staying. She knows I'll do anything for my kids. She's seen me bring in clothes for one whose family lost their house in a fire. She knows I pay off school lunch debts. She knows those kids are my world.

But what I need to do for them right now is to stand up for myself. Stand up for them. They might not get it now, but I hope maybe one day, they'll know that I did this for them just as much as me.

"That does hurt me," I say. "I love each and every one of my students. But I teach them every day to do the right thing. I teach them that sometimes the right thing isn't the popular thing, or the easy thing. And that caving to peer pressure is never a good move. And if I caved right now and didn't teach that book…if I cowered and did what was told of me, even though I knew it wasn't right…then I'd be going against every single thing I've ever taught them. And I won't do that. I respect myself too much. And frankly, I have zero respect for anyone in this room."

And with that, I turn my back, slam the door behind me, and storm to my room to collect my things.

I guess summer break is starting a little earlier this year.

3

porter

When you own a bar, there are things that just become a normal part of your occupation that no other business owner has to go through. Call it the bartender's version of the death and taxes guarantee.

Regulars will always bitch and moan about something that's wrong. They don't care that it's been wrong for twenty years, they're still going to complain. Two of my regulars, who bear a striking resemblance to the two old dudes from the Muppets, love to bitch about the lighting. That it's too dark and they can't read their newspaper. I inform them that the lighting has been the same every day since they first started coming here when my dad owned it, and maybe, just maybe, that it's their eyesight getting a little worse for wear.

They tell me to shut my trap, get better bulbs, but before I do that, pour them another beer.

There's also the guarantee that just when I'm starting to feel comfortable and things are going smoothly, something will break, burst, or catch on fire, needing me to pay a hefty repair bill. Two months ago it was the ice machine. Three before that was the fryer vent. And while I hate forking over that money, if I want The Joint to survive, I need to suck it up and pay the piper.

And lastly, and this is a guarantee: When it's a Friday night, and the drinks are flowing and the music is playing, that you will get hit on by a woman.

I'm not being conceited. It's just facts.

"Hey, Porter. What's a girl got to do to get a drink around here?"

I let out a groan as my back is turned from the voice, which gives me the chance to mumble what I actually want to say.

"Flash your tits to someone. It's what you do every fucking week."

But, when I turn around from pouring whiskey into a rocks glass, I'm wearing nothing but my signature smile as I face Emily Babcock.

"Just gotta order, Em. Whatcha feeling tonight?"

I'm purposely non-flirty with her. No use of the word "hun," "darlin'," or "beautiful." But that doesn't matter when it comes to the one woman in town I'm pretty sure every man has had a nighttime visit with—she's going to assume you're flirting with her just by speaking.

"Vodka soda with a lime. And maybe you, if you're up for it?"

"One vodka soda, coming right up."

I purposely ignore the last part as I go to make her drink. Emily has always been one to throw herself at men. Hell, she's been doing it since we were in high school, which is the only time I fell for her come-ons. But I don't remember it being as bad as it's been recently.

Then again, I've never had live music in here on a regular basis, which I have the past few Fridays. I'm going to assume that's the direct correlation.

This is what I get for trying to make an extra buck.

Some of my younger clientele—the ones who come in when my grumpy old men head home for the night—have been on me to get some sort of entertainment in here. Which, I don't know what they're talking about. I have a jukebox, televisions, and pool tables. What else do you need at a hometown dive bar?

After a while, I was tired of hearing about it, so I caved—but just to prove to them it wasn't going to work. That it wouldn't drive up business, or bring in new faces into our small town of Rolling Hills, Tennessee.

All it proved was that I don't know shit.

So now every Friday night we have some sort of musical act, my bar is busier than ever, and I have to deal with the likes of Emily Babcock more than usual.

"Here you go." I hand Emily her drink and start to take someone else's order, figuring she's going to hand me her credit card. She shouldn't need me to tell her the price. She's been coming in nearly every weekend since she turned twenty-one, so I'm a little baffled as to why she's still standing here. And why she's staring at me like she's trying to figure out a riddle.

"Cash or tab?" I ask while I gesture to the next customer. After they signal to get them two more beers, I realize that Emily is still staring.

"Did I grow a tail or somethin'?"

She shakes her head as I reach into the beer cooler to pull out two bottles. "I'm just trying to figure out who's going to be the woman who finally breaks Porter McCoy."

Now this makes me laugh. "I'm pretty sure she doesn't exist, Em. Want me to start you a tab?"

She lets out a little huff and puts her credit card down on the bar. "Sure. But I want you to know, if you're ever ready… If that big house next door is feeling a little lonely, you know where to find me."

"See ya later, Emily."

She thinks she did something there as she tosses me a wink before she turns away. I'm pretty sure a wink isn't supposed to send a cold shiver down your spine, but that's what it does when it comes from her.

"Is she ever going to stop? I think my dick just shriveled up in sympathy for you."

I chuckle at the words from my cousin, Wes Taylor, who's

now standing at the bar with his wife Betsy. I reach across to shake his hand, which ends up being pulled into a bro hug. I also lean over to give Betsy a kiss on the cheek.

"Unfortunately, I'm used to her. Dangers of the job." I look out to the crowded bar to see if the table that Wes and his crew usually sit at is open, but it isn't. "Sorry, man. If I would've known you were coming, I would've reserved your table."

He shakes his head. "No need. Just the two of us tonight. A little date night, if you will."

"Married and still going on dates," I say, pouring them their usual drinks. "Aren't you two just adorable."

"Damn right we're still going on dates," Betsy says. "I love those kids more than anything, but they're exhausting."

"But, they all had plans of their own—when you don't need to pay a babysitter, you take full advantage."

"Cheers to that," I say as I hand them their drinks. Not that I'd know the first thing about the daily dealing of children. But I can assume it's hell in a hand basket.

"You know, though, Emily did ask a good question."

I lift my eyebrow to Betsy, because I know where this is going. "Don't start."

"What?" she says in mock innocence. "I'm just saying that when you're one of the most eligible bachelors in Rolling Hills, the people want to know when Porter McCoy will go off the market."

I shake my head at my cousin-in-law and start making drinks for a few regulars that I can see need another. "How about this? When I find her, you'll be the first to know."

Betsy slightly rolls her eyes at my response. "Fine. I guess I'll accept that. Maybe you can throw in some mozzarella sticks to make the deal binding?"

I laugh and shake my head. "Mozzarella sticks for you to stop hounding me? Say less."

I don't know why the state of my love life—or lack thereof—seems to be the hot topic of conversation tonight. People know my situation. Hell, I've known most of these people since kinder-garten. They've never seen me with a woman for more than a few dates. They sure as hell have no idea about the woman I've been sleeping with for eight years. So according to them, I'm Porter McCoy, bachelor extraordinaire. And that's just how I like it.

Plus, they also know my family history, which means they know I have my reasons for not wanting a wife or family.

My family in town is sparse—just Wes and his parents. Pops died eight years ago. Mom took off when I was in middle school. I think she still lives in Indiana, but I could be wrong. I haven't talked to her since I called to tell her about his death. Silly me thought that she had the right to know that the man she was once married to, and had a son with, was dead. And maybe part of me wanted to know that I still had one parent. I know we didn't talk much, but the thought of losing the man who raised me being gone turned me into a scared kid all over again.

I should've known better. After I told her he was dying, she said that she was sorry and hung up. Didn't come back for the funeral. Didn't even send a card.

So yeah, she still could be in Indiana with my stepdad and half-sister. Could be in Alaska. Hell, she could also be dead. I have no clue.

But it is what it is. I learned a long time ago that family isn't always blood; sometimes it's the family you choose. Or in my case, the family that chose me. The people who've come into this bar faithfully since my dad opened it thirty years ago knew me since I was a straggly kid sitting at the bar doing homework. So yes, I might bitch about them, but they've been here for the good times and the bad. They're the reason my business is still alive and thriving. And why I'm slammed on this Friday night.

I'm running back and forth down the bar, hating that I keep putting off hiring someone else to help me tend the bar. I can normally handle it, but on Fridays it's been rough. And frankly, it would be nice to have a night off once in a while. But I can't think about that now. I have a bar three-people deep and there's no sign of it slowing down.

But as I top off a Long Island iced tea, I happen to catch a glance at the front door. I know most everyone who comes in the bar, but sometimes even friendly faces can take me by surprise. Which is how I feel when I see Maeve Banks walk in the door.

It's few and far between that The Joint gets a visit from the oldest Banks daughter. Not that she has anything against the bar that she took her first legal drink in—and the bar she used to steal Smirnoff Ice from when she was a teenager—but now that she lives closer to Nashville with her billionaire husband, we don't see her as much.

Right behind Maeve are her youngest sisters, Ainsley and Stella. Seeing Stella here isn't as far-fetched since she works in Rolling Hills with her brother Simon. It's always shocking to see Ainsley here since I've never seen her take a sip of alcohol in her life.

Three Banks sisters have my spidey senses tingling that the fourth might be behind. Though that's doubtful. She was just home last month, and I'm pretty sure her school year doesn't end for another month. It was rare we got a non-holiday or vacation visit from Quinn then; I doubt it would happen two months in a row.

Much to my cock's dismay.

So, as much as I'd like to stare at the door and say a prayer to the God of Hookups, I can't, as customers start shouting their orders at me. Begrudgingly I serve them, but unfortunately I now have nothing but thoughts of Quinn Banks rolling through my brain.

Fuck, what I'd give to get lost in her curves tonight. Yes, I just saw her last month. I don't think in our eight years we've ever seen each other two months in a row. But it has been three times in the past five months, which is probably why I keep looking to see if my favorite brunette is going to walk in.

Which is ridiculous. I don't stare at doors. I don't wish for women to come see me. Hell, I barely initiate small talk when it comes to the opposite gender. I've seen the worst in people and relationships. I watch grown folks cheat on each other every day in this bar. I watched my mom pack her suitcases and leave. I know Pops was strong and put on a brave face after she decided that small-town Tennessee life wasn't for her, but there were nights I heard his tears. I know he wasn't the same man after she left. And like hell I'm ever going to risk my wellbeing for the chance that maybe I'll be on the slim chance of a happily ever after.

It's why Quinn and I are perfect together. I only see her when she comes home from Arizona. We have incredible, string-free sex. She flies back home. I go back to my life. We don't text in between. We don't call and pretend to catch up. It's all physical. No more, no less.

The round of applause from the patrons to the entertainment for the night breaks my thoughts as I turn my back to grab a bottle of tequila. But the thoughts don't stay away for long as the tequila makes me now think of the one night where I licked this same brand off of Quinn's luscious body.

That was a good night…

"Jesus Christ, Porter! What's a girl gotta do around here to get a drink?"

The voice stops me on a dime. There's no other woman that could scream at me like that, and yet I find it so fucking sexy.

I don't turn around. I don't react, except for the smile that no one can see.

Because Quinn Banks is home.

guide to love rule #17

Sometimes you need a girl's night to make
you forget your problems.
Sometimes you need a dick appointment.
Both have their benefits.

4

quinn

I didn't really want to come to The Joint tonight. First, no one knows I quit my job, and being around liquor isn't the best idea when I'm trying not to blab.

Second, I didn't shave my legs.

The first is the most important, because I'm currently fibbing to my sisters about why I took an impromptu trip home on short notice. So far, they're buying the bit about a long weekend and expiring airline miles. But because they think nothing is wrong, I couldn't put up a fight about coming to The Joint since none of them had plans.

So now I have to figure out how to not blurt out that I quit my job, but also make sure I don't accidentally go home with Porter tonight. Because while a hookup might soothe the ache of my life being in shambles, I doubt I'd wake up tomorrow morning feeling any better.

Sated? Yes. Sore? Depends on how adventurous we're feeling. Still depressed? Very much so.

All of this is going to be easier said than done. I'm one slip of the lips from my sisters calling me on my flimsy story. And those jeans Porter is wearing should be illegal. No man's ass should look that good in a pair of Wranglers.

God, I really am weak…

And I'm just going to keep staring at it until he acknowledges me. I know he heard me. He might not have turned around or made any sort of noticeable movement, but when you sleep with a man for eight years, you know how to read his body.

When he slowly turns toward me, the cocky smile says it all. To any other woman in this bar, they'd think it's the classic Porter flirty bartender smile. And to the untrained eye, it looks just like that.

There's just one exception: the smile he gives me pops a dimple that sends shivers down my spine every time I see him.

Fuck my life! Why didn't I shave my legs before the plane this morning…

"Well, look who's back."

I purposely don't give him a reaction, because that's how this game goes between us when we're in public. He openly flirts with me because he's a bartender and he can. I pretend I'm not affected because I have a reputation to uphold, or something like that. Then, give or take a few hours, and after one of us says the code phrase, we're ripping each other's clothes off. Most of the time we make it back to his house. Sometimes we fuck in his office. I've always wanted to do it on the bar, but I'm still wrapping my mind around the logistics of that.

All in all, it's a solid system that's been honed and perfected for nearly a decade.

And I'm the dumbass who forgot to shave her legs.

"I don't know what you're talking about," I say in my casual way. "I'm just here wondering if I can get a round of drinks for my sisters?"

The glint in his eye says more than any words could say as he goes and starts pouring the drinks he's memorized that we've ordered for years in this establishment—beer for me, Jack and Diet Coke for Maeve, vodka and soda for Stella, and a club soda with a splash of cranberry and a lime for Ainsley.

"What brings the lost sister home?" he says as he hands me

Ainsley's drink. "Another family party that you just *had* to come home for? Maybe your niece is having another milestone you just *can't* miss?"

This is what I get for telling Porter why I've been home more often than I have been in years. Those *were* the reasons I came home. But my dumb ass just had to overly defend that I was home for my family and not to see him.

I wasn't.

Mostly.

"Actually, this was a spontaneous trip," I begin, figuring it's best to stick with the same lie for the time being. "I had a long weekend and expiring travel miles. Figured why not come home for a few days."

Porter raises an eyebrow. "Really? That's it. No other reason? None at all…"

God, he looks good. Too good. His brown hair is messy, but you can tell it started the night styled. Actually, it looks like when I try to rip it out of his head when his tongue is trying to kill me. His sleeves are rolled up, showing off forearms that shouldn't be sexy, but they are. And is his drawl thicker? I feel like it is. Either that or I'm just thinking about how deep it gets when he tells me to suck his cock.

"Nope," I say with a pop at the end. "Just wanted to hang out with my family. Nothing more. Nothing less.

He gives me a "I don't believe you for a second" nod as he hands me my beer. "That's good. Family's important."

"I agree."

"I'll start you a tab," he says as he arranges the drinks on a tray for me to take back to the table. But just as I'm about to pick it up, he crooks his finger for me to come closer.

What is he doing? It's one thing to flirt with me—Porter is known for being a shameless flirt behind the bar—but to bring me in like he's telling me a secret? This feels a little bold. A little dangerous.

A lot hot.

"Good to see you. I hope you order the chicken wings tonight."

I swear my body has a Pavlovian response to that phrase. And while I know that probably by the end of the night I'm going to be ordering, for now I feel like I need to play it cool. A little mysterious. A girl can't be too eager, you know?

"Maybe later," I say coyly as I back away. "Not sure if I'm in the mood tonight."

This makes him chuckle. "We'll see about that."

I don't say anything else as I pick up the tray of drinks and make it a point not to show that my heart is beating faster than I'd like it to as I walk back to the table my sisters snagged. I mean…sex does sound good. Especially Porter sex. Not that I've had other sex in the last…I don't know when…but that's because what Porter is able to do to me makes every other man pale in comparison. I figured that out when I tried to date a guy back in Phoenix. The first time he went down on me, he bit my clit. Not nibbled. Not sucked a little too hard. No, the motherfucker nearly took a chunk out.

Clearly he took the phrase "eating out" a little too literally.

But not with Porter. I bet that man would say that he literally didn't care about my stubbled legs and still throw them over his shoulders. I wish my brain was functioning enough this morning before I got on the plane to think about that. In my defense, I just wanted out of Arizona. I couldn't bear spending any more time in my apartment, staring at the wall, wondering what the hell I'm going to do with my life.

"Hey! Watch it!" I stumble backward, not realizing who I just ran into. "Oh. I'm sorry. I didn't realize Big Girl Banks was coming through."

Ah yes, a trip to The Joint just wouldn't be complete without Rolling Hills' off-brand Regina George.

"Hi, Emily. Always great to see you. How's the chlamydia?"

Did I start that rumor in high school? Yes.

Did she have it? Maybe.

Will I ask her about it until the day she dies? Fuck yes.

"Grow up Quinn. Let me guess. Here with your sisters?"

"Yes. And let me guess. Here to see which man here you haven't fucked?"

She rolls her eyes before walking away.

"Bye, Em! Always a pleasure!"

I laugh under my breath as I finally make my way to our table.

"What was that?" Maeve asks.

"Just Emily being Emily," I say as I pass the drinks around.

"That's not what I meant." She tilts her head back to the bar. "You and Porter. Was he telling you a secret or something?"

Shit, shit, shit… What was he thinking? What was *I* thinking for being so obvious?

Okay, Quinn. Think fast. Keep your face right. Don't blow this.

"Oh, nothing," I say. "He wondered why I was home. Told him. That was it."

Maeve's face clearly says she doesn't believe me.

"Why are you home?"

This question comes from Stella, who I'm going to guess has put on her bedazzled FBI hat and has already poked holes in my story.

"I told you. Expiring flight miles and a long weekend."

"I'm sorry, but you're lying," she says. "I checked your school calendar, and it isn't a long weekend. Plus, even if it was, when have you ever come home for a trip this short just because?"

I start to defend myself when Stella holds up a finger, clearly not done presenting her case.

"Whatever you're going to say, save it. It didn't sit right when you said you were coming home, so I started lurking around social media. I stumbled onto a post from a group of moms claiming that a teacher who recently was fired should never be hired again in any school district ever because not only did she repeatedly use the f-word against them and told them that they had botched plastic surgery done, but she also refused to listen to parents concerns about teaching books about murder. And if that doesn't sound like Quinn Banks, I don't know what does."

I don't try and defend myself, but simply look at Ainsley, the only sister who may be able cushion this blow. "Do you have anything to bring to the interrogation table?"

Ainsley Banks is the quiet one of the sisters. A little shy. I'm not sure if she's an actual empath, but this girl can feel one's emotions better than anyone I've ever met. So when she takes my hand and gives me that Ainsley look, I know I'm about to spill my guts.

"Nothing specific. But I'm worried. We all are. When I picked you up from the airport, you barely said two words on the drive down here, and that's not the Quinn I know."

Who knew me not saying something would be my giveaway?

"I hate that you all know me so well," I say, gripping onto my beer bottle with each hand.

"Did you really get fired?"

I shake my head, close my eyes, and take a deep breath. "I beat them to the punch. Quit before it could happen. What you read on Facebook? Those were my parting words to the moms of my school district who made my life a living hell this year."

I bring my beer to my lips when I look over to Maeve. "Thoughts, big sister?"

She shakes her head. "I have a lot, but I'm going to withhold them until I hear the story. Because I'm guessing there's a story."

"Oh, there is," I say, turning to signal for my favorite bartender to bring us a round of shots. "Hold on to your butts. You won't believe anything that I'm about to tell you."

———

"Their name wasn't actually penis, was it? You're making that up."

"You're fucking right it was!" I say to Ainsley. "I got fucked over by P.E.N.I.S.!"

This is apparently the funniest thing I've ever said, as all of my sisters, even a sober Ainsley, are falling off their chairs in laughter.

"I'm not laughing at the situation. The whole thing fucking sucks," Stella says as she tries to catch her breath. "But man, if anyone is going to quit a job, that's how you do it."

I tip my beer to her before taking a sip that's more like a chug. "At least I'll be remembered."

I was never going to completely lie to my sisters about my employment status, but I didn't want to do it here. I still haven't processed everything, considering it happened two days ago. But as soon as I started talking, I felt lighter with every word.

The shots of tequila that we ordered helped too.

"In all seriousness, Quinn, I'm so sorry," Ainsley says, wrapping me in a hug like only Ainsley can give. "I know how much you loved your students. And how good of a teacher you are."

"Thanks," I say as I feel the tears starting to well. I really don't want to cry in the middle of The Joint, but between Ainsley's hug, the booze, and all of the emotions coming back to the surface, it's hard to keep them at bay. "I know it was the right thing to do, but it fucking sucks."

"Of course it does," Stella says. "You built a life and a career out there. Now I'm sure you don't even know which way is up."

"I don't," I admit. "It's why I came back here this weekend. Sitting in my apartment made me feel like I was trapped in this box. I didn't even want to go out for groceries in case I'd see one of those bitches, or worse, one of my students. I don't know what the school told them. Do they think I'm coming back? I mean, they have to know by now but still… I can't face them yet. Maybe ever. It hurts my heart to even think about it."

Fuck, here comes the tears. I'm not a big crier. But the

thought of not getting to say a proper goodbye to my students guts me every time I think about it.

"They'll understand," Ainsley says. "Maybe not now, but one day, they'll know that you stood up for them and what you thought was right."

"I can only hope," I say as I rest my head on her arm.

The table falls quiet, which is when I realize that I haven't heard my big sister offer any words of advice. Which is very unlike the one we fondly call Mama Maeve for her want to fix everyone's lives. Though maybe now that she's getting regular dick, she's less bossy? One can only hope.

"Quinn, I don't mean to be this person…"

Never mind that thought. "Yes, you do, so just say it."

Maeve shakes her head, but not in a disapproving way. More in the she hates to be the bearer of bad news way. "I support you one-thousand percent in the decision you made. But what now?"

And there lies the million-dollar question. One I don't have an answer to.

"Don't get me wrong, I love what you did," Maeve quickly says. "That took bravery that not a lot of people have. But with that bravery comes the next chapter."

"I know," I say, pushing back another wave of emotion that was threatening to come over me. "Can I say I don't know yet?"

"Of course," Stella says. "This has been a roller coaster for you. No one blames you for not knowing what's next."

I nod, though I wonder if Maeve agrees with my baby sister's sentiment. "I know I need to figure it out. And I plan to. But not tonight. Tonight I want to be in my drink-until-I-forget stage."

I look to Maeve, needing her seal of approval on this. "Fine. But know we're here for you. You've been here for all of us. This is the least we can do in return."

I reach my arm across the table we're sitting at. "Thank you. Thanks to all of you. I needed this."

Stella and Ainsley join our hands, and the four of us share a silent moment.

These women…I don't know what I'd do without them. Or how I got so lucky that when God created the universe, she said, "Quinn Banks, you're going to be a fucking mess. But we're going to give you sisters to make up for that."

And you know what? I'm good with that. Because I love me. I love the mess and chaos that I am. I love that I stand up for things that are right and tell people what I think. And if they don't like me? Fuck 'em.

Most of all, I love my sisters to the ends of this Earth. We're opposites in so many ways. But the one thing we have in common is that we love and support each other without hesitation. So whether it's a shoulder to cry on, getting your sister drunk after she quits her job, or doing borderline illegal things to get back at ex-fiancés, we're here for it, no questions asked.

Especially that last one. I hated Stella's former fiancé, and taking him down was a highlight of last year.

"All right, ladies, here we go."

Seemingly out of nowhere, Porter is at our table, delivering us a tray of food that I don't think anyone ordered.

And did he put on cologne? The one he knows I like because I stupidly told him I did in a semi-sober state?

"What's this?" Ainsley asks.

Porter starts setting down the arrangement of bar food. "I figured that no girls night is complete without snacks. So these are loaded cheese fries, some fried pickles with extra ranch because I know you'll just ask me for more so I saved a trip, mozzarella sticks, jalapeño poppers, and of course, chicken wings."

Oh that sly fucker…

"Really? Chicken wings?" I ask as my sisters start reaching for baskets. "Bold of you to assume we want chicken wings."

"But it was the right assumption," Ainsley says as she reaches over for the basket. "Who says no to chicken wings? I always want them."

Poor thing has no clue what she's saying, or why Porter is

snickering. And it's taking every ounce of my being not to crack up, especially since the debate is heavy in my house on whether Ainsley is still a virgin.

"I hear ya, Ains. They always hit the spot." Porter picks up our empty glasses before looking at me. "Anything else?"

The silent conversation we're having in our eyes would be fascinating to watch if anyone around us had any clue what was happening.

I'm trying to act cool and calm and that maybe I won't be at his house tonight.

He knows I'm going to be.

I try to play it off.

He gives me a subtle wink that makes my pussy clench before he walks away.

Goddammit, I'm having sex tonight…

"Porter's the best," Stella says in between bites of a mozzarella stick that leaves a touch of marinara on the corner of her mouth.

"Yes he is," I say on a sigh, making sure he's out of eye shot before I take a wing. "He really is."

5
porter

I REALLY CAN'T COMPLAIN ABOUT LIVING NEXT DOOR TO THE BAR. It's convenient when I need to get there quickly. I save a shit ton of money on gas. And on nights like this, when I was stuck inside for hours, it's nice to breathe in the air during my hundred-yard walk.

Usually, I'd take my time. Go over anything I need to remember—like making it a priority to hire a second bartender. Breathe in the crisp air. But not tonight. No, tonight I need to get home.

I've got the best kind of surprise waiting for me.

How do I know? When you've slept with a woman for eight years, you get to know their looks. Their body language. And the smile that Quinn sent me before she left with her sisters? I only get that smile when she's feeling extra feisty.

It's about to be my lucky night.

God, she looked so good. You'd think since I just saw her a month ago she wouldn't have this kind of effect on me. It was actually the opposite. From the second I saw her in that tight white blouse, her hair messy on top of her head, I wanted to turn off the "open" sign and fuck her right there on top of the bar. When I was at her table, I wanted to sit her on my lap, just so I could feel her against me. And when she leaned over the bar tonight when I stupidly told her to come closer? She knew what she was doing when she gave me the perfect view of her tits. The woman knows they're my kryptonite.

Which is why I'm sprinting home. When I walked out of the bar and looked toward my house, I could see a faint light coming from my bedroom. I take the porch steps two at a time and throw the door open, kicking off my shoes as I all but sprint to my bedroom, thankful I showed her where I hide the spare key years ago.

I take a second to catch my breath—I have to keep some sort of cool about me—before opening the door. Now, I could find her asleep. There have been nights she's come over and used my spare key when I've had a late-night closing. When that happens, I wake her up by her favorite way—with my tongue between her thighs.

Except when I open the door, I see that Quinn is definitely not asleep.

No. She's sitting up in my bed, gloriously naked, legs spread, and staring right at me.

"Took you long enough."

I grin at her words as I slowly start making my way toward the bed, unbuttoning my shirt as I go, tossing it to the side as I stand in front of her.

"Did you start without me?"

She coyly shrugs. "Maybe."

I crook my finger, silently asking her to come to meet me at the foot of the bed. She never takes her big brown eyes off of me as she maneuvers to her knees, crawling to me.

I swear the woman is a fucking goddess.

But as she comes closer, I realize that there's more than fire in her eyes. Hurt? Vulnerability? That's not something I normally see from Quinn, especially in this bedroom. I don't think I've seen that look on her since our first night together eight years ago.

"Can you do something for me?"

Quinn Banks just crawled to me, and now her tits are pressed against my chest. Right now I'd commit murder for her, especially after I tip her chin up and stare at her red lips.

"Anything."

For a second, I see that sadness back in her eyes before she pushes it away. "Make me forget."

I wasn't expecting that.

"Are you okay? What happened? Did someone—"

She shakes her head. "No. I've…it's been an epically shitty week. I'm sad and confused. I stole my mom's car to drive back over here. So what I need now is for you to not push me on anything and just fuck me. Fuck me so I forget that my world is upside down. Can you do that?"

Shitty week? World upside down? What is she talking about? "Qu—"

She quickly puts a finger in front of my lips. "Please. Don't ask. I've talked a lot today. I'm going to have to do it a lot tomorrow. And everything will be public knowledge soon. But just—please—tonight…fuck me until I forget."

I do have a lot of questions. A ton, actually. But that's not my job right now.

She wants to forget? Done.

I lower my hand from her chin, giving her a quick kiss on the lips before I have both hands on each of her perfect ass cheeks, tipping her back onto my bed. The mattress is so soft that she bounces a little, which gives me a spectacular view of her flawless tits bouncing on her chest. I know I just saw her a month ago—and we usually go much longer between our rendezvous—but my mouth is salivating at the thought of getting to feast on those tonight.

But that can wait. Tonight isn't about me. Tonight is about making sure Quinn forgets her name, where she's at, and that she forgets to say that this is the last time.

I quickly unlatch my belt and snap it off my waist, pushing

my blue jeans and boxer briefs down as Quinn positions herself on my bed just where she thinks I want her.

"Where you going?"

She gives me a questioning look as she lays in the spot where we usually start. "Where I normally go?"

"Oh no," I say, crawling up to her, trailing small kisses across her soft skin. "If you want to forget, then this isn't going to be like it normally is. If you want to forget everything, and feel nothing but my cock, then this is going to be different. You good with that, Hurricane?"

The fire is back in her eyes, and all traces of that vulnerability are now gone. "Do your worst, McCoy."

"That's my girl," I say, crashing in for a hard kiss before pulling back. "Now hold on."

As soon as she has her hands on the bars of my headboard, I pull her down as far as her outreached arms will go. I spread her legs apart, displaying her already wet, and always perfect, pussy.

"You already wet for me?" I groan as I lean down, brushing a finger across her slit before inserting two fingers.

"Yes," she moans, her body starting to writhe as I immediately go for the spot I know will make her come apart. "I've been waiting."

"I know you have," I say as I continue to work my fingers in and out of her, harder and faster with every pump. "And you looked so fucking pretty and needy sitting up in my bed for me."

I insert a third finger, making her body convulse. "Were you getting anxious for me to come in and touch you?"

"Yes."

"Were you thinking about me? How I'd be sucking on your tits tonight? Eating this pretty pussy?"

She doesn't answer for a second, which I know is because I've brought her close twice now, only to pull the brakes slightly so she's not coming just yet. But that doesn't mean I don't pinch her nipple, sending a shock directly into her pussy that's now holding my fingers like a fucking vise.

"Answer me, Quinn. Were you thinking about my mouth on them?"

She lets out a yelp as I twist her nipple. "Yes. I was thinking about you. Your mouth. How turned on you get because of me."

She's right about that. I've always been a tits guy. I blame nineties television, specifically *Baywatch*. But nothing, and I mean nothing, could've prepared me for the first time Quinn and I were together and feeling those two, soft, round, perfect tits in my hands. I think I camped out there for an hour, just kissing and sucking on them. Getting lost in the feel of her.

And then there was the time I made her come just from nipple play. That was fun. We should do that again sometime.

Except she's probably going to give me the bullshit that this is it. I mean, she's always gone back on her word, but do I want to chance that? I've never been a gambling man, and I definitely don't want to take the chance that tonight is indeed the last night and I didn't do every single thing I want to do with this woman.

"You know me so well," I say as I bring her just to another cusp of an orgasm before removing my fingers. The sudden emptiness makes Quinn gasp and her eyes immediately look to see what I'm doing. "I also know you very, very well."

She wants to say something, but she's stopped the second my teeth lightly latch on to her nipple. I let go quickly, letting my tongue explore before my mouth takes over.

"Porter, please...I need to come. I'm so close."

"Shhh...." I say, taking my coated fingers and tracing them around her other nipple. "You asked me to make you forget, right?"

She nods, her eyes now glued to my hands.

"Then trust me. Lay back. Just focus on my mouth. I'll do the rest."

My mouth descends on her other breast, licking and sucking the wetness I placed there before inserting my fingers back inside her. The sudden action makes Quinn's hips buck into me, and as much as I'd love to take my time tonight, that's not a possibility. Especially when Quinn's desperate cries fill the room.

"Porter. God…so close. Please, God, please…"

I speed up my efforts, fingering her like I don't think I ever have before. Quinn's hands are gripping the headboard so tight her knuckles are white. But it would be a small price to pay for the orgasm I know she's about to have.

I hook my fingers just slightly inside her, and just like I expected, she detonates. Screams fill the room. My sheets are soaked from Quinn's release. I'm sweating from just watching this beautiful woman come undone from my hand.

But little does she know, she's not done yet.

"Come here," I growl, bringing her in only so I can roll her over. "I need to fuck you."

Quinn climbs to her hands and knees as I grab a condom out of my nightstand drawer. I watch her intently as I roll it on, loving how she's so ready for me.

"That's my girl," I growl, coming behind her. "Now hold on."

It only takes one thrust from me to make her lose any control of her body, collapsing to the bed as I fuck her from behind. It's fine. Doggy style has its purpose, but knowing she's so tired that she can't hold herself up, but also is begging me to fuck her harder? There's nothing hotter on this fucking planet.

"That's it," I say, which is accompanied by a smack on her ass. "I bet you can't come again."

I've found that over the years, Quinn responds to most dirty talk. But like everything else in her life, she can't turn down a challenge. Or being wrong. Or not winning. The first time I dared her to orgasm, I thought a pipe burst somewhere. I don't use this tactic all the time, but tonight feels fitting.

"Yes, I can," she says, a touch of resilience in her voice as she pushes herself back onto all fours. She turns over her shoulder, looking me dead in the eyes. "Fuck me like you mean it, McCoy."

I can only smile as the heat in our eyes meet. "Yes, ma'am."

And I do. I fuck her harder than I've ever fucked her. The only sound in the room is our bodies coming together and the eventual screams of our orgasms.

"Holy shit," Quinn says, her body once again collapsing onto the bed. Only this time, mine follows behind her.

"Yes indeed," I say, kissing her shoulder as I roll to her side.

Neither of us say anything as we catch our breaths and come down from the highs. Normally, this would be the time we make idle chit chat and I eventually ask her to stay. But I know better than that tonight.

I slowly roll off the bed to go dispose of the condom. I quickly clean myself up and splash some water on my face, which doesn't take me more than a few minutes. However, when I come back into my bedroom with a warm washcloth for her, I notice Quinn is still lying face down on the bed. When I approach, I hear the tiniest of snores coming from her lips.

"Get some sleep, Hurricane," I say as I do my best to clean her up while not waking her. I toss the washcloth in the hamper before carefully climbing into my side of the bed. For starters, I don't want to wake her. She has to be exhausted if she let herself fall asleep here. And two, it's taking every ounce of willpower I still have to not throw an arm around her, bringing her into me so I can feel her against my chest.

But I'm not going to do either of those things. I know better than to press my luck.

So I'm going to enjoy this moment while it exists. I don't know how long she's going to sleep, or if she'll be here when I wake up, but I'm going to sleep now, knowing Quinn Banks is in my bed.

And that I fucked her so hard that she forgot to leave.

guide to love rule #48

If you're sneaking out for a hookup, always make sure to have your story straight and an extra pair of panties. You never know when either will come in handy.

6
quinn

I'M THIRTY-FOUR YEARS OLD. I'M PAID—OR RATHER, WAS PAID—TO mold the minds of the future. To teach them right and wrong and how to make good decisions.

Which is rich, because I don't think I've made a good decision since, well…

Shit. If you can't think of anything besides the day you decided to get a cat then you probably haven't made many good decisions.

Though that one good decision was the best choice I made. I know I'm biased, but Turtle is a superior feline, and there will be no debates on that topic.

But other than that, every other decision? Trash.

Oh, and it's usually a decision I made without thinking through things at all. Consequences of my actions? That's future Quinn's problem.

Take, for example, in high school, when I ran for class president. It wasn't because I had this need for political service. Nope, I just didn't like the girl who was running. We never got along, she was a horrible bully, and she ratted on a bunch of us who threw a party and didn't invite her.

But being class president was her entire personality. So I ran against her solely for the plot.

Then I went and won. Which meant instead of cruising in my senior year, I was leading meetings, speaking at graduation, and now apparently in charge of class reunions for the rest of my life.

No one told me that part.

Then there's how I ended up in Arizona. Now, not living in Rolling Hills was a definite—no one could've paid me to live in the town where the Emily Babcocks of the world and people who otherwise knew me as Hurricane still resided. But it's the story of *how* I ended up on the other side of the country.

I threw a dart at a map, and that's where it landed.

Fast forward thirteen years later and now I'm not sure if that was my best move.

Then there's last night, where I did the stupidest thing I could ever think of doing—I spent the night with Porter.

After sex.

I don't spend nights.

Ever.

I'm a hit it and quit it kind of gal. Get out of there before the sun comes up. No awkward conversations. No chance for anyone to say that they'll call when they won't. And most importantly? No cuddling.

Cuddling leads to feelings. And we don't have room for feelings here.

I don't even remember falling asleep, which is probably because the man fucked me into a coma. One second I'm actually begging for him to fuck me, the next I'm waking up having to go to the bathroom. I thought I'd just closed my eyes for a second. So consider me shocked when I realized it was five-forty-five in the morning and Porter's muscled arm was draped across me. I don't know how I Houdini'd myself out of his bedroom, or his hold, but somehow I did.

Either that, or he pretended to sleep and let me think I won.

Which, if he did that, will earn him a future blow job. It's the least I can do.

Knowing I was going back to Porter's after Ainsley dropped me off, I stopped drinking way before my sisters did. That way I could pretend to go inside and then wait a few minutes until she drove away before grabbing the spare keys for my mom's car. And now, luckily, because the sun isn't up, no one is around to see me drive away from his old farmhouse and make the ten-minute drive to my parents.

"One of these days, Quinn, you're going to stop being dumb," I say to myself as I turn onto the empty road. "Obviously not today. But one of these days."

What was I thinking last night? Oh. I know. I was horny and sad. That's what I was thinking. Which means now I'm doing a true walk of shame while simultaneously praying that my dad sleeps in today and doesn't get up at his normal six in the morning.

"For once in your life, Dad, remember you're retired and stay in bed."

I shut off the car, take a breath for good luck, and make my way to the front door. Over the years, I got really good at turning the lock with minimal noise. It was clutch in high school. Who knew it would be a skill that would come in handy later in life?

I slowly open it, doing my best to minimize the sound, and at first, I don't hear anything. I let out a sigh of relief, knowing I just have to make my way up the stairs then a quick turn into my bedroom before I'm scot-free.

I slip off my shoes, not wanting any extra weight for noise, and just as I hit the third step, I hear a voice that stops me cold.

"Good morning, Quinn."

And suddenly I'm sixteen again, getting busted by John Banks after sneaking out to a senior party even though I was only a sophomore.

Ha! Funny enough, I think that was the first night I hung out with Porter.

"Hey, Dad."

"Do I want to know?"

I don't turn around. I can't bear to look at him and his likely disappointed face as I'm still wearing my clothes from the night before. "Nope."

"Are you okay?"

"Yup."

He lets out a sigh. "I thought once you moved out of my house we'd be done with this."

"Believe me, so did I."

Neither of us say anything, and I'm too scared to turn around. Luckily, he breaks the silence.

"Go get some sleep. But when you wake up, you know we're going to need to talk. About *everything*."

It's the way he emphasizes that last word makes me turn to face him.

Now, this scene right here is not the first time I've been busted by my dad sneaking into, or out of, this house. And yes, I was always punished. But I never thought it was unfair. Dad was a lawyer for forty-two years, and I always appreciated the way he weighed out the crime and balanced the punishment.

Having more than a few run-ins like this in my teenage years, my dad and I got really close. Which is odd to say for the troublemaker kid, but our punishment sessions always ended up more than just him grounding me. And with that, we came to really know each other. I could always tell when he had a bad case and something was bothering him about it. On the other end, he could sense when I was hiding something. The man could read me like no other.

So with him emphasizing "everything," I have a feeling that he's not meaning to talk to me about stumbling in during the morning hours. No, he knows this is more than a weekend trip home.

John Banks just knows me that well.

"We will, Dad. I promise."

He nods, and signals for me to go up the stairs. "Get some sleep. I won't tell your mom you stole her car. Again."

That makes me smile. "Thanks, Dad."

He just shakes his head and mumbles something about pain-in-the-ass daughters as I make my way to my old bedroom.

I immediately fall onto the mattress, but sleep doesn't come easy. My brain is running a million miles an hour.

Thoughts of Porter and I last night.

Admitting to my parents that I quit my job without any sort of backup plan.

My ass hurting from Porter spanking me.

Wondering what the hell I'm going to do with my life.

Porter coating my nipple in my own come.

Can I apply for unemployment?

My brain goes in a loop like that until I eventually fall asleep, with the last thought being Porter's arm on me as I woke up this morning, holding me like he didn't want me to go.

———

"Good morning, sleepyhead. Or should I say afternoon?"

I groan at Maeve's words as I come down the stairs to see not only my mom and dad sitting in the living room, but all of my siblings. My eyes are still filled with sleep from the nap I took, but from the looks of it, the whole gang is here, minus partners and children.

Which kind of sucks. I was hoping I could use my niece or nephew as conversation shields.

"I didn't realize I was walking out to a family reunion."

"Well, we didn't realize that you were coming home on a whim, so you can say we're all surprised."

I ignore my brother's dig and bypass everyone as I go straight to the kitchen to get a glass of water. I stand at the sink, chugging the cold, refreshing goodness. Have I drank anything since last night? I don't think I have. I usually live in a constant state of dehydration, but this is bad, even for me.

"There's a Gatorade in the fridge and an iced coffee for when you need it."

I turn to Ainsley, the caretaker of our group, who's leaning against the breakfast bar.

"Thank you," I say, polishing off the water before grabbing the two drinks. "How long has everyone been here?"

"About an hour," she says. "We're worried about you."

I shake my head. "No one needs to worry."

She gives me a look as if she's not buying it. "But we are. Especially me."

"You always worry about me. I'm going to be fine. Once I—"

"Where did you go last night?"

I'm known to have the best poker face out of all the Banks siblings. But even I couldn't be ready to steel my face from that statement. "What do you mean?"

"I saw you pull out of the driveway." She pauses for a second to make sure no one else is in earshot. "I dropped you off and got a little ways down the road when I realized I had to go to the bathroom. I was not going to make the forty-minute drive back to Nashville and everything was closed. So I turned around to Mom and Dad's, and that's when I saw you pull out of the driveway. Where did you go?"

Fuck. Eight years. I've done this for eight years and have never been caught. Figures it's Ainsley who finally catches me. It's kind of poetic that the wild Banks child is busted by the angel.

"I'll tell you later, but can it wait? I can only handle so many confessions in one day, and I have a feeling the gallery needs to know the important one first."

She nods and takes my hand in hers. "Of course. But just let me know you're okay."

"I'm fine," I say as I give her hand a squeeze.

Very fine…

"Okay," she says. "Let's go. The quicker you tell them, the quicker it's over."

I know she's right, so when we get back to the living room, and a hush falls over the room as I sit down on a couch. I do as Ainsley suggests and rip the Band-Aid.

"Family, I didn't come home because I missed all of you. I'm home because I quit my job, told a group of awful mothers to go fuck themselves, and don't know what I'm going to do with my life now. I'll now be taking questions from the floor."

I think it says a lot about who I am as a person that not one person in the room gasps. No flabbers are ghasted. Granted, my sisters know the story. But I was hoping maybe a little bit of shock from my mom. A groan from my dad. Simon to be… well….his normal, over-the-top, self.

But nope. Nothing.

"Okay," Dad begins as he lets my words sink in. "Tell us the story."

And I do. Probably with a little more of a clear head than last night, and even through a few parts, I can tell that I did leave out some details. But by the end, the words and outcome are the same.

I don't have a job, and I have no idea what's next.

"Wow," Mom says. Finally, someone who's a little surprised at my antics! "Their name was really P.E.N.I.S.? I feel like that was a short-sighted choice on their parts."

There's a moment of silence before an absolute eruption of laughter takes over the Banks living room. Leave it to Demetria Banks for the unintended comedy relief.

"Oh, wow, Mom," I say, wiping the tears from my eyes because I'm still laughing. "I needed that."

"And I need to give them a piece of my mind," she says. "How dare they think that they know better than teachers?

Teachers are a blessing on this Earth. Because I tell you what, if I would've had to stay home with all five of you for every one of your eighteen years, well...I..."

"We would've gone mad," Dad says, finishing her statement. "Quinn, I know this is sudden, and you probably are trying to get a handle on a lot of things right now. But I need you to know, I'm proud of you. We both are."

Dad reaches over for my mom's hand as she nods in approval.

"Really?"

He nods. "You stood up for what's right. For what you believed in. You five might've turned out very different, which we love, but we taught you all to have beliefs and to be true to them. And that's what you did. And that takes a lot of courage that not many have."

Now the tears are coming out for a whole different reason. "Thanks, Dad."

Each one of my siblings comes over to me, giving me some sort of awkward hug.

It's at that point that I look over to Maeve, who I know is dying to repeat the question she had for me last night.

"I don't know," I say, answering before she can say it. "I don't know what's next. I don't know what I'm going to do. I...I don't know anything."

"Um, that's not the right answer," Simon chirps up.

"Excuse me? I know you think you know everything, but I'm pretty sure you don't have my right answer."

"Oh, but little sister, I do," he says with a smirk. "You're going to move back here."

I have to blink a few times to make sure my brother said what I think he just said. "Did you say move back here?"

"Oh yes! Quinn! Please move home!" Mom leaps from her seat next to my dad and scooches her way in between me and Maeve so she can wrap me in a hug that feels more choking— smothering—than comforting. "Come to where you have family.

You know me and your dad miss you. Your sisters miss you. You have a niece and nephew I know you miss. Why do this alone in Arizona when you can figure out what's next here?"

"I—" I start to object before I realize I don't have a lot to object about. Yes, I have some friends, but none that I feel like I need to stay for. I'm sure word will travel around Phoenix about what I did and said, making it so no school in the area will ever hire me again.

But...moving back to Rolling Hills? Doing the one thing I vowed to never do?

I don't think I can commit to that in this kind of emotional state.

"I don't know," I say honestly. "First, where would I live? Mom, Dad, I love you, but I'm pretty sure none of us would love each other if I moved back in this house."

"Oh, you aren't moving back here," Dad says. "I'm done having to worry about when you're coming and going."

He gives me a wink as we share the inside joke.

"Easy," Simon says. "The apartment above Mona's Diner is open. You'll stay there."

I shake my head. "Simon, that's great and all, but you're not going to just give me an apartment. I'd pay rent."

He waves me off. "That's the last thing I'm worried about. But I don't want you not having a place to live being the reason you don't get your ass back here."

I let out a sigh as I turn to look at my sisters, who are all now sitting and looking at me with pleading, puppy-dog eyes.

"I know you three have to be loving this," I say. "But if I agree to do this, I need you to know that this isn't permanent. It's just for now. Until I figure out my next move."

The three eagerly nod their heads before Stella speaks up. "We miss you, Quinn. However long you're here, we're glad to have you back."

Maeve takes my hand. "Let us help you. This is going to be a big thing to figure out, and you shouldn't have to do it alone."

I finally look at Ainsley, even though I know what she's going to say. "Any chance you're going to be the dissenting vote?"

She shakes her head at my attempt at a joke. "Absolutely not. Come home, Quinn. Where you belong."

7

porter

People hate Mondays. Not me. The Joint doesn't open until four, so I have the morning and early afternoon to catch up on life. Run some errands. Go to the gym.

But most importantly, I have time to sit down and get breakfast at the best damn diner in all of Tennessee.

Mona's Diner is a staple of Rolling Hills and has fed generations in this town. After my mom split, Pops and I started coming here each Saturday morning. What began as a way for him to distract me from the fact that it was just the two of us quickly became our weekly tradition. As the months and years went on, it became our time to catch up. He'd talk about the bar and his pals. I'd talk about school, football, and whatever else I had going on.

Pops has been gone eight years now, and I still can't bear to come in on a Saturday morning. But even though it's now been sold to Charlie Bennett, soon to be Banks, I still make sure I'm here once a week.

"You know the only reason I know it's Monday is because you come in," Charlie says as I walk up to the breakfast counter.

"I'm glad I can serve as your calendar," I say. "What's the special today?"

Charlie picks up the pot of coffee and pours me a mug. I might change my order every week depending on my mood, but I'll never change that I need two cups of coffee. Whatever she puts in this stuff is addicting.

"I'm testing out fried chicken and waffles. I also have a vegan—"

I hold up my hands, because whatever she was going to say was *not* chicken and waffles and nothing vegan was going to come close. "Say no more. Test it out on me. And add a side of bacon, if you don't mind?"

"Just one side?" she asks, apparently knowing my stomach better than me.

"Fine. Make it a double. Crispy."

She shakes her head, but sends me a warm smile. "Like I'd serve it any other way."

"You're the best, Charlie!" I give her a wink as she heads back to the kitchen. In turn I take my mug of coffee and walk around the corner to my normal back booth.

One of the things I love about a small town is that whether it's here or at the bar, regulars have their own spots. Take today, for example. The group of older men who come in every morning for their coffee and bitchin' pull together two tables at the front of the diner. You know, because everyone needs to hear them complaining about technology and young people today. It's also the last Monday of the month, which means the town's planning committee, a group of women who've made it their life's mission to make sure that every holiday has some sort of extravagant event around it, is meeting at the long table that runs along the windows. I say hello to them as I pass by, and notice that pictures of American flags are spread out on the table. I'm guessing they're finalizing plans for the Memorial Day parade and town festival.

Then there's me. I choose to sit in the back booth that's just a little bit removed from the main part of the dining room. It's quiet. No one bothers me. Hell, no one ever sits back here, so I can enjoy my breakfast in peace.

Except today, when I turn the corner and see someone sitting there.

And not just any someone.

A someone I'm *biblically* familiar with.

"Quinn?"

Her face was buried in her phone, so she didn't see me coming, but I'd know that top knot anywhere.

"Oh! Porter! Um…hi."

It only takes me a few more steps to get to the booth, where I slide in across from her. "What are you doing here?"

"Getting breakfast. What else would I be doing here?"

I narrow my eyes, because she has to know what I'm actually asking. But if I know Quinn like I know I do, I'm going to have to pry this information from her.

Seeing Quinn on a non-holiday is unusual.

Seeing her twice within a few months' span is rare.

But now three times in two months? And two of those in a two-week span? Something is up. Something big.

"You know what I mean. Why are you in Mona's Diner, in Rolling Hills, on a Monday morning in the spring?"

Because of the nature of our relationship, we don't regularly talk. We have each other's numbers, but we rarely use them. I just assumed that after she snuck out before the sun came up, that she was headed back to Arizona.

But did she go back? Or did she stay? No. There's no way she would've flown under the radar in town for the past week. Someone would've said something. Quinn "Hurricane" Banks is infamous around this town due to her years of pranks and general spectacles. And if she were back, the Facebook group, the old men's bitching group, and every other clique would be whispering nonstop about the lost Banks sister back in Rolling Hills.

"I'm back in town. Temporarily."

Her words are quiet, but I heard every one of them.

Quinn Banks is back in Rolling Hills.

And even though I'm doing a little dance inside—my sex life just got a lot more interesting—I can tell by her demeanor that this isn't a happy return. So I do the gentlemanly thing and temper down my excitement.

Much to my dick's dismay.

"Is everything okay? Wait, is this what you were—"

She holds up her hand, knowing where my words were going and when she said them to me. It's then that I really look into her dark chocolate eyes and can see the gamut of emotions running through them.

"I quit my job. So I'm back here while I figure out my life."

"Wow." I wasn't expecting that. "What happened?"

She shakes her head. "The story is way too long for the lack of energy I have this morning. Short version is that I got into it with a group of parents. They'd been fighting with me all year. And I finally had it. Dropped a few f-bombs. Called them names. Not-so-subtly accused one of having a lavender marriage. And then I quit."

"Damn. If that ain't the most Quinn Banks way to quit a job, I don't know what is."

She laughs softly, but not enough to wipe the pain off her face. "That's what my family said."

Mention of the Banks crew makes the rest of the pieces fall into place.

"Is that why you were home a couple weeks ago?"

She nods again, holding her iced coffee between her hands. "I'd quit a few days before. I was going stir-crazy in my apartment. And I think my cat was worried about me. So I found my cat a sitter and booked a flight home. I didn't know where else to go."

My heart breaks a little more with every word she says. I also didn't realize she had a cat. Knowing Quinn, it's some random name or something like Bob.

"I'm sorry," I say. "If there's anything I can do…"

She shakes her head and pushes her shoulders back, doing everything she can to look like she's not about to fall apart. "Thanks. It's just all hitting me now. I went back last week to gather some of my things. I flew back yesterday with overly stuffed suitcases and my cat in a carrier. But it wasn't until I woke up this morning that this feels real, you know? It might be temporary, but I don't know…things feel real today."

"I can't imagine."

"I don't regret what I did. I did what I thought was right, and I stood up for what I believed in. It's just…today was the first day I woke up with the thought that I'm thirty-four and starting my life over."

"Change is scary," I say. "Especially when it's sudden."

At least, that's what I've heard. I'm not the guy who changes much. I've worked at the same bar since Pops was legally allowed to hire me, and even before that, I was washing the dishes for payment under the table. I live in my childhood home. I serve the same food and pour the same drinks that he did when he was alive. When I added the live music, people thought I lost my fucking mind.

"It is," Quinn says. "All I can do is take it one day at a time. One task at a time."

"That's a good plan. What's on today's agenda?"

"A job," she says with a little more confidence. "Today's task is to start looking for employment. I might only be here for now, but now still requires money."

"Okay, then," I say, suddenly getting an idea. Because luckily for her, I'm hiring. "Have you ever bartended?"

She gives me a confused look. "Yeah. In college. Why do you ask?"

I clap my hands. "Then it's settled. You can work at The Joint. I need a bartender. You need a job. Two birds. One stone. Look at me! Monday morning and I'm solving problems."

Her raised eyebrows and tilted head signal that she's not as excited as I am. "Really, Porter?"

I shrug. "Yeah? Why not?"

She just stares at me like I'm supposed to know what she's thinking. I'm great at reading her mind when we're in my bedroom, but apparently in the light of day, not so much.

"Porter. I can't work for you." She leans down closer to whisper the next part. "Not with our…history."

She makes it sound is so dirty.

Which I mean, it is.

Dirty. Spontaneous. Hot. Intense.

Unexpected.

That's actually the word I've always felt best describes us. Nothing about us was expected. Not that first night and not in any nights since then.

Our saga started eight years ago. I'll never forget it, because it was the night of Pops' funeral. I had private services and burial for the family, but I knew that the town wanted to pay respects. I figured there was no better way to do that than a true celebration of life at The Joint in his memory.

It was the only night in the history of the establishment that it was truly an open bar.

I shouldn't have gotten as drunk as I did, but then again, I felt like my world was flipped upside down. The man who raised me was gone. The bar that he built with his own two hands was now mine. And while I was honored and touched by all the people who came out to pay respect to the life of Frank McCoy, I just wanted to be alone.

So I did what I do best when I've had one too many: I said an Irish goodbye and snuck out the back door. I planned to go sit on the front porch of my house, close enough if anyone needed me, but far enough way to catch my breath. But when I walked out of the back, I saw Quinn, who was home during her summer break, sitting on an empty crate, beer between her hands, and tears pouring down her cheeks.

. . .

"Quinn?"

She jumps at the sound of my voice as I take a few steps closer to her.

"Hey, Porter. Sorry, I'll get out of here."

"No, stay," I say, taking a seat next to her. I know I came out here to get away from people, but I'll always take the chance to hang out with Quinn. "Everything okay?"

She nods and tries to wipe away her tears. "Yeah, I'm fine."

I don't know much about women, but I know that doesn't mean fine.

"Bullshit."

She turns her shocked eyes to me. "Excuse me?"

"You're not fine."

"And how would you know that?"

"Because I might not've seen you much over the past few years, but I can tell when someone is trying to put on a brave face."

I should know, because that's what I've been doing for the past week since Pops passed away.

She lets out a deep sigh and her shoulders fall a bit. "You're right. I'm not. But I'll be okay."

"Want to talk about it?"

I figured out a while ago that I have the bartender gift of being a good ear for someone who's crying in their whiskey. And if that someone happens to be the girl I had a crush on back in high school? Then I'm all ears.

"I appreciate the offer, Porter, but it seems pretty selfish of me to complain about my love life when you buried your dad today."

"Please, I insist." I swallow the slight amount of jealousy I'm feeling for no good reason. "Between you and me, I need a distraction from everything. This week has been…"

I trail off, because any words that could finish that sentence aren't strong enough for what I've had to go through.

"I can't imagine having to bury a parent," Quinn says. "I mean, I

know realistically one day I'll have to. But I selfishly know Maeve will take care of everything. I'll just have to show up. I'm so sorry you've had to do this alone."

I hang my head, because I think that's been the hardest part. Yes, my Aunt Peggy has helped a lot. She was his sister and the only other family I've still got. God knows my mother couldn't be bothered to show an ounce of sadness, or God forbid, show up.

"I thought I was ready," I admit. "Pop hadn't been doing well. He never really bounced back after his heart attack."

"Is anyone ever ready?"

"I'm beginning to think not," I say. "This week has just been so damn hard. I feel like as soon as I get one thing organized or figured out, six more things end up on my lap."

"Have you had anytime to grieve? Or process it?"

I take a breath and look up at the stars. "Every night I've come out here, or sat on my porch, and just looked at the stars. I'm not sure if I believe in heaven, or an afterlife, but...I don't know...somehow looking at the sky has made me feel like he's still here. That he's gone, but not really. Does that make sense?"

I take a second and push back the tears.

"Hey," she says as she reaches for my hand. "Let it out. I'm the one interrupting your time right now. Don't hold back because of me."

I look down to where our hands are connected. What I would've given years ago to hold this girl's hand. Yes, she was a few years younger than me, but she never acted like it. She was funny. Smart. Likes hockey—and what girl likes hockey in Rolling Hills? A little crazy. A whole lot of beautiful.

Exactly my type.

There was just one problem; Quinn wanted nothing to do with me. I asked her out a few times—movies, a high school basketball game, that kind of thing—and she always laughed me off. She said we could go as friends. Or with a group.

After a while, I stopped asking. An eighteen-year-old guy can only be turned down so much, you know? Plus, I realized not too long after that single life was the way to go. No hearts are broken. No one leaves you. No shattered pieces to pick up.

So it's funny that now, when I'm feeling more alone than I've ever felt in my entire life, it's Quinn Banks to comfort me.

"Have you ever felt completely alone?" I ask.

She huffs out a laugh. "Every day."

I know it was a rhetorical question, but her answer still surprises me. "Really? Quinn Banks, the most extroverted person I've ever met, feels lonely?"

She nods. "All the time. I live three time zones from my family. Sure, I've made friends. Up until today, I had a boyfriend. But you can be surrounded by people all the time and still feel like you're the only one in the room."

Well that takes me by surprise. "Boyfriend?"

"You caught that part, huh?"

"Are you all right?" Not that I can do anything to him, even though the thought of some douchebag hurting her makes my blood boil.

"As all right as a woman can be when she finds out the guy she's been seeing for a year has been cheating on her for the past four months."

"What!" I bark out, probably a little too loud, but seriously, what the fuck? "Did you catch him?"

"More or less," she adds. "Stella asked to see pictures of us. That turned into her digging into his social media, and she asked about a woman I never noticed before. She was in the back of every picture he took when he was out with his friends. Before I knew it, Stella created a fake SnapChat and Instagram, friend requested the woman in question, she accepted, and then saw story after story of them together. I called to confront him and he admitted everything. Didn't even try to lie. That's how little he cared."

"Fuck, Quinn," I say, inching a little closer to her once I realize that she's now crying too. "He's a fucking idiot."

She just shrugs, looking all sorts of defeated. "It is what it is."

"No, it isn't," I say. "You're a beautiful woman, and any guy

would be lucky as hell to be with you. And any fucking prick who doesn't realize that doesn't deserve you, and you sure as fuck don't deserve him."

"Thanks," she says, giving me a playful push with her shoulder. "And you don't deserve to have to go through all of this alone."

We sit there for a second, Quinn's head on my shoulder, the warm summer air feeling a little cool as it gets closer to midnight.

"We're a mess, aren't we?"

I can only laugh at her comment. "Two peas in a pod."

I don't know if it's the booze right now, Quinn this close to me, or how lonely I've felt all week, but the combination is about to make me say something really stupid.

"Quinn?"

"Yeah?"

I nod back to my house. "Want to get out of here?"

She looks to my house, then back to me. "Yeah. I do."

And that was the night that started it all. Two sad souls needing to find comfort in something. Instead, we found each other.

We've never said it out loud, but we both thought it was going to be a one-time thing. Hell, when we were done, we both got dressed and went back to the bar.

Little did we know, eight years later, here we are…

"Come on, Quinn, we're adults. And friends. We can work together. Unless you don't think you can keep your hands off me."

Quinn's eyes narrow, and just as she's about to probably tell me off, Charlie interrupts us with my food.

"Here you go. Chicken and waffles with two sides of bacon," Charlie says as she sets my plates down. "Oh! Look! Now you have a friend to sit with."

I snicker as I take a sip of my coffee, while Quinn looks mortified.

"Charlie, why don't you tell Quinn that she should come work at The Joint?"

Quinn's now giving me a full-on scowl while Charlie claps her hands in excitement. "Oh my God! Yes! That would be perfect."

"I don't think it would be," Quinn defends. "Plus, I have a few interviews lined up over the next few days. Porter will have to look somewhere else for a new bartender."

Charlie starts to say something else, but is called away by one of her cooks, leaving me and Quinn back to our game of cat and mouse.

"Where are the interviews at?"

Does she really have them? Or is she lying to save face? Most importantly, who does she think would hire her? Not because she's not qualified. I'm sure she would be. But this is the woman who once somehow coordinated a town-wide event when every phone rang at the same time for an hour straight. It drove the chamber of commerce businesses nuts.

"I don't want to jinx them," she says. "You'll know when I walk into The Joint tonight and order a celebratory cocktail."

"I like the confidence," I say. "And you know what? When you get that job, that drink will be on the house. I'll even throw in an order of chicken wings. Sound good?"

I've always loved flustering Quinn. But rarely do I get to see her face turning red in the middle of the day.

"I appreciate that, but now that I'm back in town, I don't think I should have wings anymore. Actually, I think I'm going to become a vegetarian."

This makes me laugh as I pick up a piece of bacon for extra emphasis. "Whatever you say, darlin'. Whatever you say."

guide to love rule #31

The world would be better off if
we didn't need jobs.
Or men.

8

quinn

"So, Quinn, why do you want to work at Rolling Hills Credit Union?"

I don't want to work here, Lacey. Just like I'm sure you didn't want to marry the douchebag who knocked you up at seventeen, but here we are.

That's what I want to say. It's on the tip of my tongue before I pull it back.

Actually, want is the last word I'd use to describe my intent for this job. I hate numbers. In my experience, math usually doesn't math. It's why I teach words. And I surely don't want to work for Lacey. I can tell she's trying to put on a professional face, but she and I both know that we didn't get along in high school. It might've been because I started a rumor she had a sixth toe. In my defense, she was bullying my chemistry lab partner. And I wasn't having that shit. She was a nice girl and did all the hard work while I did anything she asked me to because I knew she was carrying my ass.

But this is a job interview, I need money, and Rolling Hills Credit Union is one of the few places hiring. But I didn't know that I'd be working for Six Toes McGee.

However, the biggest reason I need this job is because I may have...possibly....perhaps...stretched the truth a bit this morning when I told Porter I had interviews.

As in plural.

I have one interview. This interview. So I can't fuck it up. I can't start my temporary relocation in Rolling Hills having to admit that I lied, or worse—admit defeat, to Porter McCoy.

It'll lead to sex. I just know it.

Which means that right now I need to suck it up, put on my big girl panties, and lie through my teeth to Lacey about how much I'd just *love* to work here.

"Rolling Hills Credit Union is where I had my first bank account," I say, hoping my touching anecdote will charm her.

"We all did, Quinn," Lacey says, a touch of condescension in her voice. I'm going to go out on a limb to say she remembers the sixth toe thing.

"Yeah, I guess you're right," I scramble to figure out what I can say that will get me the job without completely lying. So I just kind of lie. "But why do I want to work here? I'm all for local businesses, and working for one is a nice thought. Plus, since I've been away, I'm out of touch with a lot of people. This might be a great place to see some familiar faces and help them with their banking needs in the process."

"Interesting to assume people want to catch up with *you*."

Yup. Definitely remembers the sixth toe thing.

And this right here is why living in Rolling Hills is only going to be temporary. Because no matter how many minds I've molded, or how much I've tamed my crazy ways from my teenage years, I'm always going to be the troublemaker of the Banks clan.

See, we all had our roles. Teachers knew them. People around town. Each of our reputations preceded us.

Simon was the teacher's pet who could give one grin and make anyone cave to his ways.

Maeve was the smart one.

Ainsley was the good girl.

Stella was the popular cheerleader.

And me? Well, I was the true middle child. The feral one. The one in detention the most. The one who organized the senior pranks. And no, not just for my class. I gained such a reputation at school for the stunts I pulled—highlighted by helping Simon's graduating class build a General Lee replica car in the gymnasium—that every class above me, and a few after, sought my guidance.

But I'm not that girl anymore. I'm slightly less crazy. Now instead of pulling pranks on teachers, I apparently tell off parent groups.

Personally I love the evolution for me.

"Lacey, I know that—"

"No, Quinn. You don't get to tell me what I do and don't know," she says, clearly asserting her bank manager authority. "I know that I'm holding your future in my hands."

"I'm not sure about future," I quip. "I'll be honest that I don't see myself doing this forever."

"Why not? Are you going to go back to teaching? Oh wait. I heard you got fired from your last job. No school will hire you, I bet. Which frankly, I don't know how you got hired at a school in the first place."

I take a deep breath, wanting to make sure that I don't blow up at her. "No, Lacey. There was a disagreement I had with the administration and a group of parents. I chose to leave."

She lets out a loud guffaw in place of a laugh. "Let me guess, you're one of those 'woke' teachers trying to indoctrinate students? I should've guessed."

It wasn't until right now that I truly didn't realize how triggering that word is with me.

And it's also at this moment I know I'm *not* going to be working at Rolling Hills Credit Union.

"You know what, Lacey? Fuck you and your sixth toe."

She lets out a gasp. "You don't get to talk to me that way! I'm this bank's manager! And I don't have a sixth toe! I don't know why everyone has always thought that!"

"Oh! Impressive. I didn't realize I was at the *foot* of royalty," I say as I stand up. "And get off your fucking high horse. You peaked in high school, got this job because your uncle is on the board of trustees, and you're only working here because your husband has a gambling problem so you can't stay at home like you want. I might only visit a few times a year, but even I know that one. And as for my teaching, I stood up for what I thought was right. I stood up for my students and my principles. And I'm going to do that again by walking out of here, because I refuse to work for someone who still wishes it was the senior year of high school. Peace out, Six Toes."

————

I didn't want to work at the stupid bank anyway.

Now that I'm thinking about it, sitting at a teller window for eight hours a day would've just driven me more crazy than not working at all. I'm used to being up. Walking around. Talking a lot. That's what's going to be more suited for me.

Great job justifying it. Keep it up!

Now knowing that about myself, I scoped for jobs that will keep me moving. Allow me to have conversations with people. Which is how I ended up at Marvin's Furniture Outlet.

Yup. I'm selling couches, sectionals, and anything else you'd like to take a nap on.

It might not be my ideal job, but I one time convinced the debate club to filibuster our history class to get out of taking a test. How hard can it be to convince someone to buy a bed set?

And even better? Marvin is the uncle of one of my high school best friends. He's well aware of my past antics and even said that his store could use my spunk. I was hired on the spot.

"I don't know. I like the set, but that's not my color."

"Oh! Well, I can fix that Mrs. Wolfe!" I say as I go to grab the upholstery color options. "Here we go. A binder bigger than my head with every color option imaginable. Did you have one in mind?"

"I don't know, maybe a gray?"

"Gray! Love it. Classic."

I don't know if it's classic or not. But it felt like the right thing to say. My apartment in Arizona was all white because I didn't know what would go with what, but I knew white went with everything.

I start to flip to the gray section and get there quickly, because apparently there really are fifty shades of gray.

"Oh my," Mrs. Wolfe says. "I'm going to need a second to look."

"Take your time," I say as the telephone starts to ring. "I'll leave you to browse while I go grab the phone."

Mrs. Wolfe nods and I walk over to the oversized desk where the only telephone resides. And of course, it's not cordless. Or a cell phone.

"Marvin's Furniture Outlet. How can I help you?"

"Marv?"

Really? Do I sound like a sixty-eight-year-old man? "No ma'am. This is Quinn. Marv went to the bank."

"Quinn? As in Quinn Banks?"

Oh, here we go… "The one and only! Who am I speaking with?"

"It's Freda Applewood. Remember me?"

"Of course," I say through gritted teeth. "How could I forget?"

Freda was the elementary school lunch lady. She didn't like me. Or any student.

"So Marv isn't there?"

"No, ma'am. But I'd be glad to help you. And if I can't, I'll make sure Marv calls you right back."

She lets out a sigh that screams of her disappointment. "Fine. I was seeing if my desk came in. Can you check on it for me?"

I let out my own sigh, but this one of relief. "Easy enough, Freda. Just hang on for a second."

"It's Mrs. Applewood to you."

I purse my lips. "Apologies. Again. Just hold on for one minute."

I hit the button to put her on hold as I start making my way to the back room.

"How you doing Mrs. Wolfe?" I call out as I walk past her.

"Oh, I'm doing fine," she says. "So many options."

"I'm sure!" I give her one more look to make sure she's actually okay, which is how I don't make the turn quick enough and ram my shin right into the corner of a bed frame.

"Fucking dammit shit fuck!" I scream out, not able to hold my tongue because it feels like I was just speared.

"Quinn? Are you all right?"

"Fine!" I say through gritted teeth as I pay more attention as I weave my way through the beds and to the warehouse. The good thing about Marvin's Furniture Outlet is he has plenty of options. The bad part is that to make your way through the store, you feel like you're a real-life Pac-Man, and instead of ghosts, it's pieces of furniture that are there to block you at every turn.

When I finally make it back to the warehouse, it doesn't take me long to find Freda's desk. I look for a phone so I can report back to her—and answer any other question that I'm sure she has—when I realize there is no other phone.

Because of course there's only one phone for the entire store.

And it's a landline.

I mumble some more swear words in the name of first-world problems as I head back to the front. I swing open the door and as soon as I take a step out, pain shoots up my right leg. I can't see through my leggings, but I'm going to guess I already have a pretty nasty bruise from my furniture collision. I do my best to gingerly walk through the sea of furniture, but it's basically a limp as every time I put down weight, a sting of pain shoots through me.

"Quinn? Can you come help me? I can't decide between these eight."

"One second Mrs. Wolfe!" I continue weaving around when the telephone starts ringing from the front desk at the same time that bells ringing at the front of the store chime. Those two things are just enough for me to take my eye off my trail for just a second.

"Damnit!" I yell as I run into yet another bed frame. This makes me stumble back, basically on one foot, which is how I run into a book case.

Which I knock over.

Which knocks over another bookcase.

Then another.

And another.

And one more.

I'm out of my body as I watch in horror before I snap out of it, realizing that if I don't race over to the last one soon, it's going to hit the row of glass lamps. Pain races through my legs as I dodge and weave between rows of bookshelves that are now just falling all around me, heading straight toward the lamps. I'm pretty sure one bookcase just crashed into an antique table, but I can't focus on that as I try to race to the things made of glass.

I lunge at the last book case, but come up short as it crashes into a host of glass and ceramic lighting fixtures.

I hear the crashes around me as I lay on the ground, defeated, sore, and wondering what the hell just happened.

"Quinn?"

"Yeah, Mrs. Wolfe?"

"When you get up, I could really use your opinion. I've narrowed it down to three shades."

Of course she's not checking on me. Does she even realize what just happened? She had to, right?

"They're just gray, Mrs. Wolfe! Pick one! Light. Dark. Charcoal. It's your world, and we're just living in it!"

I slowly start to get up again, but fall in defeat when I hear the telephone start ringing again.

And it's that moment I admit defeat. And I just lay there.

I don't know how long I'm on the floor with broken lamps and discarded book cases when I see Marvin step over me, a mix of concern and horror in his elderly features.

"You okay?"

"I think."

"That's good. You…Well…"

Poor guy. He just wanted to go to the bank. I know what he wants to say, or rather do, and I feel like the least I can do is put him out of his misery.

"I'm going to go grab my things."

He lets out a breath of relief. "I think that would be wise."

————

Actually, this is better.

Dog walking. What could go wrong?

I'm getting exercise, which I admittedly don't get enough of. I'll always be on the go, which is what I wanted. And I'm around animals. Granted, I'm more of a cat person, but dogs still have to be better than bitchy bank managers or a walking death trap furniture store.

"Hello, Quinn! You're a life saver."

I can't even say a hello back to my parents' next-door neighbor, Mrs. Pacer, before she shoves a leash into my hands.

"Well who's this?" I ask as a pogo stick of a dog jumps in front of me.

"That's Richard. He's my pride and joy."

I choke on my own saliva. I'm all for naming pets human names, but Richard?

"Richard? You named your dog Richard?"

"Yes, after Richard Burton. He was my favorite of Elizabeth Taylor's husbands."

"Oh, well then," I say, not knowing what else to say, so I lean down to scratch his head. "Good to meet you, Dick."

"No! Not Dick!" she scolds me. "Richard."

I nod and start pulling the dog out of the doorway. "My apologies."

"Now, just make sure he gets some exercise and does his business."

"Easy enough," I say, swallowing the joke that I know is somewhere. "See you in a bit."

I start walking down the sidewalk to the dog park that opened a few years ago. I put in my AirPods, figuring I can listen to my audiobook, but just as I do, I feel the leash pull tighter. Next thing I know, my arm feels like it's being pulled out of its socket, sending my AirPods flying and nearly having me trip over my own feet.

"Richard! What are you doing?"

Once I get my bearings, I realize the dog is pulling at his leash and ferociously barking—well, as ferocious as a terrier can bark—at an unsuspecting golden doodle walking toward us.

"Stop," I command, though I don't know if little Richard here knows any commands. "I'm so sorry."

The owner gives me and Richard a dirty look before walking away. Which, I get. "Come on. You're giving me a bad rep on the first day."

The next hundred yards is okay, until I feel the jerk of the leash again, only this time, it's accompanied by Dick picking up into a full-on sprint.

Toward a squirrel.

"Richard! Dick! Stop!"

I do my best to pull at the leash, but it's no use. The little fucker is strong. Before I know it, I'm in a full sprint, which is against everything I am as a person.

I don't run. But it's either run after Dick or explain to my parents' eighty-year-old neighbor that I couldn't keep up with her dog.

"Slow down, you asshole!" I yell.

I don't think my words are going to work, but somehow they do. And since I clearly wasn't ready, nor did I see Dick's brake lights go on, the dog stops on a dime, but I don't, sending me straight to the concrete.

I lie there for a second, mentally assessing my injuries. My leg hurts, obviously, since it was already injured from the furniture store of death, and I think my arm is scraped, but everything else feels okay. Dick slowly walks over to me, and for a second I think he's going to check on me. Which would get him back on the good boy list.

But no. Not this dog. Instead of comforting me in my time of agony that he caused, he decides to hump my leg.

Because why not.

"Nope. Can't do it." I say, suddenly finding the energy to lift myself off the ground, nearly kicking Dick off my leg, and start speed walking back to Mrs. Pacer's house with the horny dog in my arms.

"What's the matter?" she asks as she curiously opens the door that I was pounding on.

"Sorry, Mrs. Pacer. Your dog's a dick. Pun intended."

I nearly toss the dog into Mrs. Pacer's arms and make a beeline to my car that's parked in my parents' driveway. I don't wave to my dad as he mows the lawn. I don't stop to say hello to my mother.

No, I just get in my car and drive to the one place I don't want to go.

Because I need to admit defeat.

9

porter

"HURRICANE! I'VE BEEN WAITING!"

Quinn holds up a hand that signals for me to stop before I go any further.

Which of course I'm not. It's cute she thinks I will.

"Are we here to celebrate?"

I get my answer by the way Quinn plops down onto a barstool and drops her head into her crossed arms. George and Harry, faithful regulars and two of my dad's best friends, look over to her then to me, clearly confused about Quinn's dramatic entrance.

"Are you going to check on her?" George says.

"I heard she was a bull in a china shop yesterday over at Marv's," Harry adds.

"Y'all shush," I direct, earning me some snickers from my ornery, elderly duo. If that did happen—I mean, I heard about it too—I'm guessing Quinn doesn't want to relive it right now. At least, I know I wouldn't.

Though I wonder if Marv has security video of it…

I stare at her for a few seconds to see if she's going to make eye contact, but after nearly a minute, I'm wondering if she's just going to stay there for the foreseeable future.

"Quinn?" I whisper, leaning down to maybe a see a sliver of her face. "You good?"

"No."

The single word comes out muffled and a little sad.

"Want to tell me what happened?"

She lifts her head up just enough so I can see those big brown eyes that right now look like they're fighting back tears. "I suck."

In any other scenario, I'd be making some sort of dirty joke. Especially if we were the only two here. But I can read a room, and clearly Quinn is defeated. I doubt she needs me kicking her while she's down.

"I'm sorry," I say as I reach into the cooler and grab her favorite beer. "The job hunt not going so well?"

She stares at me, then looks over to the wall where the tequila rests, then back to me again. "Retelling the events of the last seventy-two hours is going to take more than a bottle of beer, Porter."

I let out a laugh, because somehow, even when she's likely at one of the lowest points of her life, Quinn Banks still finds a way to crack a joke.

"I think I can make that happen." I grab a shot glass, the salt shaker, and a lime from the well and set it down in front of her. I barely have it on the bar before she shoots it back—no chaser— and directs me to keep the bottle in front of her.

"Shit…that bad?"

She shakes her head. "Whatever you're thinking, make it ten times worse."

Over the next thirty minutes, Quinn tells me, George and Harry, and a few other regulars, the two jobs and one interview she's managed to fuck up. Every new person that walks into the bar joins Quinn's story time, each of us hanging onto every word that she says.

Even if every word that comes out of her mouth is more unbelievable than the last.

Take that back—each one of us could believe how the bank turned out. We've all met Lacey.

But jaws were on the bar when she retold the furniture story. Apparently, her demolition through the bookshelves was worse than the guys had heard.

And no one, and I mean no one, was prepared for the dog named Dick story.

"Holy shit," I mumble when she's done. No one says anything else, because what do you say? Sorry? Better luck next time? Beware of humping dogs?

Quinn is just staring at the tequila bottle like it's going to give her guidance. I want to say that my job offer still stands, but I know she'll shut it down. Which fucking sucks. I need help, and I have a feeling, especially after seeing her interact with this ornery bunch, that she'd fit right in with the clientele. But I know this headstrong woman well enough to know that the last thing she wants now is me offering her a job—especially one she already turned down.

I swear she's just as stubborn as she is beautiful.

And damn if she isn't beautiful. Today she looks like she went through a tornado. The only makeup she has on is dirt streaked on her face. Her hair is messier than normal. There's even a little hole in her T-shirt. Yet there's something about her that pulls me in. Always has. Probably always will. And now that she's back? I'm going to have to get myself in check so I'm not openly staring at her every time I see her.

I decide to leave Quinn be and go check on my other customers when a hand furiously slams on the bar, making me jump out of my skin. Quinn nearly drops her beer bottle. Before I can figure out who did it, a shout cuts through any other conversations.

"That's it!"

The cry, and I'm guessing the assault to my bar, comes from George.

"What's it?" I ask.

"Quinn can work here!"

I can't help but spit out a laugh. Quinn nearly chokes on the pull of beer she just took.

"Sorry to break your heart George, but Quinn already turned me down."

"When?" Harry chimes in. "We didn't hear about it. I thought we were part of personnel decisions."

"First off, you're not," I say. "And she did Monday morning. Broke my heart."

I can feel the daggers Quinn is shooting at me before I even look at her. "What Porter is trying to say," she begins, "is that yes, he did ask me. And it wasn't so much me turning him down but rather me thinking I had other options in front of me."

"Well you did then, but now you don't," George says. "Porter needs some help. You need a job. I don't see a problem with it."

Oh, if George only knew…

I'll never admit this out loud to her, but she's right. We do have a history. If it were one shift, I'm sure I could control myself. I'm an adult and a professional. Then again, I know that after it was over, we'd probably not even make it home before ripping each other's clothes off.

But if she was working here regularly? I don't know if I'm strong enough. This is the only woman I've slept with more than twice. She's the only one I've ever asked to stay. The only one who can get me hard with just a look. Working with her would be a disaster.

Though it would be worth it to see that perfect ass bending down into the beer cooler…

"Mr. Baskins…"

George scoffs at the use of his last name. "You're about to start working here, Quinn. You can call me George."

She smiles at the man who used to own the convenience store in town that every kid in Rolling Hills used to visit for their beverage of choice before school. "George, I appreciate what you're trying to do. But I don't think I'd be a good fit here."

"Can you sling drinks?"

"Yeah. I mean, I haven't done—"

He cuts Quinn off before she can continue.

"Can you count money?"

"Yes, but that's not—"

"Are you going to kick out any assholes who forget the manners their mamas gave 'em?"

"I think everyone knows that I don't have a problem—"

"Then that settles it!" Harry exclaims, clapping his hands together for extra emphasis. "You're working here. Porter! Hire the girl!"

My snickers turn into full-blown laughter as I watch Quinn's eyes get so big they might pop out of her head.

"What'ya say, Hurricane? When do you want to start?"

———

"Jaw up, boy. Can't be staring at the help."

I don't offer a comeback to Harry, though I do make sure to close my jaw, as I watch Quinn gliding around the bar in awe.

In my defense, I think I'd be in a trance even if I didn't know what she looked like underneath her T-shirt and jean shorts.

When I asked Quinn when she wanted to start, I didn't think it would be immediately. But when she muttered the words, "Fuck it. Let's go," that apparently meant we were starting now.

Luckily, there's not much to train when it comes to working here. She was quick to pick up my basic POS system, even having a few drinks in her. I told her how to take food orders to get it back to the line cook. Other than that, it's just a matter of familiarizing yourself behind the bar of where certain liquors and beers are kept.

And she picked it up in no time. Which I expected. It gave me a chance to sit at the end of the bar, catch up on some bills and invoices, while she tended to the Tuesday night patrons who come in for fifty-cent wings.

The only problem now is that I haven't looked at one number on any of these bills because I can't take my eyes off her. Which apparently Harry has noticed.

"I wasn't staring," I finally say in my defense, making it a point to focus back on the water bill for the month.

"I get it, boy. She's a stunner," he says. "A spitfire, from what I remember. But that's good. You need some of that in your life."

Harry and my dad were friends since I was in diapers. I think he was The Joint's first customer, and if he has his way, he'll die on this barstool. With that kind of history, he likes to give me advice. Usually it's about the bar and the things that day that are annoying him. Today, it's about my newest employee.

"I'm just fine," I grumble, though that's probably not believable since I accidentally lifted my eyes to catch a glimpse of Quinn reaching up for the top-shelf whiskey.

"You aren't. But I'm guessing you're like your daddy and going to tell yourself that until you die alone."

I don't bother arguing his point. He's right. Though I would defend that I'm not as much stubborn as I am determined.

Determined to not go through what my dad did.

Determined to live the life I want. A life that's going to make me happy and not worried that at any second the rug is going to get pulled out from under me.

And right now, determined to not go behind the bar and press my body behind Quinn's.

Fuck! No! What am I thinking?

She's now my employee. I give her a paycheck. I can't be fantasizing about fucking her behind the bar. Frankly, I shouldn't be thinking about it at all.

Because Quinn is back. And yes, it may be temporary, but this isn't like our weekend hookups. She's going to be here the next day. The next week. The next month.

Which means she can't be in my bed.

I signal for Jenny, my one and only waitress and the woman who truly keeps this place running, to come and watch the bar.

"Quinn? Can you follow me into the office?"

She gives me a confused look. "Don't tell me I'm fired already. I need to have one job that goes more than four hours."

I shake my head. "Nothing like that. Just want you to fill out some paperwork and go over a few things."

"This feels so official," she says as we both take a seat—safely apart, as my desk is between us. "Then again, I didn't get to the point of filling out paperwork for any of the jobs I've had so far."

I chuckle but don't make a motion to grab the W2s and other tax information I'll eventually need from her. Instead, I clasp my hands and rest my elbows on the desk.

"You're right."

Her eyebrows shoot up. "I am? I mean, I usually am. But about what? Just so I know for posterity."

"This." I point back and forth between us. "You. Me. We have history. And as much as I know we're both adults, what we were can't keep going."

I don't know what I expect Quinn's reaction to be, but I wasn't expecting a devilish smile.

"You're smiling about this?"

She shakes her head. "Not because it makes me happy. I'm just basking in the 'you were right' glow."

I lean back in my chair, thankful for Quinn's humor that will keep this conversation from not getting too heavy. "This is serious, Quinn. I know you said that this was going to be complicated with our history, and I dismissed it. I was wrong to do that. It…well, it hit me today that you're here. And staying here. At least for a while."

She nods in understanding. "Now I'm not leaving."

I see a flash of sadness over her face before the mask she likes to wear reappears. It was quick. If I'd have blinked, I would've missed it. But I've learned to not blink around Quinn Banks. If you do, you might miss something. And you never want to miss a thing around this woman.

"You're right," she continues. "Me leaving is what worked so well for us. Neither of us ever wanted anything serious. Me leaving every time and going back to Arizona made that happen. And now…"

"Now you're here."

"In Rolling Hills."

"In my bar."

"The complete opposite of leaving."

The two of us fall silent as our situation unfolds before us. Our eyes are locked with each other, a little sadness in hers, and I'm sure in mine. But both of us are smiling, because at the end of the day, Quinn and I are friends. We always have been. Always will be. It might've come over the years in the form of roasts, teasing, and quick fucks, but at the root of everything was friendship.

And that's what we'll be again.

Friends.

Boss and employee.

That's it.

"It was a good run," she says.

"It was. Eight years is a long time."

"Longest relationship of my life," she jokes.

"Mine too."

We both stand up, and it feels like we should shake hands or something. Never in our eight years of doing this, or even the years before of hanging out from time to time, have I felt awkward around Quinn until right now.

"Let's not make this weird," she says, clearly feeling the same thing I was. "We know what we did. But it's in the past. Officially now."

"You're right."

The biggest smile crosses her face. "Twice in one day? Porter McCoy…you spoil me."

I know she didn't mean it the way my teenage brain is taking it. Or maybe she did. This is the woman who once dared me to see how many different ways I could make her come in a three-hour time span.

"Get out," I say. "Close the door behind you."

"Whatever you say…*boss*."

I don't miss the extra emphasis she puts on the last word as she exits my office. And I'm going to tell myself that it was my mind playing tricks on me and that she didn't send me a wink before she made her way back to the bar.

But I don't follow after her. I know I should, to make sure she's okay, as it's her first shift. Instead, I take a moment to close my eyes and take a few deep breaths.

I did need help. Hiring Quinn is what I needed to do. And she's going to be great.

But I have a feeling this decision might be the death of me.

Because working around Quinn Banks every day—and resisting her—might be the hardest thing I've ever had to do.

guide to love rule #115

Every small town should have a bar where everyone knows your name. Bonus points if the owner is your fuck buddy.

10
quinn

The Joint is one of those places that every resident of Rolling Hills has fond memories of.

It's always had good food at reasonable prices, so it's not unusual for families to come in for some burgers or wings before the bar rush hits.

And for many of us who grew up here, this is where we took our first legal drink.

Emphasis on legal.

Let's be real, most of us were drinking in a random field on the Rolling Hills city line before the days of Life360. Which, thank God. If John and Demetria Banks had known what I was doing—or really, any of their kids besides Ainsley—none of us would be alive today. And frankly, none of us should be. How I survived the days of Four Loco I'll never know.

So even though I was attending the University of Tennessee when I turned twenty-one, I made sure to come home the day before my birthday so that I could make sure my legal first drink was at my hometown bar. It's Rolling Hills tradition.

Which is why it's giving me a great pleasure to pour this birthday girl her first legal drink.

"Here you go! One green tea shot on the house. Happy birthday!"

Her friends, and what looks like her parents, all line up their phones to take photographic evidence of the drink, cheering her on as she slings it back. The lack of recoil on her face, or even the tell-tale look of liquor hitting your system, clearly says this is in no way her first drink.

Mom looks shocked.

Dad looks pissed.

And for some reason, I feel oddly proud.

"What are you smiling at?"

I nod my head toward the birthday girl, not making eye contact with Porter. Which is hard. I swear I get a hot flash every time the man is near me.

This is the third shift we've worked together this week—and our first Friday night—so there have been plenty of encounters, none of them overtly sexual. But that didn't stop my body from having a reaction. He brushed behind me once as I was making a drink because he needed to get to the wine cooler. We ran into each coming around the bar at the same time. I looked into his eyes to see if he had any sort of reaction when my chest was pressed against him, but nothing.

That was a little disappointing.

Then there was last night when he walked in as I was cleaning a toilet in the women's bathroom when we were closing. Nothing is more unsexy than that. And yet, the way he stared at me made me wonder if that we could lock the door and see what kind of workmanship they put in on those counters.

I need to stop it. Snap a rubber band on my wrist or something every time my mind wanders. Because he's right. I'm here now. We can't do it. Especially because Porter is Mr. Calm, Cool and Collected while I'm over here being Miss Hot and Bothered.

So there's only one thing I can do until I can retrain my body —don't look at him unless absolutely necessary.

"I remember my first legal shot and pretending around my

parents it was my first. I did at least pretend to choke on the whiskey. This girl didn't even try."

Porter lets out a small laugh as he grabs a beer for someone who just made their way to the bar. Not that I was watching him do it. I caught it out of the corner of my eye.

"Did I hear you say that it was on the house?"

"Yeah," I say with a shrug while also suddenly feeling the need to wipe down the cooler. It's better than looking at his ass as he digs for a Miller Lite.

"You know we don't do that?"

I figured he didn't. But I was hoping he wouldn't hear me say that so I could sneakily slip the money into the drawer when he wasn't looking. "You should. It's good will. Plus, every person deserves a birthday shot."

"I didn't even get a free birthday shot, and my dad owned the place."

Now I can't help but look over to Porter, who's now nonchalantly pouring four drinks at once and is completely unbothered by the statement he just said. "Really? Not even one?"

He shakes his head as he grabs the soda gun. "Nope. He didn't believe in free anything. I'm pretty sure he even paid for food he brought home for us."

"Okay, that's insane," I say as I glance up and down the bar to make sure no one needs served. "The man owned this place for what? Thirty years? You're telling me in three decades he never gave, or took, anything?"

Porter thinks about it for a second as Jenny flags me down to make her drinks to take to her tables.

"Nope. Not once."

"Jenny? Is this true? Porter's dad never gave out a free drink?"

Jenny is just as much a part of The Joint as Porter is. I'd guess she's in her mid-fifties and has been serving here since she was old enough to pour a beer. The town loves her, she doesn't put up with anyone's shit, and if she serves you once, she'll remember your drink for the rest of her life.

She also knows more gossip than anyone in town. If it's happening, Jenny knows about it.

"Not a once," she says as she organizes the Jack and Cokes on her tray. I feel Porter getting closer behind me, but I don't turn to take in his proximity. "Actually, I think the only night we've ever given free drinks was Frank's wake."

"Oh wow," I say, trying to keep my face even as I turn away from Jenny. But just as I do, I actually run into Porter's broad chest. I'd have bounced back if his hand wasn't there to catch me.

The feel of his hand at the small of my back, and Jenny talking about that fateful day has my memory flooding back to that night.

And judging by the heat in Porter's eyes, he's thinking about it too.

The night that started it all.

Is this happening?

Am I really walking next to Porter, his hand on the small of my back, as he leads me up the stairs to his bedroom?

At his house? Where he sleeps?

I realize I sound like I'm sixteen years old again, but that's because I feel like it. Because if you would've told that version of me that she was about to go have sex with one of the hottest guys at Rolling Hills High School, she never would've believed you.

But here we are.

How is this happening? I didn't even want to come out tonight because of the Douche Who Will Not Be Named, but my sisters reminded us that everyone in town needed to pay their respects to Frank. And that's true. The man was a Rolling Hills institution. But the more the drinks were flowing, the more sad I became, which is why I stepped outside. I needed some air. I needed to cry in private.

Never did I think I'd see Porter.

And never did I think I'd be here right now.

His bedroom is dark, but I can still see remnants of the older guy in school who always made me smile. I'd heard that he moved back in with his dad after he had his heart attack a few months ago. But the room is like I'm stepping back into a time machine: Football trophies and track medals are lined on a shelf. A bookcase with a few books and some pictures. A sparse desk and a queen-sized bed fill the space.

How is this real life? I had a crush on this man for years. I mean, most girls did. I knew who he was growing up—he was in Maeve's class and played football with my brother. But when I saw him on my first day of Rolling Hills High School, I was immediately smitten.

And then, somehow, by the grace of God or Kelly Clarkson, Porter started talking to me. Me! Quinn Banks. The pain in the ass of the Banks children—which says a lot considering who my brother is. The girl who was always in trouble, but never really punished. The girl who became famous for her pranks and antics. Everyone's friend. But no one's love.

But I was okay with that. I get it. I wasn't beautiful like my sisters. I always struggled with my weight, had a smart mouth, and generally never cared what people thought of me.

At least, that's what I portrayed. And after a while, I started to believe it.

Which is why I always turned down Porter when he asked me out. I knew he wasn't serious about it. He couldn't have been. No one else in that school ever asked me on a date, and you're going to tell me that Porter McCoy, one of the most popular guys at Rolling Hills High School, was the one to do it?

Please. I'm the Queen of Pranks. I can see one coming at me a mile away.

I always told him no, even though parts of me wished it were real. But I knew it wasn't, so I saved both of the us the embarrassment. Because I know he would've gone through with it if I'd have said yes. And then I would've had my heart broken when I found out it was just a joke, or him being nice.

No. Turning him down kept my heart intact.

Which is why right now I need to tell myself that this is just one night. I can't think about my crush. I can't think this is more than two people needing comfort on a very shitty day.

And most importantly, I can't spend the night. I can't wake up in his arms or feeling him next to me.

I won't be able to take it in the morning when he tells me it was a mistake. Or when he asks me to leave with regret in his eyes.

So no. I'll let myself enjoy tonight. I'm going to let my body enjoy this. But without a doubt, I'm going to protect my heart.

And I did. That night was like no other. The way Porter kissed and held me? It was like nothing I'd ever felt in my life.

At that point, I'd been with a few guys, and the sex was enjoyable-ish. But nothing that made me want to write anonymous posts on the internet bragging about the earth-shattering orgasms I'd just received.

Over the years, I tried to date, even as Porter and I were in the midst of what we were. I didn't feel bad. We were just having fun. And I assumed he was dating while I was away too. But I found that, at least in my case, the men who wanted to be with a bigger woman didn't want to date her. They just wanted to fuck her like a dirty little secret that they could only have in their bedrooms but God forbid take her to an Olive Garden for some breadsticks.

Then I'd come to Rolling Hills, be with Porter, and remember why at least in the bedroom, no man was stacking up. He turned on a switch in me that's never been turned off.

Porter and I are still standing pressed against each other, neither of us moving. He's so close. I could just tilt my head up and easily kiss the scruff of his jawline. He hasn't shaved for a few days, and right now he's sporting the perfect amount of beard that I don't even have to close my eyes to remember how it feels between my thighs.

God, how am I going to be able to do this? I'm not strong. I'm just a weak bitch with a good vibrator. I told Porter for years that we weren't going to do it again, and every time I crumbled at the first mention of chicken wings. Or a wink he'd send me across the bar.

"Quinn…" My name on Porter's lips is more of a groan than anything. But before he can finish, the deafening sound of glass breaking snaps us out of our trance.

"Oh my gosh! I'm so sorry!" The apology is coming from the birthday girl, who apparently dropped her drink. "But everyone! It's my birthday!"

The crowd cheers and forgets about the glass breaking. And if they were looking at Porter and I, their attention is now diverted.

Thanks, drunk birthday girl.

"I'm going to go clean that up," Porter says, giving his head a shake before turning to walk the long way around the bar so he and I don't have to touch for him to make his exit.

I in turn head to the ice chest and take a few cubes out to rub them on the back of my neck and drop a few down my bra for good measure.

Because I might've turned the light switch off in theory when it comes to Porter, but apparently the fucker still has current flowing to it.

11
porter

"ALL RIGHT, PORTER. I'M OUTTA HERE!"

I don't know if I've ever heard George say those words in my life. "Where you off to?"

He points outside as he fixes his trucker cap. "It's a beautiful day and the lady wants me to go to the greenhouse or some shit. But then she promised steak tonight, so to the greenhouse I go."

I laugh and wave goodbye. "See you next week."

He tips his cap to me and walks out the door, leaving me alone at The Joint on a Saturday afternoon.

I don't know the last time I worked a Saturday day shift. Jenny usually holds down the fort and I come in at night, but because Quinn's in the fold, Jenny was able to take the day off and after a week on the job, Quinn said she's ready for a solo night weekend shift. Which left me here for the day.

Alone.

I have some bills and invoices I need to go through, but it feels weird being able to catch up on paperwork during normal business hours. Also, what am I going to do with a Saturday night off? I haven't had one of those in…I don't even know. Maybe I'll get out of town. Grab a drink at a bar that's not my own.

Or, more than likely, I'll sit right here at the end of the bar and pretend not to stare at Quinn.

After last night's shift, I probably need to give myself some space from her, but I don't know if I have that in me. When she was pressed against me last night—purely on accident on both our parts—after Jenny made mention of Dad's wake, I could tell we had both been transported back to that night. I was *this* close to kissing her in front of everyone and not giving a flying fuck.

Over the past week I had to ball my hands into fists to stop from touching her. But last night? Last night was the closest I've come to kicking everyone out of the bar, grabbing her by the waist, and fucking her on a barstool.

The worst part is that she's not affected in the least bit. Hell, she's barely looking at me, just going about her shift, smiling and talking to every customer that walks in. And there I am, sitting back, staring at her, and wondering how in the world we got here. I also wonder at least five times a night if she's trying to kill me with those shorts and fitted tank tops that perfectly hug her chest.

It's probably a good idea that today's shift is by myself. It'll give me time to catch up on paperwork, clear my mind, and have a Quinn-free day.

I grab the old ledger book that my dad used to keep the books and start the painstaking process of balancing the ledger. My dad was old school in everything he did. And for the most part, I'm the same way. There are a few things I've modernized since taking over—I'm sure he rolled his eyes from the grave that I'm now taking credit cards.

There are a few other things I've upgraded since he passed, but mostly I've kept everything just like he had it. I still pay everyone by check. The requesting time off is just a piece of paper thumbtacked to a cork board. And when it comes to balancing the books, I still use the same brand of ledger Pops used for thirty years. In a weird way, it makes me feel still close to him. That he's still a part of this bar. Which I know is silly. But this was his place. His baby. And I'm going to keep his memory alive here for as long as possible.

I grab a pen, open the ledger, and grab the top invoice off the pile without looking.

So much for having a Quinn-free shift. Because why am I staring at the invoice for the chicken wings that were delivered this week?

Thanksgiving Eve in the bar industry is, without a doubt, anyone's busiest night of the year. And don't get me wrong, last night was a good night.

But tonight? Tonight is going to be the start of something big.

For the first time in The Joint's history, I've decided to open the bar on Thanksgiving. I splurged for a DJ—also a first in this bar's storied history, as every song has only ever been played from the old jukebox that Pops bought when he first opened the place. I even came up with a special drink of the night.

Is this my way of avoiding the fact this is the first holiday without my dad? Without a doubt. But I also think he'd get a kick out of me turning a day that I would've been moping around into a night of celebration.

At least, I hope he would.

Thanksgiving was our day. We'd watch football, head over to Aunt Peggy's for dinner, then all of the guys would head to the backyard for some football of our own. As adults, we still did all of that, save for the football playing. These knees aren't meant for backyard football.

I knew this day was going to hurt more than others, so I knew I'd need the distraction. And what better distraction than making a few bucks with the slogan, "You've been with family all day. I know y'all need a drink."

And apparently everyone in Rolling Hills does. The place is packed from wall to wall—much busier than it was last night and any other night I can think of. I had to bring in two extra bartenders for the night, and none of us have had a chance to stop for hours. Yet, even in the sea of people packing my bar, I can still see Quinn Banks like she's the only one here. She's on the dance floor, having the time of her life, her smile a mile wide, drink in the air and looking fucking gorgeous.

I haven't seen her since the day of Pops's wake. Or should I say the night of? That night was…fuck. What's the word to describe it? I feel like a teenage girl if I say it was magical. But it was. I don't know if it was because we were both in vulnerable states. Or maybe because I was finally getting the chance to be with the person I'd been infatuated with for years.

I'd also be a liar if I said I hadn't thought about that night more than a few times. I mean, how can I not? I can still feel her soft curves in my hands. See the image of her lips around my cock. And when I made her scream? How she threw her head back and shouted my name? It's a moment I'll never forget.

I take a peek back out at the dance floor, and Quinn is now holding court like only she can. She might've earned the nickname "Hurricane" over the years, but everyone loves her except the ones who didn't, but that was usually because they were jealous of her or she called them out on their bullshit. So it's no surprise that she's chatting away, smiling from ear to ear, nearly glowing despite being in a dimly-lit bar.

I smile as I start pouring another round of shots. I'm glad she's seemingly bounced back from that asshole who cheated on her. I hope she's happy now. Maybe she started dating again and he's the reason there's a smile on her face.

Except that thought shoots a burning rage through me that nearly has me breaking the empty beer bottle I swipe off the bar. I know she's not mine. We hooked up once, five months ago. We haven't even spoken since then. Yet, the thought of another man touching her makes me want to punch a hole through the wall.

"Porter!" Quinn's scream snaps me out of my ridiculous jealousy. I take the extra second I need to pull myself together before turning to her.

"Hurricane!" I greet her like I didn't know she's been here for exactly two hours and fifty-two minutes. "Happy Thanksgiving."

"Thanks," she says, her head wobbling a little bit. I'm guessing

she's drunk, but since she hasn't been up to the bar, I have no idea how many drinks she's hud bought for her.

"How you feeling tonight?"

"I'm feeling grrreat," she says, her words a little slurred.

"That's good. What can I get ya?"

Instead of asking me for her normal order of a beer or vodka tonic, she leans up on the bar, which I'm sure is sticky as hell on a night like tonight, but she doesn't seem to notice. I raise my eyebrows at her actions, but she only answers me with a curl of her finger, signaling for me to come closer. I reluctantly do, because I know if I'm that close to her, I'm going to be a high school boy and look down her shirt.

God, her tits are perfect.

"You know what I want tonight?"

Her whispered drunk talk makes me laugh. "What's that?"

"I want chicken wings."

My hushed laugh is now full body. "You needed to tell me that you want chicken wings as a big secret? Hurricane, how much have you had to drink tonight?"

"Not that much," she defends. "And plus, I don't want chicken wings. I want chicken wings."

Why is she putting a weird emphasis on chicken wings and now wagging her eyebrows? Also, she's trying to wink, but I don't think she can. "Okay… The cook's still here. I can put in an order for you. What flavor do you want?"

Quinn shakes her head and asks someone sitting down on a barstool if they can move so she can climb on it. Just when I think she's going to climb onto my bar and start dancing, I realize she's just sitting on her knees, allowing her to get closer to me.

God, she smells good…

"You. The flavor is you."

She might've whispered the word, but even in the loud as fuck bar, I hear it crystal clear.

I pull back a little bit so I can get a good look at her. I need to make sure that's actually what I heard.

"Yeah?"

She nods slowly, and even though she's drunk, I know she has every faculty about her right now.

"Okay then. Chicken wings. I'll have them ready at closing time."

I give her a wink that I've given plenty of times to women at this bar over my life, only I know this one's a little different.

Because that came with a smile. A smile that I'm pretty sure only Quinn Banks brings out in me.

That night I rank in the top three of hottest nights of my life. Our first time together was a little more emotional. A little sloppy. We were drunk and sad and just wanted to feel. The hottest was probably a random summer night about four years ago when we couldn't wait and I fucked her outside the bar.

But the night I'm remembering? I knew when I walked up to my front porch and I saw Quinn sitting on my steps, a devilish grin on her face and her shirt unbuttoned, that it was going to be a good night.

And it was. Holy shit was it ever.

I smile and move to slightly readjust myself when I'm blinded by the light of the bar door swinging open, letting in the piercing sun from the midsummer May day. From where I'm sitting at the corner of the bar, I can't see who's walking in. Once my eyes adjust after the door closes, I can tell it's a slender woman, but that's about it.

I get up to walk behind the bar and assume my position. As she comes closer, I'm starting to get a better look at her. Long brown hair that's slightly covering her face. Even if I could see all of her, I'd know she doesn't live in Rolling Hills. I know every person in this town, and she's never sat at one of my bar stools. Yet, at the same time, there's something familiar.

"Welcome in. What can I get ya?" I ask, grabbing a cocktail napkin.

"Hey, big brother."

Her words shake me. Because the only person who would

call me that lives in Indiana, and I still think of as a two-year-old. That's when I really look at her—and recognize the emerald green eyes she got from my mother.

"Missy?" I blink a few more times, everything now in focus as I stand in front of my estranged half-sister.

"Surprise?"

I can't even laugh. I'm speechless. I have so many questions sprinting through my head right now I don't even know where the hell to start.

I'm not lying when I say the last time I saw Missy she was a toddler, which was the last year I saw my mom as part of court-ordered custody visitation. Funny enough, that was the last time I saw Mom, too.

The divorce happened when I was in eighth grade, and it's sad that I wasn't fazed that she didn't fight for custody. It didn't matter, though—I would've stayed in Rolling Hills no matter what. Pops was my best friend. We went hunting and fishing together. I used to sit at the end of this bar doing my homework while he served drinks to his buddies. We never had a ton of money, but I never wanted for anything. And most important? It didn't matter the event, he was there. Football games. School functions. You name it, that man was front and center.

As for Mom? I barely remember her at anything growing up. I do remember her complaining for years about being stuck in this "podunk town." When I was younger, I remember feeling like it was my fault somehow. So when she picked up and left, I felt nothing but relief. Especially when I found out she was never coming back. I did get a good laugh when I learned that even though she despised small-town living with every fiber of her being, she ended up in a smaller town in Indiana. Pops once got drunk and joked that's as far as she could get on a bus ticket. He probably wasn't wrong.

But she wanted a new life and she got it. She remarried and had Missy, who is apparently sitting at my bar. I'm guessing she's still alive? I haven't seen her since my last visit when I was seventeen. She didn't bother coming to my high school gradua-tion. The last time I talked to her on the phone was when Pops died. Other than that, I had no contact with her before it was the cool thing to do.

"What are you doing here?"

I feel like that's the safest question to start with. And frankly, no other answers are going to make sense until I know the answer to that one.

"Would you believe me if I said that I wanted to come visit the famous Joint?"

"No, because I know for a fact this place isn't famous. I'm shocked you even knew about it."

"Of course I knew about it. Mom used to talk about it all the time. That it was your dad's pride and joy. Next to you, of course."

"Try again. Mom hated this place. Always accused my dad of loving it more than her."

Not that I blame him…

She lets out a sigh. "I'm in Nashville on a road trip with some friends."

"Why didn't you just tell me that?" Though that doesn't answer why she's here.

She shrugs. "Felt weird just dropping by."

That I can understand. "Listen, I know my relationship with Mom isn't…well, there. But that doesn't mean I hold you in any ill will. And I don't know what your relat—"

She stops me there. "If I never see Bonnie again it'll be too soon."

"Oh," I say, noting she's using our mother's government name. "Still mother of the year?"

This makes her laugh. "To say the least."

I grab a glass from the bar and fill it up with ice water for Missy. She stares at it for a second before taking a drink while I try to study her. Something is off. I'm not sure what, but her short answers are sending warning signals. Then again, I don't know her at all. The only thing I have going for me is years of bartending experience that's taught me how to read people.

And I might not know my sister, but I do know something's not what it seems.

"Okay, so you're in Nashville. And you thought to take time out of your day to drive down and see your half-brother?"

She doesn't respond to that. Instead, she stands up off the bar stool and starts walking around the bar. I watch as she looks at every picture. She even goes down the hallway that has the office, restrooms, and supply closet. Does she also moonlight as the health inspector?

"Everything okay?"

She walks back out, eyes still looking around. "This is a nice place. A little empty, though."

Gee, thanks. "It's a nice day. Who'd want to be stuck inside when they could be enjoying the sunshine?"

She walks up to a picture hanging on the wall of me and Pops. It's from my high school graduation. The one my mother didn't show up for.

"Is this your dad?"

"Yeah," I say, as we look at the nearly twenty-year old picture. "So you don't talk to Mom. What about your dad?"

I watch as her shoulders slump, and for the first time since she's come in here, I think this is a genuine Missy.

"He died. Six months ago."

"Fuck. I'm so sorry."

"Thanks," she says as I watch a single tear fall from her eye. "It's been hard."

"I get it," I say, empathizing with her more than she knows. "I get it more than most."

She nods. "Exactly. Actually, there's—"

I feel like she's about to say something else, but at that moment, the front door swings open, bringing in Harry and George. Their eyes immediately take in the sight of me standing next to a much younger woman whom they don't know.

Oh hell, the town Facebook page is about to go nuts.

"I gotta go," Missy quickly says.

"Wait. Stay for some food. You're here. We can catch up."

She shakes her head. "Maybe some other time. Good seeing you, Porter."

Missy all but sprints out of The Joint, nearly hitting George and Harry in her exit, leaving me questioning what the hell just happened.

"Who was that?" George asks, who I'm now guessing didn't go to a greenhouse.

"I don't know who she was, but she's the spitting image of Porter's mama," Harry says.

"Holy shit!" George yells, looking out the door, then back to me. "Does that mean it was who I think it was?"

I quickly point to their stools. "Get over there and forget about what you just saw."

"Sorry, Porter. No can do," George says. "If that girl was your half-sister, Rolling Hills is about to be aflutter wanting to know what she's doing in town."

Me too, George. Me too.

guide to love rule #66

Having a shoulder to cry on is always a good thing. If that person can also make you orgasm? Even better.

12

quinn

Something's off.

I know I've only worked here a few days, and tonight is technically my first solo bartending shift, but as soon as I walk into the bar, I can tell the vibes are off.

There's music playing, but normally you have to strain to hear it over patrons talking. But I can hear every word of the classic rock song that I've heard more this week than I have in my entire life. And it's not because the bar is empty. Far from it. The crowd is decent for a Saturday early evening. But everyone is talking in low whispers, looking around like someone might hear what they're saying. It's like top secret information is being passed around.

What's even stranger is that Porter is nowhere to be seen.

"Oh, thank God you're here," Jenny says, looking exhausted and it's only six o'clock.

"Are you okay? Where's Porter?"

Jenny tilts her head back toward his office as she pours a Beam and Coke. "He's been back there for a few hours now. Asked me if I could watch the bar for a bit, which was fine because we didn't have many customers. But he hasn't come back and I've been too busy to check on him."

Shit. That doesn't sound like Porter at all.

"Do you want me to see if he's okay? Help you? Tell me what you need."

"Can you please make these drinks for me so I can go to the bathroom? I'm dying."

I wave her off. "Go. Leave me your order."

She drops her notebook and sprints to the back, leaving me to make the drinks. They aren't anything hard—just two gin and tonics. I also notice she needs some food rung in, so I do the nice thing and send it back to the kitchen when I hear a "psst" from the end of the bar.

When I look over, Harry and George are leaning down, signaling me to come over to them.

"Why are y'all whispering, you weirdos?"

Seriously. What the fuck is going on in here today?

"Did you hear?"

I want to chuckle, because there are a few things this town could be known for. One is Mona's Diner. Best fucking pancakes and french toast in the world. And the second would be this town's gossip mill. It's unparalleled and could put any national tabloid to shame. Who needs the *National Enquirer* when you have George and Harry, the mean old men who sit at the diner each morning, and the Bingo ladies on the case?

In my week working at The Joint, I've been more than caught up on the town news. There are the few rumors about some marriages that might be on the rocks—of course solely based on people's Facebook profile pictures. Whether or not the empty lot on the outskirts of town is going to become another dollar store. My favorite, though, has been Harry learning what Only Fans is because a girl who graduated with Stella is apparently now making a killing on it.

That was hilarious.

"Did I hear what? Is it why everyone in here looks like they're playing a bad game of telephone?"

"Yes." Harry signals me to come closer. "When we walked in today, Porter was here. Alone. With a woman."

I take a step back from the bar as my heart drops into my stomach. I think my face is turning white. Am I about to pass out?

Wait. Stop. No. Wrong reaction to have. If he was here with a woman, that's his prerogative. We're nothing. Especially now. And even before, he could see whoever he wanted.

I quickly fix my face to make sure that I don't have a visible reaction. Not that these two would've picked up on it. I've seen the size of their bifocals. "Do we know who she is? An ex?"

George shakes his head, his white hair sticking out of his trucker hat. "Not an ex. His sister. Well, half. Daughter that his mama had after she ran off and left Porter and Frank."

"Sister?" I say as I let out a big breath. Couldn't these two have led with that? "I didn't know he had a sister."

"She's never been here," George continues. "When we walked in here today, boy looked like a deer in headlights."

I look back into the office, the sudden urge to run back and check on him is overwhelming.

"You're the best," Jenny says as she ties her apron back around her waist and interrupts my gossip session. "I'm good now."

"No problem," I stutter. "I think I'm going to go back and check on Porter."

"You do that. Just don't you disappear on me, too."

I quickly weave out from behind the bar, through the tables, and down the hallway to Porter's office. I gently knock, but no one answers.

"Porter?" I ask as I try the knob, but it's locked. "Porter? You in there?"

I stand there for a second, but I don't hear anything. I start to grab a bobby pin from my hair, wondering if I still remember how to pick a lock from the time I broke into the teacher's lounge. Which I wouldn't have had to do if they would've just put a microwave in the cafeteria.

"Quinn!" Just as I'm about to insert it, I hear Jenny calling for me. "Need ya. Bikers just came in off a ride."

"Be right there," I say, looking to the door for a second before I move.

"You should've called me," I whisper, giving one more look to the door before hustling back to the bar.

———

Eight hours, three birthday shots, and one minor bar fight later, The Joint is finally closed up for this Saturday night.

"Holy shit," I sigh as I collapse on a bar stool, Jenny across from me pouring herself a Diet Coke from the soda gun. "Should I be this tired?"

She laughs. "You'll get used to it. You did good tonight, kid."

"Thanks," I say. "And thanks to you for defusing that fight. I couldn't get over there in time."

Jenny waves me off as she chugs her drink. "That was nothing. Those two know they can't drink bourbon. Makes 'em mean."

I laugh and force myself to stand up, because if I sit any longer, I might pass out. "Hey, did you ever have a chance to talk to Porter?"

She shakes her head. "Never had the chance. I figured he'd pop back in after close and I'd make sure everything was okay."

I look back down the hallway where Porter would normally be at this time of night, counting money and going through receipts, when I see a sliver of light creeping through the bottom of the office doorway. Except I know a few hours ago when I went back to grab vodka out of the closet that no lights were on. I checked.

"Ready to go?" Jenny asks as I see headlights pulling up to the front door. "Like clockwork, my ride awaits."

I look back to Jenny, then back down the hallway. "You go ahead. I have to go drop the money back in the safe."

Jenny looks past me and down the hallway before raising an eyebrow. "You sure?"

I nod, not really knowing what else to say. We both know that I'm staying to talk to Porter. I don't think Jenny knows our history, but if anyone in this town did, it would definitely be her. The woman has waitressed at the town bar for more than twenty years. She could write a best seller with the things she's heard and the secrets she knows.

Oh! Jenny needs a reality show. I'd watch the shit out of that.

"Be careful, Quinn."

Now that surprises me. "Of what?"

"I didn't mean it like that," she explains, but adds in a nod down the hallway. "He doesn't talk about his mama a lot. And if that girl *is* his sister like people are saying, that's going to bring up some wounds that he let scar over a long time ago."

"Good to know. Thanks."

I follow Jenny to her car, giving her a wave as I shut and lock the door. I then make sure to grab the moneybag before heading to the office. I need to put it in the safe anyway, so at least it gives me a reasonable cover story.

In all the years Porter and I have been…well, Porter and I…I don't think he's ever talked about his mom. Not even the night of his dad's funeral.

I knew she wasn't around. Everyone in town did. But I never asked about her. Fuck buddies don't ask questions about personal lives or childhood traumas. That's too…relationshippy. Too personal. Too real.

And yes, Porter and I might've been real in what we were doing, but that's the only sense. And that's how we both wanted it.

But now things are different. We're…friends. Yeah, friends. Plus, he's my boss. Employees can check on their bosses to make sure they're okay, right? If they can't, I know friends can.

Now whether he wants me to? That's a different question.

The closer I get to the office, the more I see the light beaming from under the crack. I gently knock, not wanting to scare him, but part of me has to think he knows at some point I'm going to come back here.

"Just leave the money on the bar, Quinn. I'll get it later."

I shake my head and push open the unlocked door. "Sorry. Can't do. I'm very responsible with money, and for all I know Harry and George are going to come in and swipe it."

My joke falls flat as Porter just stares at his computer screen. I take another step in to get a better look at him, and my heart breaks seeing the blank stare on his face in contradiction with a million emotions dashing through his brown eyes.

"Want to talk about it?"

I walk around his desk, propping myself on the corner of it. I take a look to see what he's staring at, only to find that it's a picture of a much younger Porter—I can tell this was high school because I remember that Rolling Hills football T-shirt—surrounded by a family I've never seen.

"This was the last time I visited," he says, his tone somber. "I was going into my junior year. I was pissed because I had to miss the first week of football practices. I was angry that whole trip."

I don't say anything, because what do you say? He's clearly going through it right now, so I'm going to do something I rarely do—just shut up.

"I only went on those summer trips because Pops made me. Said it was the right thing to do. That she might've left, but she was still my mom. I told him she never paid attention to me while I was there. That I sat in the guest bedroom the whole time and played on the computer. He said it was still better that I was showing effort. And that it was her decision not to show any."

"Wise words." I nod to the computer screen. "Was this the last time you saw her?"

He shakes his head. "I visited one more summer. But she

never came to graduation. And at that point I was eighteen. Both my dad and the state of Tennessee said I was free of visiting obligations."

I have no words, because the idea of not seeing either of my parents for years at a time—or ever—unfathomable to me. Even living away, I made sure to get home at least twice a year and my parents visited plenty of times. "You couldn't have imagined what would happen. Not with your dad's passing. Not realizing that you stopping to visit meant never seeing her again. Not with…"

I was about to say "not with your half-sister showing up out of nowhere," but I'm guessing I'm not supposed to know that.

"If you meant to finish that sentence with 'seeing my sister for the first time since she was in a diaper on a random Saturday,' you win."

Holy shit. For once George and Harry had their stories right. "Yeah…something like that."

Porter leans back in his chair, rubbing his hands across a face that is clearly well past the five o'clock shadow window.

"She just showed up out of nowhere."

"Did she say why?"

He shakes his head. "Said she was visiting Nashville and wanted to come down and see me, but something felt even off about that. We talked a little before she ran out of here."

That's random. Nashville's only about a forty-minute drive—hour if the highway is backed up—but it seems weird to come all that way for a quick visit.

The confusion I'm feeling is nothing compared to what I'm seeing in Porter's eyes. The man looks haunted. Lost. Just staring at the computer like he's trying to find the answer in this twenty-year-old picture.

"You know you can let it out, right? Say what you need to get off your chest. I know it's been a minute, but if you do remember, I'm a pretty good listener."

He shrugs, and suddenly I'm transported back to that first

night. Granted, that talk was out back. But the emotion is right on par.

"She has my mom's eyes."

Now things are making a little more sense. Jenny was right. Seeing his sister today opened up a whole big-ass can of worms. "I'm guessing you thought you were never going to see those eyes again?"

Porter sits back up. "Not in a million fucking years."

He recounts the events of the day. As he's talking, I'm listening, but I can't stop staring at the emotions tugging at his features. His eyes are a mixture of confusion and anger, but there's a sadness to the rest of his face. He looks defeated.

I hate seeing him like this. Porter is a good man. Has made a life for himself and kept his dad's legacy alive in this bar. He sponsors Little League teams and donates to town festivals.

And in the blink of an eye, a blast from the past knocks him off kilter.

"Damn," I say when he finishes. "No wonder your head is spinning. I still wonder what she wanted, because you're right—something is off."

"Right? It's just…I feel like she was about to tell me something before she got spooked and ran off. I don't have her number, and God knows I'm not at the point yet to call my mom to ask her for it. I just can't get out of my head that she was here for a bigger reason."

"Did she ask for money?"

"No, but that would've at least made sense," he says. "I would've given her some. She's my sister, no matter how long it's been since I've seen her. But I feel like she wouldn't have sprinted away if it was just about borrowing a few bucks."

"Think she was casing the place? Or is that my too many hours of *Law & Order* catching up to me?"

My second attempt at a joke falls flat. I'm really off my game tonight.

"What could she have wanted, Quinn? I think not knowing is worse than anything she could've asked me for."

Porter gets up and starts pacing back and forth in his small office. "I hate that this is going to keep me up, but I can't stop thinking about the worst. That she's in trouble or something. Or maybe you're right. Maybe she was going to rob me tonight. She was looking around the bar. Maybe it was for security cameras."

"No, don't let my warped mind take over." Porter walks past me, and without thinking, I take his hand as he's mid step, stopping him in front of me. "You're a good guy, Porter McCoy. Don't think the worst."

He laughs, and apparently Porter's body is also separate from his brain because he takes my other hand in his. "Don't let it get out. I have a reputation to uphold."

"I'm serious," I say as I look up into his eyes. "You're worried because you care, even if you don't know her. It's okay to be confused. If she really needs your help, she'll be back. And if she doesn't, well, then this is just a very weird day in your life. But don't put any blame or worry on your shoulders. That's not your responsibility."

He nods and neither of us say anything else. The only thing making a sound in the office is the humming of his computer and the air conditioning roaring to life. The cool air isn't helping, though. Being this close to Porter has me getting warmer by the second.

That and the way he's looking at me.

Caring eyes. A little hurt in them. A lot of confusion.

A whole lot of want.

I know that look. It's how he looked at me eight years ago.

"Quinn?"

"Yeah?"

Holy shit, the deja vu is strong. Back then I didn't know what he was going to say next. Never in a million years did I even begin to dream he'd ask me back to his house.

Only now I know him. I know his looks. His touches.

And I know exactly what's about to happen.

guide to love rule #103

When you find a good hairdresser, you don't try others just to make sure. The same can be said about dick.

13

quinn

Before I can get my bearings that this is about to happen, Porter's lips crash into mine. His kiss is hard and claiming, which isn't out of the ordinary for us. Every time we've been together has been like that. We both knew it was only a few hours before I disappeared into the darkness. Plus, even long-term friends with benefits don't do romance. There are no flowers or candles or beautiful words spoken. Sure, there's fore-play—both of us are big fans of both giving and receiving—but there's no caressing or cuddling. There's no slow kissing before eventually getting to the good stuff.

It's just sex. Raw, unfiltered, fucking amazing, sex.

Yet, right now, there's something different, yet vaguely famil-iar. Everything about Porter feels desperate. Needing. Just wanting to feel anything that's not sadness.

Oh my God, that's it. This really *is* like that first night. When we both needed to feel…something.

He was obviously devastated and feeling alone after the passing of his dad. And me? I was stupidly heartbroken over the dickwad who cheated on me, though looking back, he did me a favor. We were dating in the base sense of the word. We had dinners at my place. I spent the night at his. But that was it. I never met his friends. He refused to meet mine. And when I asked him to come with me to Rolling Hills during that fateful vacation? He said he couldn't get time off work. A good excuse in theory, but bad execution on his part. Once Stella got into the girlfriend's social media, we found out that he couldn't come with me to Tennessee because he was in California on a wine tour with his new girlfriend.

I was devastated. Crushed. He basically told me that I wasn't the person he saw himself with in the long term but didn't know how to tell me.

Translation: You don't want to date the big girl. But you want to fuck her.

And that's not me being down on myself; it's what I've discovered after years of analyzing evidence of past dates and boyfriends. The fact of the matter is that while I may love my body, and have finally learned to love the skin I'm in, I tend to attract the men who want to keep me hidden. I don't know if I'd go as far as to say they're ashamed to be seen with me, but until I'm proven otherwise, that's the running theory.

So that night when Porter found me crying behind the bar, I just wanted to feel something. I realize that a drunken hookup with a man I'd crushed on for years probably wasn't the best decision, but I was sad and had six Lemon Drop shots in me. I certainly didn't think we'd still be doing this eight years later.

And like that first night when we stumbled into his bedroom, hands everywhere as we tried to strip each other down, this night is playing a mirror image. I stumble backward, Porter's lips still on mine, as I slam into the wooden door of the office.

I yelp out in surprise, but it's quickly swallowed by Porter's mouth. Our kisses are big and sloppy, which are only in unison with our hands fumbling at our clothes. There's no sensuality in what we're doing. I'm shoving down my shorts as I hear the whip of his belt coming off before I'm greeted by the vision of him taking off his white T-shirt with one hand.

How do men do that? No. I don't want know. I just want them—specifically Porter—to just keep doing it.

"Come here."

His words are a growl as he grabs the back of my neck and pulls me into him. He doesn't let go as he moves my head where he wants it as his other hand brings my leg up, giving him access to my throbbing pussy.

"Oh!" I gasp as he inserts two fingers. My head falls back and hits the door, but I'll take the likely bump that's going to form tomorrow because I can already tell this is about to be one for the ages.

"You're always so wet for me," he grunts as I feel the palm of his hand against my pussy, his fingers completely inside me. "Always wet. Always perfect."

My moan starts as a hum when his mouth descends on one of my breasts. My nipples were already peaked from the cool air of the office—or at least, that's what it should've been. I have a feeling they knew Porter was here, though.

And Porter is their biggest fan.

My knee nearly gives out as his mouth starts sucking like he hasn't tasted them in ages. I reach down for his dick, wanting to feel something of his. Holy shit is he hard. It feels like steel in my hands as I stroke it as best I can from this angle. It must be working because I feel the vibration of Porter's moans on my skin before he gives one last suck on my nipple that ends with a pop.

Porter lets down my leg before spinning me around, the front of my body now pressed against the wooden door.

"Bend over. Put that marvelous ass in the air for me."

I do as he says, bending at the waist so I'm nearly at a right angle. The only thing that's holding me up right now is my hands against the door, my chest pressing into it, and my wobbly legs. That's until I feel Porter behind me, his hands spreading my ass before I feel the first swipe of his tongue on my center.

"Holy fuck!" I yelp, my elbows nearly giving out from the

sensation. "Don't stop. Please for the love of fucking everything, don't stop."

And I mean that. I think if Porter were to stop right now I'd cry actual tears. Which is madness. This whole scenario is. I just came here to check on him. I didn't expect to be naked, pressed against a door, Porter going down on me in a way he never has before.

Why is this so intense? Is it the act? I mean, sure. Porter's mouth devouring me from behind is hot as hell. But it's more than that. This whole situation was sudden. Unplanned. And frankly, the hottest I've been for him maybe ever. Which is saying something. Once when I was home, he snuck me out back, fingered me behind the bar, and then told me to go wait for him in his bed. And that if I wasn't waiting naked, or had gotten myself off again before he got there, I'd be punished.

The part of me that always bent the rules wanted to see the punishment. The part of me that has a hidden praise kink listened, knowing the pleasure was going to be too good to pass up for the sake of curiosity.

Spoiler alert: It was. The man made me squirt that night.

Though, if I really think about it, every pleasurable experience or feeling that my body has felt during sex over the course of my lifetime has come from the hands, mouth, or fingers of Porter McCoy. The man knows my body better than I do. He sure as hell knows it better than any of the clowns I tried to get with in Phoenix.

None of them know about the spot on my neck, just above my pulse, that make me shake in seconds. None of them could ever get me off with just a few fingers, yet Porter has done it on multiple occasions. Hell, he can make me come with just nipple play. And they definitely don't know how to talk to me in the bedroom.

Nope. That's only this man right here.

"Jesus Christ, Quinn, you taste so fucking good." He stands

up, which feels like a drastic contradiction to the words that just came out of his mouth.

"Then why are you stopping?" I'm panting, now just realizing how close I was to coming before he abruptly halted.

He grabs me around the waist, spinning me to him. Our bodies are pressed together, his dick hard as stone between us.

"Because I need to fuck you. I need that pretty pussy to grip my dick like you know I like it. I want to make you scream and wake the neighbors. You okay with that, Hurricane?"

And there it is. My kind of dirty talk. The kind that has a bit of a challenge to it. A little edge. A little bit of a dare.

And let's be real, Quinn Banks could never turn down a dare.

I mean, any guy can throw in a "shut the fuck up" and "good girl." Some think that they can ride the line between bossy and douchey, but they can't.

But Porter? The man could teach a masterclass.

"Do your worst, McCoy."

That's all the encouragement Porter needs before he pulls me away from the door and expertly maneuvers me back to the desk. I watch in awe as he shoves off every piece of paper with a swipe of his hand.

"Sit," he commands. "Let me look at you."

I'm butt-naked, sitting on Porter's desk. I'm sure my cheeks are flushed and my hair that was in a messy bun probably looks like a hornet's nest right now. My chest is heaving in anticipation. And my heart is pounding out of my chest with the way Porter is looking at me.

"You look so good like that," he says, at some point finding his jeans and pulling out his wallet, grabbing a condom from within. "Now spread those legs for me."

I do as he asks, because why wouldn't I? By the look in Porter's eye, and the way he's stroking himself as he fits the condom on his cock, this is about to be an epic dick down.

When he gets within a step of me, his hand is wrapped around my neck, urging me to his mouth. He doesn't let go, applying just enough pressure to make me gasp, but not hard enough to cut off the airflow.

Just like we both like it.

His kiss is intense as he steps between my legs, using his other hand to line himself up just right before he drives into me.

"Gah!" I gasp, my head falling back as Porter's thrusts begin with a fury. I throw both of my hands back on the desk, praying that they're able to hold me up. Hell, the way Porter is fucking me right now, I just hope this desk holds up. I'm not a tiny girl, and I wasn't great at physics, but I have to think that this desk is about to fight for its life.

But Porter doesn't seem to care. If anything, he's doing his best to bust it *and* me. Good Lord, this man is possessed right now. His mouth is sucking hard on my tit while he's thrusting into me like it's the last time.

Like it's the last time…

This time wasn't supposed to happen. Is that why he's like this right now? Figuring that if we slipped he might as well go out with a literal bang?

Well, if that's the case—which I secretly hope it's not, because I'm sorry, this is too good to stop—then I better hold up my end of the bargain.

"More," I say, though it sounds like I'm begging. "I need more, Porter."

He releases my breast to look me in the eye. "More?"

I nod, biting my lip for some extra flirt. "You wanted me to scream, didn't you?"

A new fire blazes through his eyes as he pulls me up, spinning me around so I'm bent over again, only this time on the desk. The sound of his hand smacking my ass echoes around the room as my body nearly collapses on the desk as he enters me again.

"Like that?" he asks, but both of us know that there isn't going to be an intelligible answer that leaves my lips. Not when

Porter's hands are digging into my hips, fucking me with all his might and bringing me very quickly to the brink.

"Yes. So close."

His thrusts only speed up, Porter knowing exactly what I'm going to need to send me, as well as him, over the edge. Without asking, he reaches around, rubbing my clit before giving it the perfect amount of pressure.

And just like that...I'm a goner.

"Fuck!" I scream, my orgasm crashing through me like a freight train into a brick wall. I feel Porter's hands dig into my hips, his tell that he's not too far behind me.

"Damnit Quinn! Ah!"

He stills inside me, his chest breathing heavy against my back, as we both come down from a high like no other. I feel like we're joined together for minutes like that, both of us trying to find our breath, and bearings, as the world stops spinning.

I must say, if this was the last time, I can't complain with how it ended.

Porter helps me stand up before he quickly grabs his jeans and steps into them, running out of the office and coming back a minute later with a damp towel.

"Here," he says, cleaning me as I try to gain my bearings.

"Thank you," I say, suddenly feeling bashful of my nakedness in the light of the office. Porter must pick up on it as he immediately looks for my bra, shirt, and denim shorts and hands them to me.

I shimmy off the desk and step into my shorts when I see Porter put on his T-shirt and then slumping onto the corner of the desk.

"Is everything okay?"

I'm really concerned. Porter usually doesn't have a regretful look after we have sex. And I don't know if this is necessarily regretful, but he doesn't have the post sex glow like I want him to have.

"What are we doing, Quinn?"

I'm halfway to putting my shirt back on when those words leave his mouth. Shit…after eight years, is Porter *now* wanting to have the "what are we" talk? And with remnants of orgasmal bliss still in the air?

I mean, he *has* asked me to stay. Is this the new version of that? And shit…I don't fucking know. I can barely stand on my legs, let alone put together a coherent answer. This always worked because we were casual and on the same page about not wanting to be in a relationship. Or so I thought.

"You can put away the panic," he says before I can say anything. "I wasn't trying to ask you to be my girlfriend."

I let out a big breath, which earns me a laugh from him. "Geez, don't get too excited."

"No, it's not that," I say. "It's just…now more than ever, I'm not looking for anything serious. I don't know how long I'm staying in Rolling Hills. Everything about my life is up in the air right now. The last thing I want is anything serious."

"And you think I do? I'm not going to be sleeping tonight, wondering if my sister is coming to rob me."

Oh, shit. How did I almost forget about that?

Oh. That's right. The orgasm.

"So what are you asking, then, Porter?"

"I…I don't know, Quinn. All I know is that I should stay away from you, call tonight a slip and go back to us just being boss and employee, but I don't know if I can."

That makes two of us.

"I mean, us going back on promises of 'the last time' is kind of our thing, isn't it?"

He bumps my shoulder as we lean back against his desk. "We could do this, couldn't we? What we've been doing before, only now more frequent?"

"Porter McCoy, are you asking me to be in a situationship?"

He laughs. "Do you think a word like that would ever come out of my mouth?"

"No, but it's fun to think about." I step in front of him, taking hold of his white shirt so I can press into him slightly. "But you're right. We can do this. We're consenting adults. Both on the same page of what we want. Why deny ourselves?"

"Exactly," he says, his arms now pulling me in as they rest on the small of my back. "We just need some guidelines. Boundaries. It'll keep us in line."

I nod. "Normally, I'm not for following the rules, but in this case, I think it's best."

"Agreed. So nothing during work hours."

"Absolutely no flirting at the bar. Oh, and the only time anyone is allowed to say 'chicken wings' is when we're relaying an order to the kitchen."

"Good call," he says. "And, I think it would be best if no one knows. This is just between us. No one needs to know our business."

I do my best to not have a reaction to that statement, even though it feels like a punch in the gut. Which is ridiculous. If he didn't say it, I was going to. But still, hearing it from his mouth stings more than it should.

"Obviously."

Porter tilts his head. "You okay? If you don't want—"

I put my finger to his mouth, needing to distract him from asking any further questions. "I'm fine. And I do. In fact…" I trail off as I push my hands under his T-shirt. "I think I want to do it again."

"Really? Round two?"

I lift my shirt over my head before lowering myself to the ground. "I'd rather call it 'things I didn't get to earlier.'"

14
porter

I SMILE AS I CASUALLY SLIP MY PHONE INTO MY BACK POCKET AS Harry flags me down to grab him another beer.

"What has you smiling like that?"

George smacks his best friend on the back of the head. "What do you think? Or has it been that long since you've been with a woman that you forget the dipshit smile you have the day after?"

"It's not like that," I say, doing my best to throw these two off the scent. I usually have a pretty good poker face, but then again, I've never had sex with Quinn Banks multiple nights in a row. I'd guess that I'm smiling like the damn Joker right now. "Just been a good few days. Can't a guy smile?"

Both of them look at each other before giving me a once over before Harry speaks up. "Guys? Yes, *guys* can. You? Well, you're not really the smilin' type."

"Unless you're flirtin', then you're all smiles."

Can't argue with him there. At least with what these two have seen from me over the years. I've been known to turn it on to appease customers, or back in my manwhore days, to whatever lovely lady I wanted to take home that night. But that version of Porter has gone to the wayside over the past few years. "I promise you both, it's nothing to get your boxers in a bunch over. So go back to watching whatever god forsaken show you made me turn on and drink your beer."

I turn my back from them, wanting to make sure I don't give anything away as I feel my phone vibrate in my pocket. I grab a bucket of beers for the construction crew that rolled in about an hour ago before reading Quinn's response.

QUINN

Sounds good. I'm *very* hungry.

PORTER

You are, are you? Even though you had them last night? From what I remember, you swallowed every last bit.

QUINN

I did. And I enjoyed every last drop. But I'm always ready for more.

Indeed she did. Quinn came in last night under the guise of a beer and wings for dinner.

I knew exactly what that meant. And because I'm the owner, and I can do whatever I want, I sent Jenny home early, telling her I could handle it, locked the door when the bar emptied out at midnight, then proceeded to fuck Quinn over a bar stool before she sucked me off in my office while I was trying to count money.

Trying being the operative word.

PORTER

You're bad.

QUINN

You love it. My place after close?

PORTER

I'll text you when I'm leaving.

QUINN

I'll be the one naked and ready.

Before I can reply back, Quinn sends me a selfie that somehow I can tell she's completely naked, yet only teases me with the parts of her that make me salivate at the thought of kissing and touching every piece of skin she's showing me.

Hell, who am I kidding? I'd worship that woman's body every day, twice on Sundays, and throw in an extra service on Wednesday nights just to make sure I've properly paid respects.

PORTER

Fuck. You're killing me woman.

QUINN

Good. See you tonight. 🐱

Now I really need to keep my face hidden from Harry and George, or any other customer for that matter. I don't know what's going to be more obvious, the red I can feel on my cheeks, the smile I can't seem to put away, or the bulge growing in my pants. So to be safe, I shout for Jenny to watch the bar while I go grab something from the office.

I shut the door behind, me, taking a few deep breaths to calm myself from all thoughts of Quinn Banks. The only problem is that now this whole office has her scent on it. I can barely be in here anymore and not think about Quinn beautifully laid on my desk as I fucked her until we both screamed.

That night was…God…nearly two full days later and I still haven't been able to make my brain come up with words to describe it. Yes it was hot. Probably the hottest time we've ever spent together. I don't know if it was the emotions, or the place, or what, but I know that if there's ever going to be a memory of

Quinn burned into my brain, it's her bent over this desk, her perfect ass bouncing on my cock as I left her ass red.

I had no intentions of doing anything with Quinn that night, I really didn't. Hell, I didn't think I'd come back to the bar after I slipped out the back door to get my head right after seeing Missy. I knew the rumors were going to go flying around the bar, and it was just a matter of time before Quinn or Jenny would come check on me under the ruse of needing to grab something from the office.

But at some point in the night, as I was sitting in the darkness of my living room, I felt like the walls were starting to close in on me. I don't have many places I can go and just think. But one place that never ceases to come through is the bar's office. I don't know what I believe when it comes to life after death, but when I have a problem, or am in a funk, I sit in the office and I swear I can feel Pops' presence. And if I ever needed to feel like he was here with me, it was that night. Unfortunately, the more I sat there, the more questions I conjured in my mind of why the hell Missy showed up out of the blue, and why she ran off like a bat out of hell.

I knew it was only a matter of time before Quinn would force herself in to check on me, but even then I figured I'd just vent to her. Had to be better than keeping everything inside, right? But what happened after…holy shit, I wasn't ready for that.

Though I should've been. I'm really some sort of idiot if I thought I could be alone with Quinn Banks and keep my hands to myself. I don't know what kind of spell that woman has cast over me, but it's strong and potent. Part of me hopes it never fades away. The other part of me is scared shitless for thinking that.

A knock on the door thankfully breaks my thoughts from whatever road my Quinn-filled mind was about to take me. I also breathe a little because I know it's not Quinn. It's not her knock.

"Yeah?"

The door cracks open to show my favorite cousin standing on the other side.

"Can I come in?"

"Always," I say, pointing to the seat on the other side of the desk from me. "What brings you by?"

Wes takes a seat, and by the concerned look in his eye, it's not to talk about the upcoming Nashville Fury football season. "Thought I'd come and check on you."

I sit back in my chair. "You heard?"

"Everyone in the city limits heard. Hell, my brother heard, and he's on vacation in Aruba right now."

Damn. News travels fast and far. The post office could use some pointers from this community. "Thanks, but I'm okay."

Clearly my half-truth isn't convincing. "I'm going to call bull-shit. So when you're ready to actually talk, I'll be sitting right here. Though I could use a beer."

I laugh and reach over to the mini fridge I keep for myself, and grab one for each of us. "Honestly, I could too. Nothing like unpacking family trauma without a cold one."

We tip the beers to each other and each take a pull. "But in all seriousness, I'm fine. Well, now I am. Still a little shook, because seeing Missy wasn't something I'd planned on. But I haven't heard from her since she ran out of here."

Wes leans forward, elbows on his knees. "She really didn't say anything? Ask for anything?"

"Nope," I say. "I could tell she was making some things up. Too jumpy, you know? But she wasn't here long enough for me to get a real read on her."

"Do you think maybe she just actually wanted to connect?"

"Maybe," I say. "And I thought about that when she mentioned that her dad passed. But then why dart out of here when Harry and George walked in? What would she have done if there were people here when she arrived? Nothing makes sense."

"So odd." Wes pauses for a second before asking me the one he knows is going to hurt. "Did she bring up your mom?"

I nod, the pain of having to think about my mom after all these years being the worst part of all this. "Apparently Bonnie hasn't changed her ways. I think Missy was lying about a lot of things, but the one thing she was truthful about was that Bonnie was still the same ol' woman."

Wes's eyebrows shoot up. "Bonnie? I know you don't talk about your mom a lot, but I don't think I've ever heard you call her by her first name."

"Guess I finally realized that to be called Mom, you have to act like one. She sure as shit hasn't. "

"That's the fucking truth," Wes said. "Okay, so back to Missy. She hates Bonnie too. She randomly popped in here. Was jumpy. Made a lot of random small talk. Then left? Just like that."

"Just like that," I say with a nod.

"So weird. Something's off."

"Is this what family drama is like?" I ask.

Wes shakes his head. "Slightly. But then again, you never had to deal with a crazy ex-wife or a custody battle. So maybe I'm biased."

I laugh, because he's right. Then again, having a crazy ex would require me getting married. And that is one thing I've never wanted.

God love being a child of divorce with a mother who doesn't give two shits about you.

"Well, if she comes back, keep me in the loop, won't you?" Wes says as he stands up. "Oh, and the fact my mom had to hear the news from one of the Bingo ladies did not sit well with her."

I laugh and stand up as well. "I'll call Aunt Peggy and apologize."

"You know an apology will require you to come over for dinner."

I nod. "I think I can live with that."

Wes and I exchange a slap-your-back hug before he exits my

office, me following behind. When I go back into the bar, it's the normal, slow, Monday crowd. Good. When it's slow like this, I can leave Jenny to tend bar and handle the tables. More money for her and a break for me.

And after the weekend I've had, I could use a break. Plus, maybe now a certain guest can come over a little earlier.

Yes. I like this plan.

"You good if I take off?" I ask Jenny as I open the register to grab my keys.

"Yup. Get out of here," she says. "I can handle these rowdies."

"Hey!" Harry yells. "I take offense!"

"You should," I joke, giving him a slap on the back. "Thanks, Jenny. I'll come back to help you close."

"No, you won't," she says. "Take the night off. Please."

The look she gives me is one a mother would give to her child. And technically, Jenny is old enough to be my mom, though I'd never say that to her.

"Thanks," I say, sending her a wink. "Call me if you need anything."

I say goodbye to a few guys playing pool as I slip down the hallway and past my office. Except as soon as I take a step past it, I realize that it's cracked open, which is not right. I distinctly remember closing it when Wes and I stepped out.

"Hello?" I ask, wondering if one of the cooks came in to grab something. But I don't hear anything as I push the door open and flip the light on.

But as soon as I do, I can't believe what I'm seeing. I just left this room not even ten minutes ago.

And now, sitting on top of my desk, is an infant carrier.

And looking at me, with the brightest green eyes I've ever seen, is a baby.

guide to love rule #69

Stay up to date on current lingo and slang. It'll help in many aspects of life, including, but not limited to, deciphering booty calls.

15
quinn

"How is it that I've been back in town for two whole weeks and this is the first time we're getting together for dinner?"

The question is floated in generality to my sisters as I sit down in a booth at Mona's Diner, but Maeve is the first to answer.

"I'd also like to know how we're having dinner at the establishment you live above and somehow you're the last one to show up."

I wave off my sister as I settle into my seat. "I just wanted to make a grand entrance."

"Well, we were tired of waiting for the fanfare," Stella says. "We ordered cheese fries."

"No complaints here," I say as I grab one and my own side of ranch. Because ranch as a condiment is elite, and I'll be taking no arguments on that fact. "I do appreciate you already having my drink ready for me."

Ainsley shakes her head at me as I take a big sip of my fountain Coke. Because that's the only acceptable Coke. "I'm going to go out on a limb and say you've already drank three iced coffees today."

I hold up two fingers. "Only two, thank you very much."

"Still, you had two iced coffees, and now you're drinking a Coke. You're going to be up all night."

After the text exchange with Porter this afternoon I can only hope.

"I appreciate your concern, Ainsley. Helps having a nurse in the family."

"I'm a labor and delivery nurse. I care for babies and mamas. And this isn't nurse care, this is general worry about your state of dehydration, which has to be off the charts."

"I'm fine," I wave off. "I think the real concern is how you work multiple overnight shifts, and ones that go for ten to twelve hours, and you *don't* drink coffee. Or any kind of caffeine. That's really what's concerning."

Ainsley shrugs as she takes a sip of her water. "Just that good. You could learn a thing or two."

I snicker at my sister's demure, yet cutting, answer. Ainsley has that way about her. She might be the good girl of the Banks bunch, but the woman can throw a quiet shot and have it cut just as deep as a profanity-laced dig.

"Okay, enough about un-caffeinated Ainsley being better than all of us," Stella says. "No offense, Ains."

"None taken," she says. "You're right. This isn't about me. Tonight's about Quinn."

I nearly choke on a cheese fry. "What do you mean tonight's about me? I thought we were just getting together for a sisterly dinner?"

At least, that's what tonight was spun to *me* as. Since the bar is only open a half day on Mondays, Porter told me I'd always have the whole day off. Which is great since I'm now working weekends. I thoroughly enjoy a reset day. I sit back, relax, think about meal prepping for ten minutes before I don't, and in the meantime, I ponder my existence.

You know, adulty things.

So when my sisters asked me if I could have dinner tonight—Stella works in town, Ainsley had a day shift at the hospital, and

Maeve was free of all of her commitments—it felt like a great night to catch up.

Little did I know this was some sort of weird intervention.

"It is," Maeve says, reaching across the booth and taking my hand. "We just wanted to talk to you. See where your head's at."

"My head is fine," I defend.

"We're not saying it's not," Ainsley adds. "It's just that last time we all really talked, you hadn't made a decision on whether or not you were staying."

"And you hadn't started at The Joint yet, and we wanted to see how that's going."

I make sure to hide any sort of reaction after that statement from Stella. My sisters don't need to know what kind of benefit package I'm getting by working at the town bar.

I also have to swallow a laugh at my use of the word "package" because apparently hanging out with adolescent boys for years has given me their humor.

"Everything is fine," I say. "It hasn't even been a month since I quit. I'm barely settled here. I started at the bar last week, which has taken up a lot of time. So yeah, I haven't really gotten to 'plan rest of the life' yet on the to-do list. But I promise it's coming."

Is there snark in my voice? Of course there is. But even for me, it's a little sharper. I mean, what do they expect? The wound is still fresh.

Though judging by Maeve's look, she's not amused by my tone.

"Words of wisdom from Mama Maeve?"

She shakes her head. "All I was going to ask is if you've truly processed what happened."

Processed? Yes. Recovered? Not even close.

"I'm fine."

"No, you're not," she says. "You came here in a whirlwind. I know we thought this was going to be good for you to sit back and think about what you wanted. But now I'm worried that you've thrown yourself into working at the bar, just delaying the process you'll need to go through to come to terms of what quitting actually means, and what's going to be next."

Okay, she's getting a little too close to the wound. Time to deflect.

"I know. I thank you. And so does future Quinn. Those are her problems."

Maeve, nor do any of my sisters, think that joke was funny. "Quinn. Be serious about this."

"I am," I defend. "I just…it's a lot, you know?"

Ainsley reaches over and places her hand on top of mine. "We know, Quinn. Please know and we acknowledge that."

So much of me wants to spill and tell them everything that's going on in my head right now. Because while I might be deflecting, or filling every waking hour with staying busy so I don't have to acknowledge my life, I think about it every day and every night.

Each night when I lie in my bed, Turtle next to me, the silence of Rolling Hills is deafening. Somehow the silence of the small town is a loud reminder that I'm back in the town I swore I'd never call home again. I cry every day when I wake up in the morning and I remember I'm not going to school. We should be in the thick of *The Westing Game*. We should be getting ready for end-of-year field trips and game days. When those emotions take over, I want to book the first flight back to Arizona, talk to the school and tell them I made a rash decision, and see if I can get my job back for the next school year.

From time to time, I wonder if I could start fresh again. Throw a new dart at the map. I hear Oregon is beautiful this time of year.

Then there are the days here like this one, when I wonder if living in Rolling Hills would be so bad. I'm having dinner on a random Monday night with my sisters. I see my niece daily at the diner when Charlie or Simon brings her in. I get to eat my mom's home cooking and have chats with my dad.

And I kind of like working at The Joint. Besides the dick perks, talking to the people who've lived here for years has been more fulfilling than I thought. I figured they'd still look at me as the crazy Quinn who once listed the high school's address as a property for sale on Craigslist. Instead they've been nothing but nice and welcoming to me. I don't know if it's a job I'd want to do forever, but it's been a nice addition to my temporary life here.

Now, will I tell them any of that? Absolutely not. They might be my sisters and the best friends I could ever ask for, but they don't need to know that Quinn Banks, famously for taking everything in stride, is hurting.

And questioning her life.

No, I'm the sure one. I'm the one who makes instant decisions. And for now, that's what I need to be.

"I acknowledge that everything y'all have said is true. And I also acknowledge that I can't make a decision yet." I don't want to give too much away, but I know I can't be vague right now. So maybe a little will go a long way. "When I start thinking about everything, it just feels too big. Too soon, you know? It's overwhelming frankly. So I push it to the back of my brain and open my Kindle."

"Ah, avoidance," Stella says. "I'm very familiar. When I get like that, my therapist has told me to make tiny decisions and do little things. And then you can open your book."

"You're in therapy?" Ainsley asks.

"Of course," she says. "My ex cheated on me with a dominatrix, and I'm a pathological people pleaser. Of course I'm in therapy. And frankly, everyone should be. We're all a little fucked, if I'm being honest."

She's not wrong about that.

"I'll try it," I say. "I know at some point I have to make a decision, but I just need a little more time. Maybe one decision at a time is the way to go. But I promise when I'm ready to talk more, you three will be the first I call."

Or I'll just do everything on my own time and tell them at the end what I decided. That's probably more how it'll go.

Ainsley wraps her arms around me. "And we'll be here. Always. Whatever you decide, we'll support you no matter what."

"Even if you move back to the desert."

I stick my tongue out at Stella for her comment as I lean into my sister's hold. And I must admit, a hug from Ainsley is putting a whole lot of points in the Rolling Hills column. No one can comfort you like Ainsley Banks.

"Thanks everyone," I say. "But next time, can you tell me when the intervention is coming so I can plan for it? Or better yet, maybe have the spotlight focus on someone else. I mean, why can't we grill Ainsley about her life? She's got to have something going on."

"Nice try," Ainsley says as the waitress approaches our table with our orders. "I deliver babies for a living, volunteer on the weekends, and haven't drank since college."

"Whoa!" I yell. "That! We need to go into that! I didn't even know that happened!"

"Another time," Ainsley says. "I need food."

Somehow, the conversation of Ainsley *ever* drinking is brushed away and replaced by four starving sisters. Which, I mean, I get. Charlie and her staff make one hell of a sandwich. I've become quite fond of the turkey, bacon, and ranch, which I'm about to take a bite of when the sound of a door slamming open takes all four of us by surprise.

"Unacceptable!"

Each of us puts down our sandwiches as Simon marches to our table. "How many times have I told you that I have FOMO? I can't believe you didn't invite me! Again!"

"It's not that we didn't invite you, it's that you shouldn't have been available now," says Stella, who also serves as my brother's office manager and therefore is the keeper of his schedule. "You had a late afternoon and evening showing. And

Charlie has the night off, so shouldn't you be spending it with your fiancée and daughter?"

He waves Stella off as he pulls up a chair. "The showings were done an hour ago. And it was my beautiful fiancée who told me about this little dinner. How dare you not invite me!"

"Can't we just have some sister time?" I ask. "I promise we'll invite you next time."

"You said that last time."

"Fine, we'll invite you to the next sisters' dinner."

Simon holds out his pinky, apparently my words not enough to seal this promise.

"Thank you. Now, what are we talking about? What's the tea? Isn't that what the kids say? Is Quinn staying in Rolling Hills or leaving us again?"

"Nope," I say. "I've already done the debrief. Someone else fill him in."

Maeve draws that short straw, and I dip my sandwich into the puddle of ranch on my plate when I feel my cell phone vibrate in my back pocket. Since all of my siblings are here, and no one from my old school district has bothered to reach out since I sprinted out of town, I have to assume it's Porter.

I grab my phone and stand from the booth, turning away from my siblings so no one can see the hopeful dirty text my now-permanent fuck buddy has sent.

Only when I open the text, I'm very confused by the contents.

PORTER

What in the emoji word scramble filter is this shit?

"Quinn? You okay?"

"Yeah," I say, though I trail off as I try and decipher what the hell Porter just texted me.

QUINN

Care to translate?

I stare at my phone, but Porter doesn't type anything back, which only leaves me staring at the screen and confused as all hell.

Okay, the winky face, the spicy pepper make sense. A little flirty intro.

I'm pretty sure the next one is a trench coat. Does he want me to come over wearing only that? Do I even own one?

Moving on to the eggplant. That's easy.

Peach? I hope that means he wants to spank my ass again. Because if the eggplant before the peach means what I think it means, we need to have a conversation about out holes and in holes.

If all of that is correct, the devil face makes sense. But the poop emoji? That one is really throwing me.

"You look confused," Stella says. "Who is it?"

"Porter," I say without thinking, so I hurry and cover. "He needs me to come relieve him at the bar tonight."

"Everything okay?"

I nod to Ainsley's question before I help myself to a to-go box. "I'm going to go upstairs and get changed. I'll text you guys tomorrow."

Simon starts to say something before I finish. "And I'll make sure to use the all-siblings chat and not just the sisters chat."

"Thank you," he says. "You were always my favorite."

"Hey!" Stella yells. "I run your life. Doesn't that count for anything?"

The voices fade of my squabbling siblings as I head to the back of the diner and up the stairs to my temporary apartment. I check my phone again to see if Porter texted me back. Still nothing.

Turtle meows at me as I walk into the apartment, but can't be bothered to do much else. It's why we get along so well. We both like our space. He does his thing. I do mine. Occasionally he cuddles with me.

Holy shit, I have a situationship with my cat...

I can't think about that right now as I dig through my underwear drawer for the one piece of lingerie I own. I can't help but think that this whole thing feels a little off. We were already planning on meeting tonight. Dirty texts had been sent. And I know the bar can be slow on Mondays, but sending me this now is confusing. Does he mean that I should come now? Or is this a message for later and I should come over at the previously agreed upon time?

PORTER

Okay then. Message received. We're starting earlier than planned. And I guess at his place?

"Porter McCoy, be ready for a night you'll never forget." I adjust the royal blue lace one piece that leaves nothing to the imagination. I take the extra few seconds to slide on the thigh highs and straps that came with it.

I only bought this to go under a dress I wore to a coworker's wedding. It was sexier, and more expensive, than I needed. But it had a halter neckline and a low back, and when you're a 42DD, bra and lingerie options are far and few between. And it came with thigh highs and fasteners. I told the saleswoman I didn't need them. She told me to take them just in case.

I don't know her name, but I could kiss her right now. I barely recognize myself. I feel sexy. I like my body—well, now. It took me a while to get here. But even though I'm comfortable in my skin, rarely do I use the word "sexy" to describe myself. But the way this lingerie is snatching my waist, while also pressing my boobs together in a way that I know is going to drive Porter insane? I've never felt better about myself.

Oh, tonight is going to be fun…

I quickly throw on a little makeup, fluff up my hair, and grab my long rain jacket because I don't have a trench coat. As I tie the knot to close it, I check out of the window to see if my siblings are still here. They were all parked on the street, so I have a clear view of their whereabouts.

"All gone," I say as I pull the jacket a little tighter. "Turtle, how do I look?"

My cat stares at me like I'm crazy, which is valid. But since he doesn't have an answer for that, I doubt he'll help me decide on whether to wear my black high heels or my comfy slip-ons. I decide to wear the flats in case someone sees me—wearing high heels on a Monday night is sure to raise suspicion if anyone at The Joint sees me—but I throw the black heels in a bag to hopefully slip on later.

I sneak down the stairs, making sure no one from the diner sees me as I get into my car and pull out of the back parking lot. Normally, the drive across town to The Joint takes five or ten minutes, depending if I hit the two stop lights along the way, but tonight it feels like it's taking forever. I've never done anything like this before. Even though Porter told me to come—in his own weird emoji way—I've never been summoned like this. I've never taken the time to doll myself up. Yet tonight I had no qualms of doing either. In fact, everything about this has been exciting. Hot. And we haven't even gotten to the good part of the night yet.

It's nights like this I wish my sisters knew about me and Porter. I'd love to have girl talk about the man who makes me feel beautiful. The man who makes me scream. And the man who can't keep his hands off me when we're together.

But I can't. Not that they wouldn't keep my secret. I know they would. But me telling them I'm in a sexual situationship with Porter and don't want any more will only have them playing therapist with me and trying to convince me that relationships aren't all bad. And after dinner tonight, I think I'm getting enough therapy from them on my life.

I park at my normal spot in the back of The Joint, feeling like that will raise the least amount of suspicions. I speed walk through the parking lot, knowing I probably don't have a lot of time before someone comes outside for a smoke. I hurriedly slip off my comfy shoes in place of the black heels and give myself one more shake of my hair before knocking on the door.

I quickly unbutton my jacket, knowing only Porter will see the lace number I'm wearing when he opens the door. My goal is for his eyes to pop out of his head.

And when he opens the door, his eyes are indeed big.

They are arguably not in his head.

But his face is also white.

I don't think he's breathing.

And, this is just a guess, but I'm pretty sure it has nothing to do with what I'm wearing.

"Porter? Why are you holding a baby?"

16
porter

"GET IN HERE!" I WHISPER-YELL, PULLING A HALF-NAKED AND fucking smoking hot Quinn inside my house.

She hurriedly ties back up her jacket, which makes me cry on the inside because I didn't get to appreciate what she was wearing nearly enough. She follows me into the living room, where I sit the baby on the couch, encased by pillows so she doesn't fall. I learned this trick an hour ago when she wasn't having the baby carrier anymore and I was losing feeling in my arms.

"Porter. What the fuck is going on? Who is that baby? And, you know, why do you *have* a freaking baby?"

I start pacing in my living room, trying to get my thoughts together. When I stop to take a breath, I realize that not only Quinn, but also baby girl, are looking at me with similar confused expressions. It'd be hilarious if this whole thing wasn't absolutely insane.

"She—her—the baby…on my desk…in the bar…"

Quinn snickers. "There was a baby? In a bar?"

"Yes. Didn't I just fucking say that?"

Her laughter is now gone from a snicker to a snort. "Why are you laughing? This isn't a joking matter, Quinn!"

"I'm sorry," she says, her laughter escalating. "When we get this figured out, I need to have you watch *Sweet Home Alabama.*"

I shake my head in frustration, confusion, and hoping that if I shake it hard enough, I'll wake up from this dream. "This isn't a joke, Quinn. Wait. Why are you here? And why are you dressed like that?"

I didn't mean for it to come out biting, but this whole situation has me losing my cool. Especially when I see Quinn look at me like I'm the dumb one.

"You told me to," she says. "You texted me."

"Yeah. We both did. But I didn't think you'd take that as *come over now*?"

"No. *You* texted me an hour ago. I took it as you were ready."

"I promise I did no such thing, because for the last three hours I've been trying to figure out what the hell to do with a random baby that showed up in my office!"

"Oh my God, Porter! I'm not lying!" She grabs her cell phone out of a tote bag. "See!"

She hands me her phone to a text string between us. And she's right. After our promise to meet later tonight, is a whole new set of random emojis.

"I promise you I never sent these," I say. "I never use emojis. I don't even know what this means."

"Really, Porter? Then who sent them to me? And who else would send an eggplant and a peach back to back? Also, if you're into that sort of thing, just let me know. I'm not opposed, but we need to talk about a lot of things in regard to that. Mainly prepping."

"Quinn, I promise you, I didn't send these. I don't even know who would or how—"

Before I can finish the sentence, the sound of babbles and incoherent sounds come from the couch. She's even clapping like she's trying to tell me something.

And that's when I remember...

"No..." I say, going to sit down next to my unexpected guest.

"No what?"

"This little one, a little over an hour ago, I put her down because my arms were tired. And I needed to go to the bathroom. I had my phone out because I was looking up if I could leave a baby alone. I couldn't find the answer I was looking for when I was about to call you in a panic. She was on her stomach, and it was sitting next to her before I walked out of the room…"

Quinn's horrified look quickly turns into a fit of laughter. "Okay, I don't know who this kid is, but she's officially my favorite."

I let baby girl take my finger as I stare at her. "I wish I knew who she was, too."

Quinn gasps as she sits across from me on a chair. "What do you mean? How do you not know who she is?"

"I have a feeling who she came from, but that's it," I say. "I was getting ready to leave the bar. I walked down the hall and noticed the office door was open, which I knew I'd shut. When I opened it up, there she was, staring at me like she'd been waiting hours for me. Then I panicked, grabbed her, and raced back here. The rest is a blur."

"Okay, then." Quinn trails off as she looks over to the baby. The two of them make eye contact, and Quinn gives her a little wave. Baby girl is all smiles toward her, which makes me relax slightly. Then the loudest, and smelliest, fart I've ever heard comes from my cute guest.

"What the fuck was that!" I yell, coughing once the scent hits my nose.

"That, my friend, was her letting us know loud and clear that she needs a diaper change."

"A what?"

Quinn's staring at me like I grew a second head. "Her diaper, Porter. She's wearing a diaper. It needs changed. This is where you come in."

"Oh no!" I say, jumping up from the couch, hands up in

surrender. "I don't know how to do it. What if she poops on me? It's going to fucking smell. I can't. You do it."

Quinn lets out a sigh before standing up and picking up Baby Girl, which is her name until further notice. "I'll do this, but at some point I'm going to be teaching you. It's not like I can be here twenty-four-seven, on diaper duty."

"Yeah, yeah," I say, sitting back down because my head is spinning. I watch as Quinn picks up the bag that was left next to the baby carrier and starts digging in it for Lord knows what. I'm going to assume diaper things.

I'm not a baby kind of guy. I wasn't around when Missy was a baby. I barely held Wes's kids when they were young. Hell, I specifically didn't take home economics in high school because I didn't want to do the weeks where we had to take the baby doll home. I knew even back then I didn't want kids.

I watch in awe as Quinn—wearing nothing but lace lingerie and a rain coat—kneels on the ground as she spreads out some sort of pad before laying the baby down on it. She then reaches back into the bag and grabs a diaper and some sort of wipes before pulling out an envelope.

"Did you see this?" she asks. "It has your name on it."

"No. I never even opened the bag," I say, reaching for it. And yup, clear as day, in pretty cursive handwriting, is my name.

I rip it open, and from the first word I realize who this is from. And suddenly, the events of the last two days make a hell of a lot more sense. And why baby girl's green eyes hit me in the heart from the second I saw them.

PORTER,

IF YOU'RE READING THIS, YOU'VE NOW MET GRACE. SHE'S GOING TO BE ONE IN JUNE. SHE'S YOUR NIECE. AND I NEED YOU TO RAISE HER.

I SHOULD START BY SAYING THAT I'M SORRY. THIS

isn't how I wanted to do this, but I couldn't take the chance that you'd say no if I asked you the other day.

Because last year when I became a mother, I was scared. I didn't want her, but I also couldn't bring myself to have an abortion. You know our mother, so you probably know how she reacted to finding out my news. My dad said he was going to help, but he was sick and died soon after she was born. I thought I could do it on my own, but I can't. I'm not built for this. And then, out of the blue, I met a guy who wants the same things I do. To travel. See the world. We want to live in a van and see every sight we can.

I wasn't meant to be a mother. I don't know how to do this. And I want to live my life. I can't raise this baby. She doesn't deserve me. She deserves stability.

Someone like you.

I don't take a lot of stock into what Bonnie has said over the years, but one thing she once said always stuck with me. After your dad died, she went on a drunken rant about how "Porter has everything figured out." She said you didn't need her. Never did. She was trying to say it as a dig. But when something got to her like that, it's because it was true.

So when I knew I couldn't do this, when I had cried too many nights to count because I couldn't do this, I remembered that. So I came here. Saw the life you've built for yourself. That you were those things Bonnie said.

Everything she isn't.

YES, I KNOW WE'VE BARELY SPOKEN OVER THE YEARS, AND I KNOW THIS IS THE BIGGEST THING I COULD ASK SOMEONE, BUT I NEED YOU TO DO THIS FOR ME. WHILE I KNOW I CAN'T DO THIS, I ALSO DON'T WANT TO PUT HER IN AN UNSAFE SITUATION. IT MIGHT SEEM LIKE I'M NOT, BUT I AM DOING THIS FOR HER. AND I NEED YOU TO HELP ME WITH THAT.

PLEASE DON'T TRY TO CONTACT ME. ALL OF THE PAPERS YOU SHOULD NEED ARE IN THIS ENVELOPE. SHE'S YOURS, PORTER.

I JUST ASK THAT ONE DAY WHEN SHE ASKS ABOUT ME, TELL HER THAT I DID WHAT WAS BEST FOR HER. HOPEFULLY SHE'LL UNDERSTAND.

MISSY

———

I don't know how much time has passed. But I do know that I've read Missy's letter no less than twenty times. I've stared at the birth certificate, immunization records, and a letter from Missy herself saying that she has given guardianship to me.

I feel the air hitting my skin. I see Quinn out of the corner of my eye holding Grace, letting her flip through a children's book that makes noises. I even pinched myself a few times to make sure this isn't some sort of fucked-up nightmare.

I'm not. This is real. So fucking real.

"You okay?"

I snort out a laugh, because I don't know how else to respond.

"I'm sorry, bad question." Quinn says. "I just…I don't know what to say right now, but the more you don't say anything, the more worried I get."

I look over to Quinn, who's since changed out of her lingerie and raincoat into a pair of my sweatpants and a T-shirt. I'm so fucked up in the head right now I can't appreciate Quinn Banks in my clothes.

"I just don't know what to say. Or think. Or do."

"I get it," she says, setting Grace on the floor with a few toys she found in her diaper bag, though she seems to be more interested in the remote control. "I mean, I'm rarely speechless, but a situation like this would cause it to happen."

"I just don't know what to do," I admit. "I've never wanted children. Or at least, I never saw myself with one."

"Same," she says. "I'm built for the life of the cool aunt."

"But that was then. She's here. Missy is gone, and from the sounds of this letter, wants nothing to do with her or motherhood. If I don't take her in, then what happens to Grace? Also, why would she think that I'm the guy for this job? She doesn't know me."

"An estranged relative who isn't an axe murderer is better than foster care," Quinn says. "I saw that happen a lot back in Arizona. Kids had parents who weren't equipped to take care of them, and didn't have family who could help out, went into the system."

"No. Absolutely not." I look down at Grace, whose big green eyes are already putting a vise grip on my heart.

Green eyes that seem to run in the family.

But it's not just her eyes. Maybe it's her full cheeks that have a little red in them. Or her small pink lips that are amazingly quick to smile. Or maybe it's the part of me that knows she's blood. And you do what you need to for family. Even if it wasn't in the cards.

"And that's why she picked you."

I look up to Quinn. "What?"

"You asked why Missy, who doesn't know you, would ask you to do this. Because in that one meeting you had, and the little she knew about you, she knew that you'd be a safe place for her daughter. She made an impossible decision, Porter. But I have a feeling she didn't do this lightly. You don't want her to go into foster care. And Missy is gone who-knows-where. So what are you going to do, Porter McCoy?"

I stare at Grace. I'm not sure how many words she knows, because I know literally nothing about babies, but I swear this little thing is staring at me and daring me to let her go.

And it's in this moment that I realized I'm already fucked when it comes to this kid.

"I don't know how to do this," I say in a panic, as the realization of what I'm about to do takes over. "I've never changed a diaper. Hell, the only reason I have any idea of how to hold a baby is because of Wes's kids. And even then I was always scared I was going to drop them. What does she eat? When does she sleep? How will I know when to change her diaper? She can't talk. How do I know what she needs? And all of those things are just the generic things I know I need to know about babies."

"You know more than you think," Quinn says as she moves closer to me. "First-time parents only know what they read in books. And even then, there's stuff that happens every day that they were given zero warning about. Plus, you did your first Google search about baby things. You're basically a pro."

"You're not making me feel better about this," I say. "What would've happened tonight if you didn't show up? One second I'm panicking, next second I'm still panicking but you're taking over and changing diapers and feeding her and doing things that I knew nothing about. If you weren't here…"

"No. Don't think like that," she says. "Eventually you would've called me, or Jenny, or even Wes and Betsy. You're resourceful. I did it because I was here, but you would've figured it out."

"I think you're giving me too much credit."

"No, I'm not giving you enough." Quinn takes my hand in both of hers, giving it a reassuring squeeze. "It's going to be hard. But you're going to do this. You have people who love you who will help you. Family. Friends. Hell, you have built-in babysitters at the bar."

This makes Porter laugh. "I have a feeling Grace will be watching Harry and George more than they'd be watching her."

"Probably," Quinn twists in her seat to look straight at me, but doesn't let go of my hand. "But what I'm saying is that you have a tribe here. A village. And you have me. I don't know a lot, but what I don't know I can ask Maeve or Ainsley. Hell, Simon is somehow Dad of the Year, which means anyone can do it. You can do this, Porter. I know you can."

My eyes lock with Quinn's, and the look of pride and encouragement is overwhelming. I start to lean in as does she, the emotion of the day too much to keep us apart. And just when I'm about to take that bottom lip, a squeal makes each of us jump back.

"Jesus Christ," I say, breathing a little heavy as I realize it was just Grace, who is very excited that she made the television turn on with the remote. "One day in my care and she's turning on televisions and texting."

"Kids these days, too much screen time."

I know Quinn is trying to keep the mood light, but I'm panicked right now. "Quinn?"

"Yeah?"

"Can you…can you stay tonight?"

"Um…I mean…"

"Please, Quinn. I know it's not part of our agreement, but I'm terrified right now." I take her hand because I need her to know just how serious I am. "I need help. If she wakes up in the middle of the night, I won't know what to do. And you never taught me how to change a diaper. What if she needs one changed tonight? Please, you need to stay. I'm begging."

As if Grace is realizing what I'm asking, I watch as she half crawls, half walks over to Quinn, before falling into her leg.

"See? Even Grace wants you to stay."

She leans down, picking Grace up. "You want me to stay, Miss Ma'am?"

Grace doesn't say anything, instead just squishes Quinn's cheeks with her tiny little hands.

"I think that means yes."

Quinn laughs as she takes one of her hands and blows raspberries into her palm. "Okay. I can stay. But just tonight. We'll get you settled in, go out tomorrow and load you up on essentials. Then we'll go from there."

I let out a sigh of relief, but that's until Quinn hands me Grace and goes to get her keys out of her bag.

"Where are you going?"

"Relax. She needs food. Milk. A few more diapers, to be safe. I'm going to run to the all-night market to get us through."

"Okay," I say, trailing off. "That can't wait until tomorrow?"

Quinn laughs. "Oh, Uncle Porter...I say this in the most sincere Southern way...but bless your heart."

guide to love rule #84

It's impossible to not be attracted to a man wearing a backward hat while shopping for baby clothes.

17

quinn

STELLA

QUINN ELIZABETH BANKS. WAKE UP. NOW.

I HEAR THE PHONE VIBRATE FROM THE NIGHTSTAND NEXT TO Porter's bed, Grace sleeping peacefully between the two of us on his California King. Though, the term "sleep" is relative. I maybe dozed off for a few hours, but I think we were both so nervous that something would happen to her—since we didn't have a crib for her to sleep in—that neither of us really slept more than a few minutes here and there.

And *that's* why I'm not freaking out that I technically slept in the same bed as Porter for the first time in eight years. Because it wasn't sleep. It was random naps with a baby between us.

Totally doesn't count.

QUINN

What are you talking about and why are you shouting at me?

STELLA

Um, maybe because someone saw you at the late-night pharmacy buying diapers. Care to explain, since I'm pretty sure you weren't being a good aunt and getting them for your niece?

SIMON

I can confirm that no diapers have been delivered to my daughter. Why is that? Huh Quinn? DON'T YOU LOVE YOUR NIECE?

I roll out of bed, careful to not wake Grace or Porter as I go sit in the chair in the corner of his room. I've sat in this chair many times, though normally it's to put my clothes back on before I leave.

QUINN

I'm going to need everyone to quit shouting at me.

AINSLEY

I promise to not shout, but I am going to need to know why you were buying diapers.

I let out a sigh, because I really thought I could make it more than twelve hours before anyone would realize what's happening here. Damn small-town gossip mill.

QUINN

Long story short, Porter's estranged sister abandoned her baby at the bar with a note. She wants Porter to raise her. He was panicked. So I'm helping out.

MAEVE

Holy shit.

SIMON

Another member of the Dad Squad! Love it! Tell him I'll order his shirt. Initiation will be next week.

AINSLEY

Is that why he texted you last night?

It takes me a second to remember what she's talking about. Those emoji texts feel like they happened a lifetime ago.

QUINN

Yeah. That was it. He didn't know what to do.

STELLA

Smart. Though I don't know if you'd be the one
to call.

QUINN

Hey! I kept her alive last night. And changed a
poopy diaper!

AINSLEY

I'm proud of you. How old is she?

QUINN

Ten months? She's a little doll baby.

I walk over to the bed and text a picture of a sleeping Grace next to a sleeping Porter. The scene is too cute, with his hand on her stomach, her sleeping like a little starfish under his touch.

It's enough to make the ovaries combust.

Not mine. But I'm sure someone's.

Keep telling yourself that Quinn…

STELLA

Okay, shut the fuck up. That is the most
precious thing I've ever seen.

MAEVE

Quinn? While that's adorable and all, why are
you in Porter's house at nine in the morning
taking pictures of him sleeping?

Did she have to call me out like that?

QUINN

> Part of me helping included spending the night. He doesn't know how to change a diaper, let alone what to do if she'd wake up crying. He was terrified. So I stayed to make sure they were okay.

I know at some point today I'm going to be getting a phone call—not a text—from my sister about the validity of that last statement, and if there's something more about why Porter would call me and not anyone else. In the eight years I've been sleeping with Porter, she's the only one to even sniff that there's something going on. But I'm pretty sure I threw her off the scent.

Then again, Ainsley saw me leave the night I came over after we went to the bar. Is she putting things together?

Shit. My carefully guarded secret might be slowly starting to unravel.

AINSLEY

That was nice of you. You're a good friend.

Phew. If she has any inklings, at least she's keeping them to herself. Also, I can't help but laugh at her use of the word "friend." Ainsley meant it in the actual definition. Yet, all I can think is that I have to be the only fuck buddy in the history of fuck buddies to get conned into spending the night to take care of someone else's baby.

QUINN

> Thanks. I'll probably be tied up here all day today helping him get settled. We need to get her more diapers and essentials. The only outfit she has is the one she showed up in. Probably need a crib or a pack and play or something.

SIMON

Let me go through some of Lainey's things. We
have too many clothes and Charlie will be
ecstatic that I'm getting rid of some of the
things I bought on a whim.

MAEVE

And don't buy a pack and play. I know for a fact
I still have Jayce's. I just saw it when we sold
my house. I'll get it out of storage and anything
else you could need. We'll bring them by
tonight.

QUINN

Thank you both. I appreciate you.

STELLA

And please let me know if I can help. I'm here
to pull a babysitting shift if you or Porter need a
hand.

AINSLEY

Same. We're here to help, Quinn.

I feel a tear forming in my eye. I don't know what I did to deserve this family, but I thank my stars daily that I'm a Banks.

QUINN

I love you all. I'll keep everyone updated.

I set my phone down as the cutest little cry comes from the bed. I look up to see Grace starting to stir, causing Porter to quickly open his eyes.

"I got her," I say, walking over to the bed and leaning over for Grace. "Come here, sweet girl."

She immediately comes into my arms, laying her head on my shoulder as her quiet cries come from her tiny mouth.

"You sure? I can do it," he says with his eyes completely closed. Does he think he learned to change a diaper in his dreams?

"I'm sure," I say. "But we have a big day ahead of us. Jump in the shower and get that credit card ready, McCoy. It's time to baby shop."

———

"Are you ready?"

I go to grab a buggy, setting my iced coffee into the handy dandy cup holder, as I watch Porter do his best to strap Grace into the seat of the child-friendly shopping cart.

"You got it?"

"I'm fine," he says as he bites his bottom lip in concentration as he tries to fasten the strap while little miss Gracie is wiggling around, wanting to look at every little thing. Though she's definitely not as wiggly as she was this morning when I was trying to teach Porter how to change her diaper. "Also, did you need a coffee for this? You already had a cup today."

I let out a big laugh as we make our way through the store. Little does he know this is my third and it isn't even noon. "The answer is that you always need an iced coffee. But for this kind of shopping haul? Yes. An iced caramel cold brew with an extra shot of espresso and sweet cream cold foam is needed. Now, enough stalling. Off to the baby section!"

"Wait," he says as I skillfully avoid the cookie aisle. "Why do you have a buggy too?"

I don't say anything, because in about ten steps I'm going to sit back and watch Porter's eyes as he realizes why I also needed a buggy.

Overwhelm shock coming in three...two...

"What the fuck is all this?"

And there it is.

"This, my friend, is the baby section. It has everything you're going to ever need when it comes to this little one."

Porter starts slowly walking down the aisle, eyes unblinking and jaw hanging as he starts looking at all the options, and I'm guessing by the choking sound he just made, the prices.

"I'm going to guess you didn't know this section existed?"

He just shrugs his shoulders. "I've walked past it on the way to electronics, but I never paid attention."

"That tracks," I say as I head over to the diapers. I look at the label, making sure I'm getting the right size, before tossing the biggest box I can find into the cart.

"What the hell, Quinn?" he asks. "Why would you buy that massive box?"

I swallow a laugh, but on cue, Grace lets out the most precious, and well-timed, giggle herself. "That's right, Gracie. You tell Uncle Porter that these aren't going to last two weeks."

"What?" he yells, following behind me blindly as I start loading up with wipes, ointments, baby food, formula, and all of those essential items you need for a baby. "Quinn. I thought you said we were getting essentials?"

"These are the essentials. And we haven't even made it a quarter of the way down Ainsley's list of things to get."

"Wait. Ainsley knows?"

Shit. Does he not know the whole town probably knows by now? What must it be like to not be addicted to phones and social media? "Yeah. I'm guessing you haven't checked your messages today?"

Porter pulls it from his pocket and I can see the moment he realizes that all of Rolling Hills knows about our newest resident. "How the fuck did this happen?"

"That's on me," I say, making my way to the baby bathroom aisle. "Someone spotted me last night when I ran out to get the diapers and formula. Apparently Quinn Banks buying diapers after dark is enough to set off alarm bells. Then, and this is only me assuming and knowing how our town's rumor mill goes, the Facebook group got real nosy, someone saw my car at your house, already knew something was going on with your sister, and people started talking. My family was rioting for answers this morning. But because of that, Maeve and Simon are helping out with things they don't need anymore for their kids. So that's going to save a few bucks."

Porter runs his hand over his face. "I mean, it was only going to be a matter of time. But I would've liked a few more hours to wrap my head around this before people start butting into my life."

"I get it," I say. "I can only imagine what it's going to be like tonight when you show up to the bar."

"The bar!" Porter's outburst makes me jump, which brings on the first actual crying I've heard from Grace in the hours I've known her. "Shit. I scared her."

Porter looks like a deer in headlights as Grace's cries become louder. "It's okay," I say to Grace as I pick her up, but it was meant for Porter as well. "Shhh. It's okay, Gracie Bear. Uncle Porter just got excited. But that's because he has to tell your new, non-family, old-as-dirt uncles about you."

My joke and soft tone work on Grace, who rests her head on my shoulder, but apparently not on her terrified uncle. I come over to him, Grace in my arms and my other hand rubbing his back, trying to offer some comfort. "Hey. I told you I'm here for you. For her. You tell me what you want me to do tonight. If you want me to work the bar, I can do that. If you want me to stay with her, I can do that as well. Stella and Ainsley have also offered babysitting shifts when need be. I'm sure Wes or any of his family will jump in when you need them to. Like I said, you're not alone in this. It's just going to take a little bit to adjust everything."

His head is down, but he doesn't shy away from my touch. "This is becoming more overwhelming with every minute."

"I know. I'd be more worried if you weren't acting like this. It's a lot. And no one says you have to know everything right now. But hey! Last night you didn't know how to change a diaper. This morning you learned. And right now you didn't realize that babies have hearing and will react to loud screams.

And now you do. Two new things learned in twenty-four hours."

That joke makes him let out a soft laugh. "Can I do this, Quinn? And don't sugarcoat this. I need the Quinn Banks who doesn't pull punches. Can I actually raise this little girl?"

I could answer him right away, because I know the answer is yes. But I have a feeling he's not just going to believe my words. He needs to truly believe it for himself.

"Are you going to give her a safe place to live?"

He seems shocked by my question. "Of course. Why would you ask—"

I cut him off. "Are you going to make sure she has food and clothing? You know, once you get over the sticker shock of this shopping trip."

He seems to realize what I'm doing and relaxes slightly. "I will."

"Are you going to love her? Even though you just met her. And even though she'll one day grow into a teenager who might try and stink bomb the high school. Will you love her?"

He smiles. "I already do."

"Then that's all you need to know. The rest you can figure out along the way."

Porter nods as I let my hand fall off his back. But before I can step away, he reaches for me, taking that hand in his.

I've obviously held Porter's hand before. I've held many pieces of his body. But somehow, in the middle of a baby section at a place where you can get an oil change, ground beef, and baby formula, somehow this feels like one of the most intimate moments we've shared.

And I'm pretty sure this man is about to kiss me.

"Porter…"

We start to move in closer, and Grace nearly jumps out of my arms.

"No!"

I don't think I've heard her say a full word, so having it be this one is interesting.

Oh my God…is Grace the literal voice of reason on my shoulder?

Porter steps back as Grace turns and reaches for him, which puts the softest look on his face that I've ever seen. "We should probably keep going."

"Yeah," I say, trying to not feel disappointed that we didn't kiss. I mean. We shouldn't. Fuck buddies don't kiss. Especially in public.

But I'm going to admit, over the last twenty-four hours, this hasn't felt very fuck-buddy at all. It's felt very domestic. Very relationship-y.

Which can't happen. For one, neither of us want that. Two, I'm probably only here a few more months. And three, see number one. I won't go back on my word to help with Grace. Porter needs support, and since I know a few things about babies and he knows none, I'm not going to back away from that promise.

But I am going to guard my ovaries and heart with an iron-plated shield that medieval knights would beg for. No fucking way I'm going to let a hot man holding a baby get to me. Nope. Not going to happen.

"No fucking way!" Porter laughs in the clothing section as he stops next to a display of headbands. "This bow is as big as her head!"

I laugh at his joy over a simple head band. And by the way Grace is clapping her hands, she's also a fan. "Put it on her. See if she likes it."

I stand back and watch as he slips it over her ears, and while she does try and grab it, he's able to get it in place. And yup… the bright pink bow is roughly the size of her head. And cute as hell. Also, clearly this is a diva in training, because Grace is nothing but smiles as Porter lights up at her new look.

Stella is going to be obsessed with her.

"Do you like that?"

Oh shit...Porter McCoy using a baby voice. I didn't see that coming.

Grace giggles as Porter nuzzles her nose. It's the most precious thing I've ever seen.

Yup. Going to need that shield. Do they sell those here?

"Well, we're buying that," he says, grabbing five more in different colors. "Now, where are the highchairs? I need one of those, right? Wait—I should get two. One for my house and one for the bar. She's going to need her own place to sit."

Ah, fuck me. There go the ovaries.

18

porter

"Come on, Grace…I really need you to stop crying, baby girl. If you do, I'll buy you a pony. Or a car. Literally whatever you want. Just please…stop crying for Uncle Porter."

In the thirty-six hours I've had Grace, I've learned so much about her. I've learned that she might be cute but her shits are vile. I've learned that her little laugh might be the best sound in the world. On the complete other side of the sound spectrum are her cries.

Also, who knew that babies have different cries? There are the little ones. Then the ones that come and go in a matter of seconds that confuse me more than anything. And then there's this cry, a pure wailing that hasn't stopped for hours, and I'm about to cry along with her because I can't figure out what's wrong.

I've changed her diaper. I've tried to feed her but she keeps shoving it away. I've tried to rock her. I've tried to bounce her. I just tried to even lay her down, wondering if she's just over me and needs her space.

None of it has worked. It's now two in the morning, I don't think I've slept in twenty-four hours, she won't stop drooling, and if this keeps going, I'm going to have my own breakdown.

I continue pacing back and forth with a crying Grace in my arms, her distress physically stabbing me in the chest because I don't know what's wrong with her.

Maybe I can't do this. I know if Quinn were here, she'd tell me that it's okay because I've been doing this for a day. But maybe this is a sign… Grace's way of telling me that I'm not really cut out for this and to take all of the baby items back to the store while I can still get my money back, because there's no timeline or dimension on this planet, or any other, that I'm equipped to be a dad.

No. Guardian. Uncle. Stand-in dad? Wait. Why am I thinking about my title when right now the only one I deserve is "moron who can't get the baby to stop crying."

"Is everything okay?"

I spin around to see a concerned Quinn standing in my living room. I had her work the bar tonight because I didn't feel right about pawning Grace off on her—and I wasn't ready to face the firing squad of my customers. But maybe I should've sucked it up and gone. Clearly I'm doing a bang-up job here.

"Yup. Great. Just having a middle-of-the-night scream party. I read on a baby blog it's good for their lungs."

Quinn laughs, even though this is not a laughing matter. "I didn't realize a sleep-deprived Porter had my level of sarcasm."

"Well, stupid questions get stupid answers," I bite. "Clearly I'm not doing okay and neither is she."

Quinn puts up a hand. "Okay, first, I know you're tired and apparently are dealing with a screaming baby, but there's no need to bite my head off."

"I know, I'm sorry," I say as Quinn comes over and relieves me of my Grace holding duties. Unfortunately though, Grace doesn't stop crying, though the way she curls into Quinn's shoulder at least lets me know the child is seeking comfort. We just can't find it. "She's been like this for hours."

Quinn's eyes are double the size as she turns to me. "Hours? Porter. Why didn't you call me?"

I fall to the couch and run my hands through my already disheveled hair. "Because I can't call or run to you every time she cries. Grace is now my responsibility. Not yours."

"You dumb, stupid, man." Quinn quits talking and I fall over into a lying position, closing my eyes as I try to even myself out. Which is hard, because just as it seems like Grace's cries are coming to a stop, she starts all over again.

"Hey, take her," Quinn says, and just as I'm opening my eyes, Grace is laying down next to me and Quinn is…texting? What the fuck?

"What are you doing? Who the fuck are you texting now when we're in the middle of a crisis!"

"Calm your tits. I'm going to go raid your kitchen. Because if me, Ainsley and Google are right, you're about to owe us for life. Also, do you have any bananas?"

"Yes?" I ask, and I'm pretty sure even if I wasn't on the edge of insanity, I'd be confused by her question. And really that whole monologue in general.

"Great. Be right back."

I just lie on my couch, a crying baby next to me, as Quinn disappears into my kitchen.

"What is she doing?" I ask Grace. Not that I was expecting an answer, but the fact that she's quieted down a little does make me think that she's also in a state of confusion.

"Here we go," Quinn says, bringing back what looks like to be a washcloth and a cup of ice water. "Can I try?"

I pass Grace back to her. "Try whatever you want. Please."

Quinn positions Grace in her arms so she has access to her mouth, dips the washcloth into the ice water for a few seconds, before inserting it into Grace's mouth. She protests for a second, trying to push Quinn away, but soon she stops squirming. She stops fighting.

And even more amazing, she stops crying.

"What in the Hogwarts shit did you just do?"

My comment seems to surprise Quinn. "Okay, when we're

not in the middle of the baby crying torture chamber, we're definitely having a further discussion on that reference. But we have much more important things to do."

I watch as Quinn continues to dip the wash cloth in cold water, then go back to putting it in Grace's mouth.

"She's teething," Quinn explains. "The cold compress helps with the gums to numb them a bit because you try being a baby and having things pop out of your mouth suddenly. You'd be screaming, too."

I'm in awe as I watch this unfold. "How did you know she was teething? And how did you know how to fix it? Also, why did you ask me if I had bananas?"

"I really didn't know for sure," she begins. "I remember a teacher friend a few years ago talk about when her kid was teething that it was the worst cries she ever heard, and she included herself giving actual birth in that comparison. There was a bunch of drool coming out of her mouth, so I took a guess. Now the next part, I can't take credit for. That was Google and Ainsley. Also, get on Amazon right now and order teething toys. You're going to need them."

I do as she says, ordering ten different kinds because I don't know the difference and I'd spend a million dollars if I thought it would make her never cry like that again. "How was I supposed to know that she was teething?"

"You weren't," Quinn says, holding Grace as she continues to dip and dab the washcloth into her mouth. "The fact that she barely cried since she's gotten here wouldn't have given you a clue, but yeah, if she's about ten months like Missy said, Google says this is prime teething time."

I fall back into my couch, thankful the cries have stopped, but horrified that I didn't think to use things like a search engine. "I'm fucked, Quinn. I can't do this."

"Porter, you have—"

"No! Don't give me your bullshit," I say as I stand up off the couch, starting to pace in circles, which is apparently what I do now when I'm freaking out. "I can't do this. I learned to change one diaper today, thought I was a fucking pro, and told you go to cover the bar. And look what happens!"

"She was teething, Porter. I'm sure her diaper is fine."

"It wasn't! I fucked it up six times before I got it to go on."

"Is it on now?"

I snap my gaze to her. I know she has a habit of cracking jokes, but this isn't the time. "This is serious, Quinn. What was I thinking? I can't do this. I'm not equipped for this. I thought that an industrial size box of diapers was going to last me months, not days. When does she eat? When do I do formula and when do I do food? Ainsley can't keep making me a list forever. And how do I know she'll like it?"

During my pace I happen to take notice of an outlet, also known as a death trap for babies according to one blog I read today during hour two of the crying. "Oh! And then there's the fact that my house is not baby proofed in the slightest. It's essentially a walking death trap."

"I wouldn't go that far," Quinn says. "And you can get socket covers. Did you already put in the Amazon order? Add some to the cart."

I stop mid-pace to look at her. "How are you making jokes right now?"

"They're not jokes," she says as she starts rocking Grace a little, who seems to be starting to doze off. "If they come out that way, I apologize. But nothing I've said isn't true. You can buy socket covers. You can call over a few guys and have this place baby proofed in a day. You found out about her yesterday, Porter. *Yesterday*. In what universe were you going to be ready for this? None that I'm aware of. So give yourself some grace and give yourself some credit for the wins you have today."

She's right, but my stubborn ass refuses to admit it. "Wins? What wins?"

"Well, let's see. She's alive. Always the biggest win of the day when it comes to kids."

"I told you no more jokes."

"And I'm not joking. Ask any parent, teacher, or babysitter. Rule number one of every day is keep the kid alive. And you did it, Porter. Congratulations. And let's not forget that both of you are probably confused and scared shitless right now for this new world you've suddenly both been thrust into."

I fall back to the seat, my hands all but scrubbing my face as I try to make sense of this new reality. "I didn't know anything. She's just a baby. And I–I'm fucking this all up."

Quinn doesn't say anything immediately, which makes me think for once she's going to agree with me. But then I look up to see Quinn taking a finally calmed down Grace to the pack-n-play Maeve dropped off tonight, laying her down in there. I try not to stare as she bends over, but that's hard to do. I try to push aside how beautiful she looks as she maneuvers Grace into what I've learned is a sleep sack. But what I can't push aside is how much of a godsend she's been to me these past two days, and how I don't know if I could ever do this without her. Sure, I could've called Wes or my aunt. I'm sure Jenny would've known what to do, or maybe a few others at the bar who I know are parents, but I didn't want any of their help. No. Somehow I knew Quinn could help me. And somehow tonight, she knew I needed her, even when I was too stubborn to ask for help.

"Are you okay?" she asks as she sits next to me, taking my hand in hers.

I shake my head. "I don't know. I didn't know anything. And then you…you just walked in out of thin air and knew every-thing to do."

"That's a bit of a stretch."

"It isn't," I say. "You've known everything. You knew she was teething. You knew what to get her last night. You knew what to buy today."

"That's not because I'm some sort of baby whisperer. I have

friends with kids. I'm an aunt to two, and their mothers talk a lot about baby growing stages. And I babysat three times in high school when families really wanted Maeve but she wasn't available. That barely qualifies me as some sort of genius."

I fall back into the couch. "What am I going to do, Quinn? She would've been crying all night if you wouldn't have showed up."

"Well, then, you're lucky I did," she says, looking over to Grace, then back to me. "She seems to be out for a bit. The banana, per your question earlier, is for her to chew on when she gets like that again. It's currently in the freezer for when you need it."

She starts to stand up, but I pull her back down. "Where do you think you're going?"

"Home?"

"Why?"

Her eyes are darting around the room like she's looking for an answer. "Because I'm tired? And it's where I live?"

Panic races through me. She can't leave. Not now. Not ever…

"Stay. Please."

I know I sound desperate, but that's what I am right now, and I'm not afraid to play the tired new-dad card.

And if it comes down to it, the "I'll never give her another orgasm" card.

"Fine," she says with an exaggerated exhale. "I'll stay another night. But I'm going to need clothes again. These fucking stink."

"No," I say hurriedly, now pulling her back to the couch with me.

"No, I can't have a T-shirt and shorts? Come on, Porter. I'm not the girl who's going to steal your hoodies."

"No. Take them all. I don't care. I just…move in with me."

There have been a few times in the course of our…history… that I've scared Quinn Banks speechless. Until now, the most frightened I've ever seen her was the first time I asked her to stay the night. The immediate panic that flooded her eyes would've been laughable if it didn't stab me straight in the heart.

However, that night has been replaced by this. Because I'm pretty sure Quinn is as white as a ghost, and I'm not sure if she's breathing.

"Quinn?"

"Yeah?"

"Can I explain my reasoning?"

She starts nodding like a bobblehead—all while still not breathing or blinking.

"You know way more than I do. And when I'm thinking clearly, which might not happen again until she turns eighteen, I'm going to be playing behind the eight-ball. You know more than I do. You can help me curve this gap. I need you, Quinn. Grace needs you."

"Porter, I can be here—"

"Yes, I know you can be here when I ask. But what if I take the asking out of it? Move in. Please."

She doesn't respond right away, which I'm glad for. Because while she's coming up with a million reasons why she can't, I'm coming up with a million reasons why she can.

"You know I don't know how long I'm staying in Rolling Hills," she begins.

"That's fine. For as long as you're here, or I actually get a grasp on this, will be the timeline. Whichever event happens first can be your out."

Judging by the look on her face, she wasn't planning on me having a comeback that quick. And honestly, I'm kind of proud for being this on top of it with the lack of sleep I'm currently operating on.

"If I come, it's with Turtle."

She has a turtle? "When did you get a turtle?"

"No, Turtle is my cat."

"Your cat's name is Turtle?"

"That's what I said."

"You couldn't have named it Whiskers or Baxter?"

She narrows her eyes. "First of all, do not talk about my son like that. Second, is this really the time to bash the name of my pride and joy, considering what you're asking of me?"

I hold my hands up in surrender. "No, you're right. Turtle is more than welcome."

Judging by the look in her eye, I think she thought that was going to be her out. I'm trying not to get my hopes up, but I'll literally say yes to anything right now if it means she'll move in.

"If I say yes—and that's still a big if—there's one rule that I need to put down. And you can't say no."

"Anything."

She's quiet for a second before her eyes meet mine, more serious than I've ever seen them in my life.

"You. Me. If I move in, we have to be over."

Shit…I didn't think of that, that's how fucked my head is right now.

"You're probably right."

"Not probably. I am." She turns to look me straight in the eye. "If I'm going to be living here with you, what we've been doing has to stop. And this can't be one of my empty promises, or us thinking we can keep things professional. This has more riding on it than just us and no real consequences. I'm doing this for Grace. You're asking me to do this because you want the best for Grace. And I'll do it, but you have to promise me that you know it's temporary, and you have to know that what we were in the past is gone."

For years, Quinn Banks has had the reputation of the wild child. The slightly unhinged Banks sibling. The girl who uses rules as loose guidelines. Which is how I know how serious she is about this.

But she's right, it's what I have to do. Because at the end of the day, I need help. And there's no one else I trust more in this world than this woman sitting in front of me.

A woman I'll have to fight not to touch every day.

A woman whose lips I'll stare at, remembering every time I felt them against mine.

But if this is what I need to do for Grace, then I'll do it. No questions asked.

"I promise."

guide to love rule #93

News travels fast in small towns. So keep your secrets guarded. And keep your hidden looks to yourself.

19
quinn

I'm living with Porter...

I'm living with a boy...

I'm living with a boy who I've ridden reverse cowgirl...

"Hey! Hurricane! Come back to Earth and quit spilling my beer!"

I jump a little, beer running over the glass and down my arm, as I hear Harry call me by the nickname that he heard Porter use once and now everyone at the bar is using. It would be cute if it wasn't a constant reminder that people still think of me as the crazy Banks.

"Shit, sorry about that," I say as I wipe up the spill and hand him his beer. "Zoned out for a bit."

Harry tips his glass to me before taking a drink. "That's what'll happen when you're raising a baby. I don't think I slept for two years when my middle child was born."

Two years? That's so long. Surely Grace likes me enough that she'll start sleeping through the night soon. And I'll be gone away before—

"Whoa! What do you mean *raising a baby*?"

I've been staying with Porter for three days now, but we haven't told anyone about our arrangement except Jenny. And she only needs to know so she can cover the bar for the few minutes that we play tag back and forth from the bar to the house so Grace isn't alone. My sisters don't even know. They still just think I'm just helping out. And I sure as shit would've told them over my grumpy regular who thinks that advice you can get on a fortune cookie constitutes a tip.

"You and Porter, raisin' that little girl. I think it's admirable what you two are doing. Having her mama left her all alone."

"Okay, we need to back up," I say as I rest my elbows in the bar. "Where did you hear that?"

I mean, he's right. I just want to know. Wait! Does he also somehow know I saw Porter this morning shirtless, in pajama pants, and carrying Grace? No. He couldn't know that. But I sure as shit will never forget that image.

"Everyone knows, my dear. Everyone knows."

"Everyone? Who's everyone?" Because for Harry, this could mean just the guys at the bar. But how he uses his finger, gesturing for me to turn around, I realize at that point he actually means *everyone*.

The Joint is steady right now, as we're starting to get in the after-work crews for happy hour, and until now, I thought people were staring at me because Porter normally works this shift. But now I'm thinking this is more than customers clocking our shift rotations.

"How did people find out?" I swear to God, that fucking Facebook group…

"Really, Quinn? I know you've just gotten back to town, but you had to realize news like this was going to spread like wildfire."

I mean, I did figure, but I thought we were careful. I also thought we were careful about the other secret. Do people know about that too?

"I'm just staying for a little bit to help him out until he gets a handle on everything."

Harry starts cracking up as George slides in next to him.

"What's so funny?"

"Hurricane over here didn't realize we all knew about her and Porter playing family together."

Now George joins in on the laughter. "Oh, yeah. Y'all are the talk of the town. Especially since you kids think you're keeping it some big secret."

"We…I…it's—"

Both of them start laughing as they reach for the television remote that they one day took control over and never let go. "You keep searching for the words, Hurricane. We're going to watch our program."

I walk away from Harry and George, but now can't help but feel like everyone is staring at me. Are they whispering? What do they know? I can't ask them, but I have to assume if they knew the really long secret, that it would be the gossip right alongside us living together. As much as I'd like to study how everyone is looking at me, a group of guys playing pool wave me down for a bucket of beers.

I'm glad now more than ever that I told Porter we have to be over. If people really did know about us, it would be chaos. And frankly, it's none of their business what went on between me and Porter.

But more than that, and what I've never said out loud to a soul—not even Turtle—is that I don't want to deal with the looks. Or the snickers. Or the "is that the best Porter can do?" talk.

I've been that girl before. I've been that girl many times. Too many to count. So I did what any naturally sarcastic, stubborn, woman would do: I built up a wall of jokes and self-deprecating humor to give people the idea that I don't give a shit what people think of me. But I don't need a therapist or one of my sisters to tell me that it's really because I care a lot what people think.

Probably too much.

Which is why we need to get ahead of this. Well, as much as we now can.

QUINN

So everyone knows.

I set my phone down on the bar and start wiping it down as Porter immediately texts back.

PORTER

What do you mean?

QUINN

I'm pretty sure the town knows I'm living with you. And that it's because of Grace. Who they keep calling "the baby." Our idea of keeping things mum is now officially out the window.

PORTER

Fuck. Don't these people have lives of their own?

QUINN

I think you know that answer. So what's the plan?

PORTER

Just hold them off the best you can. I'm on my way. I think it's finally time that Grace meets her Joint family.

QUINN

You sure? I can just tell them it's none of their business and to fuck off.

PORTER

While that's great in theory, I know these folks. They won't stop. They've got nothing but time on their hands, and happy hour doesn't end for another two hours. Plus, we knew it was going to come out sooner or later.

QUINN

You're right. Just pick out a good outfit for her.
First impressions last a lifetime.

PORTER

I mean…she's wearing this?

Porter proceeds to send me a picture that immediately makes me smile.

And makes my heart, and other body parts, clench.

Grace and Porter are standing in front of a mirror in his hallway. She's looking up at him like she's very confused—which I've learned is her normal resting face and it's cute as hell—as he's looking down at her through the mirror to try and get her to look at her reflection. She has on a little pink T-shirt with the cutest jean overalls. And of course, a matching, and insanely large bow, on the top of her head.

While that would be cute enough in its own right, it's the smile on Porter's face that's grabbing my attention. I think it's the first real, and not scared, smile, he's had since Grace showed up in his office. The man has been stressing and worrying, and honestly, I don't blame him. So seeing him smile? Seeing him relax a little? It's a good look on him.

Really good…

QUINN

Did anyone ever tell you that you could be a
baby fashion stylist?

PORTER

Let's not get ahead of ourselves. I just guessed.

QUINN

You did good. I'll see you soon.

I put away my phone, put in a few orders and make a few drinks, and when I finally get back around to checking on my favorite ornery duo at the bar, they've picked up a guest.

And not just any guest. The woman who changed my life with a side-swept, short hair-do I'll never forget as long as I live.

"Mrs. Metcalf? What are you doing here?" I sprint around the bar and nearly tackle my former middle school librarian. "Oh my God, it's so good to see you."

"Now, now, Quinn, you don't need to be squeezing me, I'm not going anywhere," she says with her light tone. "But it's good to see you, my dear."

I don't know if this woman truly understands how much she meant to me when I was growing up. After I discovered my love of reading, I was a permanent fixture in her library. At first she thought I was pulling pranks in there—and given my track record, I don't blame her for that. But soon we started talking. She was the first adult, maybe besides my parents, who I felt like was actually listening to me and not just thinking of me as Simon or Maeve's sister. Or the girl who brought Crisco to school and greased all the doorknobs. We talked about books and life, and I'd tell her the drama going through Rolling Hills Middle School. While every other kid could only check out one book at a time, I was allowed five. She'd show me pictures of her cat, and I told her about how one day I'd have one of my own and I'd name it Turtle.

Oh, I can't wait to tell her about real life Turtle!

Some days when I was having a bad day, or I just needed a break, I'd just go into the library to sit with her and read. She never asked questions. She never sent me back to class. She just knew I needed it.

She's an angel. A saint. And I know for a fact that she changed my life.

"What are you doing? Are you still at the school? And wait —" I trail off as I realize she's choosing to sit next to George and Harry. No one chooses to sit next to George and Harry. "What are you doing sitting next to these fools?"

"Hey!" George yells in protest. "This is my lady."

If I had a drink, I'd spit it out. "You? And Mrs. Metcalf?"

"Quinn, my dear, it's been more than twenty years since you've sat in my library. You can call me Shirley."

I vehemently shake my head. "Absolutely not."

"Well, you could call her Mrs. Baskins if she'd ever say yes to my proposal."

"Mrs. Metcalf! Are you keeping this man dangling on the hook?"

She gives me a wink. "He knew when he first asked me out that I wasn't interested in getting married again. But the man is stubborn and just keeps asking."

George shakes his head. "I'm wearing her down."

I let out a laugh. "Sure you are, George. Sure you are."

Mrs. Metcalf and I keep chatting as I pour her a glass of Pinot Grigio. Turns out she's still at the school library—when school lets out in a few weeks it'll conclude her forty-second year of teaching. That doesn't shock me. I always thought she'd die in that library. But what *does* shock me is that she and George have been dating for five years now.

"I didn't think I'd date after my husband passed away," she says.

"Why did you?" I ask.

She looks at George, and the soft smile she gives him through her bright pink lipstick gives me the warm fuzzies. "Sometimes you think something is wrong. You convince yourself all the reasons why you shouldn't do it. But then one day you realize those reasons are a bunch of horseshit."

I know I was paranoid earlier about people knowing about me and Porter, but does Mrs. Metcalf know? I mean, I always thought she was psychic, but damn, that one hit a little too close to home.

Also hearing my middle school librarian swear is weird.

"That and he drives a nice car. I've always been a sucker for a Corvette."

"Damn straight!" George says, making everyone laugh before the room falls to an eerie silence.

I look toward the back hallway, where everyone seems to be looking.

Ah, now I get it.

"Everyone! I hear that I'm the topic of conversation these days," Porter says, holding Grace in one arm and pushing her stroller in another. And wait. Did he put on a pink T-shirt to match her? Holy shit, he did. "So if everyone could have a seat, we're going to clear the air and set the ground rules."

I know teachers who didn't have as much command over their students as Porter does right now. Seemingly everyone rushes to a seat, and as if somehow people know what's about to happen, they start pouring in the front door. Was there an announcement? There had to have been, because how else would my brother Simon, who just walked in the door, be here?

"Everyone, this is Grace. Grace, these are the idiots who can't keep their mouths shut."

A chorus of little hellos in tones I've never heard from these patrons fills the air. I think Harry even does the baby two-finger wave. And poor Grace…her confused face is now scrunched and she buries her head into Porter's shoulder.

"I'm not going to go into every detail of how Grace came to be in my care, because they're none of your business, but here's what I'll tell you so you can all shut up. She's my niece. Yes, her mother is my half-sister. And she has asked me to raise Grace. And I've agreed to do it."

After a second of shock, the mumbles start mumbling. Which then grow into shouting. People are trying to ask Porter questions. Some are just talking loudly amongst themselves. Plain and simple, this is a middle school classroom gone rogue.

"Hey!" I yell, channeling my teacher voice that apparently hasn't gone away. "Shut it so he can tell y'all the truth, so you can quit running your mouths!"

I watch as everyone's eyes go wide, then they quiet and find their seats again.

"Thank you."

I catch a glimpse of Mrs. Metcalf, who shoots me a wink. "I always knew you'd have that teacher voice in you."

I return the wink as Porter starts talking again.

"This is going to be an adjustment for me, clearly. Which is also why Quinn is going to be staying with me." The crowd starts ooohing and ahhing before Porter cuts them off. "And minds out of the gutter, people. This is nothing more than her helping me with Grace and helping me out here. We're just roommates. Nothing else."

I see everyone's eyes turn toward me. "That's exactly right. It's nothing more. Just a friend helping a friend."

Porter and I share a look of understanding before the mob swarms him to get a better look at Grace. Which is fine by me. Let them look at her. Because that means no one is looking at me.

Roommates only was my idea. It was my demand. I needed that boundary. *We* needed it.

So why does it hurt so bad?

"You know, Quinn, fences are meant to be burned down."

I do a double take to Mrs. Metcalf, who I think is the only one in the bar not fussing over Grace. "What was that?"

Mrs. Metcalf gives me her warm smile that comforted me so many days all those years ago as she signals for me to come closer. "Fences. Walls. Boundaries. They're never meant to be permanent. Even ones made of stone eventually fall."

I think I know what she means, but that would mean she knows what I'm thinking, and that can't be because she's not really a mind reader.

I don't think.

But, just to make sure, I offer a reply back. "But they're meant for safety."

"That's true. But sometimes the danger is inside the house, and a fence doesn't help with that."

Yup. It's confirmed.

She's a witch.

Though I think by living with Porter, I'm the one about to get burned.

20

porter

WHEN I WAS ASKED WHAT I WANTED TO BE WHEN I GREW UP, MY answers would vary. Football player. Fireman. Garbage man. I think I even went through an astronaut phase.

But no matter what I said at any given age, there was one thing they all had in common—none of them required wearing a suit to work.

And after spending all day in the only suit and tie I own at a family law office, I now know that seven-year-old me was right.

Suits are the worst.

"Hello? Where's everyone at?" I walk through my front door, immediately loosening the tie and kicking off the most uncomfortable shoes known to man. Quinn doesn't answer me, but I do hear noises coming from the kitchen.

As I make my way there, tossing my jacket over the couch so I can roll up my sleeves, I let the information that I got today run back through my mind.

I knew, even with Missy's letter, that it wasn't going to be easy gaining custody, though it did help. What I didn't realize is how long it's going to take, or the hoops I'm going to have to jump through to make sure that Grace is taken care of. But I'll jump through a hoop of fire into a pit of snakes if it means that little girl stays with me. She might only have been here for a few weeks, but she already has me wrapped around her little finger.

I never wanted a family, which stemmed from not wanting to get married. Being a child of divorce, and having a mother who had no problem leaving you, does that to a guy.

But over the past week, I've been reminded how much family doesn't have to be blood. And the best ones rarely are. It can be extended family that helps out in a pinch. It can be the found family at the bar you own who has taken it upon themselves to decorate and fence off a corner of the bar for your niece to have as her play area.

And it can be the woman who stepped up when she didn't need to, helping you in ways you never thought imaginable.

The woman who's currently having a little dance party in your kitchen, trying to entertain your niece before dinner.

"All right Gracie, here's what we got tonight." I lean against the doorframe of the kitchen as I watch Quinn bargain with a ten-month-old. "We're doing peas. Now I know you're probably going to hate them. Let's face it, they're gross. But! If you eat the peas, I'll buy you your first car. Deal?"

Grace's confused face is loud and proud as Quinn scoops a little bit of peas onto a spoon. My smile is big as I watch her lean down, doing her best to coax her mouth open. Grace opens, and I see the moment Quinn thinks she's won.

But after two swirls around her mouth, I watch it play out in real time.

"Shit!" Quinn yells and I start chuckling as Grace furiously swats the spoon out of Quinn's hand, making the peas go flying. If she was playing basketball, it would be an impressive block.

Note to self: Get her a mini basketball hoop.

"Don't you laugh, mister," Quinn says as she does her best to wipe the pureed peas off of her face. "We tried prunes today. And you're going to be on diaper duty tonight to make up for the fact that I did every meal today."

"Fair enough," I say as my laughter dies down. "I take it we can put peas on the no-fly list."

"It's currently her most hated food. Though that can be said about most green veggies."

I grab the dry erase marker to add peas to our list that we've been keeping of foods that Grace has vehemently rejected, which right now include mashed potatoes, eggs, green beans, and now peas.

"We'll find something," I say as I look over the six-foot-white board that I mounted on an empty kitchen wall. "At least she likes some vegetables. That has to be a win, right?"

"We'll take what we can get. Oh! And add squash to the yes column. That was a hit during lunch."

I do as Quinn says, while internally patting myself on the back for this idea. The last week has been a whirlwind in so many ways. One of the biggest ones that neither of us realized was that we knew nothing about Grace, in terms of her likes or dislikes. We didn't have ten months to get to know her, or even know what she's tried. So we're starting from scratch.

Which is why I came up with the board. That way even if one of us isn't here, it's an easy way to let the other know what the goods and bads are. What a new habit is. Little notes for when we play tag to and from the bar. With as much information as we're both dealing with right now, anything I can use a cheat sheet for, I'm going to do it.

"Should I ask how the rest of your day was?"

I pull a bottle of beer out of the fridge before sitting down across the table from Quinn and Grace—who's now happy as a clam shoveling fistfuls of pasta into her mouth.

That's number one on the good food list.

"We had a good day," she says. "I finally finished unpacking. She watched Miss Rachel. And Turtle only knocked down four things today. Wins all around."

"Turtle did what?"

On cue, Turtle jumps onto the table and sits in front of me, staring into my soul as if I'm going to dare reprimand him for tearing my house up. I didn't know cats could be so destructive.

"You're lucky I need your mother. Otherwise you'd be on the streets."

"How dare you speak to my son like that!" Quinn says, reaching across the table and bringing Turtle into her arms. "He's just a little boy, and he's in a new house. He doesn't know better."

Now, I know cats don't really understand English. But I swear, at this moment, that little fucker turns his head to me and tells me through his eyes that he does in fact know better, and he's going to do it again tomorrow just because he can.

Asshole.

"My apologies," I say as I take a pull of my beer. "So everything went well besides the peas?"

Quinn nods as she sets Turtle on the floor, only so she can pull Grace out of her highchair. "Yup. And honestly, I can't even be mad at her for that. I hate peas, too."

"Really? I don't mind them. I've always thought they got a bad rap."

"Blah," Quinn says, which makes Grace giggle. Also I didn't know that baby laughs were like drugs. Hearing that little sound is addicting. "Nope. I'm with Grace. Team No Peas."

I sit back and look at Quinn, who's still making Grace laugh with her little noises and faces as she finishes cleaning off peas, pasta, and who knows what else that is covering that child's face.

"Why are you staring at me?" Quinn says, though I don't know how she saw because she's still making direct eye contact with Grace.

"I didn't know you hated peas."

"Why would you? I don't think I know your least favorite food."

"I know. It's just…When you know someone…how we know

each other…I guess I thought I knew everything about you. But now that I think about it, I don't know if I know anything."

Quinn gives me a raised eyebrow. "You know plenty about me. In fact, you know things about me that no one else does."

"That's not what I'm talking about," I say, figuring she means that I'm the only one who knows that if she wants a quick orgasm, that doggy style is the preferred mode. A smack on the ass also helps. "What's your favorite color? Do you like pineapple on pizza? Why the fuck did you name your cat Turtle?"

Quinn gives me a soft smile as Grace reaches her arms out for me. I gladly take over the holding duties, wondering how in the matter of such a small time I could go from being scared to hold her to craving baby snuggles.

"You want to know the first date questions."

"First date questions? I just wanted to know your preferred pizza toppings."

"Which is a first date question." Quinn turns to me, her arm resting on the back of the chair casually. When she turns to me, I realize that in Grace's pea launching, a spot landed right on Quinn's boob.

Boobs that I've done my best not to stare at. But when she's wearing a white shirt and there's a green mark right where I know her nipple is, it's kind of hard.

I do my best to get my brain back on track. Luckily, Grace bounces herself on my knee to be let down, which helps.

"People are asking pizza toppings on first dates?"

"Well, if they meet on dating apps, that's usually covered then. But yeah, that's a normal question."

"Do they also want to know your favorite color and how you take your coffee?"

Quinn nods. "Normally, yes. See, the locations or activities might change of said date, but it doesn't matter if you're going out with a coworker, a guy you met online, or a stranger from the grocery store, no matter what, the questions are always the same. It's why I call them first dates interrogations."

"Interrogations? I know I haven't dated in a while, but I feel like even then I was doing it wrong if this is what it's supposed to be."

"Oh, it shouldn't be. They just are," Quinn clarifies. "First dates are interviews. You're trying to feel each other out if you have enough in common, or can answer the basic enough questions, to get you to date number two. It's like interviewing for a job. The first interview is always the basics because they need to weed the applicant field down."

"That sounds awful," I say. "Both the dating and the interviews."

Especially the picture I'm getting in my head of Quinn on dates with other men.

Oh God…is she going to try to date while she's living here? How did I not even think about that possibility?

"Wait!" Quinn's exclamation breaks the image of some asshole kissing her goodnight on my front porch. "Have you never been on an interview?"

"No. I worked at the bar in high school bussing tables and washing dishes. I mowed lawns and did odd jobs for some extra cash, but none of them needed a resume, let alone an interview. And then I took over the bar. The rest is history."

"Fascinating," Quinn says. "Well, if you are curious on how to make a resumé, I'll be updating mine soon."

That takes me back. "Really? Why?"

"Because I can't work at the bar forever, Porter. I have a degree. I'm a teacher. Or…at least I was."

Quinn gets up from the table and quickly makes her way into the kitchen, pulling an assortment of vegetables out of the refrigerator before taking out a cutting board.

"I'm sorry," I say as I follow her. "I didn't mean to sound like that. I know the bar isn't going to be the rest of your life."

She shakes her head, but doesn't look up at me. "You're fine.

The problem is that I don't know what *is* the rest of my life. I thought I did, but now I'm not so sure."

I lean against the counter and look at Quinn, who's doing her damnedest to not make eye contact as she whacks at the cucumber. And I know why. I might not know her favorite potato chip flavor or what her first concert was, but I know when she's trying to hide her vulnerability. She tries to retract in herself. She's probably thinking of some sort of joke she can make to take the heat off of her having to open up at all.

And maybe before, I'd let her. I'd know that I only had one night with her, so in the rare case when she was a little sad, I'd let her handle it her way.

But not anymore. Because for as much as she's helping me with Grace, trying to help her work out this stretch in her life is the least I can do.

"Hey," I say, walking over and tipping her chin up, our eyes meeting. "Talk to me."

For a split second, I see her try and reinforce her determination. Her eyes narrow a bit and her cheeks start to redden. But I don't let go. I don't waver. I tighten my grip. Because if knowing Quinn has taught me anything, it's that sometimes she just needs pushed out of her comfort zone.

"Don't put this off, Quinn. Don't let it fester. Though I have a feeling you already have been."

Her resolution only lasts for a second before she drops the knife and her walls start to break.

"I miss them." Those three little words are enough to send her into tears as she falls into my arms. "I didn't get to say goodbye. I went to the principal's office, got in a fight with parents, and walked out with my middle finger in the air. My kids didn't deserve that. I'm not mad about quitting or leaving that toxic school district, but I regret every day doing it in a way that hurt them."

"Let it out," I say, rubbing slowly up and down her back. "I've got you."

And she does. For minutes we stand in my kitchen as I hold a crying Quinn. Every once in a while she'll say a little something about problems she was having at the school, and I think at one point she starts talking at penises, but I could be mishearing things against the sound of her tears.

The way she's crying in my arms, I have to think this is the first time she's truly grieved what she lost in Arizona. She's been here for more than a month. Has she really not dealt with this at all? By the way she's crying, and the confession she just made, I don't think she has. At least fully.

"I want to teach again," she says as she starts to pull back from my hold. "I want to be around that environment. But I just…I don't know where. I don't know how."

"But you know what you want," I say, leaning down a bit so I'm eye level with her. "And that's the first step."

She nods. "You're right. Thank you, Porter."

"Anytime, Hurricane," I say, giving her hand a squeeze before turning back to Grace, who has started babbling something as she plays with her blocks.

"What you got there, baby girl?" I kneel down next to Grace, but as soon as I'm crouched down, I hear Quinn's scream.

"Ouch! Shit! Fuck, fuck, fuck!"

I'm up in a flash and turn around to see a horrified look on Quinn's face. It's then I see her holding her finger, and blood gushing from it.

"Quinn!"

It only takes me three steps to get to her, grabbing her around the waist and all but carrying her to the sink. I flip on the water and hurriedly put it under the running water.

"Here, hold it there."

She doesn't argue as I start tearing apart my cupboards for my first-aid kit. Of course it's in the last cupboard, but luckily it has gauze, ointment, and various sizes of bandages.

"Here," I say, grabbing her hand again, and wrap the gauze around her finger, holding it tight to try to stop the bleeding.

"I swear I've cut vegetables before," she says through her tears. "I just—"

"Hey. It's okay," I say, holding her finger a little tighter, which brings us closer together, as Quinn is a little off balance. "Just breathe. Let me take care of you."

Our eyes are locked as I hold the gauze around her finger. Minutes pass in silence, and I have to remind myself to check if she's still bleeding, or worse, that she'll need stitches.

The bleeding has stopped enough that I can put on some antibacterial ointment before securing the new bandage.

There's just one problem. Even though the bleeding has stopped and the bandage is on, I don't let go of her hand. I also don't break the stare we're sharing.

She's right there. I could just lean down and take those lips that I miss every day. I can smell a faint bit of her perfume, and it's enough to drive me wild.

I want to drive her wild.

I want to walk into this kitchen on an exact day like this and kiss the hell out of her.

I want her. All of her.

"My favorite color is red."

Her words are a whisper, and the only reason I know she spoke was seeing her lips move. Because I was staring at them.

"What's that?"

She swallows the lump in her throat. "You wanted to know my favorite color. It's red. And pineapple doesn't belong on pizza unless ham and pepperoni are involved, and even then it's debatable. And Turtle is the name of a character from my favorite book as a kid. I always said that if I had a cat, I'd name it Turtle."

"Thank you," I say, bringing her bandaged finger to my lips and placing a soft kiss on it. And then I do the hardest thing I've had to do in a very long time.

I drop her hand and walk away.

guide to love #94

Women are strong beings—until we see a hot man with a child.

21
quinn

"WE NEED TWO GLASSES OF WINE, A CLUB SODA, AND THREE CRISPY chicken salads."

"And don't skimp on the ranch!"

"Please!"

I turn around from the tedious task of wiping down the liquor bottles to see my three favorite women walking into The Joint.

"Well, well, well…what do I owe this pleasure?"

"Maeve and I have the day off, so we figured we'd make the trip down from Nashville," Ainsley says. "You know, just a nice lunch."

I raise an eyebrow as I pour my sisters their wine. "Really? This is what you two are choosing to do on your day off?"

"Why not?" Maeve asks nonchalantly. "It's not like this is the *only* way we get a chance to see our newly-back-in-town sister since she's basically ignoring us."

"And maybe we just want to see where her mind might be since the last time we talked," Stella says. "You know, if she made any big decisions, like moving, she wanted to talk to us about."

"Or maybe catch a glimpse of that baby. Considering I've

been your twenty-four-seven phone-a-friend, it's the least you can do."

I set down their drinks with a little more force than necessary. "Next time, give me a heads up when you're planning on having another Quinn-tervention. Also, it's highly unfair that y'all can drink through this and I can't."

"Not an intervention," Maeve says before shooting a look to Stella. "Remember? We promised this was just a visit."

Stella rolls her eyes. "Fine. But if it comes up naturally, I'm not dropping it."

"No need to bring it up," I say as I send their order back to the kitchen. "I still don't know what I'm going to do."

None of my sisters say anything as I pour myself a glass of water—which of course complements the iced coffee I grabbed earlier today—and go take a seat at their table. We're pretty slow right now, so no one will mind if I join them for a few minutes.

"Really? You don't know?"

I give Stella a hardened look. "I don't. I've thought about it a little. I miss the kids like crazy, but I hate the politics that has overtaken our schools. If I go to a new school and they have their own P.E.N.I.S. Posse, which most schools do these days, I'll quit before I start."

"Maybe it would be different at another school district?" Ainsley suggests. "Or, you know, one that you once attended?"

I let out an audible "Ha!" before realizing that Ainsley's serious. "Really? You want me, the girl who's not allowed within fifty feet of the chemistry lab, to go teach in Rolling Hills?"

"That's not true," Stella says. "Plus, that chemistry teacher is gone. They probably wouldn't remember that you once filled it with foam."

Well, that's good at least. "I know where your heart is at, Ainsley, I really do. But me teaching in Rolling Hills is out of the question."

"And girls, let's not forget she has no time to think, you

know, what with helping raise a baby with her hot roommate and all."

I narrow my eyes at Maeve. "Smooth transition, sis."

She shrugs her shoulders. "Let's consider it payback for when you not-so-subtly asked me about my husband's dick size."

Stella and Ainsley can't hold in their snickers as I tip my glass to Maeve. She's right. I did not so subtly dig for details. Though, in my defense, at the time they weren't even fake married. She was just his interior designer.

"For one, you're a married woman, you shouldn't be calling other men hot."

"I'm not married so I can say it. He's hot, Quinn. Very hot."

I gasp at Ainsley. "Ainsley Mae!"

"What? I may be sweet, but I'm not blind. And neither is any other woman in this town. So spill. Or next time you message me about the baby, I'll leave you on read."

"I liked you a lot better before you realized you held a superpower," I say to her, but she only flashes me the sweet-and-innocent smile that I'm starting to think might not be so sweet and innocent. "But there's nothing to dish. Yes, I moved in to help him. Yes, we're just roommates. That's it. I'm only there until he gets a handle on things with Grace or I move to my next stop. Whichever comes first."

I know Porter was scared when Grace first arrived. But I must say, he's adapted faster than I expected. He mastered diaper changing within a few days and only threw up once during an especially epic poop from his little princess. He was very proud of himself when he came up with installing the whiteboard—which was started for foods and now has grown into an "everything about Grace" board. Foods, nap schedules, milestones, you name it, the man is tracking it.

It's kind of adorable.

But only kind of.

"That!"

Maeve's outburst scares the shit out of me. "What?"

I frantically start looking around the bar to see if I missed someone come in, or if maybe the kitchen randomly caught on fire. But when I see nothing, I turn back to Maeve, who's pointing straight at me.

"That look!" she yells. "There *is* something going on between you two."

Now, I have a split second to make a decision here. I could finally come clean to my sisters about what had been going on with Porter and I for longer than Maeve's son has been alive. Or, because it's not happening anymore, I could continue to keep mum about the only secret I've ever kept from them.

"Sorry to burst your bubble, Mama Maeve, but nothing is going on between Porter and I. I'm just his roommate."

"That's how it *always* starts," Stella says. "One second you're living together, raising a baby. Next thing you know you're bumping into him coming out of the shower and oops! Towel falls down. I wonder what will happen next."

"You're ridiculous," I say as I stand up from the chair. But only because I don't want my face to give me away, because I have seen Porter in just a towel. And it should be criminal for a man to look like that, well, ever. "I'm going to go get your salads. When I come back, let's maybe find a new topic of conversation that doesn't revolve around my life. Oh! Remember when Ainsley said she drank in college? Let's finally circle back around to that."

My sisters snicker as I walk back to the kitchen to grab their salads. Honestly, the bell notifying me that their food was ready couldn't have come at a better time. Just going back to the kitchen, grabbing the dishes, and an exorbitant amount of ranch, gives me enough time to compose myself. Because truth be told, every day I live with Porter is one more day I have to remind myself that I shouldn't be staring at him.

Or sneaking looks at him anytime we're in the same room.

Or trying to forget how I almost kissed him the day I cut myself.

I've been so close to breaking so many times. Between the way he held me when I finally grieved the loss of quitting my job, to taking care of me when I nearly sliced my finger off. Which I didn't. I didn't even need stitches. But the way he came running to me, and looked at me with such concern…fuck, it was hard to resist.

And when he kissed my finger? I nearly melted on his kitchen floor.

I always knew Porter had a sweet streak in him. Granted, for years, I mostly saw the dirty-talking side that chokes me from time to time. But seeing him over these last few weeks? The sweetness is undeniable. It's pure. And it's been there the whole time, and yet, I never got to know it.

Or, more accurately, I never allowed myself to.

I kept it casual. I made sure I never spent the night. I made sure it was sex and sex only. There's no room for sweetness in the situation I carved for us.

But not Porter. He's the one to always clean me up after. Make sure that I'm okay after I come down from the high he's given me. He's the one who always demanded a text message to let him know I got home safely.

And he's the one who asked me to stay.

Then there's me: The one who leaves as soon as she can. The one who wants to make sure this is a secret. The one who draws the line in the sand.

The one who never believed a man like him could actually love a woman like me.

The one who feels her carefully constructed walls breaking a little more every day.

"Dammit, Porter McCoy…what are you doing to me?"

———

Usually it takes me all of two minutes to walk across the parking lot from The Joint to Porter's house. But today I take my sweet time.

Not that I don't want to get home to spend my night with Grace, but I don't want to see Porter.

I mean, I have to at some point, and it will only be a few minutes before we play tag for Porter to head over to the bar. But after the talk I had with my sisters today, and the emotional floodgate that opened, my head and my heart need a little bit of a break.

Even if that comes in the form of walking extra slow and then sitting on the front porch to scroll through my phone.

Out of habit, I check my emails, which I don't know why I do. It's not like I have a job offer sitting there, or a formal apology from my school district telling me that they realize that the P.E.N.I.S.s are horrible and they'd love to have me back. No, I'm usually just looking for good coupons so I have an excuse to shop for things I don't need under the impression that buying will make me feel something.

I delete most of them, saving a few for possibly an online shopping dopamine hit later tonight, when I see an unusual email from something called "Quinn's Crew Book Club."

I probably would've scrolled right past it if it wasn't my name. And, don't get me wrong, I get plenty of spam and random emails every day, but after a while, you start becoming familiar with the senders. And I know for a fact I've never seen a sender of anything with my name.

Curiosity getting the best of me, I ignore every email training I've ever had and open it.

TO: Quinn Banks
FROM: Quinn's Crew Book Club

Miss Banks,

We need to talk. You owe us. And I'm not just talking money from the Bruh Jar.
Here's a Zoom link. Meeting time this Tuesday.
Sincerely,
Quinn's Crew
P.S. Some of our moms know we're doing this, but the not-cool ones don't. Just thought you'd like to know that.

I laugh out loud, because I have no idea which of my former students is behind this, but it's too good. And Quinn's Crew? I'm here for it. Even if they're doing this to yell at me for quitting how I did, I'm going to commend their creativity and their initiative to make contact.

I save the meeting in my calendar before checking the time. And while it's a beautiful day, I probably need to go inside and face the music.

I quietly walk into the house, knowing this is usually Grace's nap time, and I'm glad I do. Because as I turn the corner into the living room, I see Porter and Grace napping together, Turtle joining them from his spot on top of the couch.

And this isn't just any nap.

Porter is shirtless, and the gray sleep pants he wears have traveled dangerously low on his hips.

Oh, and then there's Grace, napping on top of him, her little hands holding onto him like she's afraid he'll sneak away.

Oh, baby girl…that man isn't ever going to let a thing happen to you.

And I bet if I let him, he wouldn't let anything happen to me either.

No, no, no! Stop it Quinn! Right the fuck now!

In an absolute panic, I sprint upstairs and shut my bedroom door before throwing myself onto my bed and screaming into my pillow, thinking that somehow might stop my ovaries from trying to combust. Or stop my heart from beating faster. Or regulate my body temperature that suddenly could benefit from a cold shower.

Newsflash: it doesn't.

Seriously, what is happening to me? Am I that weak? Why am I reacting like this? Why do I want to go back downstairs and curl up on the couch with them? Why do I want to ask Grace if I can take a turn lying on top of him?

And why the fuck does a slight part of me now want to see that image every day for a very long time?

Oh, that's right. I've said it before, and I'll say it again.

I'm a weak, *weak* woman.

22

porter

"There he is! The newest member of the Dad Squad!" I look up from my menu at Mona's Diner to see Simon clapping as he makes his way over to my booth. "Where's the little one?"

I stand up as we slap hands and exchange a back-slapping hug. "On her way with your sister. I had a few errands to run, and Grace was having quite the morning, so Quinn said she'd bring her over so we could have breakfast."

"Awww, the little family going for breakfast," he says. "But beware of Quinn when it comes to biscuits. She'll eat them all if you give her the chance."

"Good to know."

Yet another thing I didn't know about the woman. I never pegged her as a biscuit girl. Does she like them with honey? Is it a biscuits and gravy situation? Jelly? Should I order some for her so they're here when she arrives?

Every day with Quinn I learn something new about her, which is funny because I thought all of my learning these days would be about how to raise a kid. But nope. I'm learning more and more about the woman who is unknowingly driving me wild every single day.

For example: Since she never spent the night, I didn't realize she likes to sleep in boxer shorts that she rolls up so high that the bottom of her ass cheeks hang out. I also didn't know that she likes to dance when she doesn't think anyone is watching and that she has a tendency to talk in her sleep. Oh, and she refuses to ask me for help when it comes to getting lids off of jars. Though I don't push back too hard. It's cute to watch her bite her lip when she gets that determined look in her eye.

"Oh! I almost forgot!" Simon yells as he claps his hands. "I have a present for you. It's next door."

"A present? For me?" Did I miss something in my Quinn daydream? "Don't you mean Grace? Which by the way, thank you for everything you've given us. You have no idea how much I appreciate it."

He waves me off. "Happy to help the newest member of the Dad Squad."

"Is he still going on about the Dad Squad? You can't just make fetch happen, Simon. " Charlie asks as she comes over to pour me a cup of coffee. "Don't listen to him, Porter. This is not a real club."

"Yes I can, and yes it is," he says, giving her a quick kiss on the cheek. "Be right back!"

Charlie and I watch in confusion as Simon runs out of the diner and makes a sharp right into the space next door that houses his real estate firm.

"He's a lot," she says. "But he's all mine."

"And Rolling Hills thanks you for that," I say. "Oh, is there a highchair I can use? Quinn is bringing Grace."

"Of course. Let me go grab it for you."

"No. I got it," I say. "But can you bring over Quinn's coffee order? I think it's a caramel cold brew? With sweet cream cold foam?"

This makes Charlie's eyes light up. "You remember her coffee order?"

I shrug, not wanting to make a big deal out of it. "She drinks enough of them."

"Sure…that's it," Charlie says. But before I can ask her what that's supposed to mean, Simon comes flying back in, a wrapped box in his arms.

"What the fuck?" I ask as he slides into the booth, a little out of breath. "You were serious?"

"As a heart attack," he says as he passes it across the table to me. "On behalf of the Rolling Hills Dad Squad, I hereby bestow upon you your official membership gift."

"So there are others in this group?"

"Right now it's just me and Wes. I want Maeve's husband to get in, but he lives in Nashville so I have to check the bylaws," he says. "I have some holdouts, but that's just because they're grumpy bastards. But it's going to take off. Just wait and see. Especially since now we can have our monthly meetings at The Joint."

"You're ridiculous." I start to open the box and am for some reason nervous, though that has to do with Simon's excitement and Charlie's look of exasperation.

"It's a polo shirt!" Simon yells before I can even see through the tissue paper.

And yup, underneath the pile of tissue paper, is a pink polo shirt. And not just any shirt, one with the embroidered logo "R.H. Dad Squad. EST: 2025."

"Every new dad is going to get this," Simon says. "We went with pink because Grace is a girl, but if you're opposed, or if Grace isn't a pink kind of girl, we have yellow and green. You know, because we're inclusive as fuck."

I laugh and fold it back up to put in the box. "Thanks, man. I appreciate it."

"Anytime," he says. But before he can say anything else, the front door swings open, and in walks my two girls.

No. My one girl, and the woman whom I wish was mine.

"There she is!" Simon jumps up from the booth and runs to the door, snatching Grace out of Quinn's hold. And in true Grace form, she just looks at him like he's the strangest man in the world.

My niece's confused face never seems to disappoint. Combine it while she's wearing a huge blue and white checkered bow, and it just makes the interaction that much funnier.

"Good to see you too, Simon," Quinn says as she pulls her arm out from his as it got tangled in the baby transfer.

"Oh, shush. You're old news. But this one...well, this one here is all the talk of the town, aren't you, sweet girl? When are you going to come play with your future best friend Lainey?"

Simon tries to make baby faces to Grace, but she's not having it. No cries. No laughter. Just a deadpan stare.

"I know, Gracie. He's just an odd man, isn't he?" Quinn takes Grace back and puts her in the highchair.

"That makes zero sense. Babies love me!"

"No, your daughter loves you because she has to," Charlie says, bringing over our coffees, mine hot, Quinn's iced. "Now let them have their breakfast. You need to go to work."

"Fine," he grumbles, but not before trying to get a smile out of Grace.

He fails. Miserably.

"Oh we're going to be best friends, little one. Just wait and see."

"Get out of here!" Quinn yells. "Let me have my breakfast in peace!"

Simon grumbles as he walks out of the diner as I put the shirt back in the box and tuck it next to me.

"Sorry about him," Charlie says. "What can I get you both?"

"I thought maybe we could split a few things. Also that way we can see what Grace here likes?" I say.

"Oh that sounds good," Quinn says. "But make—"

"We'll take biscuits and gravy. Oh, and just plain biscuits with some jelly and honey on the side." I begin. "And french toast. Pancakes and waffles, obviously. And throw in some bacon and sausage if you can? Did I get it all?"

Quinn's eyes are unblinking. "Yeah. That sounds great."

I hand Charlie the menus, and the smile on her face is knowing and also a little curious.

Damnit, she knows.

"Did you get all your errands ran?" Quinn asks, clearly not seeing Charlie's wink as she walked away.

"Oh. Yeah. Bank checked off the list. Had a good phone call with the lawyer. There's apparently a program in Tennessee about being a relative caregiver that Grace and I qualify for. He's going to set that up for me as we work through everything for me to become her legal guardian."

"That's awesome," Quinn says. "Seems like things are moving in the right direction."

"They are," I say, though I can't help but feel a little sad about that. Because like she said, when I have a handle on things, she's moving out. I'd never stall that process just to keep her around, but part of me wishes that it wasn't going so well. "What about you? Any news on the job or teaching front?"

She shakes her head. "No. I did update my resumé just in case. But I have to make a decision soon about going back to Phoenix. My apartment lease is up in a few weeks. I either have to renew, which means I'm looking for a job out there at a different school, or I need to move the rest out."

"I see."

I have a million follow-up questions. Most of them around if she doesn't return to Arizona, would she be staying here, or finding a new place to land? Obviously, I want her to be here, but I know the thought of living in Rolling Hills terrifies her. Though she's never said why…

"Can I ask you a question you don't have to answer?"

She chuckles as she hands Grace her sippy cup. "Go for it."

"Why won't you live here? In Rolling Hills?"

I watch as Quinn contemplates her answer, but before she can, I feel someone walk up behind me and stop at the edge of my booth.

"Now who is this precious little thing?"

I watch as Quinn's eyes narrow before I turn to see Emily Babcock standing behind me.

Fuck my life…

"Good morning, Emily."

It's the nicest words I can say to a woman who rarely has anything nice at all to say to anyone. Except to me. But that's just because she's trying to fuck me.

I don't have a lot of regrets in life, but hooking up with her all those years ago in high school probably tops that short list.

"Hey, Porter." She gives me a wink before turning to my roommate. "Quinn."

"Town bike. How we doing today?"

I nearly bite my lip off by Quinn's greeting. I mean, she's not wrong. But only Quinn Banks has the balls to say it out loud to the person standing in front of them.

"Probably better than you…Big Girl."

"What the fuck did you just call her?" I bite out.

Emily has the audacity to wave me off. "Oh, it's nothing. Just a little joke between me and Quinn. Isn't that right?"

I look at Quinn and see the split second that Emily's comeback got to her. However, I don't think Emily did as she's now leaning over, frankly, way too close, to Grace. "I heard there was a new little baby so I had to come see her. Aren't you just so cute? Yes, you are. Oh yes, you are."

Now, I've done more baby talk over the past month than I ever thought I'd do. It's like, all of a sudden, I just started doing it the second Grace was dropped on my desk.

But mine is nice. Soothing. Emily's is just weird.

And I'm not the only one who thinks so—Grace's "what the fuck" face is as strong as I've ever seen it.

"Come here, baby girl," I say to Grace as I purposely move her away from the crazy woman standing at my table. "Actually, you know what, Emily? I think it's best you leave."

Apparently Emily didn't hear, or is choosing to ignore me. I'm betting the latter. "Baby girl? Oh, Porter. That's such a sweet nickname. But of course, you're a sweet man, and she's just a precious little girl."

I'm guessing my expression at Emily's theatrics are the reason Quinn is snickering. If I had to guess I'd say my look probably matches Grace's.

"What are you laughing at?"

Quinn shakes her head and fans herself to stop crying. I can tell she's being dramatic, but that's the fire you have to fight when it comes to Emily. "Oh nothing. I was just thinking about how sweet he is at home. I've seen such a new side to Porter. He really just is the best person to take care of this little girl."

This gets Emily's attention. "Home? How do you know about his home?"

And now I see what Quinn's doing. And you know what? Fuck it. It's always good to have a show with a meal.

"Oh, you didn't know? Silly me, I figured everyone in town knew, you know, with how the gossip mill runs around here. Then again, no one tells you anything because most of the time the gossip involves you and which marriage you're trying to break up this week. But yes! I moved in with Porter and Grace. We're just one little happy family."

"You. And Porter." Emily looks back and forth between Quinn and I. "You're together?"

"We're raising Gracie here together, yes," Quinn says. I don't miss how she doesn't answer the question exactly, but does so just enough to piss Emily off. I'm both disappointed and impressed. "It's been amazing. Playing with her. Family dinners. Oh, and you should see the way Porter twirls her around, making her laugh and laugh. Oh! And then there was the other day when she was napping on him as he was shirtless," She sighs dramatically. "It was a sight to see. You really should've been there, Emily. Because let me tell you, it was perfect."

Emily's eyes are so narrow I don't know how she's seeing out of them. But what's getting my attention is how Quinn's not breaking her seething glare at Emily. She's standing her ground. Daring her to have a comeback.

Also, I didn't realize Quinn saw me the other day when Grace fell asleep on me. Interesting…

"Well, that's just great for you," Emily says in her fake nice way. "I mean, after you were fired from your teaching job and everything, it's good that you could make yourself. Let's be real —who in this town would ever give Big Girl Banks, the terror of Rolling Hills, a chance. Of course Porter would, he's too good of a guy."

She turns to me, her eyes showing nothing but mock sincerity. "Just know Porter that if you ever need *any* help, with *anything*, you know where to find me. I'm always going to be here for you. Just like I used to be."

Oh, fuck her. Why is she making this seem like what we had was a thing? It was one drunken hookup at a party when I was in high school.

I look over to Quinn, hoping to somehow let her know that it wasn't like that with me and Emily, only to see a fury of emotions playing through her brown eyes.

She's pissed. She's mad. She's hurt.

And no one hurts Quinn Banks while I'm around.

"You know what, Emily? Fuck you." I stand up, Grace in my arms as she drinks out of her sippy cup.

"Excuse me?"

I also realize an audience is gathering, but I don't care. Emily and her antics have been ignored far too long in this town.

"You heard me. First off, where do you get off going around calling people names? Especially something so juvenile. It's classless. Just like you."

Emily's mouth drops a little, but she has no idea what's coming. "I could go on and on about how no one in this town likes you. How you've ruined relationships and friendships. Marriages. But you know that. You just don't care. But you know what, Emily? I'm not going to let you ruin my life. I'm not going to let you ruin Quinn's. And I'm sure as hell not going to have you sticking your nose into my business. *Our* business. Because my family? No one talks about my family like that."

I look back to Quinn, her mouth open in awe. Emily might not realize what I'm saying, but Quinn sure as hell does.

"But Porter!" Emily squeals. "What we had—"

"Oh, for fuck's sake, Emily. What we had was a dumb, drunken, hookup when we were in high school. It wasn't this great love affair that lives in your delusion. I was a dumb kid who was hurt because the girl I was in love with didn't want me and you were…well…*available.*"

Emily gasps, and the gathered audience snickers at the show in front of them. "Porter…you don't know what you're talking about."

"Oh, I do, Emily." I take another step closer to her, and I realize at this point I shouldn't be holding my niece, but we're in it now. Plus, this is good for her, to learn how to stand up for the people that mean the most to you. "What I'm going to need you to do is walk out of here. I also need you to never come back into my bar. Hell, you should probably look for a new town to live in. Because if you ever, and I mean ever, talk to Quinn like that again, or even look at my child, you're going to wish you moved a long time ago. Because I will make your life a living hell. And that's a promise."

"Uh! Ah! Uh!" are the only noises that comes from Emily. And as I stand there and wonder why she hasn't left yet, it's then that I witness, as if in slow motion, as my niece picks up her sippy cup, winds her arm back, and whips it at Emily. And no shit, it's a perfect bullseye off the forehead. With some speed to it. The cup bounced back and everything.

That's my girl…

"Ouch!" Emily squeals as she finally takes the hint and turns on a heel to leave. This makes Grace start clapping and laughing as Emily storms out of the diner.

But as Grace's laugh fades and I put her back in the high chair, I turn to Quinn, who's still sitting in the booth, motionless. Speechless.

"Hey," I say, as I quickly sit back down and reach for her hand. "Talk to me."

She shakes her head. "You want to know why I won't live here? That. That's why."

I look back as Emily stomps across the street. "Her? Quinn. She's not going to be a problem again."

"It's not just her. But what she said? It's what most people in this town still think of me." She's quiet as I can tell she's trying to figure out what to say next. "Forever I'll be Quinn Banks, or, as our peers liked to call me, Big Girl Banks, because that's what happens when you're sisters with supermodels and I'm…me. Or if I'm not known as that, I'll forever be the prankster who rigged the homecoming queen ballots to make sure that bitches like Emily didn't win. And no matter how much I change, or what good I did as a teacher, none of it matters. Everyone knows by now what happened in Arizona and have put it down to me being same ol' Quinn and not the teacher who stood up for what she believes in. To this town, I'm always going to be that girl. And even though you defended me against her, you can't be there for every time this is going to happen. Because at the end of the day, I'm still the same Quinn Banks."

"Quinn—"

"I'm going to go." She quickly grabs her keys, and before I can stop her, she runs out of the diner.

I stand up, grabbing Grace's things to follow her, before Charlie puts a hand on my shoulder.

"Don't. Let her go."

I look out the window to Quinn, then back to Charlie. "But—"

She shakes her head. "But nothing. Let her go. She needs her space. Trust me on this."

I do as Charlie says and sink back down into the booth.

I'll let her go for now.

But I won't let her go forever.

guide to love rule #89

The hardest thing to decide in life is what to do with your future. Oh, and what to eat for dinner tonight.

23

quinn

I'M NOT USUALLY A NERVOUS PERSON. WHEN YOU HAVE A SUIT OF armor made from one-hundred-percent, fake-it-till-you-make-it, Teflon, it allows you to walk into any situation with false hope and a brush-it-off attitude if things don't go well.

Yet, I'm oddly nervous about what I'm about to walk into with this Zoom call.

For one, is it really my students? I'm trusting it is based on the knowledge of the Bruh Jar, but maybe one of the parents knows about it and is tricking me? Maybe this is the P.E.N.I.S. Posse setting me up to having communication with the students, which many would deem inappropriate. Then again, I'm not their teacher anymore, so is it? And it's not like I'm texting them every day or sharing memes.

And really, part of me hopes this really is them. I want to properly say goodbye and tell them what happened. And for all I know, this is them being savvy and demanding the farewell I never gave them. Which, honestly, they deserve that much. And if I piss off a few parents in doing it, well, that's very on brand for me.

I check the baby monitor to make sure that Grace is still napping, and yup, my girl is out. It was really convenient that the Zoom call that I have no control over happens to coincide with her sleep schedule. And since she was up half the night crying, I knew she'd nap good today.

When she sleeps, baby girl sleeps.

I check the time to see that it's promptly three o'clock and I click on the link. Again, smart? No. But if I started making smart decisions now, then who would I be as a person?

I expect a blank screen—if I learned anything from pandemic teaching it's that students conveniently don't know how to work technology when you need them to. But to my surprise, not only am I the last one to seemingly arrive, but there are rows and rows of my former students.

All with their cameras on.

And every one of them is holding a sign with a heart on it.

"What are y'all doing?"

I don't even try to fight the battle of keeping my tears back.

"We're having our first meeting of the Quinn's Crew Book Club."

That statement comes from Axel, who I had a feeling was behind this. "What?"

"Hold up." This comes from Antonio. I laugh through my tears, because of course he's going to be the one to challenge anything. "We've got a few things to discuss, bruh."

I wipe away my tears. "I'd tell you to put money in the jar, but I can't anymore."

"And that's why we needed to talk with you," he says. "Is it true? Did you quit?"

I nod, but I know I need to clear up a few things first. "I'll tell you my side of the story, but first I need to know how many of your parents are okay with y'all being here?"

Everyone but Makayla raises her hand, which tracks since her mom is the reason I'm sitting in Rolling Hills right now. It's also at that moment that Daniella's mom pops onto the screen.

"Hi, Miss Banks!" I wave back to her, but I'm too in awe to say anything. I think these kids thought of everything. "Just wanted to let you know that all of their parents gave permission, and I told them I'd be around just in case. And well, Makayla…"

"My mom is at her weekly facial. I've got two hours."

I know I shouldn't be laughing, but Makayla's rebellion right now is giving me life. "All right then, here's the story."

For the next twenty minutes, I'm brutally honest with my kids. A little too much? Probably. They might be barely teenagers, and they're still figuring out the world, but that doesn't mean that I should sugarcoat what happened. They deserve to know the truth, the whole truth, and nothing but the truth, so help me Dolly Parton.

"Damn," Antonio says after I've concluded. I probably should reprimand his language, but he's not wrong.

"And I need to say how sorry I am to each and every one of you." I take a deep breath, ready to say what I've wanted to tell them for weeks now. "I didn't want to leave like that. I wanted to come tell you all goodbye. I wanted to spend the Bruh Jar money on an epic last day party. I wanted to read *The Westing Game* with you. But I let my emotions get carried away, and I had to leave. And you didn't deserve that. It probably felt like I abandoned you, and I did. And I'll never be able to fully apologize for that. But please know, I've been thinking about y'all every day. And I hope that one day you realize that what I did was because I love each and every one of you, and you deserve better, and this was my way of telling people that."

I was hoping for a chorus of "It's okay Miss Banks" or maybe even a round of applause.

But what I wasn't expecting was a bunch of snickers.

"What? I just poured my heart out! Why are y'all laughing?"

Axel raises his hand between his own laughter. "You say y'all a lot now."

The rest of my former class continues to laugh. And honestly, his joke helps me laugh away the tears. "Well, I'm living back in Tennessee. I guess being back around it has brought out the Southerner in me."

"You're back in Tennessee?" Axel asks. "So you're not coming back, ever?"

I shrug. "I'm not sure yet, kiddo. I'm not sure."

A somberness hangs over the call, so I do what any good teacher does when she's losing the class—change topics.

"But enough about me. This is your Zoom. I doubt that you came up with a covert email, got parental permission, and organized this way just to hear my apology."

I notice everyone's mic's go to mute, except for Makayla.

"We never got to read *The Westing Game*. And we were wondering…"

She trails off, and Axel turns his mic on. "We were wondering if we could start a summer book club and read it together?"

It takes a lot to make my jaw drop. I'm not easily shocked. But it's safe to say that my jaw is firmly on the floor.

"Are you serious?"

"No cap, Miss Banks. You hyped it up so much and then you bounced," Antonio says. "Plus, our parents said we needed to find something else to do this summer besides play video games. So let's read."

"That was only your mom, Antonio," Makayla says. "But he's right, Miss Banks. We were looking forward to it. And… well, I know that you didn't want to quit. I live with my mom. I get it."

Oh, this poor girl. But good on her to realize the devil is in the house.

"We could read it on our own, but that wouldn't be as fun," Axel says. "So we thought, what if we started a book club? We can meet each week on Zoom. You tell us how many chapters to read, you can talk about everything you were going to teach us, and we can talk about what we liked and didn't like. Isn't that what a book club is?"

I nod through my tears. "That's exactly what it is, Axel. That's exactly what it is."

"So you'll do it?" Makayla asks, a hopeful plea to her voice.

"Just remember, you ditched us, Miss Banks. You owe us this."

Everyone in the chat starts laughing, Daniella's mom included.

"I'd love to," I say. "But wait. Not everyone has books. I think it's on an eBook, but I'd have to make sure I can get copies for everyone."

"No worries, Miss Banks. We got it covered."

I raise an eye to Antonio. "May I ask how, or is that making me an accomplice?"

He shakes his head. "Nah. I took the books out of your room. Every copy. So technically, I'm just holding on to your property."

"Excuse me what!"

Snickers start from my students again. "Well, I saw Hargrove and the mean moms come into the room, and they said they were looking for the books. I couldn't let them take those. They were your babies! So…"

"I caused a distraction with my mother—told her I ate gluten and didn't feel good—and Antonio grabbed the books and we all shoved them in our backpacks."

"Makayla!" I gasp. "I've never been more proud."

She shrugs. "It felt good. I've never done anything like that before."

"What am I going to do with you kids?"

"Easy, Miss Banks," Antonio says, holding up his copy of my favorite book. "You're going to read with us."

———

If one thing is for certain after today's Zoom call, I want to teach again.

The question I guess now, is where?

I sat in shock for an hour after I hung up the Zoom call with my kids, and then the second Porter got home, I sprinted out the door, telling him I needed Jenny to cover my shift. I needed to think, I needed to process. Which is how I ended up at the town park.

It's a beautiful day, so I'm not the only one here. But this is the last place any of my family, or Porter, would expect to look for me, so right now, that's as good as anything.

Because I need to cry.

And think.

And not puke.

Because the decisions I've left for future me are now in the present. And present Quinn doesn't know what the fuck to do.

Since I ended the Zoom call with the kids, all I can think about is how much I missed them. And how much I know I'll miss working with students in the future if I don't get back into a classroom. I might hate the way some things in education are going, and I'll never understand every decision an administration makes, but I wanted to teach English to make sure every child, especially the ones like me, got a fair shake. And I'm not doing that when I'm not in a classroom.

But where? Where the hell would I go? If I went back to Arizona, I couldn't go back to my district. That bridge is burned. But there are others within driving distance, so I wouldn't have to get a new apartment. As long as they'd be okay with how I left my last district.

On that note though, I'd still likely see people around town. I'd probably get glares and whispers, snickers and eye rolls. And if I wanted that, I could just stay here in Rolling Hills. Porter might've set Emily straight, but that doesn't mean her clique isn't still around. Or a person who remembers the time I organized every driving student in the high school to line up our cars and surround the high school so no teachers could leave during an in-service day.

No, I couldn't live here. Too much history. Too much baggage. But yet, every time I think about leaving, I feel sick to my stomach. Saying goodbye to my family—and even more so, Porter and Grace—is something I can't even fathom right now.

"Well, look who we have here."

I look up and push my tears aside to see Mrs. Metcalf pushing what looks to be a cat stroller. Oh! Maybe I should start walking and going outside more, so I can get one for Turtle.

"Hey, Mrs. Metcalf," I say, scooting over on the bench. "What brings you here?"

She maneuvers the stroller around so she can sit next to me. "Out for my daily walk. I don't like going this late, but I had to do some things at school today, so here I am, an early evening walker."

"Isn't it summer break? Shouldn't you be living it up?"

"Oh, Quinn…" she laughs as she pats my leg. "I'll have plenty of time for that once I get everything in order. In fact, George and I have a nice cross-country trip planned starting in August."

In order? What is she talking about? "August? Doesn't school start then? How long are you guys going to be gone?"

She smiles and watches the handful of children running through the park. "I'm retiring, Quinn. It's time. Paperwork is ready to go, I just have to turn it in. My time in public education has come to a close."

"What!" I cry out. "No. You can't retire. Who's going to run the library? No one knows that place like you. Also, why wasn't I invited to the party? Is it because of the time I rigged the Battle of the Books because I wanted the pizza party? I apologized for that."

She laughs and pats me on my knee. "There was no party, if that makes you feel better."

"Slightly. But why? You're an institution. You deserve a sendoff."

"It was just my time." Her voice is soft, but surefooted. "Forty-two years in that library. I always knew when it would be my time to go. And it is."

We sit in silence for a second as I process what Mrs. Metcalf is telling me. I know every teacher deserves to go when it's their time, and I know I don't live here or have children who go here, but I always thought that she'd be there forever. I hoped every student had the same fond memories of that library that I did. And that won't happen unless she's there.

"You know you were my favorite student."

"Yes!" I say with a fist pump. "Vindication!"

"Oh, you knew it," she says, taking my hand in hers. "Students like you are the reason I became a librarian."

"Dammit, Shirley, don't make me cry," I say. "I've already had a very emotional day today. I don't know if I can take any more."

"You're strong. I think you can take anything," she says. "Do you remember the first time you came into my library?"

I laugh. "You mean the time I got detention?"

"No, Quinn. The time after. The first time you returned a book."

I have to think about it for a second, but the memory starts slowly coming back to me.

"I asked if I was allowed to take another one."

She nods and gives my hand a squeeze. "The hopeful look in your eye was one I've never forgotten in all my years. Knowing that I could give you a place to retreat to, a place where maybe for a little bit you weren't such the prankster—"

"Well, that didn't work out too well, did it?" I joke through my tears.

"Perhaps not. But I know what books did for you. I saw the change in you from that moment on. When I was feeling down about things, or kids not wanting to read as much anymore, I'd remember your face that day. And always after I'd remember that moment, when a new student would come up to the counter asking me what kind of books they might like. And *that*, my darling, is why I kept going for forty-two years."

Well, shit. I didn't know I needed a whole ass box of Kleenex for this outdoor excursion.

"So why now?" I ask. "Granted, I don't know if I would've had forty-two years of public education in me. I couldn't even make it to fifteen."

"Yes…I heard about your fallout in Arizona," she says.

I can't help but groan. "I promise you, whatever you saw on Facebook isn't the truth. Well except a few names I called them. That's the truth."

She laughs. "Oh, I stay away from that social media garbage. No, I heard it from your mother. I ran into her at the grocery store."

I let out a sigh of relief. "Good. The last thing this town needs is more ammo on me and how I can't control myself."

"You did what you needed to do," she says. "I know you, Quinn. You wouldn't have done something like that without strong reasoning."

I nod, my eyes downcast as I think about the twenty-six faces smiling at me today. "I did it for the kids. I know it doesn't seem like it, but I did."

"You don't need to explain it to me," she says. "You're the reason I'm retiring."

I do a double-take. "Did you start a new conversation and forget to tell me?"

"No, my dear." She takes both of my hands in hers, turning me slightly to face her. "I retired because you're here now. You're back. And I want you to take over the library."

Excuse me what…

"Me?"

"Yes."

"You want me to work at Rolling Hills Middle School?"

"The very one."

"The school that still has a 'Most Wanted' picture of me in the office?"

She waves me off. "They got rid of that a long time ago. Plus, that principal retired. You'd be starting with a fresh slate."

Now that's laughable. "You and I both know that when it comes to this town, I'll never have a clean record. They still call me Hurricane at the bar. Plus, I don't even know if I'm staying here. So while this is flat—"

She holds up a finger, which was always her universal signal to kindly shut the hell up. "I didn't expect an answer today. I just want you to think about it. Because there's no other person in this world who I'd leave this library too. It's yours, Quinn. That is, if you want it."

I throw my arms around her. "I don't know what to say."

"Just promise me you'll think about it." She pats my back, holding me for a few seconds. "I truly believe everything happens for a reason. And you being back here means something."

"Really? I never took you as an astrology girlie."

"Oh, I'm not. But I believe in the power of a fairytale. And Quinn, I think you're starting to live yours right now."

24

porter

The house is quiet as I walk in from my day shift at the bar, which isn't surprising. We've gotten into a good groove where Grace's afternoon nap straddles the time where Quinn and I are coming and going.

On a normal day, Quinn would be in the living room, most likely reading. Maybe in the kitchen making dinner. Then again, the last few days have been anything but normal.

I took Charlie's advice and gave her space after the incident at the diner. The problem with that, though, is that it's now it's been two days, and I've barely said two words to her. I thought I could yesterday before we traded shifts, but she nearly knocked me over as she ran out of the house.

Something's going on with her, and I think it's more than just Emily's bad behavior. As much as Quinn talks, not a lot of it is about her or her feelings. Which I get. But it's driving me crazy knowing that something is going on with her and she, like always, thinks she has to deal with it herself.

The woman is nothing but stubborn. Beautiful. But stubborn.

I quietly walk through the house and see Quinn's bedroom door open. I peek in and gently knock, but it's empty. That's when I hear the faint sound of a lullaby coming from down the hall.

The door is cracked, and I push it open a little more. Quinn hasn't noticed me, so I take the opportunity to just lean against the door and observe. Because how can I not, when she's holding Grace, rocking her, and my niece is looking up to her with all the wonderment in the world?

"I mean, on one hand, I'd love to live here. I never thought I could move back, but maybe I was being stubborn? My sisters are here, and they're just the best. Just wait until you go shopping with Stella. And, I did always miss them when I lived in Arizona."

Grace starts baby blabbering as if she's answering Quinn. I have to bite my fist from saying anything, because I don't want to interrupt, but this interaction is hitting me straight in the heart.

"I know. So many things. And! You're here, and you're just too adorable. I'll also be really mad if I leave and then the next day you finally take your first step. Which, by the way, my phone battery is starting to lose steam because it's always on just in case. So if you could hurry that up, that would be great."

Until the diner incident, I hadn't really thought about Quinn leaving. But that was purely out of denial on my part. I mean, the odds are against Rolling Hills for multiple reasons. But, the more she talks, maybe they're more fifty-fifty?

Grace doesn't answer this time, instead just reaches up for Quinn's face and smooshes it. "See. How can I move away from this? No one else would smoosh my face."

Quinn takes Grace's hand, gives it a kiss, before her tone turns more serious.

"And of course, there's your Uncle Porter. You two are kind of a package deal these days. And this needs to be our little secret, but I'd miss him too. I'd miss him a whole lot."

She'd…miss me? Did she just say that?

I know I'm now officially in eavesdropping territory, and

she'll probably deny that she said it later, but I'd do it again to know that behind the strong walls Quinn puts up, that she's also feeling a little of what I'm feeling.

Because if she left tomorrow, I'd do a hell of a lot more than miss her.

I'd ache for her. I'd beg, borrow, and steal from the devil to have her with me. In my house. In my bed. In my life.

Because somewhere along the way, sometime between hookups and touches, kisses and glances, laughs and tears, I fell in love with Quinn Banks.

Hell, I think I've always been in love with her. From the time I first met her in high school, I knew she was different. That mischievous smile took my breath away. The way she handled herself against anyone was admirable. Her humor? Undeniable.

Since she's been back in town, I'm realizing now that I've fallen in love with her a little more every day. Getting to see her with Grace in moments like this. Laughing and brushing shoulders when we tend bar together. Seeing her genuine smile when she interacts with her sisters or the regulars. She's a light. A star that doesn't know how bright she burns.

And she could be gone in an instant.

"I don't know, Miss Ma'am. What should I do? Do I go to a new district that probably has mean moms? Or do I stay in Rolling Hills and work at the school and deal with the mean moms here? Only these meanie heads know me from when I used to start rumors about them in school. In my defense, they deserved it, but still. Big Girl Banks can't be the middle school librarian, can she?"

I don't know if I accidentally said something, or if the universe just tapped Quinn on the shoulder that there's a visitor, but at that moment, she lifts her eyes to mine. And I make sure I say everything silently that I need to.

Fuck yes you can.

Stay.

I love you.

Quinn doesn't answer me, telepathically or otherwise, as she stands from the rocking chair and walks Grace to her crib. She places her down and flips over the speaker from the lullabies that had been playing in the background to the white noise that seems to soothe her. I quietly step out of the door, but only into the hallway. Because we need to talk.

Now.

"You know you're a shitty eavesdropper," Quinn says as she closes Grace's door. "How much did you hear?"

Since I don't know when she actually started, I can't say everything. "Enough."

She motions for me to follow her, and we turn into her bedroom. "So then I take it you've heard about the job offer?"

"Yeah," I say as I sit next to her at the edge of the bed. "When did that happen?"

"Yesterday. After the Zoom call with my former students that had me for two seconds thinking I needed to go back to Phoenix."

Wait, what? "A Zoom call? How much has been happening that you haven't told me about?"

She quietly laughs. "A lot. But remember, this all happened in the matter of twenty-four hours."

Quinn goes on to tell me about her former students, who seem to have picked up a penchant for rowdiness from their teacher, and them asking to start a book club with her. How she gladly accepted, but that interaction made her realize she needed to be back in a classroom, and she needed to figure out where.

Not going to lie, the knife hit the gut deep when she said that.

But as soon as that pain hit, a surge of hope ran through me when she told me about her conversation with Shirley. George had told me in passing that she was thinking of retiring, but I never knew that it could be this soon. Or that she wanted Quinn to take over.

"Wow," I said, giving my head a little shake, because if I'm overwhelmed by this information, I can't imagine what she's feeling. "No wonder you've been M.I.A."

"Yeah, sorry about that," she says. "I'm not great at decision making—which I think has been well documented in my life. I just…I needed to try and think, but every time I sit down and do, my head starts spinning. Though, this is probably what I get for never having *actually* thought something through before. Karma man, she really is a twat."

I try not to laugh at Quinn's joke, but since she is, I'll join with her. "I think you're being too hard on yourself."

She shakes her head. "I'm probably not being hard enough. Because this is a major decision, and the last major decision I made was quitting my job without a second's thought. I moved to Arizona by throwing a dart at a map. I've always been act first and figure it out later. But this? I know I can't do that. There's just…there's too much riding on this."

"Yeah, it is," I say. No need to lie to her or sugarcoat her situation. But I know I can't say anything more than that. This has to be her decision. Not her choosing to stay here because I blurt out something stupid like, "I love you."

"When do you have to make a decision?"

"In theory, soon," she says. "Mrs. Metcalf only has so long that she can file her retirement paperwork before the next school year begins. Or, if I go back to Arizona, I'd need to start applying for jobs. And my lease is ending soon. Or if I want to go somewhere else, I need to figure that out. I'm just overwhelmed. So I figured I'd ask Grace during our daily chat."

"Daily chats with Grace? Did she suddenly start talking and you forget to put it on the board?"

"Unfortunately, no. Though I think she either said apple or asshole today. Not sure. But, she is a good listener. Like her uncle. Only she doesn't talk as much, which is great for me."

I bump her shoulder as we share a small laugh. But it soon dies out, because we know the gravity of the decisions she's about to make.

"So what's next?"

"That's the problem. I don't have a fucking clue."

I don't say anything. God knows I don't have any helpful, unbiased advice to give. Because the more I sit here next to her, and the more she's in my life, the more I realize the only reason I didn't fall in love with this woman years ago was because she always left.

This time she stayed.

I've had a taste of what life with Quinn Banks could be like, and now I want more.

I want forever.

"Can I say one thing?"

She nods but doesn't say anything else.

"I'd miss you too. More than you know."

Her eyes snap up to mine as I stand in front of her, leaning down to kiss her forehead. I let it linger longer than I probably should have, but I don't care. I need her to know where I stand.

And before she can say anything else, I walk out of the room.

guide to love rule #126

No one knows you, or knows how to call you an idiot, quite like a sister.

25

quinn

There are specific siblings you call for certain things.

When you need sunshine and rainbows, you call Ainsley.

When you need money, you call Simon.

When you need a slap across the head, that's a Maeve call.

When you need to know a person's detailed life history but only have a first name, you call Stella.

The problem is, when you need someone to get you drunk and tell you the hard truth, you call me.

Which is a problem, because I'm the one who needs to get drunk.

Correction: I am drunk. Now I just need a sibling to come over and tell me what the hell to do with my life.

To tell me to get my head out of my ass and stay in Rolling Hills.

And, to see if they know if I'm actually in love with Porter McCoy.

Because I think I am.

Fucking forehead kisses. They get you every time.

Which means that I have to tell my sisters the secret I've been keeping from them for eight years.

QUINN

SISTERS!!!! MOUNT UP!

MAEVE

What the fuck, Quinn?

STELLA

I know you keep bartender hours now, but you know the rest of us don't.

AINSLEY

Is everything okay?

QUINN

No, everything is not okay!

STELLA

Are you drunk?

QUINN

Maybe. A little.

AINSLEY

Where are you?

QUINN

The diner.

STELLA

Why are you drunk at the diner?

QUINN

Because I can't get drunk at the bar.

MAEVE

Why can't you get drunk at the bar?

QUINN

Because they know me there.

STELLA

Everyone knows you, Quinn.

QUINN

Exactly. That's why I have to be stealth. And
you need to be stealth when you come meet
me. Wear all black. Oh! Maybe we can—

MAEVE

Stop what you're thinking right there. I'm a
mother and married to a man who the tabloids
love, I can't be causing havoc in my hometown.

STELLA

Also, who said we're coming to meet you? I'm
in my pajamas.

QUINN

Well then let's have a slumber party! You come
here and tell me what to do with my life,
because I clearly can't make that decision. And
in the morning Charlie will make us waffles.
What do ya say, sisters?

MAEVE

I say you're drunk. But I'm never going to pass
up a chance to fix your life.

QUINN

There's the Mama Maeve I know and love!

AINSLEY

I'm coming in my pajamas.

STELLA

I'm not even putting on a bra.

An hour later—which also could be counted in four shots of
whiskey—my three sisters walk into the dimly lit diner, where
I'm currently slouching in a booth with one phrase bouncing
around in my head.

I'd miss you too…

What the fuck did he mean by that? Clearly, he heard what I
said to Grace, but did he have to say it out loud? With a forehead
kiss.

A forehead kiss!

I never understood the hype of those. They seemed kind of silly when I'd hear women talking about them. But I get it now. It's because you can still feel it hours later. And somehow, it's the most intimate thing we've done, which says a lot.

"Why are you down here?" Stella asks. "And why are the lights off?"

I shrug as I spin the shot glass around in my hand. "I didn't expect to end up here, and I didn't bring my apartment keys. But I knew Charlie hid a stash of booze in the cabinet, and I caught one of the cooks who was leaving. My timing was impeccable."

Maeve slides in across from me. I know she chooses that seat because she likes to look me in the eye when she's telling me what to do. "What happened?"

Ainsley places a tray of waters down before sitting next to me. "Or did it finally hit you that you need to make a decision about, well, everything?"

"Oh Ainsley Mae, so much has happened over the last two days that I don't even know where to start."

Maeve rips the shot glass from my hand and replaces it with a water. "At the beginning. Talk. Now."

Because I'm drunk and slightly scared of Maeve in this moment, I do as she says. It's a longer story than what I told Porter earlier, but that's because drunk me keeps trailing off. But by the end, I tell them about Quinn's Book Crew and my not-really, but kind of, offer from Shirley.

When I wrap it up, everyone's eyes are on me, but it's Stella's that are making me curious.

"What?"

She tilts her head like she's trying to figure out a clue. "There's more."

How does she know? I mean, I know there's more, I'm just not ready to tell them yet, because if I say words out loud it makes them real. "There's not anything more."

Stella shakes her head. "Sorry, sis. Not buying it. Because while your little army of rebel readers is cute and all, and I can see where that, combined with your talk with Mrs. Metcalf, can have you a little flustered, it wouldn't be driving you into the arms of Jack Daniels."

When did Stella become Maeve? "It's nothing."

God…why can't I bring myself to tell them? I want to. That's why I called them down here tonight. It's on the tip of my tongue. But now that we're here, I can't seem to form the words.

"Bullshit," Maeve says, her mean mom face on. "Tell us why we're here and what's really fucking you up right now."

"It's…" I try and rack my brain for the words. "I…Well, see, what hap-happened was…I've…Back a long time ago, in a galaxy…"

"Oh my gosh! Just say it!" Ainsley yells. "Say that you've been hooking up with Porter and now that you moved in with him things are weird. And I'm guessing because now that you're drunk and have been crying, you realize you love him?"

I'm rarely shocked. Like, it takes a lot for me to be still and speechless.

But if I wasn't sitting down right now, I would've pulled a fainting goat and dropped right down on this floor from Ainsley's outburst.

"How…what…when…what the fuck, Ains?"

"Actually," Stella says. "We all know."

My head snaps to the other side of the booth, where both Stella and Maeve are fully smirking.

"What do you mean you all know? Who's you all?"

"In our defense," Stella begins. "We only just figured it out. But when we started piecing together the clues, we realized that if we would've talked much earlier, we could've solved this puzzle weeks ago."

I try to open my mouth to say something, but when nothing comes up, Ainsley reaches over and helps snap it shut.

"There we go."

"Can someone please fill me in, because I was supposed to be dropping the bombs on you guys tonight, not the other way around."

"Gladly," Stella says, sitting up a little straighter. "We all first noticed things the night we went to the bar when you first came back. Right after you quit. We thought it was weird that Porter brought over all that food."

"Which we were thankful for," Maeve said. "But we've been going to The Joint for years, and Porter has never brought over free food like that. Also, there were looks."

"There were no looks." I protest.

There were definitely looks.

"And then there was the night when I saw you driving away from mom and dad's," Ainsley says. "I might've never had a one-night stand, but I know that you only leave a house at two in the morning for one thing."

"Maybe I needed something from the pharmacy?"

Ainsley quirks a brow. "Did you need something from the pharmacy?"

Stella holds up a finger. "That would be called a dick-scrip-tion, I believe. Take once a day for glowing skin and sore legs."

The three sisters are cracking up at Stella's joke, which I'd find funny if this didn't have to do with me.

"Okay, enough!" I yell. "So what, because he brought us food, a few looks, and Ainsley saw me leaving the house for an unknown booty call, all of a sudden y'all knew?"

Maeve shakes her head. "You know, I had a suspicion last year. So after that night, I started a chat to ask them—"

"Whoa!" I interrupt. "You have a side chat without me?" When the dust settles, that might be the thing I'm most mad about. Now I know how Simon feels.

"It was to confirm suspicions."

"But still, that's not confirmation," I counter.

Stella is then all smiles. "That's where I come in. Well, and Jenny."

I'm slack-jawed as Stella tells me about how she put on her rhinestoned FBI hat to start investigating if there was something more between Porter and I. All it took was one visit to The Joint when Jenny was bartending to get all the dirt.

And not just from Jenny. Harry and George, too. The biker guys who come in on the weekends after rides. Even the customers who only come in once a month said they suspected something.

"So you're telling me," I say slowly, still processing. "That not only do you three know, but every customer at The Joint knows? Which means…"

"Every person in Rolling Hills knows."

Ainsley wraps her arm around me. "Congratulations, sister. You and Porter are officially the worst-kept secret in Rolling Hills."

I dramatically throw my head into my hands on the table. "We were so careful. So cool about it. For so long we did so good!"

"Apparently not cool enough," Stella says. "The only thing that no one can put their finger on is how long it's been going on."

"Because if my suspicion was right," Maeve continues. "Combined with stories that Stella heard at the bar…then this has been happening well before you came back to town."

I nod. Guess I'm airing out all the secrets tonight. "I need y'all to promise that you're not going to freak out when I tell you."

Stella and Ainsley both draw Xs over their hearts. Maeve just lifts an eyebrow.

"Eight years."

There's silence for a second before Ainsley whoops in a cheer. "I win!"

Of course my siblings would take bets on this. Hell, if this wasn't about me, I would've organized the pool. "What was your guess?"

"Right on the money," she says. "When we were chatting, for some reason I remembered the night of Porter's dad's funeral. I never thought about it until we started putting the pieces into place, but you two were both gone for a long time that night. And because I was the only sober one there, I think I'm the only one who realized it. I always thought it was coincidence until…"

"Until you realized the only relationship I've had in that amount of time was a friends-with-benefits who I used to have a crush on in high school?"

Ainsley nods. "Exactly."

"You liked Porter?" Stella asks. "How did I never know that?"

"One, most girls did. He was that guy. And two, because she never told anyone," Maeve says. "Because our sister here turned him down every time he asked her out."

"What! Why?"

I look to Maeve, who probably knows the answer, even though I've never said the words out loud. Back then I told her I didn't like him like that. We both knew I was lying, but she never called me out on it. But since tonight seems to be about truths, might as well be honest with them.

And to myself.

"Because back then, I was convinced that guys like Porter McCoy didn't date the Big Girl Bankses of the world. And I thought that if I said no, I'd save myself the eventual heartbreak when he woke up from the weird dream state he was living in where he asked me out on a date."

"You know that makes zero sense," Stella says.

"To sixteen-year-old Quinn it did," I defend. "I convinced myself it was going to happen."

"But why?" Ainsley asked. "You were Quinn Banks!"

"Exactly," I say, but not with the enthusiasm that Ainsley just had. "I was Quinn Banks."

"What does that mean?" Ainsley asks. "I'm not being funny. Talk to us Quinn, because I have a feeling whatever that girl was going through, you're still battling that demon."

God, she's right. Did she transfer to the psych floor at some point?

"I learned early on that being funny got me attention," I begin.

"A case study should be done about how stereotypical middle child you are," Maeve jokes.

"Exactly. Once in elementary school, a kid called me fat. A little bully being mean. But instead of telling the teacher, or calling him a name, I pulled a prank. Now, instead of kids laughing at me because a kid was being mean, they laughed with me because of the awesome funny thing I did. And thus began thirty-plus years of using humor, pranks, and sarcasm to deflect any words that could be thrown at me."

"Honestly, that makes complete sense," Stella says.

"In high school, I realized that my pranks came with popularity. All of a sudden, I was a little cool. Seniors knew who I was, and not because I was Simon or Maeve's younger sibling. The day Porter started hanging around me, I didn't know what to do. I mean, he was hot, you know?"

"Still is," Stella says with a smile.

"You don't have to tell me. He does this—"

"Quinn!" Maeve yells. "Focus."

"Oh. Sorry. Where was I?"

"Porter started talking to you and you freaked the fuck out."

"Oh! Yes, anyway. When he asked me out, I couldn't believe he was serious. I thought he was being nice. Or he was bored. Because I knew the name Big Girl Banks was being thrown around in his circles. And in my mind, no one with that nickname really could go out with a guy like Porter."

"Oh, Quinn," Ainsley gives me a side hug. "I hate that people made you feel like that."

"If it had only stopped there, I probably would've been okay.

In college, I tried to start dating. I felt confident. It was a new start. People didn't know about my antics in Knoxville."

"You tried to date when we were in college?" Maeve asks. "Did I never meet any of them?"

I shake my head. "No, because there weren't any. You don't get dates when stereotypical sorority girls exist. I wasn't skinny or perky. I wasn't in a sorority. I was a big girl with a weird sense of humor who cursed more than the baseball team."

I pause for a second when I feel Maeve take a hold of my hand across the table. "Take your time."

I nod and suck in a breath, knowing it'll just be easier if I keep it going.

"College came and went, and then I needed to figure out what was next. I didn't want to stay in Knoxville, and all I could think was that if I moved back here, I'd forever be Big Girl Banks, the girl who once hid all the spoons in the cafeteria. I needed a fresh start, and the dart hit Arizona."

"It still pains me to know that's how you picked where to go," Maeve says.

"I know, but it worked. That's when I thought I truly found where I was supposed to be. I was a teacher. I had my degree. It was a new city, where no one knew who I was. I even started dating."

I trail off, remembering the douchebag that really I need to thank for starting this whole saga.

"The guy I caught cheating on you," Stella says.

I see light turn on for Maeve. "The night of Porter's dad's funeral."

"And then you disappeared for a while…"

I nod, not needing to confirm anything. "That was the first night. We thought it was going to be a one-and-done."

"Until it wasn't."

I tap my nose to Stella's observation. "One time became two. Two became three. Before I knew it, every time I was home, it happened."

"Wow," Ainsley says. "That often? For that long?"

"I don't know whether to be mad or impressed."

Same, Stella. Same.

"That's our history. Things started hot when I came back to town, but I cut everything off when I moved in. I thought we could quit cold turkey. And we have, don't get me wrong. It's just… Tonight he kissed my forehead and said that he'd miss me if I moved. And he stood up to Emily the other day for me at the diner and that was hot as fuck, watching him go all alpha like that. And oh, did I tell you he always tries to slide me a water because he's insistent that I'm dehydrated?"

I didn't expect a rousing answer to that last question, but I didn't expect silence either. "What? Why are y'all looking at me like that?"

"Are you serious?" Stella asks. "Do you really not know?"

"Clearly I don't, or y'all wouldn't be here."

The three of them have a silent conversation in front of me—kind of rude—before I'm struck on the back of the head by a hand I didn't see coming.

"Ouch! Ainsley!" I rub the back of it because I didn't know she could hit, let alone hard. "What's that for?"

"Because, we love you, but you're being an idiot."

"Harsh words from the nice one," I say.

"Okay, you want harsh words? Listen up."

Oh shit. Mama Maeve's being mean.

"You love Porter. You don't know it yet, which is fine, but you do. I'm going to guess he loves you because forehead kisses aren't casual. And I've seen the way you look at him and now that I know what the looks mean…well, frankly, you've loved him for a lot longer than before tonight, and you're just a little slow to the game."

Ainsley chimes in. "And then there's the fact that you send us twenty pictures a day of a baby that's not yours, so I know you've grown attached to that little angel."

"And let's talk about the job," Stella says. "I know you think everyone in this town still think you're the hot mess from high school, but it sounds like the perfect job is at your feet, and only idiots would pass that by. And you, my sister, are no idiot. Though maybe you are if you didn't know that you've been in love with Porter for years."

I hear my sisters' words. I really do. But…

"Whatever you're thinking, stop it," Stella says. "Speak the words out loud. Don't be in your head."

Damn them for knowing me so well.

"It's just…can I come home? I know I can, but it's fucking terrifying. And Porter? What if he doesn't want this? What if I'm making it up? What if he still is just being the nice guy from high school and I'm reading things wrong?"

"Or, what if *you're* wrong."

I look over to Ainsley, who's apparently channeling her inner Maeve right now. "Excuse me?"

"I said what if *you're* wrong. What if everyone wants you back? What if Porter wants you to stay? What if the school would love to have someone with your experience? What if for once in your life you stop thinking that everyone is still calling you names and you finally see that everyone wants you here, where you belong?"

I know I'm still a little drunk, but Ainsley's words are blowing my mind.

"Damn…" I say. "I expect that shit from Maeve."

She laughs and takes my other hand. "Well, I had to get mean to get through to you. I apologize."

"Don't," I say as I wrap my arms around her. "It's what I needed to hear."

The rest of the night is spent sobering me up, and stealing leftover pie from the coolers, as I tell them the rest of the Porter story over the years. The details I wanted to share but didn't. The times we almost got caught. We laugh, and I do feel lighter when we say our goodbyes.

But still, as I walk up to Porter's house, there's one question I can't get out of my mind: What if?

What if I move back?

What if I tell Porter I want more?

What if I let myself be brave and do things I never thought I'd do?

What if I'm vulnerable?

Just…what if?

guide to love rule #38

Make sure you're alone when using your battery-operated friend and moaning your roommate's name.

26
quinn

I can't sleep.

I've been home from the diner for hours now. It's currently three in the morning, I already have a hangover, the house is eerily quiet, and all I can do is stare at the ceiling and think those what-ifs that have been plaguing my mind.

Specifically: What if I told Porter I didn't want to go.

Or, the scarier thing, what if I told him I love him.

Because Maeve was right. I love him.

And I don't want to go.

I want to stay here. In Rolling Hills. With him.

And while I know it's what I want, doesn't make it any less scary.

What if he doesn't want this? What if he said he'd miss me because he's a nice guy? Or that he'd miss me helping him with Grace? What if I'm misreading the looks and the glances? Or the little touches. What if the heat I still feel between us is just left-over from our eight years of situationship?

Fuck, I'm going to drive myself crazy. And I hate that the only way I'm going to know is that if I actually talk to him about it.

But that requires truths and realness and not making a joke out of something.

All things I don't do well.

I sit up in my bed, wondering what he'd do if I just knocked on his door. No. I can't do that. It's the middle of the night. You can't have life-altering conversations at three in the morning.

No, I'll do it in the morning. Yes. That's a good idea.

Which means that I'm going to now lay here all night and thinking of the worst-case scenarios, because that's what I do.

No. I need a distraction. I need something to take my mind off of the fact that I'm actually going to lay my heart on the line with no idea how Porter is going to react. He could kiss me. He could sweep me off my feet, tell me he loves me too, and we could live happily ever after.

Or, he could let me down gently and tell me that he just wants to be friends. And oh yeah, by the way, you need to move out, because he has a handle on things and I just made our friendship awkward as hell.

God, I'm an idiot. Years of "protecting myself" now has me lying in a bed, my body and heart aching, hoping against hope that I haven't screwed this all up.

Because I want him. All of him.

And that if he wants me too, I'll stay here.

I'll stay the night.

I'll stay forever.

I'll stay for the family we've become and the family who has supported me through thick and thin. I'll stay and become the librarian at the school where I once stole the keys to the teachers' lounge and distributed copies around the school.

But most importantly, I'll stay for love.

Because I love Porter McCoy.

I think I've loved him for a while now.

The only question is, does he love me?

"Oh God, Porter…" I fall back onto my bed and close my eyes, begging the melatonin I took to finally kick in. I don't know why my treacherous brain is doing this, but instead of peacefully falling asleep, it's taking me back to the last time we were together.

That night in the office was like a greatest hits album of all our times together. It was heat and passion. But it was also filled with emotion.

I let my hands roam my body, stopping on all the places Porter loves to touch. I twist my nipples just like he does, thinking back to all the times he has told me to lay back so he can get lost in my breasts. My hand travels down to my center, under the sleep shorts and my panties, needing to relieve the building pressure. I start rubbing my clit, and I can tell that I'm already wet just thinking about that night, and really, every other night over the years we've been together.

Needing more than just my fingers, I roll over to the night-stand and take out my vibrator. I haven't used it since I moved in. I've never shied away from owning and using this, but it felt awkward with Porter on the other side of the wall and a baby sleeping nearby. I know it's basically silent—the technology these employ these days is quite impressive—but in my mind, the vibration will be able to be heard over the whole house.

But tonight I frankly don't give a shit, because if I don't get some relief soon, I might actually die. And it would be really shitty to die just when I finally just got my head out of my ass.

I have no idea how loud my groan is when I slide off my shorts and place the toy that I bought solely for the tag line "this is the only situationship you need" and slowly insert it into me.

Oh, shit…I feel it in every cell of my body. This is exactly what I need. And forget how loud the vibrator is. I have to make sure I keep it down, because fuck…I need this so damn bad.

I let out another, and likely louder, moan as I turn up the speed, letting the toy do the thrusting while also perfectly stimu-lating my clit. I arch my back, wanting more from the vibrator as I turn it up to another speed. And while it's doing the trick, it's still not what I *actually* want.

Because it isn't Porter.

My mind starts wandering again, only this time it isn't going back to a time we had before. No, this is a complete fantasy. We're standing in front of a mirror, both of us completely naked. Even in this dream scenario I want to retreat into myself, being on display like that for him in the open. I know he's seen me naked, but it's usually under sheets and dark in the room. But here there's light and nothing hiding us.

But then I picture how he's looked at me before, and how he's looking at me in this dream. The heat in his eyes. The way his hands can't stop touching me. How he always makes sure to worship every part of me.

He wants me. All of me. Exactly the way I am.

I hear noises coming from my mouth, but I don't know or care what they are or what I'm saying. How can I when I'm now perfectly picturing Porter's hands all over my body, his dick between my tits, and his eyes looking down on me like I'm the most perfect being he's ever seen? I pinch my nipple as the vibrator continues to work me, imagining that it's Porter's hands making me ready to come.

I insert the vibrator a little farther as my fantasy continues. I don't have to think too hard about how my body would react to his hand coming up from my tit to around my neck, putting just enough pressure on it to make me gasp.

"Porter," I moan as I turn up the vibrator to the max speed. "I want you. I want to stay. Please let me stay."

I don't know who I'm talking to or why, but the words are just falling out of me. It's like I'm in this weird dream state where I'm awake but I'm so far into my fantasy, I don't know what's real or fake.

That is until I feel the beginning of my orgasm start to build in me, which is a thousand percent real. I squeeze my eyes shut, letting my hips work with the vibrator as I mumble words that probably aren't English.

All except one word.

"Porter!"

I keep my eyes closed as I let the orgasm run through me. The pounding in my head from the intensity is loud, but it's nothing compared to the beating of my heart.

I love Porter McCoy. And it's about damn time I realized it.

I turn down the speed until it's eventually off, slowly taking it out of me. After a second of catching my breath, I'm finally able to open my eyes. Only when I do, Porter is looming over me.

"Porter! What are—"

"Shhh…" The fire in his eyes is undeniable as he leans down and kisses me quiet. And not just any kiss—a hard kiss that I feel all over my body.

I try to speak when he breaks the kiss, but between the orgasm I just had, and the one Porter's about to give me from just a look, I can't.

"Did you have fun without me?"

I nod, unable to say anything else.

"I figured you did," he says as his hand starts tracing up and down my bare leg. "I heard. A lot."

I was in a daze before, but not now.

He heard a lot? How much? What did I actually say? And what is it with this man and eavesdropping?

Oh shit. Did I say that I loved him out loud? No…maybe? Fuck my life.

"Did you forget already?" Porter sits down on the bed next to me, cupping my still throbbing pussy. "You screamed my name."

That I remember. "I know."

"Did you wish it was me?"

I nod again, only this time it comes with a whispered "Yes."

"Do you remember what else you said?"

Porter starts leaning close, his fingers now toying at my entrance. I try to thrust my hips toward him, needing the relief again even though I just came, but every time I do, he moves them just slightly to keep me away.

"I don't."

"That's too bad. I don't think I can give you what you want until you do."

Oh this motherfucker...how am I supposed to remember what I said five minutes ago? I feel like that's really unfair.

"I said..." I trail off, begging my mind to remember the nonsense it came up with. Knowing that the reward will be will be worth it. "I said..."

"That's it. Use your words, beautiful."

My eyes find his, and then it hits me.

He heard what I didn't want to say out loud.

The words that still scare me to speak into existence.

The words that will change everything.

"I want to stay." My words are barely above a whisper, but the slight smile on Porter's face tells me he heard it loud and clear.

"Say it again."

"I want to stay."

His fingers start to insert a little more, but not nearly enough for my pleasure. I try to find my voice when I feel his other hand take my wrists and pin them over my head.

"Say it, Quinn. Say it all. Say what you want."

Porter has pushed me in the bedroom plenty of times. It's one thing when it's orgasms. It's another when it's your heart.

But I'm tired of hiding. I'm tired of shielding. I'm tired of being on the defensive.

I'm ready to jump.

More importantly, I'm ready to land.

"I want to stay. Here. With you."

27

porter

STAY…

That one word releases the floodgates I've been holding onto for eight years.

Quinn Banks is staying.

And whether she realizes it yet or not, she's mine.

I crash my lips to hers, falling down to the bed as our mouths meet. The second I feel the heat from her body, I'm a goner. I have no thoughts except that this woman isn't getting on a plane again. When this is done, she isn't going to run out of here and say this was the last time.

She's staying.

In my bed.

With me.

Forever.

Her arms wrap around my neck as she deepens the kiss, her nails slightly digging into me as if she's scared I'm going to go somewhere.

I'm not going anywhere, Quinn. Not now. Not ever.

"Mine," I say as I break the kiss just enough to slide her T-shirt over her outstretched arms, bearing to me what I've been suffering without for weeks.

"Yours. I'm yours."

I groan into her tits, bringing one to my mouth and while massaging the other. I never thought I'd held back when it came to Quinn, but right now? I'm a mad man. Out of control. I'm likely bruising her as I take turns sucking on each one. If I'm leaving a mark, she doesn't seem to care. If anything, she's only encouraging me, holding my head to her like she never wants me to stop.

Say less.

I switch my mouth to the other side as she holds one in her hand, pressing it against my face so I feel like I'm surrounded by her fullness. This. This is heaven. Hearing the sounds Quinn makes when I suck on her, feeling her nails dig into my skin when she wants more, how I know that she's going to be wet as hell for me when I'm done, it's perfect.

I somehow pull myself away as I stand up from the bed, needing to slide my sleep pants off and free my aching cock. I want to go back down, my body already missing her, but I can't help but look down, in awe of the beauty laying before me.

"Do you know how fucking gorgeous you are?"

"Porter…"

My name trails off on her lips, but that doesn't distract me from the second of doubt I see in her eyes. It's the same look she had that day that her and Emily had that run in at the diner. It lasts for just a second. But it's there.

Not anymore. I won't let my girl think for another fucking second that she's anything but perfect.

"Come here," I say, holding my hand out for her. She looks confused, but doesn't waver in giving it to me as I stand both of us up from the bed. "Good girl."

I step closer to her, bringing her lips in for another kiss. My tongue starts getting a mind of it's own, searching her mouth wanting more, before I have to pull away.

I'll have plenty of time to kiss her later. If I have it my way, the rest of our lives. But first, she needs to know exactly how I feel.

"I want you to know, that when I say that you're beautiful, I mean it. With everything in me."

My hands start running down her arms and I feel the goosebumps form on her skin. "Our first night together. I know you probably thought that I was just sad and lonely. And I was. But it was more than that. That night, my wishes were coming true. That I had to go through the worst thing of my life to finally feel like what it was like to have you."

I kiss her again, this time letting my lips trail down her neck, over her shoulder, and across her chest. With each kiss I pepper on her smooth skin, I feel her body relaxing just a little more.

"I thought our first time was going to be it. You were gone again. I didn't know when you'd come back to visit. And even then, how would we act? Would we still be friends? Still joke around with each other? And then you ordered chicken wings, and my life changed from there."

She softly laughs as I lower myself to my knees in front of her, continuing to kiss every piece of her soft stomach I can. "Quinn, you are perfect. In every way. And every day it's been harder for me to resist you. And not because of our history, or because you're living with me. It's because of you. It's always been you, Quinn. From the moment I first laid eyes on you in high school, to right now, as you're looking at me like you can't believe the words coming out of my mouth, it's always been you."

I need a second to gather my words, and I was sure she'd try to object. But since her jaw is open and her eyes are double the normal size, I'm pretty sure I've done the impossible and rendered Quinn speechless.

"Since you've come back, and moved into my house, I've fallen more in love with you every day. Seeing you each day with Grace…watching you slowly make this house a home…

seeing you read on the couch...watching as you do your little dances in the kitchen when you think I'm not looking...to embracing life at the bar...you fit in my life more than I ever could've dreamed."

I kiss her again at her stomach, holding it there for a beat before I pull back. "I never thought I wanted more. I never thought I wanted forever. But I do, Quinn. And I want forever to start now. With you."

Quinn lowers herself to the floor with me, both of us on our knees with our eyes locked. Her hands are cupping my face, and the more silent she is, the more worried I am that everything she said was in the heat of the moment. That I've now scared her back to Arizona with my admission. But when she brings my face down to hers and kisses me with a softness I've never felt from her, I know that this is it.

This is where our story truly begins.

"I love you, Quinn Banks. I think I've always loved you. And I don't care what anyone in this town thinks or says—you're perfect in every crazy, beautiful, maddening way. You're perfect just the way you are. You're perfect for me."

She bites her lip before saying anything. But when she does, it's the most beautiful words I've ever heard.

"I love you too, Porter."

If I thought my willpower snapped when she said she's stay, it's nothing like my body's reaction to hearing those three words.

Our mouths are together in an instant as our bodies go tumbling on the floor. I don't think about the scratch of the carpet against my back. I don't think that it would take five seconds to move us to the bed. All I can think of right now is that Quinn is on top of me, straddling me, her tits are there for the grabbing, and I'm in fucking heaven.

"So fucking beautiful," I groan as her hips start circling around my hard cock. "You're already so wet."

"For you," she says as she leans down on top of me, dropping a tit into my mouth. "Only for you."

I suck at it as her hand reaches back, starting to stroke me like I need any sort of workup. Hell, I could *think* about Quinn and in two seconds I'd be ready for her.

Our mouths connect again as I roll her over, not breaking the kiss until I lean just enough away to slide into her heat. But just as the tip goes in I freeze.

"Shit. Quinn. I need—"

She grabs my face and stops me mid-sentence. "No."

"No?"

She brings my face down to meet hers, giving me a kiss I feel in every cell of my body. "I'm on the pill. And…well…it's only been you. For years…only you."

My heart doubles in size, knowing that it wasn't just me in denial about what we meant to each other. "Same. I'm clean."

"Then what are you waiting for, McCoy? Make me yours."

I can't help but groan as her words ring through my body. "Gladly, beautiful. Gladly."

I spread her legs just enough to push into her heat. The gasp she makes as I enter her, combined with the moan that escapes me, fills the room as we settle into each other.

Holy shit, does she feel good. Perfectly tight around my cock. Wet and perfect.

I slowly start working in and out of her, because I want to feel every second of Quinn's perfect pussy around my cock. She's wet and tight and her hands are flat on my stomach, as if that's going to support her. Her back is arched, her head is thrown back, and her eyes are closed as she feels every inch of me.

"That's my girl," I say as I continue to work her. "Take all of me. Every inch."

Her legs go up and around my ass, hooking me tighter into her. Normally I'd try and keep my weight off her, but clearly she doesn't want that. And, well, feeling her perfect body against mine is too good to pass up.

But what I wasn't ready for is Quinn opening her eyes. We've looked at each other during sex, but then it was usually one of us daring the other to do something. Or a little teasing.

No, this time is nothing but desire. Want.

Love.

"That's it," I say, as our slow motions begin to pick up speed. "Just like that."

I feel her nails dig into my back, which is how she's always said she wants more. Maybe she doesn't realize that's what it's saying, but I know my girl.

I reach my arms under her back and sit her up on my lap, making sure our bond never breaks as she straddles me on the floor.

"I love you, Quinn Banks."

Her smile would knock me on my ass if I were standing up. "I love you, Porter. So much."

Our lips come together again as our bodies start speeding up. The position we're in, it's like we never are too far away, yet somehow every time she comes down on my cock, it feels like she's deeper.

"Close, Quinn," I whisper in her ear, bear hugging her into my chest.

"Yes," is her only reply as her fingers comb through my hair. "So close."

With one pull of my hair, I lose it. I start pumping her faster, Quinn bouncing on my cock as her head is thrown back.

"Yes, Porter! Ah!"

Her scream is loud, but not louder than the howl that leaves my body as I come inside Quinn.

I hold her to me, long after I'm empty, because I can't let her go. I don't want to.

Then I remember that she's not leaving.

She's staying.

And tomorrow, I'm going to wake up with this beautiful woman in my arms.

"Whoa! What are you doing?"

I stand up, Quinn still in my arms, as she holds onto me tighter. Her giggles fill the hallway as I kick open the door and walk our naked selves down the hallway.

"I'm taking you to my bed."

"What? Why? I don't know if you realized this, because you chose to not use it earlier, but I do have one of those."

I lay her down on my mattress, following quickly behind her because it's been too long since I've kissed her.

"Porter…"

"Because, Quinn…this is the first night you're staying with me. The first night you're falling asleep in my arms. And like hell it's going to be anywhere else but in my bed."

A small "oh" pops out of her mouth before I kiss her again.

"And not just that," I say as my hands start freely roaming her sweaty body. "When I wake up in the middle of the night and want a snack? Don't be surprised when my face is between your legs. And in the morning, when you feel me against you, be ready, because I do plan to fuck you first thing in the morning."

"Interesting." A devilish smile crosses her face. "There's just so much to look forward to."

"Exactly." I know I'm tired and not recovered. Hell, I didn't even clean us off. But I can't stop kissing her. Or touching her. Because Quinn is here.

And I'm not letting her go.

"Can I ask one question?"

"Um-hmm," I say though my mouth doesn't move from her chest.

"What about breakfast? Does this plan come with waffles?"

I laugh because of course she'd make a joke. "Whatever you want, Hurricane. Whatever you want…"

She lifts my head up, but only so she can summon me with a kiss of her own. I want to object that she stops it sooner than I'd like, but I don't say anything as she rolls me over, placing her head on my chest.

Just where I've always wanted her.

"You know, if you keep this up, I may never leave."

I tilt my head down and kiss her forehead. "I'm counting on that."

guide to love rule #6

Flings are temporary. Falling for the single dad could be forever.

28
quinn

My eyes are barely open when I feel Porter's hand pulling me back into him.

He did this a few times last night. It's like every time he felt me move, he needed to make sure I didn't go too far.

Which, I don't blame him. I'm nothing if not a flight risk.

Except that every time he pulled me closer, and I felt his chest against me, I knew I was right where I belonged.

It only took me eight years, quitting a job, one baby, and four determined sisters, to realize it.

"Good morning."

Porter's gravelly morning voice sends a shiver through my body as he pulls me in even tighter, which I didn't know was possible.

"Good morning to you."

Porter's lips graze my shoulder, leaving small kisses in its path. When I finally roll over, I have to blink to make sure this is real life.

God, he's even more handsome in the morning. Maybe it's the light. Or his hair that's a mess from our night and sleep. Or that his bare chest is quite a sight to see before my morning coffee. And even more so, the way he's looking at me? A small smile that's filled with warmth. Calm eyes as he traces his fingers up and down my arm. He looks completely content.

Happy.

With me.

"You think a lot in the morning."

I laugh as he pulls me closer to him, our faces the perfect distance away to sneak a kiss here and there.

"Believe me, this isn't normal," I joke. But when the laughter dies on my lips, I'm left silent, wondering how I tell him all the things I need to say.

All the things I *want* to say. Things I've been scared to admit for eight years.

"Hey," he says, tipping my chin up. "Breathe. Take your time. I'm not going anywhere."

His words of encouragement help a little as I take a few moments to actually think before I speak.

Wow. So many new things in such a short amount of time…

"Do you know why I never stayed?"

I'm not sure if this is the best place to start, but it's going to come up at some point, so might as well lead off with it.

"I've had my suspicions," he says. "They ranged from not wanting to do a morning walk of shame in front of your parents to that you turned into a hawk in the morning and didn't want me to see your transformation."

I think I stop blinking. "You know *LadyHawke*?"

He sends me a wink. "There's a lot you're about to learn about me."

Damn. How does a man knowing a 1980s romantasy cult classic movie suddenly make him instantly hotter?

"Okay, well we're diving into that later," I say, as I need to get back on track. "But it was none of those things."

I take a breath, and for a second I consider making a joke and weaving my way out of this. But then I feel Porter's hand at the tip of my chin, his thumb lightly stroking my skin. He doesn't say anything. He doesn't need to. Somehow, just his touch and a simple look is all I need.

"I didn't want this moment," I begin. "Well, not this exact moment. This is great. Perfect. Ten out of ten. But what I didn't want was the next morning. You looking at me in the morning light. I didn't want to take the risk that when you woke up the next day, that you'd regret what we did the night before."

"Quinn…I nev—"

I hold up my finger to his lips. "You never, and I mean ever, did anything to make me think that. This was all me and my self-doubt creeping into my head. You did nothing wrong."

I let my finger slip away, but not before he takes it in his hand to bring it to his mouth. "I hate that you felt that way. Please know, that when I asked you to stay, each and every time, it's because I wanted this moment. And maybe some morning sex."

I laugh, thankful that he's helping me keep this as light as possible. "I've actually never had morning sex."

"Really? Does that mean…"

I nod. "Even if I was dating someone, I never spent the night. I was always gone before they woke up. Because even though I've learned to love myself, and most days I'm confident with my life and body, there are times where I'm still Big Girl Banks. And when those thoughts creep in, usually when I'm naked and in the light of day, I go back to high school, where I lived with the belief that guys like Porter McCoy really didn't want to date girls like Quinn Banks, let alone sleep with them."

Holy shit. I said it. The thing that scared me the most in the entire world. The thing that always kept me at an arm's length from any man I ever dated.

What held me back from falling in love with the man lying next to me.

"Thank you for telling me that," Porter says. "And if there's ever, and I mean ever, any time those little nuggets of doubt creep in, you just give me the signal. I'll make it my personal mission to remind you that I'm obsessed with your body, and it would be my honor—nay, my duty—to remind you that you're by far, without a doubt, the most beautiful woman I've ever seen."

I lean in for a kiss that becomes heated in an instant. I mean, how can I not? I'm lying here in a bed with a hot as hell man who hasn't been able to keep his hands off me since we fell into this bed together, who last night told me he loved me and just made me feel completely at ease with my deepest, darkest confession?

Oh shit. I almost forgot that he told me he loved me.

Porter loves me.

Me. Hurricane Banks. And while that's shocking enough on face value, it's not as shocking as me knowing without a shadow of a doubt that I love him.

I love how he has embraced instant fatherhood. I love how he bites his lip and squints a little when he's trying to figure something out. I love how he might come off as the flirty, and sometimes a little broody, bar owner, but in reality he's sponsored more Little League teams and festival booths than anyone in this town. I love how he's kept his father's legacy alive at The Joint while also making it his own place. I love that he somehow knows when I need words of encouragement, or if I just need silence to figure something out.

And I especially love how he's now deepening the kiss, rolling me to my back for the all the mornings we've never had.

"So long," he mumbles as he starts kissing down my body. "I've waited so long for this."

"No more."

I let myself and lay back, the sun now directly shining into the bedroom, as Porter's tongue begins to do what it does so well. I throw one arm up lazily over my head as I let the other one comb through his hair, making it messier than it already is.

Could this be it? Could each day be like this? I mean, I'm not demanding that Porter eats me out every morning—though I wouldn't be complaining—but could lazy and romantic mornings like this exist? I feel like they could.

Wait, is this what it would've been like? If I would've stayed, if maybe just once, is this what the morning would've been? Porter's tongue taking its time as he licks and sucks while I lay back in complete bliss? Part of me thinks that yes, the act would've been here. But the emotion? The love? I don't think Quinn from eight years ago would've been able to handle this. Hell, I wouldn't have been able to handle it last year.

No, everything happens for a reason. And maybe Mrs. Metcalf was right. Maybe my fairytale is just starting.

Though I never read the one where the prince ate pussy like it was his last meal. I would've for sure read that one.

I moan and let my hips writhe against his mouth as he starts teasing my center with his fingers.

"Fuck yes," I whisper.

He doesn't speed up his efforts, instead making sure he's hitting every spot just right. And holy shit is he. The feel of his fingers now inside me, the flick of his tongue against my clit, it's all too much.

I feel my orgasm start to build up and I reach back for the bar on this headboard, begging it to come through me. And just as I feel it in the pit of my stomach, it immediately curls back into me with the telltale sound of Grace's small cries.

"No, no, no!" I yell, begging my orgasms to come back. "I'm so close."

Even though I know this is not a two-way monitor, it's like Grace knows what's about to happen, and her cries go from small to consistently even. And so sad.

"Ugh," I blurt out, my body falling limp as Porter's mouth and fingers also stop working their magic.

Kids, cockblocking parents and guardians since the beginning of time.

"Note to self: remember to work quickly in the morning as a child will apparently somehow have impeccable timing."

I laugh as Porter crawls his way back up to me, leaving a kiss on my shoulder before he rolls out of bed. "I'll go get her. Wait here."

Like I could get up if I wanted. Though, it does hit me that I'm naked and Porter is bringing Grace back to the bed, so I hurry and dig through his drawer to find a T-shirt to slip on. Just as I do, the door opens and my heart melts in an instant.

Grace's head is resting on his shoulder, the tip of her thumb in her mouth, as he carries her back to the bed.

"Hey, Miss Ma'am," I whisper, her sleepy eyes still half shut as we sit on the bed. "Did you sleep good?"

Of course she did. This girl has two modes of sleep operation —like a rock or not at all. And since we didn't hear her last night, I'm going to assume it was the first.

You know what? I'm going to give her a pass on interrupting us this morning. She's a real star for sleeping through last night.

"Here we go," Porter whispers as he lays her down between us. "I think we could all use a lazy morning."

The three of us lay there, not saying anything, as Grace slowly starts to wake up. Porter's hand reaches over her, our fingers gently playing with the others, as we just lay and watch this little girl, who I'm just realizing is the reason I'm here.

"Do you think this would have happened without her?" I ask, because until right now, I don't know if this thought really hit me.

"I'm not sure," he says. "I'd like to think it would've."

"So do I. But then again, I know how stubborn I was."

He quirks an eyebrow. "Was?"

"Fine. Am," I say as Grace starts cooing between us. "Exactly, Miss Ma'am. Tell me all about how stubborn I am."

Grace starts giggling as I rub my nose into her belly. I'm so lost in her little laughs that I don't realize until I look up that Porter is staring at us.

"What?"

He shakes his head slightly. "Just looking at my girls."

Oh damn…that hit me in a way I wasn't ready for.

"Your girls, huh?"

"Yeah," he says, picking up Grace and laying her on his stomach. He holds out his arm for me, allowing me to snuggle in with my head on his shoulder. "I never knew I wanted this. I didn't want to be a dad. I didn't want a relationship. I didn't want any of this…but now…now I can't imagine my life without it."

I understand his words completely. I never thought I wanted to move back or live in Rolling Hills. I never wanted a relationship. I never saw myself as a mother figure. Cool aunt? Hell, yeah. But keeping a human alive? Absolutely not.

But the thought of not being here? Away from him? Grace? My family? It's unimaginable.

I guess you can truly say never say never. Because there are so many nevers I'm about to break it's not even funny.

Because get ready, Rolling Hills. Quinn Banks is back, baby!

29

porter

"WHAT THE FUCK…"

As soon as I step out on my front porch with Grace in my arms—appropriately sporting a large lilac hair bow to match her party dress—I stop and look at the parking lot of my bar.

Because what the actual fuck is going on?

From what I can see, a bounce house is being inflated, farm animals are being led to a pen, and a food truck is setting up shop.

"Huh?"

"I know," I say to Grace. I don't know if that's what she actually said, but that's what I heard, and it fits. "I think it's time we find Quinn."

Now, the reason for Grace's new bow, and my matching button-down shirt, is because this is a special day. Grace is turning one next week, I got official notice that we're one step closer to adoption, and Quinn is officially moved back to Rolling Hills.

All three are big reasons to celebrate.

When Quinn and I were talking about a party, I was thinking a backyard barbecue. Friends and family. A few regulars. Something just nice and relaxing to celebrate everything that's been happening over the past few months.

Quinn's last words to me on that topic were, "I'll take care of everything."

That should've been my first clue. Because then I remembered Quinn is a Banks. And her brother is Simon, also known as the most over-the-top man in Rolling Hills. But I never expected what I'm seeing now.

"Right over here!" Simon directs, wearing his Dad Squad polo shirt as he helps back in a flavored ice truck. "There we go. Perfect!"

"Can I ask what's going on?"

He turns to me, doesn't answer my question, but does take Grace out of my arms. This man is on a mission right now for my niece to smile at him. The fact that she doesn't only makes this little game they play even better.

"This is all for you," he says in a baby voice. "Because your Uncle Porter wanted to have a party but he didn't have a bounce house guy. I have a bounce house guy. We're going to have so much fun!"

"Give her back, please," I say as Grace willingly comes back to me. "Simon, really, this is nice and all, but you shouldn't have."

"But I did," he says as he signs something on a clipboard from a passing-by worker. "Today's a big day. For all of you. Her first birthday! Did you get her a smash cake? I did just in case. And while an open bar with food at The Joint is great, it doesn't scream one-year-old birthday/return home party. Because this girl is one, and Quinn is back home!"

I smile as I realize all of that is true until I remember one thing he slid in. "Who said anything about open bar?"

He waves me off. "You did. I'm sure. At some point. It's fine. Everything is fine. It's a party!"

I stand in confusion for more than a few seconds before Grace starts squirming to be let down. I make my way inside The Joint, not wanting her to start running around in the busy parking lot, when I realize that inside is just as much of a madhouse as it is outside.

"Quinn?" I ask as I put Grace down in the "Grace Corner" as the regulars have dubbed it. In reality, it's just a portion of the bar where they built a permanent baby gate, put in a mat so she's not sitting on the wood floor, and filled it with more toys than she could ever play with. It's becoming one of her favorite places and she cries when she has to leave. "Care to tell me what's going on?"

She all but skips around the bar, balloons in her hand as she leans up to kiss me on the cheek. "We're decorating."

"I see that," I say as a host of red and pink balloons cover nearly every inch of the bar. It looks like I'm having a Valentine's Day in June event. "I don't think I've ever seen this many balloons in my bar in, well…ever."

I look around the bar and the decorations are big, bright, and I'll even admit, fun. There's a banner welcoming Quinn back to Rolling Hills. There's another one that says "Happy Birthday" with stuffed bears and birthday candles on it. Streamers hang from the ceiling and balloons float all around. It definitely doesn't look like my bar, which makes me wonder what the regulars are going to have to say about this.

"Quinn! We finished packing the party favor bags. Should we put them by the door?"

My eyes are unblinking as I watch Harry and George carrying little party bags through the bar. "Really? She got you two in on this?"

"Of course!" George says, looking at me like I'm crazy. "That angel of a woman of yours is the reason I'm able to go across the country with my lady and my RV. She could've told me to drink concrete today and I woulda done it. Plus, our little girl only turns one once!"

"I'm here for the cake," Harry says, patting my back as he

walks next to me. "Also, don't look stressed. This is a fun day. A happy day. Have some fun. Your daddy would've loved it."

I sit down at those words, because Harry's right. He might've been an aloof bar owner for his life, but he always had a sparkle in his eye when a new baby or child would come into the bar with their parents. I think if he were alive, and Missy would've brought Grace to me, he would've supported me every step of the way. And I know for a fact he would've loved that little girl as much as I do.

On that same line, he would've loved Quinn. He knew her back in the day and always laughed at her stunts. I remember him partying with her just as much as anyone on her twenty-first birthday.

Yeah…he would've approved of us. Of this. Of us raising this family together. Most importantly, he would've been thankful that I didn't end up alone.

Pops and I had talks about why I didn't date. He knew I wasn't a monk, but he also knew that I never brought anyone over for dinner. A few times he made sure to mention to me that just because he never remarried, or really even dated after Mom left, that I didn't need to stand with him in solidarity.

And I knew that. But what I didn't know until many years later, after many late nights of thinking on my front porch with a bottle of whiskey, was that Bonnie leaving me messed me up just as much as it did him.

That's why I think I was always okay with Quinn's arrangement. I *knew* she was leaving. She couldn't surprise me, or hurt me, when she wasn't there the next day. Even if I asked her to stay, I still knew what the result was going to be. It's probably why I held back my feelings for her for so long. Because I knew she wasn't going to be here.

But now she is. She's officially moved into my house. She has closets and drawers. Her cat has taken over my house and there are strands of her brown hair in my sink. She has a book in each room, an iced coffee maker on my countertop, and I now know what it truly means to binge watch a series.

And I wouldn't have it any other way.

"Hey," she says, snapping me from my daydream as she slides onto my lap. "Everything okay? I know Simon and I kind of took over. If you want—"

She doesn't finish that sentence as I lean in for a kiss. It's probably a little much for noon on a Saturday at my bar, but I frankly don't give a damn.

She's here. She's staying. And I'm going to kiss her whenever, and wherever, the hell I please.

"Well, well," she says as I pull away. "What was that for?"

"Just thinking about things."

She taps her forehead with mine, letting it rest there for a beat. "All good, I hope?"

I nod. "Not just good. Great. Especially now that you're back."

After Quinn's decision that she was staying in Rolling Hills, a few things had to happen. One, she needed to finally finish moving her things from Arizona. Luckily, her brother knows a guy with a moving company, and they had Quinn packed and back in Tennessee within three days. What she wasn't bringing she sold easily and has now officially moved in.

Once she was back—and she admitted later she probably should've probably done this first—she formally applied for the librarian's job that hadn't even been resigned yet by Mrs. Metcalf. It was an odd meeting for sure—Quinn said that it was her and Shirley in the principal's office as Shirley told him what was going to happen. And while this principal didn't know Quinn specifically, he had heard of her lore. Before Quinn knew it, she was being formally interviewed by the principal, two members of the board of education, and members of the parent committee. Since she wasn't prepared to be facing that large of an interview room, she slightly panicked, confessed to four pranks from twenty years ago, and went into more than full detail of how things ended in Arizona. I wasn't there, but she claims that she blacked out and maybe admitted that she asked them in no uncertain terms if they named their group with a dildo in mind.

Luckily for her, one of the board members was her former chemistry lab partner who vouched that Quinn always had good intentions in mind and that she'd make an excellent addition to the Rolling Hills Middle School staff.

They also empathized with her about the parent group that led to her fall in Arizona. Apparently Rolling Hills LSD has one. In a shock to no one, it's led by Emily's best friend.

While all of that was happening, I was in a courtroom taking the next steps toward adoption. Because Missy left her with me, and wrote me that letter, a judge said that I'm, for now—until they can do a further check and go through the proper channels —her relative caregiver.

Grace's coos and noises instinctively have us both looking over to her play area, making sure she's okay. She is, just curiously looking at a very bright, and very loud, interactive toy someone gave her. For only being here for two months, this child has accumulated a shit ton of toys.

"This day feels surreal," Quinn says, tilting her head so it's resting on my shoulder.

"How so?"

"Just...everything. Three months ago I had a job in another state. You didn't know Grace existed. And look where we are now. So much has happened in such a short amount of time, but at the same time, it feels like we've been doing this forever."

"I know what you mean." I tighten my grip around her waist and kiss her shoulder. "Sometimes I can't even remember my life before Grace."

"Really? You don't remember life before you knew how to change a diaper?"

"Well, certain parts," I say, remembering the days before

Grace came here, specifically my night with Quinn in the office. "Some parts are very vivid."

She understands what I'm saying as she wraps her arms around my neck. "You know, maybe some of those nights can be redone. See if the sequel is better?"

"I like the sound of that."

Our lips meet and the kiss deepens quickly, but just as fast, a door slamming open breaks us up.

"All right people, listen up!" Quinn and I both turn toward the door, where Simon is standing with a clipboard on and—is that a head set? Who the fuck is he talking to? "Guests are arriving in ten minutes, food is starting to get prepped, and we're going to have fun today. You hear me? Fun!"

"Simon, it's literally just us here," Quinn says as she and I walk toward the door, lifting Grace out of her play area. "You don't need to shout."

"I'm not shouting. This is excitement," he says. "Now get out there. It's party day!"

Simon swings the door back open and exits the bar, leaving us wondering what the hell we've gotten into.

"Ready for a party?"

Grace, on cue, starts clapping excitedly.

"All right, then. Let's party."

———

"We didn't do anything. How is today so tiring?"

That one statement makes the entire table laugh, which consists of Simon and Charlie, Ainsley, Maeve and her husband Logan, as well as Stella and her boyfriend, Emmett.

"Because this is a different kind of tired," Maeve explains. "You're probably just getting used to normal parent tired. Operating on three hours of sleep, caffeine, and a sheer will to not have the day beat you. Your body is now used to that tired and can function normally."

"But today…" Charlie cuts in. "Today has new activities. Not the normal day. And sometimes, those ones knock you on your ass more than a day where you change twenty diapers and the kid decides that she's giving up naps for Lent."

It makes sense. My body feels like it's been through it, and all I've done is guide Grace around a bounce house, help her open presents, and change her outfit three times because my girl is playing, and eating, like it's going out of style.

It's fine, though. Gives me an excuse to try on all of her new bows.

It was a buy-one-get-one-free sale. And I'm learning that I can't be trusted with a baby clothing sale.

"Well what about you two?" Stella asks. "When is our newest couple going to celebrate Quinn's return home and new job?"

We look at each other and shrug. "Not sure. I think we both kind of figured this was it?"

"Plus, when are we going to do that?" Quinn adds. "Between Grace, the bar, and the move, we haven't really had a free second."

Quinn's siblings all share a knowing glance before turning back to us.

"What are you plotting?" Quinn asks. "If this is another Quinn-tervention, I assure you, I'm healed from whatever it is y'all think you need to fix with me."

Maeve shakes her head. "No interventions. Just a night out."

I look to Quinn, who looks as confused as I do, before looking back to Maeve. "Night out?"

"Exactly," Ainsley says. "You two have been through a lot over the past few months. And while we know you said this party was for both of you, clearly, the kids are having more of a time than y'all are."

Everyone turns to the bounce house, which I didn't realize there were going to be two—one for big kids and one for Grace —where I can see Wes's oldest daughter carrying Grace out of her mini funhouse. Her cheeks are rosy, and she's clearly having the time of her life.

"Yeah," Simon says. "I probably went a little too hard into the kid activities. My bad."

"But without my brother doing this," Stella says, "it wouldn't have given us the idea to give you two a much deserved night off."

"Guys, I appreciate it," I say. "But I don't—"

"Whatever you're going to object to, we've got it covered," Maeve says. "We already talked to Jenny, and she's going to be at the bar helping Stella, Emmett, and Simon pour drinks."

"I'm like a celebrity bartender," Simon says, a big grin across his face.

"Make him stop," Emmett groans into Stella's shoulder.

Simon slaps Emmett on the back. "Nope! We're going to have fun!"

"Wow, I…" I'm speechless. "But what about Grace?"

"I'm on Grace duty," Ainsley says. "I'll take her to Mom and Dad's. That way when you get home from your night out in Nashville, you have the house completely to yourself. She'll spend the night with me over there and then I'll bring her back in the morning."

"Night in Nashville?" Quinn asks. "Why are we going to Nashville?"

At that moment, Logan hands me an envelope. "Two tickets for tonight's hockey game. I hear that it's the championship series? Or whatever the terminology is for that."

Quinn and I look at each other in shock because we've been following each game of the series every night at the bar. Tonight the Music City Rockers could win the cup.

"Logan. We can't—"

"Oh, and be ready at four-thirty," Maeve says. "That's when the limo will be picking you up to take you to your dinner at our favorite Nashville steakhouse. And before you object, it's already paid for, so you can't say no."

I'm speechless and stunned. But in the midst of that, for some reason, I happen to notice a car pulling into the parking lot. There's a sign out front that says we're closed this afternoon for a private event, but even if it was someone coming to the party, I don't recognize the car. And I would. It's a bright orange sedan, a color that would be remembered.

I stare at it for a second, and I can't see much past the tinted windows. It stops for a second, and I think my eyes are playing tricks on me, but I could swear the person driving could pass for my mother. An older version. But still, the resemblance, even through the glaring sun, is striking.

But just as quickly as they pull in, the car backs up and burns rubber out of the parking lot.

Fucking weird…

"So what do you say, you two?" Stella says, turning me back to our conversation. "Are you ready for a night out?"

Quinn and I look at each other, smiles big on both of our faces.

"What do ya' say, Hurricane? Want to go out on our first date?"

guide to love rule #88

When parents are given a night out, they should take full advantage. This includes, but is not limited to, modes of transportation that are equipped for extracurricular activities.

30

quinn

"THAT GAME WAS EPIC! I CAN'T BELIEVE WE GOT TO SEE THEM RAISE the cup."

The adrenaline is still pumping through me as we leave the arena in downtown Nashville and make our way to the limo that Logan set up for us. The air is electric around the city right now, and part of me doesn't want to leave the celebration. The other part of me wants to celebrate with Porter in the back of a limo.

Because…limo sex. Duh.

"That shot at the end? The game winner? It came out of nowhere."

"So fucking good," I say, falling into Porter's outstretched arm as we start to battle postgame Nashville traffic. "That game? Dinner? Tonight has just been—"

"Perfect," Porter says as he kisses the top of my head. "Absolutely perfect."

The limo starts to slowly move as I lay against Porter. The night *was* perfect. The restaurant that Logan and Maeve picked for us was by far the best place I've ever eaten in my life. I'm pretty sure Porter moaned when he cut into his steak. And I couldn't blame him. The noise that came out of my mouth when

I bit into my filet mignon was something that Porter's only heard in the privacy of his bedroom.

And then there was the game, which was fucking insane. One of those games that you brag to your friends about that you got to witness in person. And watching it in club seats with unlimited food and beverage? I know the next time I go and sit in regular seats I'll feel like a peasant. I really need to thank my sister for marrying a billionaire.

And even though the hometown Music City Rockers won the game, and the championship tonight, the biggest win is that Porter and I only called the bar and Ainsley twice each. We tried to call one more time to each, but the line to the bar was conveniently busy and Ainsley sent us to voicemail.

"Remind me to thank your family again for tonight," Porter says as his head falls to rest on top of mine. "This was…I can't imagine a better first date."

"We did things so ass backwards." My comment makes him laugh, but it's true. Because in nowhere in any book of how to date do you sleep with a man for eight years and then decide to become a couple. And then go out on a date.

"I think it all happened like it was supposed to. Neither of us were ready for anything serious. We had our reasons, and they were valid. I think the world worked in a mysterious way that put us together exactly when it was supposed to."

I sit up from his hold, because while this night is perfect and I don't want to ruin it, there's one thing that's been on my mind for weeks now.

"Can I ask you something?"

"Of course."

"That day at the diner, you told Emily—"

"Quinn, I hate that she's—"

"No," I shake my head, really needing to get this off my chest. "It's not about Emily. Well, directly."

He lets out a breath. "Okay…"

"When you said to her that you were a dumb kid who was

hurt because the girl you loved didn't want you, was that girl… did you mean…"

I watch as his worried look turns to relief. "Did I mean you?"

"Yeah. I mean, I know you asked me out in high school, and I was a stupid girl who said no because I didn't think you were serious. But I know you had to be asking out other girls so I don't want to be conceited enough to think—"

I have more to say, but I currently can't because Porter's mouth is on mine, his force taking me so hard that we're now lying across the perimeter seat of the limo. While I really want the answer to my question in words, this answer isn't bad. Not in the least.

"So was that a yes?"

Porter laughs as he buries his head in my neck, but doesn't make a motion to sit us back up. "Yes that was a yes. Because contrary to popular belief, I didn't date much in high school."

"Really? I always feel like some girl was hanging around you."

"They were," he admits. "And I was always nice to them. A few I went out with for a couple of dates or took to dances. But none of them caught my interest. None of them wanted to make me see them every day, or talk to them about anything and everything. But you? Now you were a different story."

I feel my face start to blush. "Really? Was this before or after I tried to invent the fake foreign exchange student?"

"Before," he says with a smile. "There was…there was no one like you. What girl could talk hockey in one breath, get an A in English the next, and then after school organize the senior prank?"

"I'm one of a kind, what can I say?"

"You are," he drops a kiss on me before slightly pulling away. "I know you're probably saying that sarcastically, because that's what you do. But I mean it in the most sincere way…

"Porter…"

"No, you need to hear this, and I hope you know how much I

mean it. But if someone were to ask me who my ideal, perfect woman was, and I had never met you before, I'd somehow still describe you."

I think with every word that comes out of his mouth, my eyes get a little bigger.

"I know you kept your heart guarded for a lot of your life. I get why. I hate that you had to, but I understand your reasons. I want you to know, though, here and now, that it's safe with me. You're safe with me. Because our timing might be unusual; our story might be the most unique and random love story ever told, but it's ours. So yes, I loved you back then, how a teenage boy thinks he's in love. And today I'm madly in love with woman you are. Because like you, us? Our story? Our love. It's one of a kind."

I've toyed with the idea of writing a book at some point in my life, but no way on Dolly Parton's green Earth could I have ever come up with words more beautiful than the ones Porter just said.

I pull him down on me, kissing him with everything I have. Who says things like that? That's the shit that romcoms are made of. And in those movies, I always figured I was the best friend. The funny sidekick. Not the leading lady.

But here I am, insanely in love with a man who loves me back. A man who currently can't put up the privacy screen fast enough so our poor driver doesn't have to see what's about to happen. A love that I never thought I could have, and this is just the beginning.

Porter's hands push up the jersey I wore tonight, and I smile as I watch in real time his reaction to what I'm wearing underneath.

"Is that?"

I sit up, giving him a hard kiss before I make my way to the floor of the limo. "The lingerie I wore the day I thought you requested an early booty call? Yes."

Porter watches as I lay back on the floor of the limo, doing my best to take off my leggings in a semi-sexy way, leaving me in nothing but the royal blue lace bodysuit. Porter's eyes haven't even blinked as I get back to my knees. "Fucking gorgeous."

"I thought it would be a nice surprise for you," I say as I work his belt loose. "Now how about another surprise?"

He lifts up slightly so I can pull his jeans and boxer briefs down, springing free his cock. I don't say anything else as I lick my lips before letting my tongue trace around the tip.

"Quinn…"

"Shhh…" I say, my hand working his dick as I lick my lips. "Now it's my turn to take care of you."

Porter throws his head back the second my mouth is on him, his body relaxing under my touch as I begin to suck. I don't know if it's the thrill of doing this in the limo, the lingerie I'm wearing, or the noises starting to come from Porter, but I feel all sorts of sexy right now. The surge of confidence speeds up my motions, my hand and my mouth bobbing up and down on him faster and faster.

"Fuck yes," he says, his hands now gripping at my hair. "God, you take my cock so good."

Never in a million years would I have ever thought I had a praise kink. But from the first time Porter told me that I was a good girl, I was fucking done. And those words? Combined with how I'm already feeling? Holy shit, I'd do just about anything he asked right now.

Including that. Yup. That.

Feeling a little daring, I open up wider and lower my tongue, taking him all the way to the back of my throat.

"Quinn! Fucking hell…"

"Shhh…," I say as I take the chance to catch my breath. I didn't realize I could actually take it all. Yay me. "He's going to hear you."

"Don't care," he says as he quickly grabs my arms and pulls me to him. "And if he didn't hear that, he's sure as hell going to hear what's coming."

Our lips connect in a frenzy as I straddle Porter, his hand immediately going for my pussy. I lift up slightly, not sure what he's trying to do, when I feel his hand moving the lace to the side, leaving me open for him.

"I need you," he says, bringing me down on his dick. "I need you so fucking much."

I feel every inch of him as he slides inside me. I can't help but throw my head back as I start bouncing on his cock, loving how he feels bare inside me.

"You're so fucking gorgeous," he says, his hands massaging my tits through the lace. "Do you know I've dreamed of fucking you in this? This lace has been the star of my dreams for weeks."

I tilt my head back up to look at him, only to see nothing but heat in his eyes. "Then let's make your dreams come true."

I continue to fuck him, but bring his head to my chest, his mouth immediately starting to kiss the exposed skin. He pushes the lace that's covering my nipple to the side, bringing it to his mouth as he continues to fuck me.

"Yes," I say, loving the two sensations at the same time. "So good."

I feel the limousine starting to speed up, which apparently kicks up a gear in both of us. Porter kisses my lips one more time before rolling me off of him onto the seat so he can make his way to the floor of the vehicle.

"Spread those legs, beautiful."

I do as he says, not able to take my eyes off him as he shoves the lace aside again as he pushes back into me. Between the speed of the limo, and the force of Porter, I feel like I'm melting into the seat. And I don't care one fucking bit because I never want this feeling to end.

"That's it," he says as my hands go around his neck, holding on for dear life. His speed is picking up, his grip on my legs becoming tighter as he drives into me harder and harder.

"Porter! Yes! Fuck!"

The second my orgasm hits me, a loud grunt echoes through

the limo, Porter collapsing on me as his does the same. I cling to his back, feeling like if I don't hold on I might fly away. The high right now is that good. He must feel the same as he has me in his arms in an instant, holding me tight as we both come down.

"I love you," I whisper into his ear. The three words are simple, and I feel so much more than that, but right now, that's all I can think to say. "I love you so much."

He brings me in, our kiss much gentler than what we just did to this poor limo. When he releases me, his hand on the back of my neck, he doesn't let me go far, our foreheads touching as our gazes lock.

"I don't know if I'll ever get tired of hearing that," he says. "Or saying it. Because I love you too."

We kiss again, and don't stop until we pull up to his driveway in Rolling Hills. In fact, we got so lost in each other that we both forgot to get dressed as the limo comes to a stop.

But that's what you do when you fall in love. At least, that's what I assume. You get lost in each other. Forget about time. Forget to put on your pants when the limo driver knocks on the door.

Because when you find a love like this, there's not a timetable. You're not counting down until you leave.

Because you know you're going to stay. Forever.

31
porter

"Porter...can you say Porter?"

"Gah goo ooo."

"Close," I say, though it's not close. But she's cute, so she gets a pass. "How about Po Po? Pah? Come on, baby girl. I know it's hard, but you can do it. You can do anything."

The more I ask Grace to say my name, even if I'm using the gentlest of my baby voices, her look to me is still the same.

Simply: What the fuck do you want me to do? Isn't it enough that I'm adorable?

And she is, especially since the bow she's wearing today is literally as big as her head. I mean, it had pasta noodles on it. How was I not supposed to buy it?

"Bah bah!"

"Yeah yeah, you got 'bottle' down, don't you," I say as I hand her the sippy cup that I realize she means. "One day, little one. One day."

"Still nothing on the name front?"

"No," I groan as Quinn enters the house and I roll to my back on the floor. The second I'm not looking at her, Grace does her downward dog/army crawl to the new toy she's been obsessed with.

It's a mixing spoon and bowl. And not even one that came in the kids' kitchen set I spotted at the store the other day that I might've bought. Nope. Just a regular old spoon and bowl.

"I know you want the words, but I want the steps," Quinn says as she sits down next to me. "She's so close."

I really didn't understand the true meaning of baby-proofing a house until the past few weekends. I thought I had it covered. But then I saw a parenting blog about when they start walking, how much more they can get into, and it's then that I realized my house was a walking death trap.

It wasn't. Just a few things in her reach that I wasn't ready for.

But, because of that, I summoned Wes, Simon, and a few of their friends to help me Grace-proof this house.

Now the house is padded, plugs are covered, and nothing is within her small reach. Now, we're just ready for the steps.

And it's not like she's behind. We're just impatient. According to the pediatrician and every baby blog in existence, she is a little delayed on her words, but we're told it was nothing to cause concern about considering the upheaval in her life, and us not knowing anything major in her developmental history. The doc even said if that's all that's wrong to consider myself lucky. He's shocked by how well adjusted she is and how good she took being thrust into a life she didn't know. She's eating well—the white board is constantly updated. She sleeps through most nights and is overall a very happy baby. When I think about it, it really makes me wonder how overwhelmed Missy had to be, or how hard it was raising her in the same house as Bonnie, for her to give her up. Because this little one is a light on a dark day, and I know my life is going to be better with her in it.

"How was book club?" I ask Quinn as she comes to lay down next to me.

"Great!" She says, sitting up, nothing but excitement radiating from her. "The kids are loving it. They're at the part where…"

She doesn't trail off. In fact, she starts talking a million miles a minute about a middle-school novel that I knew nothing about before Quinn Banks came into my life, and now I know everything. And yes, I'm listening. It means a lot to her, so of course I am. But I can't stop watching her features as she goes on about the book, the students, and how much fun everyone is having. When Quinn is like this? Free and truly happy? There's nothing more beautiful.

"Oh! And listen to this! I was talking with one of the sixth-grade teachers today. She saw me in the library and wanted to introduce herself. She came in at the end of the book club meeting so we started chatting about what I was doing. As we were talking, we came up with idea for a virtual book club for classes this year! It's like a buddy reading, pen pal thing. How awesome is that going to be?"

I lean up to meet her, because I can't help but kiss the girl right now. "It sounds amazing."

"I'm so excited," she says as she situates herself on the floor with me. "Being in that library today, even though school is still a few months away, it feels so right."

"Was it strange?" I ask. "Being back in school, that is?"

She shakes her head as she links her fingers through mine as we watch Grace bang on the bowl. "Not as much as I expected. Honestly, when they told me I could go in during the summer to get everything ready, I figured it was a test to see if the building would collapse from the second I opened the door."

"Did it?"

She looks back at me, a mocking glare being thrown my way. "No, smarty pants. It didn't. The door did get stuck for a second, so I was convinced they already locked me out, but I just gave it a tug."

I laugh. "Well, that's good. I'm glad you're liking it."

"It's going to be so great," she says. "Mrs. Metcalf left everything in perfect order. It'll take me a minute to familiarize myself with her system, but she left it foolproof for me. I've even started researching some new books to add that I know were a hit back in my former classes."

"I love this for you," I say, kissing her cheek as she cuddles into me. "Though I must say, I'll miss you at the bar."

Quinn rolls over to face me. "You'll just miss slapping my ass."

I shrug. "That, and other things."

Since it's still the summer, we're still taking shifts between the bar and Grace, though it's been busy on Fridays and Saturdays, so we've been working both nights together and have found a sitter for Grace. Luckily, Wes's daughter is more responsible than most adults I know and Grace loves her. But the time is going to come when Quinn is back at school, so I'll need to hire someone to fill her spot. She tried to say that she could do both, but I assured her I didn't want her burning the candle at both ends. When she still tried to fight me, I told her that if she was now a customer, because she was living with and dating the owner, that she got free food and beverage. Once I promised that could also apply to her sisters, she got on board.

It's a small price to pay for a happy, and relaxed, Quinn.

"You know," she whispers as she starts giving me small, but frequent kisses. "There are some things I always wanted to do at the bar. And if I'm not working there, I'm not sure if we can ever do them?"

"Oh really?" I pull her in even closer, stealing a few more kisses along the way. "Care to tell me what they are?"

"Let's just say it involves me on top of the bar. You can let your imagination take it from there."

My groan is swallowed by her lips on mine, and shit, if she keeps talking like that, I might just have her work one day a week. Just for the benefits.

I'm starting to get lost in Quinn's mouth when I hear something that I'm not used to so I slowly pull away from Quinn. Except when I open my eyes, I'm looking at something I've never seen before.

"Quinn. Quinn! She's up!"

I hurry and point as Quinn rolls away from me just as Grace let's go of the coffee table she was holding onto and starts walking toward us.

Walking!

"Oh my God, Oh my God! It's happening!" Quinn yells, rolling around like a maniac trying to find her phone. "Where the fuck is it, I'm not going to miss this!"

We both sit up, neither of us taking our eyes off of Grace as she waddles over to us.

"There we go, Grace. You got this, baby girl!"

She takes another four steps, and just as Quinn finds her phone and starts to hit record, Grace plops on her butt, a big smile from ear to ear.

"I'm so proud of you!" I scoop her up and hold her above me, kissing her all over, which always makes her laugh. "You're such a big girl! You walked!"

Her addictive baby giggles fill the room as Quinn and I love on her, setting her back down on the ground to see if she can do it again. She does, which Quinn gets on video this time, but falls pretty quickly.

It's fine. She walked. And I've never been so simultaneously proud and terrified.

"I can't believe she did it," Quinn says.

"This is cause for celebration!" I yell, picking Grace up and tossing her in the air. "Dinner. Out. We're closing down the bar tonight so we can properly celebrate. The old geezers will understand."

"Really?" Quinn says. "You're going to close down the bar for her first steps? What happens when she learns to pee in the potty?"

"Not sure. We'll cross that bridge when we get there. But tonight, this little girl earned herself all the pasta her little mouth and hands can handle."

Quinn laughs, kisses me on the cheek, before taking Grace

out of my arms. "Well then, let's take this little one for her nap. Get her nice and rested for her big night out."

"Perfect," I say, kissing both of them on the cheek before Quinn walks her upstairs.

I fall back onto the couch, the smile on my face a mile wide. How is this my life? Toys are scattered on my floor. I keep diapers in my entertainment center to save me from going upstairs every time Grace needs changed. I wash sippy cups and baby silverware every night. And yet, I wouldn't trade it for the world.

I know that if Grace wouldn't have come into my life, and Quinn wouldn't have moved home, I would've been fine being a bachelor. I don't think I would've given any thought at all to one day wanting to settle down and start a family. I can thank my likely mommy issues for that one.

But now that I know what it's like? To see how Grace looks at me each day, even in her resting confused face? Falling asleep next to Quinn every night? Mornings with the three of us snuggled in bed together? I wouldn't trade it for the world.

I push myself up from the couch, knowing I should probably take the down time to pick up the toys that will just be discarded again later, when I hear a knock on the door. It's the middle of the afternoon, so I have no idea who it could be. No one comes to my house. Deliveries get left on the porch. But after a few more knocks, clearly telling me they aren't going away, I pick myself up off the couch to open the door to see a mid-twenty something male in an ill-fitting suit.

"Can I help you?"

"Are you Porter McCoy?"

"Yes. That's me. Why do you—"

"Here." He pushes an envelope into my hands. "You've been served."

Did he just say served? As in legally served?

"What? By who?"

The twerp doesn't answer me as he nearly runs off my porch,

jumping in his car and peeling out of the parking lot and down the road.

"What was that?"

I don't answer Quinn right away as I sit on the couch and stare at the envelope. "I think I'm getting sued?"

"Sued? Who the hell would sue you? Make someone's drink wrong? They twist an ankle in the parking lot? Oh, I swear to God if Emily is on her bullshit…"

I don't blink as I tear the envelope open. I start reading it, but the words are just blurring together in my haste. I put it down, trying to refocus. The only problem is that when I do, I see words and names I never wanted to see.

"Holy shit," I whisper as I read it again.

"What? What is it?"

I look up to Quinn as I feel all of the color and blood drain from my face.

"Porter, you're scaring me. Who is suing you?"

"My…my mom."

"Your mom?" Quinn takes the papers from me.

I sit in silence as Quinn reads over the document. I feel her tense next to me when she gets to the part I just read.

A custody petition. From Bonnie McCoy Higgins. For the legal guardianship of Grace Higgins.

"Fucking Christ," I spit out as I spring up from the couch and start pacing the living room. "Last week. The party. There was a car that pulled in. I couldn't really see in it, but I could've sworn it was my mom."

"Seriously? Why didn't you say anything?"

"Because I thought my eyes were playing tricks on me. She hasn't been back to Rolling Hills in close to twenty-five years. There's no reason for her to be back here."

Except there is.

And for some reason, she wants the little girl who's become my entire world.

"Hey," Quinn says, her arms wrapping around me from the

back. "I know this is scary. But we're going to get through this. No one is taking Grace away from us."

Us...

That one word somehow calms me in the chaos that's my brain right now. Because Quinn's right—we're a team now. Together. And I don't know what the fuck my mother wants, or what her game is, but she's not going to win.

I'm not going to let her.

This is my family now. And no one, and I mean no one, is going to fuck with my family and get away with it.

32
porter

I DON'T KNOW WHY, BUT I NEVER DELETED MY MOTHER'S PHONE number. The last time I used it was almost nine years ago, when I realized Pops didn't have that much longer to live. I thought she'd want to know that her ex-husband and the father of one of her children was dying. She then had the audacity to ask me if he had left her anything in his will. I don't even think I said goodbye when I hung up on her.

I should've deleted it then. I had no reason to talk to her again after that. Yet, there was something that always made me keep it. I guess that something is today.

"Are you sure you want to do this?" Quinn asks, holding my hands as I stare down at the screen. All I need to do is hit the green button and the call would go through. But I've been staring at it, frozen, for the past ten minutes.

In reality, I've been in a daze for the past few hours. Once it hit me what she was doing, I couldn't concentrate on anything else and all thoughts of a celebratory dinner were out the window. I knew I needed to call Bonnie and try to figure out what her game was, but I didn't trust myself to not lose it and scare Gracie. So Quinn and I hurriedly packed her up and took her to Wes and Betsy's. They told me they'd keep her as long as I needed. Which is good, because once I speak to Bonnie, I have no idea what's going to happen.

"I have to. Something doesn't feel right about this. She's up to something."

"How do you know?"

"Because even though I haven't had a relationship with her since I was a teenager, I know my mother well enough to know that she wouldn't be doing this without a reason. And before I get lawyers involved, I need to know what I'm up against."

Before I lose my nerve, I let go of Quinn's hands for just the second I need to hit the call button and switch onto speakerphone.

The phone only rings once before my mother's voice sends a chill down my spine.

"I was wondering when I'd hear from you."

"Bonnie," I say evenly, not giving her the satisfaction of hearing me riled up. Or calling her "Mom," because she sure as shit doesn't deserve that title.

"How are you? How's my granddaughter? I've wanted to—"

"Cut the crap, Bonnie. What do you want?"

I hear her snicker, which is somehow more cruel than the custody petition. "Can't we catch up? It's been so long."

This woman's audacity is growing with every word that comes out of her mouth. "You want to catch up? Then meet me at The Joint in an hour."

"The Joint? Oh Porter, you know I can't do that. I don't live—"

"Don't lie. I saw you the other day. I know you're in town. Be there in an hour."

I hang up the phone before she can say anything else.

"Do you think she'll come?"

"Yeah. Whatever game she wants to play, she needs me for it. She'll be there."

"Hey," Quinn turns me to face her as the adrenaline rush crashes through me. "Are you okay? Are you ready for this?"

My head falls, suddenly the impact of everything hitting me. I'm about to see my mom. And she wants Grace.

"I have to be," I say. "I have no other choice."

"You could just get lawyers involved," Quinn says. "If it's too much to face her, let the lawyers handle it."

I shake my head. "I will if I need to. But she's here, and she's choosing to fuck with my family. And no one, not even blood, fucks with my family."

"Okay then," Quinn says as she stands up and she starts swinging her arms around.

"What are you doing?"

"Warming up," she says.

"For what?"

Quinn comes back to me, bending over with her hands on my thighs so she can look me right in the eye. "For a fight. She's not just fucking with you, she's fucking with me too. You. Me. Grace. We're a family. The people I love. And no one fucks with the people I love and gets away with it."

I let out a deep breath, and for the first time since I opened that envelope, I feel a little more at ease.

"I love you, you know that, right?"

She gives me a quick kiss. "I do. Now let's go fight your mom."

———

"Well, this place hasn't changed." One hour and fifteen minutes later, the woman I haven't seen in nearly twenty years saunters into the bar. "Aren't you gonna give your mother a hug?

My eyes are trained on her, not giving her an ounce of emotion. "Sit, Bonnie."

"My my, and here I thought I was missing out on all that Southern hospitality when I moved away from this shithole town."

Bonnie finally sits, and it's then she takes notice to Quinn.

"And who is this?"

She holds out her hand, but Quinn doesn't give it back to her. "I'm the woman you really don't want to fuck with."

Bonnie clutches her non-existent pearls at Quinn's comeback. "Porter. Are you going to let your girlfriend talk to me that way?"

I don't look over to Quinn immediately, but I can tell she's trying to get my attention through her sideways glance. Did Bonnie guess that she's my girlfriend? Or has her visit in town included some detective work?

"She's a grown woman. She can talk to you however she sees fit."

"But I don't want to be more rude than I suspect I'm going to be during this conversation." Quinn now extends her hand. "Quinn Banks. Now what the fuck do you want?"

Bonnie looks at Quinn's hand then back to me. "I remember you. Porter? You're seriously dating that awful girl who released toads in the town square?"

Quinn dramatically takes a bow. "Why, Bonnie, I'm flattered. I didn't realize I was so memorable."

The two women have a stare down, and if my entire life wasn't on the line right now, I'd think it was comical.

"How long have you been here?" My question breaks their stare.

She shrugs. "Long enough."

"How did no one see you?"

"I have my ways."

She's bluffing, or at least exaggerating how long she's been in town. It's the only thing that makes sense. Rolling Hills isn't that big. Not many people move out. Fewer move in. But if she would've made her face seen at any point, someone would have told me. Because she might look twenty years older, and on the outside it looks like she's lived a hard life, but she'll always have those damn green eyes.

Plus, everyone remembers, and hates, the woman who ran

out of town, leaving her husband and son. Someone would've told me if she was here. And since the party was just a few days ago, I have to think that's around the time she arrived.

"So these?" I toss the envelope on the table. "You had to have someone bring them to me? Couldn't do it yourself?"

"That was my lawyer's doing," she says. "But I hate that we even have to get the lawyers involved. So I thought I'd come down here and see if we could come to an agreement. Plus, I missed this town."

Now I know that's a lie, but Bonnie pretends as if she truly misses this bar as she stands up and starts looking around. It's like she's having some sort of nostalgic moment. Which she's not. This bar was my father's pride and joy. He renovated it from the shack it was and turned it into a town institution. He poured blood, sweat, and tears into this place.

And my mother had always resented him for that. Forget that this place kept a roof over our head and food on the table. To her it was just something that she wasn't a part of, and her ego couldn't handle it.

"You know, no matter what I did, your father never loved me as much as he loved this bar."

"Gee, shocking," Quinn says. "With your sparkling personality, I can't imagine why."

The two have another stare down before Bonnie turns back to looking at the wall, this one filled with pictures of Pops and I, and bar regulars, over the years. And the newest additions, pictures of myself, Grace, and Quinn.

"You know, when I left, he didn't give me a dime. I had to fight tooth and nail in divorce court."

"Do you think he was hiding money from you?" I ask. "I don't know what kind of business you think this place does, but I assure you we're not sitting on a gold mine."

She waves off my statement and comes back to sit down.

"That's neither here nor there," she says. "What I came for is Grace. Where is she, by the way? I'd love to hold her."

"Where she's at is of no concern to you," I say. "And where do you think you get off requesting custody? And why all of a sudden? Or did you just realize that your daughter and grand-daughter were gone two months later?"

"I take offense to that."

"You should," Quinn says.

Bonnie shoots a look to her. "I don't like you very much."

Quinn smirks with a nonchalant shrug. "Good."

Now, as much as I'd love Quinn to go full-Quinn on my mother, I need to get this back on track.

"Whatever this petition is, it's going to get thrown out," I say. "Missy wrote a letter specifically asking me to raise Grace. I'm not a lawyer, but that has to count for something in court."

"You think they're going to believe a single mom who got pregnant at nineteen who abandoned her daughter? Or me, her mother? The woman who gave them shelter and food because she didn't have a job?"

"Are you talking about the same woman who also aban-doned her first family twenty years ago? That was you, wasn't it? Or am I missing something?"

If Quinn didn't say it, I was going to. And frankly, her added snark made the dig that much better.

"Bonnie, why do you want custody?" I ask. "Grace is happy and healthy with me. That's all you should care about."

"That's great to hear, but let's be real, Porter, you can't raise a child."

"And you can?" I punch back. "Rich, considering I haven't seen you in twenty years, before that Pops raised me, and your daughter specifically drove down here to make sure you didn't raise your granddaughter."

Bonnie's eyes narrow at me. "Watch your tone."

"Or what? Now you want to be a mother? Practicing how you'll raise Grace? Cut the shit, Bonnie. Why do you want Grace?"

"Because I miss her!" she exclaims before her shoulders slump and her eyes turn defeated. She's trying to fake a "woe is me" act, but I'm not buying it. "She's my granddaughter. My blood. Missy… well…Missy was a difficult kid. She never understood how much I loved her. And Grace…I just love that little girl so much, and if Missy can't raise her, well, then I only think it's right that I do."

Quinn and I are both silent, because it's quite a sob story, but I'd bet the bar that it's ninety-five percent a lie.

"You want us to buy that?"

"It's the truth," she says. "And no matter what you say or think about me, I have rights too."

"Really? Rights? What kind of rights?"

Bonnie lays out the paperwork that was sent to me. I didn't look through all of them, so I'm not exactly sure what this one says. "In Indiana there's a thing called de facto custodian. And because Missy was in and out of my house the entire first year of Grace's life—she really was a horrible mother—per the law, I am considered her de facto custodian. Which, I'm sure if I took this to a police department, you could be charged with kidnapping my grandchild."

"Oh, for fuck's sake lady, the delusion is strong with you, isn't it?"

"I'd watch that smart mouth of yours," Bonnie says. "I'm petitioning the court to give me custody. And since I'm assuming that you two are going to continue to play the little family, that means they'll be visiting you both. I'm sure with someone who has the arrest record you do, it probably wouldn't look good in front of a judge."

"Hey! I resent that!" Quinn screams, standing and smacking the table. "Eight arrests. Eight charges dropped. My record is clean, lady."

Bonnie only snickers. "You two think you're so high and mighty here. Well, guess what, you're wrong. Grace is going to be coming home with me. Whether you two like it or not."

"Bring it on bitch," Quinn says as I'm too overwhelmed to speak. "You have no idea what you're up against."

The two have one last staredown before Bonnie grabs her purse and exits the bar. I don't move as she does. Because all I can think is that she's right. There's a chance, at least a small one, that a court could side with her.

And that small chance is far too big for my liking.

"Hey," Quinn says. "Don't think like that."

I don't know how Quinn could read my mind, but I'm grateful that she did.

"What am I going to do?"

"Easy," she says. "We're going to round up my family."

guide to love rule #59

Know which sibling to call when you need a body buried. If you're that sibling, make sure to bring a lot of shovels.

33

quinn

QUINN

SIBLINGS! I'm sending out the bat signal.

SIMON

Oh my God! I'm included!

QUINN

Fuck yeah, you are. There's a problem. And I
need all of you.

MAEVE

What's the matter?

AINSLEY

Is everything okay with Grace?

QUINN

Physically yes, so no one worry about that. But,
there's a situation that has come up that I need
all the Banks siblings and significant others
help with.

SIMON

What's the matter, Quinn? How deep are you
in? I knew one day I'd be bailing you out of jail.

QUINN

No bail money needed. Yet.

AINSLEY

Quinn, you're scaring me.

QUINN

It's too much to text but here's the short version: Porter's bitch of a mother is in town and served him with papers to take custody of Grace.

SIMON

Oh, absolutely the fuck not.

STELLA

I'll start digging for dirt on her. I'll have a full file by the morning.

MAEVE

We'll be there first thing.

AINSLEY

Quinn, try and get some sleep tonight. But please know, we're not going to let anything happen to Grace, or you and Porter.

"So what are your siblings going to do?" Porter asks as we walk out of the house first thing the next morning. "I feel like if one of them was an attorney, that would help more than Simon's bounce house guy."

"I'm not exactly sure, but Maeve likes to joke that each of us have a duty if a body needs buried."

"Quinn, I love you and your determination right now, but what the hell does that have to do with our situation?"

I give him a comforting smile. "Everything. Because we're going to bury Bonnie. And when we're done, she's going to regret ever stepping foot back in Rolling Hills."

Porter and I didn't sleep a wink last night, though we both pretended to. Grace stayed the night with Wes and Betsy, and they're going to keep her until at least this meeting is done. The house was too quiet, and I couldn't turn off my brain. Because while I don't think a judge would seriously grant custody to that nut job, the possibility is there.

And that's where my mind started fucking with me.

Because if we go before a judge, I know what I'm going to need to do. I'm going to have to step back and leave Porter.

I know my record doesn't have any convictions, but it isn't exactly clean either. Especially in the court of public opinion. There's also the evidence of social media posts that will live forever about the teacher who told a group of mothers to go fuck themselves.

And I might be a different person, an employee of a school and not the prankster I once was, but I know I probably can't help Porter's case.

Which is when it hit me, roughly around four-thirteen in the morning, that if it came down to it, I was going to remove myself out of Porter's life. Even if just for the time being, to make sure he stayed with Grace. I'm not going to be the reason he doesn't keep that little girl.

Now I can only hope that it doesn't come down to that.

"Your siblings are already here?"

I shake myself out of my intrusive thoughts to see that there are four cars parked out front of The Joint, and all my siblings, along with Logan and Emmett, are waiting at the door.

"You had to know I wasn't going to be here on time," I joke, hugging each one of them because I'm so freaking grateful they're here.

"We'd hoped that being with Porter now would make you punctual."

He groans as he unlocks the door. "If anything, she's rubbing off on me."

There's laughter as we walk into The Joint, but it quickly dies down as we take our seats around the big table in the middle of the bar.

"I brought coffee," Simon says, passing around cups with our names on them. "If there's an emergency that calls for a late-night text and an early morning meeting, we need to be caffeinated."

"God love your wife for knowing that the diner needed a coffee station," I say, taking a big sip of the iced caramel goodness.

"She's sorry she couldn't make it this morning, but if she needs to do anything, just give her the signal."

"Coffee is enough," Porter says. "Though honestly, I don't know what any of you can do. This…this is a messy situation that I hate getting anyone else involved in."

"Messy?" Stella says, her eyes getting excited. "The Banks family is very good at messy."

"How about you tell us why we're all here," Maeve says, getting things in order. "And then let's see how many favors we need to call in."

Porter doesn't say anything, instead just shows everyone the papers he was delivered yesterday.

"Are these what I think they are?" Maeve asks as Logan and Simon start pouring through them.

"A petition for custody of Grace? That would be correct."

For the next few minutes, Porter and I fill them in on Bonnie's sudden appearance and enough backstory to what's relevant for now. He also tells them all about Missy, more details about the day Grace was left, and the letter she included that he still has.

"Wow! What a bitch! How dare she come in and think she's going to take Grace away from you two!"

"Exactly!" I tip my finger to Ainsley, completely agreeing with her assessment of the Bonnie situation. "She *is* a bitch."

"She really just came here and demanded custody?" Stella asks. "Has she even contacted you since Missy left Grace here?"

"Not once," Porter says. "And honestly, I don't know how she even knew Missy brought her here. From what it sounded like, Missy's cut her out of her life."

"Can't say I blame her," Ainsley mutters.

"Cut out of life or not, bitch or not, this is a problem," Maeve says. "This is probably me being a little too glass-half-empty, but she is your mother and Grace's grandmother. You can't assume a court is going to give you Grace, letter or not."

Everyone falls to a silence while I notice Logan and Simon taking a look at the papers that were served.

"Are they legit?" I ask. "For all I know she downloaded copies online and paid some kid to deliver them."

Logan looks it over again before taking off his glasses and rubbing his eyes. "I'm not a lawyer, but I've seen enough legal papers over my life to be able to decipher the real ones versus the fakes. From my barely trained eye, they look legitimate."

"Do you have a lawyer?" Simon asks. "I know a few who handle family law."

Porter nods. "Yes, I have one. The only problem is that when I called him last night, he told me he's out of town for two weeks. So he can't even look over anything until then. And…I don't know, I just hate waiting on the unknown."

"And that wait will pale in comparison to how slow the courts move," Maeve adds. "Then, there will be hearings and home checks, not to mention finding Missy to actually get her to sign off on dissolving her rights. This could take years."

I feel my face fall and my shoulders slouch, the word "years" ringing through my head. I knew this wouldn't be a wam-bam-thank-you-ma'am kind of case, but I didn't expect multiple birthdays to go by.

No. It's what you need to do. For Porter. For Grace. For the family we can be.

"What's the matter?"

I look over to Porter, who has gotten really good on catching onto the split seconds where I lose my façade. "Everything's fine."

His eyebrows shoot up. Sometimes I hate that he's not like most men who don't realize that "fine" doesn't mean "fine."

"Quinn…"

"No, really, we can talk about it later."

"Don't let her," Maeve interrupts. "She'll put you off forever, always change the subject, and before you know it, everyone has forgotten the conversation until years later."

I narrow my eyes at my sister. "It's conversations like this I didn't miss when I lived in Phoenix."

She shrugs, clearly not caring. "Tough shit. Plus, if you can't talk openly here, where can you?"

I look around the table, each set of eyes on me having so much love and warmth in them. Maeve's right. This is a safe space. Doesn't make what I'm about to say any easier.

"If this goes to a trial, or whatever hearings we'll need to have in front of a judge, I'm going to step back from your life."

Porter's face drops. Ainsley gasps. I'm pretty sure if I could see Maeve and Stella, their eyes would be popping out of their head.

"Excuse me? You're going to do what?"

"This is why I didn't want to talk about it here," I say. "But if you have to go in front of a judge, and he has to come interview people in your life, I know what my reputation is in this town. It's not going to be hard for a lawyer to say that you're living with a woman who's unpredictable. I know there are social media posts that will never die. I…I just don't want to be a liability to you. I won't be one. So if I need to take myself out of that picture for you to keep Grace, then that's what I'm going to do."

There's a silence as my words hang in the air. No one moves. I don't think anyone is breathing. That's until Porter breaks the silence.

"No."

"Porter. It wasn't a yes or no."

"Oh, but it is."

I shake my head. "Porter, I—"

His finger is in front of my mouth before I can get out

another syllable. "Now it's your turn to listen. I love that you would do that for us. But under no uncertain terms am I going to do this without you. You're a part of us, and if some judge is going to take some past bad decisions and bitchy social media posts and make that the reason that Grace isn't with us? Then we didn't get good enough lawyers."

"Oh, you'll have good lawyers," Simon chimes in. "So don't worry about that."

"See? Simon's got a guy. So whatever thought you had about needing to play the martyr? I love that you would do that, but get it out of your beautiful head. We're a team. You and me. We're a family now, and no one, not my mother, not a judge, not anyone, is going to take that away from us."

Porter pulls me in, stealing a kiss that I feel all over my body. It lasts for more than a few seconds, which is when I remember my family is watching this.

"Well then," Stella says as I pull back, a little out of breath. "I didn't know you had that in you, Porter."

He turns to Stella, giving her a playful wink. "The tricks go far up my sleeve."

"All right, enough," Simon says as my sisters are all smiles. "Enough of whatever that was and let's get back to finding a solution. Hopefully one that doesn't need courts. If I do remember correctly, this family is pretty savvy into making bad people dig their own graves."

The five of us share a smile, remembering back to what we did to Stella's ex-fiancé. And though I wasn't a part of it, I know that Maeve's ex got his comeuppance last year with a little bit of Banks dramatics.

"Let's think about this. Why would a person want a baby out of the blue?" Ainsley asks. And without hesitation, Logan and Simon answer simultaneously.

"Money."

"Really?" That doesn't seem right. "I've been through Grace's diaper bag a few times. She's not carrying stacks of hundreds in there, if that's what she's after."

"Not like that," Simon says. "But I'm going to guess that Bonnie doesn't have a job, or if she does, it's probably not a high-paying one."

"Confirmed!" Stella shouts, as she spreads out printed papers on the bar. "I found all of this on her social media. She likes to make angry posts about how everyone is working against her, including her last job that she says fired her for no reason. I doubt that's true. Also, she's really not happy with a few businesses in her town. Judging by her tone, I feel like she's the woman who always wants to speak to the manager."

"Sounds about right," Porter says.

Simon picks up the custody papers again and lays them back on the table. "My guess? She wants Grace for the assistance she'd get. And that tax credit she'll get will look pretty good. If this would work, Grace is her pay day."

Porter's face starts turning red, his anger about to bubble over.

"Fuck!" he yells, pounding the table. "It's always been about money with her. I'd bet the bar that's her play."

"Are you sure?" Ainsley asks. "I know it's a motivation for a lot of people, but using a child for money? That's so cruel."

"Actually, now that y'all say it, it makes sense," I say. "Yesterday when she was here, she made a few comments about not getting her fair share in the divorce from Porter's dad. And the way that she was looking around this bar? It was like she was eyeballing every inch of it. But it wasn't for nostalgia purposes. She had a look in her eye. Maybe a little revenge. But something was definitely up."

"Okay, let's go with this theory that it's about the money," Maeve says. "We're well aware that everyone can be bought. The question is, what's her price?"

"More specifically, what will make sure she never comes after Grace again," I add.

All eyes turn to Porter. Unfortunately, at this point, he's the one who's going to have the answers.

"My dad," he says. "She always thought she got the short end of the stick. That he loved this bar more than he loved her. He might be dead, but if she got the last laugh, she'd go away. Forever."

"Well then, we need to make sure that happens," I say.

Porter turns to me, slightly confused. "And how are we going to do that? I don't want to pay her a fucking dime."

"Are you sure?" Logan offers. "If it makes her go away, I'll write you a check now."

"I can't ask you to do that," Porter says. "But we have to figure out a way that makes her think she's getting money, but in reality—"

"That's it!" I yell, suddenly for the first time in a day feeling like the gray cloud isn't sitting over our heads. "I've got it."

"Oh shit," Maeve mumbles.

"What?" Logan asks her.

"She just got the idea for a stunt, and by the twinkle in her eye, it's a doozy."

"Damn right I do. If we pull this off, it could go down in history."

I look down to Porter. "Do you trust me?"

He smiles. "With my life."

"Good," I say, rubbing my hands together. "Because we're about to get our little girl for good."

guide to love rule #138

Don't fuck with millennial parents.
They were raised on
"Knuck If You Buck" and Four Locos.

34

quinn

I FEEL LIKE I'VE EVOLVED IN MY PRANKS AND STUNTS OVER THE years.

While many of them in school were meant for laughs, more than a few were targeted at people who deserved to have bad shit happen to them.

And no one deserves to have bad shit happen to them more than Bonnie.

"When's she going to get here?" Porter asks as he paces around the bar.

"She's going to make us wait," I say. "You know, make a grand entrance."

I realize as I say those words that's the mantra I live by. Note to self: start arriving early to not be like Bonnie.

"Are you sure this is going to work?"

I want to lie and say of course, but even I don't know if this one is going to go smoothly. There are a lot of moving parts, and most of them hinge on how Bonnie reacts. I've only been able to pull off one highly timed, very coordinated prank once in my life —those fireworks were a sight to see—and I don't know if I can do it again.

"Even if it doesn't, we have four contingency plans," Logan

reassures him. "Plus, I think I'm going to play an excellent lawyer."

Did I ask my new brother-in-law to cosplay a lawyer so Bonnie would think everything is on the up-and-up? Yes.

Was Simon jealous that it wasn't him? Extremely.

But, he had plenty to do in this scheme of mine to work. And in fact, he had one of the biggest roles—get with one of his lawyer friends and draw up the paperwork for both Bonnie and Missy.

Yes, part of my plan was finding and tracking down Missy in seven days.

Unfortunately, as of right now with Bonnie only minutes away, we haven't been able to track her down.

So it's on to Plan B. Which is fine. Plan A was boring. This one is a little more...my style.

"I still don't get why Logan gets to be the lawyer," Simon pouts. "I can say legal words. 'Objection!' 'Cause for dismissal!' 'I want the truth!'"

We all just shake our heads. "Because, like I've said, we don't know who Bonnie still talks to in this town. Or what she's figured out since she's been here. But what we do know is that she has no clue who Logan is. We just have to hope she hasn't seen him on a magazine cover."

Plus, Logan's checkbook is part of Plan B, C, and E. I love my brother, and he's not hurting in the money department, but he's not a billionaire. And Logan was happy to help, and even pay off Bonnie if necessary. I believe his words were, "it makes me feel like I'm part of the family."

"Okay, here we are," Ainsley says, scaring me as she sprints into the bar, huffing and puffing as she waves an envelope. "Sorry I'm running late."

I look at my smartwatch, and yes, Ainsley is running more on my time than her normal twenty minutes early. "You're fine. She's not here yet. Is everything okay?"

"What? Yeah. You know. Nashville traffic. A real pain at five o'clock. But I got the papers, so we're set."

I look to Porter, then to Logan and Simon. Everyone's eyes are saying the same: Something's up with Ainsley.

"You good, sis?" I ask.

"Yeah, why?"

"Um, because you're jumpy, and late. And your face is beet red, and I don't think it's because you were running."

She waves me off. Literally. She even adds a "psssh" with it.

"No. Seriously. Are you ill? This isn't normal behavior, and I'm truly worried. You look…"

"Flustered," Simon finishes my sentence. "Everything okay?"

"Yeah, totally fine," she says in a tone that makes it seem that it's everything but fine. "Just ran late at the hospital, which means I ran late getting to the lawyer's office to pick up the papers. Today was a hospital visit from some of the players from the Nashville Fury. When that happens, it's always chaos."

I tilt my head, trying to figure out Ainsley's lie. She's never told one so I know that something is off, but I can't figure out what she's lying about. Lucky for her, Stella comes running into the bar, cell phone waving in the air.

"She just turned down the road," she says. "ETA two minutes!"

"Okay," I say, giving everyone last directions. "Ainsley, go put the documents in the office. Stella and Simon, just hide somewhere so she doesn't see you and…wait…where's Maeve?"

I turn to Logan, hoping he knows where his wife is.

"She's on her way," he says. "Start without her."

I want to press him more, but I can't because the front door of The Joint swings open.

Here we go…

"You ready?" I whisper to Porter as we take a seat.

He leans in to kiss my cheek, but also to whisper, "This ends today."

We give each other reassuring nods as Bonnie confidently walks to our table.

"Well, well, well, I didn't expect to hear from everyone again so soon," she says. "I'm glad I was still in town."

It's been a week since our first meeting, and one of the biggest question marks in our plans was if Bonnie was going to stay in Rolling Hills or make her way back to Indiana. Luckily, because small town gossip for once was working on our side, we learned that she'd checked into the extended stay just outside of town. And since the manager of said motel is a longtime patron of the bar, we had daily updates on her comings and goings. We were going to try and hold out for a few more days, hoping we could find Missy, but we got word that Bonnie was planning to check out tomorrow, so we had to act fast.

"Thank you for meeting with us." Logan's distinct voice draws her attention, and I'm not really sure she noticed he was here until just now.

"Who are you?"

"Porter and Quinn's lawyer," he says, making sure he doesn't need to give a fake name unless he needs to.

"Lawyer? You didn't say anything about lawyers."

"I'm doing this out of courtesy," Logan asks. "We're just hoping…well, Porter, I'll let you explain."

"Explain what?"

Porter and I share a look, and I give him a reassuring nod. The parts we're playing in this scheme are sad, but that nod? Nothing but in encouragement.

It's time to end this bitch.

"You were right."

I know it killed Porter to say that, but it certainly has Bonnie's attention. "And what was I right about?"

"That we should do everything to keep this out of the courts," Porter says. "I don't think either of us really want to drag this on."

"You're right, I don't," Bonnie says. "So give me Grace and I'm out of your hair."

"No!" I dramatically yell, throwing my head into the table, remembering a trick from middle school when I learned to fake my own tears to get out of gym class. "You can't take her!"

"What's her problem?"

"Her problem is that she loves Grace. And so do I," Porter says as I fake cry into my arm. "She's happy here, Bonnie. Really happy. We just want to give her a life, together. Can't you understand that?"

I give Porter credit, he's doing his best to play the sympathy card. Unfortunately, we're realizing that Bonnie is a cold-hearted cunt.

"And I wouldn't give her a good life?"

"I'm not saying that," Porter says. Even though she wouldn't. "I just...she's finally adjusted here. And Missy wanted us to have her."

"As I've said, Missy didn't know what she wants, or what she had. There isn't anything you can do or say that will make me leave town without my granddaughter."

I smile into my arm before putting my sad face back on. "Nothing? Bonnie, please. There has to be something. We'll do or give you just about anything to let us keep that little girl."

If Plan B is going to work, this is the opening. And this has to be the time that Bonnie takes the bait.

"Anything, you say?"

"Yes," Porter says with a deep sigh. "That's how much we love her."

Porter holds my hand tightly, both of our eyes begging Bonnie to say something, anything, that we could do.

In reality, there's only one thing we want her to say.

"I want money."

Bingo, bitch.

"Money? We just said we didn't have money for the courts.

Our lawyer is pro bono," I say, fear laced in my voice. "How could we pay you?"

Her lip curls like she's a Disney villain. "Sell the bar."

God, I can lay a good fucking mouse trap…

Porter expertly plays up his shocked face. I rapidly bat my eyelashes like I'm trying to understand what she said.

"The bar?" Porter finally speaks up. "You want the bar?"

She laughs. "Absolutely not. If I had my way, I'd burn this place to the ground. But I think it's only fair that if you want me to go away, the price is going to be high. I know how much this place is worth. So sell the bar. Give me the money. And I'm out of your life forever."

I snap my head to Porter, hoping that I seem as devastated and worried as I'm trying to portray. Because on the inside? I'm fist pumping like it's the two-thousands and I'm on *Jersey Shore.*

Plan B is officially in full swing.

"Whoa," Logan speaks up, right on cue. "It could take months to sell. Get it appraised. Actually find a buyer."

"Exactly," Bonnie says. "But I think you could get a half a million for it."

"Mom. This is Rolling Hills. Who's going to buy—"

"Half a million, Porter. That's my price. And I want it today. Or we go to court."

"Hold up!" I shout. "Where do you think you're going to find a half a million dollars?"

She shrugs. "Word around town is that your brother is pretty well off, Quinn. Maybe you can ask him for a loan. Or maybe he can buy it like the other buildings in town he has."

Shit, I didn't even think of that angle in the plan. But that actually really helps this story. Well done, Bonnie.

"This is highly unusual," Logan chimes in, doing his best to play the part of a flustered lawyer. "For this to happen, I'll need to call Simon. Get it approved by him."

"Take your time," she says, sitting back and crossing her arms. "I can wait."

Logan and Porter shared faux-worried looks as they stand up. But just as they're walking away, Porter turns back to Bonnie. "If I do this. If I sell the bar and give you the money, you'll give me Grace? You'll sign over any future claims? She's mine?"

Bonnie nods. "All yours, son."

God I love it when a plan comes together.

Porter and Logan walk back to his office, just like Plan B says to, as I turn back to Bonnie.

Now, Plan B has me sitting here, not saying anything. When we were going through the different scenarios, Porter was very insistent on that. The problem is, Bonnie's looking at me in a way I don't like, and I might be a new version of Quinn, but I'm still me.

Sorry Porter. I'm going to be asking for forgiveness on this one.

"What are you looking at?"

Bonnie smugly smiles. "He's going to leave you."

Well, that I wasn't expecting. "Excuse me?"

"Porter. He's just like his daddy," she says. "And he's going to leave you just like he left me."

Now, a bigger person would ignore this. Take the high ground because someone went low.

That's not my style. I kick at the knees. And I don't play fair. And I was raised on two-thousands rap and liquor that should have been illegal.

"Bonnie, and I say this with zero respect, but shut the actual fuck up."

She doesn't do the fake clutching of her pearls like she did the other day. Instead she just leans closer. "Big words coming from…well…I'll let you finish my thought."

I literally laugh out loud. "Really, Bonnie? Weight jokes? That's all you got? I figured you as a better opponent than that."

I lean closer, because it's been a while since I've unleashed the chamber, and I'm about to go all in on this woman who tried to rip away my life.

"Listen here you horrible, horrible bitch. First of all, everyone in this town knows you left Frank and Porter, not the other way around like you're trying to claim. I'm surprised they didn't throw rocks at you the first day you showed your face here. So that whole 'he left you' spiel? Give it up. Just like you did on trying to fix your face."

"I—"

"Oh, I'm not done yet. Also, do you find it ironic that you left this town to start a new life, ended up in a smaller town in Indiana because that's all the bus ticket you could afford, before getting married and getting pregnant again? Kind of seems counterproductive."

"It—"

"Again, I'm not done. Very rude of you to interrupt." I take a breath, and this time she listens. "I never have to worry about your son cheating on me. And I hope he *is* like his father. In fact, I know he is. He's good and kind. Thoughtful and fun. He's exactly who Frank raised him to be, no thanks to you and your deadbeat ass. And frankly? I think the best thing that ever happened was the day you packed up and left. Good riddance to bad rubbish, you know?"

She tries to open up her mouth again, but I haven't hit her with the last bit. "And lastly. You're going to get this check. You're going to walk out of here. You're going to leave us forever. I don't want to see you in this town again. I'm going to make sure no one ever speaks your name. And we'll sure as hell never think about you. And when you run out of money, because you're going to, just remember that your choices have cost you everything. You lost your family. You drove everyone away. Your daughter literally went off the grid to get away from you. You'll never see your grandchild. You'll never see Porter again. And that's on you, Bonnie. That's the bed you'll lie in every night. And I hope you fucking rot in it."

She slowly backs away, as do I, as Porter and Logan come back into the room, envelope in hand.

"Simon approved," Logan says, sitting back down. "He authorized me to pay you your sum, and we'll take care of the payments between us on the back end."

Bonnie hangs out her hand. "I need to see it. Make sure you aren't playing me."

Logan holds it up, but keeps it out of her reach as Porter hangs his head. "Proof of the check. But you don't get it until you sign the documents first."

He pushes the papers toward Bonnie. "I need you to sign these. I quickly drew them up. These say that under no circumstance from here on going forward, that you'll attempt to gain custody of Grace."

The three of us watch intently as Bonnie stares at the papers. These are legally binding. The only thing we're waiting on—and the only thing to fuck Plan B all to hell—is if Bonnie actually reads the contract. Because it doesn't say a thing about us promising her money for this signature. That way, in case something goes south, she can't sue us for breach of contract.

All three of us hold our breaths as she grabs the pen and furiously scribbles her name on the line.

That a girl, Bonnie. Stay fucking stupid.

"There!" she says, pushing the contact back to Logan. "Now give me the check."

Logan starts to hand her the check, and I realize at this point I never asked him if it was a dummy check or if she's actually about to hold half a million dollars.

"You're a sucker, just like your father," she says, the check inches away from her. "Have a good life without your precious bar."

"Absolutely not! Porter! Stop!"

Every set of eyes whips around to the front door as a young woman marches in.

Wait…is that…

"Missy?"

Bonnie said it, but we were all thinking it.

And with that entrance, Plan B has now shifted into Plan What the Fuck.

"What the hell is going on?" I whisper to Logan, who just smiles.

"We found her early this morning. Maeve went to get her. We didn't know if we'd make it in time, so we didn't say anything."

"Wow," I whisper, in awe of everything. "This wasn't on my bingo card."

I stand in awe as my hiding siblings come out of the woodwork, ready to look and watch whatever's about to go down.

"Porter. Did you really sign the bar away?"

He looks to Logan, who gives him a subtle nod. Okay, we're still pretending. "Yeah. I just did."

"Well, fuck that," Missy says, now turning her sights to Bonnie. "Really, Mom? This is what you're doing?"

"Missy, I don't know what you heard, but I—"

"Save it," she snaps. "I've been filled in on your stunt. How fucking dare you try and take Grace from Porter. This is what I wanted. But like always, you can't accept that and think that everyone's out to get you."

"You are," she says. "Taking my grand baby away."

"Please. How long did it take you to realize I was gone? Oh, that's right, two weeks. Two weeks, Bonnie, before you texted me to see where I was. Clearly you missed us so much."

"Oh damn..." Everyone looks at me after the comment. "Oh, come on, y'all were thinking it too."

Missy turns to Porter. "I hear you have something for me to sign."

He nods and looks back to Simon, who hands Logan an envelope. "We had these drawn up for when we finally tracked you down. It's permanently forfeiting your parental rights and stating that you want Grace to be raised under Porter's care."

Missy takes the documents and pen, but doesn't sign yet, instead she shoots daggers at Bonnie. "This is what I wanted. I wanted Porter to raise her. I wanted Grace permanently away from you. And I'm going to make sure that it happens."

She signs her name on the paper, slamming the pen down. "There. Now you don't have to sell The Joint."

"Ha!" Bonnie yells. "You're too late. I already signed the contract, and it was promising me a half a million to not go for custody. I'd like my check now, please."

"Actually," Logan says, ripping the check in half, "our deal is off the table."

"Excuse me!" Bonnie screams. "What do you mean it's off the table? I signed a contract. You owe me!"

"Oh you signed a contract," Porter says, holding it up. "But nowhere on here does it say anything about money being exchanged."

"But!"

"He's right," I say, taking it from Porter. "Just that you promise to never show your face in this town again. But nope, no mention of money. Sorry, Bonnie. Maybe some other time."

"What? This isn't legal!" Bonnie yells before pointing to Logan. "You're not even a lawyer, are you?"

"I'm not," Logan admits. "But it was very enjoyable to play one today."

Everyone starts laughing—everyone but Bonnie, that is.

Take that back. Bonnie *and* Porter.

"You." She walks around the table, pointing her finger at me. "This has your name all over it."

"Guilty. But like you said Bonnie, I'm memorable. And I have a feeling you'll always remember this day. Now, kindly get the fuck out of our bar before I throw your ass out."

Bonnie turns to Porter. "How dare you do this to me? I'm your mother."

The bark of a laugh that Porter lets out echoes through the bar. "You haven't been a mother to me in twenty years, so don't even try to play that card. And how dare I do that to you? You really are delusional. How about this, Mom? How dare you treat

Pops like a piece of shit when he was just trying to build a life for us? How dare you be jealous of something that not only he loved, but brought a town together? You hurt me the day you left. You hurt Pops. He was never the same again, and all because you were jealous of—what? This? How egotistical can you be?"

Porter takes a step forward to her, and as much as I want to step up next to him, I know this is his war. And he's fighting the battle that's about to end it.

"For years I didn't think I wanted a family. I was scared to fall in love, because in my mind, it didn't last. People leave. You left. If my own mother wouldn't stay, why would anyone else? You did that to me. But guess what? You lost. You lost your family—every one of them. You lost your grandchild. But I didn't lose. I won. I've found love. I've found family. And it's all despite you. So I want you to leave. I never want to see you again. And I want you to remember this day forever, because it's the day you lost *everything*."

The two stare each other down for another second before Bonnie starts marching toward the door, but not before getting one more look at Porter and Missy.

"You two are both ungrateful brats," she says.

"Learned from the best, Ma," Porter says.

"Have a nice life, Bonnie."

And with that, Bonnie McCoy Higgins turns on her heel, storms out of the bar, and hopefully, out of our lives.

35
porter

"Okay, I'm going to need you to start from the beginning," I say, setting down my pint glass of beer because I don't know what the hell just happened over the last hour. "We went over the plans thoroughly, and in none of those was Missy making a grand entrance."

"Believe me, it wasn't," Quinn says. "Though, I do commend your flare for the dramatic."

Missy shyly shrugs, clearly a little nervous about being the center of attention. "I was raised by Bonnie. I learned to be dramatic from a young age."

The table laughs at her joke, and as much as I'd love to just laugh this day away, I have so many questions.

"Can we address the elephant in the room? How the hell did you find her?"

"She didn't make it easy," Stella says. "My normal channels of digging to track people down weren't working."

"And the private investigator I hired was coming up short as well," Logan adds. "But we knew we were running out of time, and as much as I wanted to keep everything legal and above board..."

"We were running out of time, so he hacked into her email,"

Maeve says. "My computer genius husband is an amateur hacker."

Apparently I'm the only one at the table surprised by this. It's also making me very curious if Stella is a part-time private investigator, Logan can hack things, and Simon and Quinn being, well, them…what kind of family am I getting into?

Oh, who am I kidding? I'm now a part of, without a doubt, the most entertaining family imaginable.

"So once we were in the email, we were able to trace the last time she used her computer to an IP address in Wyoming. From there Stella started doing Stella things that I'm not sure I want to know about."

"You don't," she says. "But I figured out the campsite that was near the IP address, and well, we took a guess that's where she was."

"A guess!" Quinn yells. "You guessed?"

"We had to," Logan says. "Who knew if Bonnie was going to fall for the lies? We needed to try to get Missy back because she was the nail in the coffin."

Quinn and I both wide eyed as we listen to this story unfold. About how when they narrowed down the campsite, that Maeve jumped on a plane and headed to Wyoming. That once she found Missy and explained enough to get her on the plane, that they hightailed it back so Missy could sign any documents to make sure Bonnie never had claim to Grace.

"I should probably feel violated, but I'm glad you did what you had to do," Missy says. "Clearly I didn't think things through when I left Grace here. I thought my letter was going to be enough."

"Don't you dare blame yourself," I tell her. "It's not your fault our mother is batshit."

"Once we were on the plane, Maeve told me more about what was happening and my heart dropped. I specifically left Indiana to get away from her. Because she was trying to do what she did to you, trying to claim Grace as her dependent. I was already over my head and confused and questioning if I could raise a child. She didn't help. I just…I broke. Then I came here."

"There's still one thing that never made sense," I say. "How did she know you brought Grace to me? I can't imagine I was a frequent part of conversation."

"I was wondering that too," Missy says. "But then I remembered, and it was my fault."

"Nothing is your fault," Quinn says.

"I don't know about that. When I first got the idea, I needed to make sure you were still here, so I was searching on my phone about Rolling Hills and The Joint. Looking up your Facebook account. That kind of thing. Out of nowhere she walked up behind me, saw the pictures, recognized it immediately, and then threw my phone across the room. She screamed at me for an hour about how you were ungrateful—for what, I don't know, because you seemed to be doing fine—and that I shouldn't concern myself with you. My only guess is that when she didn't get the life insurance payout from Dad's death like she thought, that's when she schemed to get Grace back."

"Wow," I say, rubbing my face. "If I didn't hate her so much, I'd be a little impressed with her deductive reasoning."

"Well, that reasoning went out the door the second she saw dollar signs," Quinn says. "I swear, once she realized she was going to get money and make you sell the bar in the process, we could've told her the check was coming from the King of England and she would've believed it."

"I was holding my breath when we brought her out the contract to sign," I admit. "But I don't think she could've signed it any faster."

"Also, kudos to you, Logan, for not actually giving her the check," Quinn says. "I don't think I've ever seen a hand move so slow."

Logan takes a sip of his whiskey. "When we were in the back, Maeve texted me that she was on her way. I was stalling as much as I could. But I must say, my wife has impeccable timing."

He leans over to kiss her cheek. "I'm just glad we were able to make it. And now this saga is behind us."

"I agree." I look around the table to make sure everyone has a drink of some sort. "And I'd like to propose a toast."

Everyone holds up their glasses. "I'd like to say thanks to each and every one of you. This...I never had a big family. Sure, I had extended and the people here, but not anything like you guys. And...well...I just hope you know I'll never be able to properly pay you back for what every one of you did today."

"No thanks needed," Simon says. "You're family now. And this is what you do for family."

Glasses clink together as the chatter starts back up, which is when I see Missy stand from her chair and walk over to the picture wall. I get up and follow her, wanting a minute alone.

"I don't know how I'll ever be able to thank you," I say. "I know this isn't what you wanted to do."

She just nods but doesn't say anything as she stares at the wall that's covered in photos. Up until a few months ago, it was pictures of me and Pops. The regulars. Harry and George holding up their beer cans from their place at the end of the bar. Those photos are still up, but I've recently added some new ones.

Photos of me, Quinn, and Grace during her one-year-birthday celebration. One of Grace playing in her special corner. George holding her while she looks at him like he's nuts.

In her defense, he usually is.

"She's gotten so big. I feel like it's been a year and it's only been a few months."

"She has," I say. "We're still working on the talking. The walking thing she's getting down pretty good."

She nods, but I see a tear escape.

"You were brave," I assure her. "What you did for Grace? What you did today? You didn't have to do any of that. I just want you to know I think what you've done is courageous and a sacrifice not many would make."

"Thank you," she says, wiping the tear away. "Porter, I promise I never thought Bonnie would come here. I—"

"Absolutely not. Don't blame yourself one minute because our mother is crazy," I say. "And now we know she's in our pasts forever."

We stand there for a few more minutes, just looking at the pictures of Grace.

"Do you want to see her?"

Missy shakes her head, another tear sprinting free. "I already said my goodbyes. It's going to be best if I get going."

"I understand," I say, bringing my sister in for a hug. "She'll always know about you. About how you sacrificed to make sure she had the best life she could."

She nods against my shoulder as we continue the embrace. "Thank you."

We pull away, but not before I grab a piece of paper and pen from the bar. "Here's my phone number. Please keep it. If you need anything, ever. And…if you're ever ready. If you ever want to…"

Missy holds up a piece of paper. "I'll know how to call you."

With one more hug, Missy says her goodbyes and is out the back door to a car ready to take her back to the airport, where his plane is standing by to take her back to Wyoming.

"Hey," Quinn says, wrapping her arms around my waist. "You okay?"

"Yeah…I'm good."

I bring Quinn around to my front, needing to feel the comfort only she can bring me now, knowing this saga is over. That our lives can start now.

Our lives together. As a family.

We slowly pull apart, but I keep her hand in mine as we walk back toward the table. Which is when I notice that we have a new member to the party.

"Come here, Miss Grace!" Simon pushes away everyone as he makes his way to Wes, who I knew at some point was bringing her back tonight. "I have a good feeling about you today!"

The crowd backs off as Wes hands her over, but everyone is watching intently to see if this will finally be the moment that Simon breaks the stalemate my niece has with him.

"Hey, Miss Grace," he says, trying to bounce her to get her to smile. She's not. "Oh, come on. Don't you know what I did for you today? I knew a guy, and he made documents, and now you get to stay with us forever!"

She looks at him, then looks at everyone else, before seeing me in the crowd. Her arms shoot out, clearly ready to be away from weird Uncle Simon.

"Sorry, man," I say as I take her from him. "Plus, I haven't seen this girl in way too long."

Grace immediately starts smiling for me as I kiss her rosy cheeks and walk with her back to a table. "Hey, baby girl. I missed you."

Wes and Betsy have been angels this week, keeping Grace more than normal as we tried to figure this all out. I've seen her every day, but sometimes only at night when she's asleep. It feels like it's been days since I've just held her like this, not worried if this was the last time I was going to do so.

"I'm never letting you go," I say, hugging her tight. But unfortunately, the second I let loose she starts pushing me away, ready to go run into her play area. "Or not."

Quinn laughs as she loops her arm through mine, the two of us watching as Grace toddles—to massive applause, because most of the people here haven't seen her walk yet—to her corner.

"It's over," she says, her head falling against my arm. "I can't believe it's over."

"It almost doesn't feel real," I say. "This whole day—hell, this whole week—felt like one bad dream."

"I know. But you can wake up now."

I bring Quinn around, holding her tight to me. "I don't know how I could've done this without you."

"You need to be thanking Stella. And money bags Logan. And everyone else. I was just the chaos coordinator."

I shake my head in laughter as I kiss her forehead. "I'm not just talking about today. But everything. You…I know this wasn't your plan. I know how you ended up here was not how you wanted your life to go. But part of me believes that in some weird way, all of this was meant to happen now. Because you were here."

Quinn cups my face with her hands, bringing me in for a kiss that screams forever. "Plans change, Porter. And this life? The one we're building? Getting to love you? Getting to watch that little girl grow up? I can't imagine my life being any other way."

I tip my forehead down to meet hers as her hands loop around my neck. "This life. It's unexpected. Us? Grace? I never would've imagined this life for myself. And yet, I can't imagine the future going any other way."

Quinn lifts up on her toes, giving me one last kiss. "Just you wait. The best is yet to come."

guide to love rule #143

There truly is no place like home.

epilogue

Quinn - Six Months Later

"So what do we think the hero was trying to accomplish with his quest?"

I can't count the amount of hands that go up between the students who have piled into the Rolling Hills Middle School library and the ones who are streaming in via our Zoom feed. But it's a lot.

And it fills my heart.

"Yes, Antonio?"

"I don't think he knew Ms. Banks. He for sure didn't have a plan."

"Yes he did!" Stephen, one of my students back in Rolling Hills, chimes in. "He knew he had to go into the outer land to save the world!"

"Well yeah, he knew that. But going into an unknown world without at least a sword? Ain't no way I'm doing that. How you going to go into a quest where you're probably going to meet a dragon and not go in with a sword? It's a suicide mission Miss Banks."

I laugh, because Antonio isn't wrong. And this is the beauty of book club, one person says one thing and suddenly that's better than any topics I could've come up with.

"That sounds like a good discussion today!" I clap my hands to grab everyone's attention. As I've done this plenty of times during the months we've had our after school meetings, the students know that they need to quiet down for these few minutes. It's usually not a problem because they know they're about to get plenty of talking time. "You're going to break up into your pairs and discuss the topic 'did you think the protagonist had a plan.' When you're done with your idea exchange, you can discuss that if you were going on the quest, what would you bring to defeat your enemies."

I see a hand go up and I quickly nip it in the bud. "And no. Your phone is not an acceptable answer because, believe it or not, I don't think Chat GPT will help you defeat a dragon."

The kids laugh as the ones I have in my home library grab their Chromebooks and headphones before dispersing around the library into their small groups. I quickly glance around the room to make sure everyone is situated and I can't help but smile.

Quinn's Crew Book Club—my former students in Arizona refused to let me change the name—has now gone from a summer activity to an after school club for students. And yes, we're based in two locations because my Arizona kiddos were not going to be left out. And since they're doing buddy reads with one of the classes here, we just added them to the after school book club. So now, once a month, students come in and talk about our book of the month. We start off in a large group before breaking off into our buddy talks. The kids are talking books and making friends they never would've met before. I've even heard snaps have been exchanged. Whatever that means.

The amount of support I've gotten from Rolling Hills and, shockingly, my former school, has been amazing. The language arts teachers are thrilled with how much the kids read outside the classroom and have told me whatever I need from them to just ask. Our school had more Battle of the Books signups than ever before and I've even been asked by the county to give a talk about reviving libraries for students.

Don't get me wrong, Rolling Hills Middle School is not the same without Mrs. Metcalf. But her legacy lives on in the permanent shelf that's been now coined, "Mrs. Metcalf's Infinity Star Reads," which of course also houses a framed picture of her and I from many years ago right next to a copy of *The Westing Game*.

As for my former school…it's been a journey from what I've heard. Since I'm still in contact with my former fellow English teachers, they're more than happy to fill me in on the gossip.

And oh my, there's been tea…

Apparently my leaving started a mini revolution. Four other teachers quit before the school year ended and two teachers opted for early retirement. And that was on top of the three who were retiring at the end of the year. But the board didn't panic until no new teachers were applying for the position. Which, I'm not sure why they wouldn't be? It's not like myself and a few of the departed teachers were posting on teacher Facebook groups about our time there and how the administration didn't have teachers' backs.

Guess what? It worked. The board panicked, talked to the union, and made a sweeping declaration that all parent groups had to be board approved. Parents can still talk to the administration about specific issues with their own child, but it can't be done in groups and if it requires that, it must be brought to the board first.

I was shocked. I couldn't believe they agreed to that. Then again, that might've had something to do with someone's sister digging into social media posts and finding long and buried things about each member of the P.E.N.I.S. Posse. And weirdly, I heard that those photos and social media posts were sent to the board to let them know that these were the people trying to take over the school and curriculum.

Moral of the story: If you're going to go on spring break in Cancun and show your tits to the world, and then proceed to also have a small role in a *Girl's Gone Wild* video, make sure it's not on the internet before going into a school and preaching about moral values in education. That's all I'm saying.

Oh, and don't fuck with Quinn Banks. Ever.

And while I'm glad they now have things straightened out, I'm still glad I left. Because leaving Arizona brought me exactly to where I needed to be.

It's been eight months since Grace made her grand entrance, and subsequently turned both Porter and my lives upside down. Looking back, I wouldn't have it any other way.

After our day of reckoning with Bonnie, things sped up in terms of Grace's legal guardianship and adoption. Missy signed all necessary paperwork when she came home, and now that we had a better way to contact her, she was quickly able to sign any other further documents that Porter's lawyer needed to make sure that he had full custody of Grace.

Her official "gotcha" day was last month. If you think her first birthday was over-the-top, you should've seen that. Simon really went all out.

And no, she's still not smiling at him.

As for Porter and I, all of my things were officially moved into his house a few weeks after the dust settled with Bonnie. I had wondered if it was going to feel different because before I had outs. Exit doors. I could've moved back to Arizona. I could've gone back to the apartment above the diner. That worry lasted all of two seconds. It's kind of scary how well we've been able to settle into life together as an actual couple.

He's hired extra help at the bar so he's working mostly days. Our nights at home are so…domestic. We take turns cooking and all Grace related things. We're always finding a new show to binge because otherwise all we'd watch is Miss Rachel and Mickey Mouse Club. We've even started talking about renovating the house. Nothing big. New floors and cupboards, things like that. Shockingly, it was Porter's idea. I loved it, but I told him that we didn't have to. It was his dad's house. The place he grew up. I didn't want to take away any of that nostalgia. He answered me by kissing my forehead and telling me his dad would've wanted us to make it our own.

Which in Quinn translation means I'm getting a library.

Each night while we're laying in bed together, I still ask myself if this is a dream. Because in no fairy tale do the main characters sleep with each other for eight years, move in together platonically, then realize that they're in love, before living happily ever after.

Apparently we're the exception.

"Delivery for Quinn Banks?"

The announcement, accompanied by a knock on the library door, gets my attention. The kids have headphones on, so I'm the only one who turns to see a teenager standing with a wrapped gift.

"I'm Quinn Banks. What is this?"

"Not sure, I just deliver."

The students are oblivious to my delivery as I set the box on the table. Who would send this? Porter? I mean, my birthday *is* tomorrow, but we already lined up a sitter and have the night planned. And why would he send the gift a day early?

I almost set it aside, but it's then that I see an envelope on top of the box that says "open now." I check the room again to make sure the students are still on task, and when they are, I quickly rip it open.

HAPPY BIRTHDAY HURRICANE. IT FELT FITTING TO GIVE YOU THIS DURING BOOK CLUB.

More curious than ever, I quickly open the box and throw the tissue paper out of the way.

And then I start sobbing.

A first edition of *The Westing Game.* I carefully lift it up, needing to see the beautiful, original, cover and hold it for myself. When I open it to see the pages, I shriek when I see that it's signed by the author.

I start to hear some commotion from the kids, but nothing's on fire that I can tell, so I leave them be because there's another envelope inside the book.

A ONE OF A KIND, FOR A ONE OF A KIND.

OH, ONE MORE THING, LOOK UP AND TURN TO YOUR LEFT.

Confused, I do as Porter's instructions say. When I do, I see my students gathered together, each holding a sign with arrows pointing to the Zoom screen. I slowly look over to the projector wall, which is when I see my former students all holding signs, each saying words I never thought I'd ever see in my life.

Miss Banks: Will you marry Porter?

The kids start giggling as I frantically look around the room, which is when I see Porter walking in, pushing Grace in her stroller with one hand, and the other hand holding a ring box.

"What is going on?"

His smile lights up the room as he stops the stroller next to me, taking my hands in his. He leans down to gently kiss me, which I think I return. I'm not sure. Pretty sure I'm about to black out.

"I've been thinking for months how I wanted to do this. And every idea I came up with, nothing seemed more perfect than asking you here. Because these students, and this library, are the reasons you came into my life for good."

He lets go of one hand as he gets down on one knee, which allows my free hand to wipe away the tears.

"I told you once that our story was one of a kind, which is fitting, because there is no one in this world like you. You're beautiful and witty. Funny and kind. You love hard and you stand up for those who need it. You'll sacrifice yourself for everyone and never ask for anything in return. You moved in with me when I felt like I was drowning. You've given me comfort on days where I couldn't be convinced that there would ever be daylight again. You've made me laugh every day. And you've shown me more love than I ever thought I deserved."

Porter pauses to open the ring box, and that's when I gasp again. It's perfect. A ruby gemstone—my favorite color and definitely unique—surrounded by smaller diamonds in a halo cut. At least I think it's halo. Stella is chomping at the bit for Emmett to propose so she's been showing all of us different rings for when he asks one of us to help, we know what she'll like.

Did my sisters know about this? I mean, Porter and I talked about it a few times, and both of us agreed that we were in this for the long haul. He's it for me and at this point I'd shank a bitch if she tried to take my man. But the word "marriage" never actually came out of either of our mouths.

It's then that out of the corner of my eye I see my family at the doorway to the library, doing their best to peek in without giving themselves away.

"Quinn Elizabeth Banks, you were once the girl I had a crush on. Then you became the woman I couldn't wait to see a few times a year. In that time we became friends. You became my person. My confidant. My partner. And now, I ask you, will you be my wife?"

There's a split second of silence in the room before I scream out a "Yes!" which causes a volume of screams that should never be heard in a library.

Porter stands up as I hug him with everything in me. It's only a few seconds before I feel a dozen arms around me, hugging and jumping on me like it just happened to them.

As soon as I'm done embracing my co-conspirator students, my family is pushing through for their turn. Mom and Dad are here, along with Simon and Charlie, Maeve and Logan, Stella and Emmett, and of course, Ainsley and her new beau.

Which is a bold move on her part bringing a star Nashville Fury player to a middle school. Which is why I'm guessing that my students are suddenly very quiet. They've just realized Linc Kincaid is in their presence.

"How long has this been in the works?"

"We only found out the other day," Maeve says, narrowing her eyes at Porter. "Seems as if this guy didn't think we could keep a secret."

Porter holds up his hands in surrender. "In my defense, when have y'all ever kept a secret from each other?"

"That's true," Stella says. "Though if I do remember, you two were a secret for a very long time."

Porter and I share a smile as I quickly run down memory lane.

All the nights of sneaking around.

The trips where I'd make up excuses to come home, but I secretly wanted to see him.

Or the biggest secret that I was keeping from myself—that I wasn't madly in love with this man.

I finish hugging my family as I realize that all of my students are now completely preoccupied by a pro football player in their presence, and a few have realized that my brother-in-law invented their favorite video game. The distraction gives Porter the chance to steal me away behind a book stack, which is where I receive my proper kiss as a newly engaged woman.

Holy shit I'm engaged.

I'm going to marry Porter.

I'm going to be Quinn McCoy.

Yeah…it's going to take a minute for that one to sink in.

When the kiss is over, we don't let each other go. I know we need to soon, but I just want to stay in this moment. A moment I'll remember forever.

"How much longer is book club?"

I laugh as I take a peek around the stacks. The Arizona class has signed off, and there's now a line to get both Linc and Logan's autograph.

"I think we're about wrapped up."

"Good. I arranged Charlie and Simon to take Grace. I thought maybe we could celebrate. Maybe go get some chicken wings?"

I throw my head back as I laugh at Porter's inside joke. Oh wow, it's been a minute since we've said that.

"I like the sound of that," I say. "Anywhere particular?"

He smiles and dips me down to kiss me again—a kiss I feel from my head to my toes.

"Anywhere beautiful. As long as I'm with you, nothing else matters."

I bring him back down for another kiss, because how is this my life? How did quitting my job and moving back to the town I never wanted to live in result in me living a life I could have never imagined? One filled with love and laughter and family.

I guess you really can never say never, because if I did, I'd wouldn't be here.

And I wouldn't trade this life, my fairy tale, for anything in the world.

Thank you for reading Roommate's Guide to Love. I love these two so much and I couldn't resist writing one more chapter. So let's fast forward a few years and see what the McCoy family is up to. Click this link to get the bonus scene!

acknowledgments

I knew this book was going to be weird. Hold on, stay with me.

I like to say that my first idea isn't usually my best idea, but when I was concepting this book, everything fell into place. I knew Quinn and Porter's story instantly. Everything was so clear to me about their past, their future, and who they were.

So at that point I was just waiting for the other shoe to drop. Don't worry, it did. These two (like most of my couples) made sure to tell me what I didn't know. For example, I didn't know how much of Porter's past was going to haunt him every day. I didn't know just how deep Quinn's mask of confidence went. And I didn't know how much I was going to absolutely fall in love with these two.

Quinn is me. I am her. If you ever wonder what I'm like in real life, well, you just read her. As many know, I haven't met my happily ever after. But I do hope that if I ever find that guy, that he's exactly like Porter.

Also, if you're a teacher or a librarian, you are the ROCK STARS of the world. You should get paid one million dollars a year and never have to wait in line when you get your coffee. I know this day and age is hard, but thank you for fighting. Thank you for teaching. Thank you for being you.

Now, to the thank yous…

The biggest thank you for this book has to be the staff at Panera and my magic booth. More than half of this book was written in that booth and I know without my Unlimited Sip Club membership, this book wouldn't be complete.

To my parents. As always, you're my biggest cheerleaders even if you still have no idea what I'm doing. Mom, thanks for telling everyone at Boscov's what I do and for my Dad who was pimping my books to his nurse's during his last hospital say.

Amanda, who would have thought when we met nine years ago that one day we'd be here together? Thank you for keeping my life in order. Thank you for reminding me to drink water. And thank you for being my best friend. I promise I won't fire you this week.

Kelly, you've been with me on this book journey since day one. Not only are you an amazing alpha reader, but you are an amazing friend. One day I'll write your country star.

Valentine, thank you for everything you, your mom, and the VPR team have done for me. Thanks for talking me off the ledge more times than I can count.

To my author tribe, you make this business fun and not so lonely. Thank you to Janice for being my writing buddy every morning. To my work wife Bella for the constant cheerleading. And Julia, you keep me sane most days. Thank you for talking me off many ledges.

Kiezha, thank you for correcting my bad grammar habits and being an amazing editor. Michele and Chloe, thank you for dotting the Is and crossing the Ts.

Corinne, I'm here because of you. If you wouldn't have given me a chance I wouldn't have started writing. You forever changed my life.

Last but not least: Readers. I love you all. Whether this was your first book by me, or you've been here since Reformation, I'm truly thankful for all of you. There are so many amazing authors you could be reading. I'm humbled that you chose me.

about the author

Known for her witty sense of humor, Chelle Sloan is a former sports editor who after completing her Master's degree in journalism, decided to become a romance author. You know, because that's the normal path to writing happily ever afters.

An Ohio native, she's fiercely loyal to Cleveland sports, is the owner of way too many — yet not enough — tumblers and will be a New Kids on the Block fan until the day she dies. She does her best writing at Panera, or anywhere that's not her house. When she's not writing, she's trying to learn to bake, fixing up her condo (badly and by watching YouTube videos), or falling in love with a book.

As for her own happily every after? Maybe one day…

Stay up to date with all things Chelle & join the VIP Squad!

also by chelle sloan

THE NASHVILLE FURY, PRO FOOTBALL SERIES

Off the Record: A secret office romance

Off Track: A surprise pregnancy romance

Off Season: A second chance romance

Off Limits: A sibling's best friend romance

LOVE ONLINE SERIES

Thirst Trap: A social media romance

Match Maker: A fake dating romance

Run Run Rudolph: A celebrity, holiday romance

ROLLING HILLS

The One I Want: A single dad/nanny romance

The One I Need: An accidental marriage romance

The One I Love: A friends to lovers romance

The One I Hate: An enemies to lovers romance

GUIDE TO LOVE SERIES

Runaway Bride's Guide to Love: A brother's best friend, age gap
romance

Single Mom's Guide to Love: A billionaire, marriage of convenience
romance

Roommate's Guide to Love: A small town, single dad, romance

Good Girl's Guide to Love: A fake dating, pro football romance

GUIDE TO LOVE WORLD

Vixen's Guide to Christmas: A rivals to lovers, holiday romance